FOR A NOBLE PURPOSE

LARKSONG LEGACY • 1

FOR A *Noble* PURPOSE

KELSEY GIETL

Purple Mask Publishing
Saint Charles, Missouri

ISBN-13: 979-8-9856744-0-8
ebook ISBN: 978-0-9991105-9-1
Library of Congress Control Number: 2022904640
First Edition

Scripture quotations are taken from The New American Bible, St. Joseph Edition.

Spiritual lyrics used under public domain from *Slave Songs of the United States* by A. Simpson and Co. 1867.

Cover design by Kelsey Gietl (kelseygietl.com)
Cover photos: Face of Woman used under license by Adobe Stock. "White Flowers with Green Leaves" by Timo C. Dinger used under free license by Unsplash. Additional images from the The Metropolitan Museum of Art, New York, Open Access Collection.
Back cover photo: "Brown Cardboard Box on White Table" by Dan-Cristian Pădureț used under free license by Unsplash.

For my godmother, Mary.
I love our conversations.

And for all those trying to find their purpose.

"Every perfect gift is from above."
(James 1:17)

KEY CHARACTERS

INCLUDED IN *FOR A NOBLE PURPOSE*

THE WALCOTT FAMILY

Sarah Walcott — Missouri plantation daughter who believes herself cursed after being widowed six times. Age: 28

Martha Louis — Sarah's 30-year-old maid and dearest friend

Redmond and Elda Walcott — Sarah's parents. Age: Mid-50s

Jackson Whitticomb — Sarah's seventh and current husband

Linden Aspen — Sarah's first husband (deceased)

Morris Aspen — Linden's 61-year-old father

THE LARK FAMILY

Tobias Lark —Former South Carolina plantation son who now leads the Larksong wagon train to their new town in Washington Territory. Age: 30.

Daniel Lark — Tobias's 32-year-old brother

Garrett Lark — Tobias's 28-year-old brother

Jamison Lark — Tobias's 26-year-old brother

Cade Lark — Tobias's 20-year-old brother

Alonzo and Geraldine Lark — their parents (deceased)

Josiah — The Larks' 57-year -old former butler.

Levi and Marie Harper —The Larks' former field hand and housemaid. Age: 29 and 28. Married with five children: Jonah (8), Marilee (6), Reeslie (5), Aphid (4), and Quint (2).

OTHER CHARACTERS

Oliver Shay — Jamison's 30-year-old business partner

Coraline Shay — Oliver's 23-year-old wife

Alice Ann Owens — Coraline's 17-year-old sister

Clinton and Gabriella Reed — South Carolina cattle ranchers. Ages: 33 and 27

At the beginning of the eighteenth century,
in the first month of the year of our Lord,
The sailing ship Oblique
made her final stand against the sea.

After the earth moved and the waves crashed,
only seven of her crew remained.
Forever changed by God's great thunder,
their legacies carried on.

One-hundred-and-fifty-two years later,
this is but one of their stories...

1

Spanish lace and a cascade of hawthorn blossoms seemed a strange prelude to death, yet once again, Sarah Walcott found herself ensnared in its elusive web. She wondered how long it would be this time. Within the next hour? Two? By midnight surely. Either way, she knew with certainty that by tomorrow morning her husband would be dead.

Many called her cursed, but Catholic households didn't believe in taboos like curses and superstitions. Rather, her parents referred to her situation in more gracious terms: a string of horrible luck, a bout of unfortunate circumstances, one terrible coincidence after another.

By the time Sarah reached twenty-eight years, she had been widowed six times, always within the day. Some had been accidents, one took his own life, another was shot in a duel. A duel! As though it were 1831 on Bloody Island. All ghoulish tales not suitable for space in one's living memory, but always claiming another piece of her father's fortune. Money for the dowry, money for the wedding, money to compensate each man for his most assured reduction in life expectancy.

She accepted her latest husband, Jackson Whitticomb's hand as he led her across the pine-planked dance floor. At each corner, lanterns illuminated the garden reception atop nine-foot wooden poles, swaths of white suspended across to form a canopy. Off the north end, a four-piece string ensemble drew their bows through the refrain of Mozart's

1

"Life Let Us Cherish," the irony of the tune not lost on her or likely anyone in attendance. From the number of cashmere shawls and sweeping silk crinolines, it seemed all of Hawthorn Ridge had come out to her father's hemp plantation.

Why celebrate a seventh marriage destined to fail? The reason was simple, really. Society expected it, especially from one of the wealthiest plantation holders in the area. Redmond and Elda Walcott would not snub their affluent friends and neighbors, not when tradition detailed otherwise. Weddings equaled a hearty meal, flowing refreshments, and a boiled side of high-nosed gossip. A way to simultaneously elevate some and dismiss others in a single evening. Especially when said wedding was for yet another of Widow Walcott's many husbands.

Of course, there were other social opportunities—debutante dances and church socials—but they were more subdued. Lately, some parents preferred to present their daughters in larger cities, like St. Louis, or even farther south for their debutante balls, anxious to devise a match more affluent than a mid-Missouri farmer. A husband who could fashion their daughters in finery and provide a high level of culture, even a European tour. Perhaps the heir to a Southern plantation with two hundred acres of cotton and even more slaves. Prominent. Important. Most especially, well-to-do. A son-in-law with prestige.

Unlike Redmond and Elda Walcott, those girls' parents wouldn't whisper about *their* daughter as she took her first dance with a mediocre husband. Mr. Whitticomb wasn't wealthy or important. He was a merchant from Booneville and the only man willing to tempt fate for his share of coin. He knew substantial profit was involved, a hefty payout if he could make it through the next week alive.

Sarah studied her husband's pleasant features. He wasn't overly handsome, yet still nice enough to look at, especially when he offered a comforting smile as he was often apt to do. As he was doing now in fact. They had known one another less than six months, only since Papa posted the advertisement in the *Hawthorn Tribune*, but it still seemed a shame for such a kind smile to grow cold.

Her satin slippers pinched her toes, the thin material wetted through from the dew-dipped grass beneath her feet. It was the only part of her not perfectly clean and polished. Every other detail had been seen to, every hair pinned, every petticoat of her crinoline ironed and cinched against her bosom, hips, and waist. Her maid, Martha, had hot-ironed Sarah's blonde waves before sliding the mother-of-pearl comb straight down into the heavy mass of curls and looping it with ribbon.

Mr. Whitticomb chose that moment to move his smile closer, speaking softly. "Blue is a most fetching color on you, Miss Walcott."

Still Miss Walcott? she thought. She did not correct him into addressing her as Mrs. Whitticomb, nor did she suggest he use her Christian name. Requesting such familiarity seemed inappropriate for two near-strangers soon to be parted.

Instead, she glanced down at the pale cornflower satin swishing against her crinoline as the gown circled her knees in time with the music. Like a bell swaying after a funeral knell, its clapper no longer falling far enough to strike the curve. For nine years, she had been in mourning, ever since Linden Aspen's death in 1843. The only time she wore color was at her weddings, conveniently scheduled only weeks after she emerged from mourning.

She forced her eyes back to Mr. Whitticomb's. They were a lovely hazel. "Thank you. Blue is one of my favorites."

"It suits you well. I plan to buy you several more like it." He smiled again and she dearly wished he would stop. A rough knot lodged between her ribs and it wasn't caused by the rigidity of corset stays.

The violins drew their final bow and appreciative applause scattered around her, its intensity muffled by gloved fingers. Judging by the number of pieces played, the hour must be nearing nine. It wouldn't be long now.

"Excuse me, Mr. Whitticomb. I need a breath of air."

"We're out of doors—" he began, but she stepped into a muddled curtsy before he could draw her back beside him. She wove through the crowd, accepting congratulatory kisses and insincere smiles while replying with her "many thanks." She desperately wished to do something else with her life than accumulate failed marriages. But what else was there for a woman? She could stitch and paint and read lovely sonnets, all skills worthless for any life except the one she knew. No one would consider her of worth without a husband by her side.

Even if she tried to make her own way, she knew she would eventually return. Her family was too precious. It would break her parents' hearts to let her go.

"May I offer best wishes to the bride?"

Turning to the next well-wisher, she met stillwater brown eyes, speckled with silt as the Missouri River flowing north of her father's farm. With one arm behind him and the other folded across his middle, the gentleman dipped into a slight bow, revealing a cowlick behind the oiled center part in his sandy hair. The holster at his waist sported a revolver, not uncommon for Hawthorn Ridge. Most of the gentlemen at the wedding carried them even now. It surprised her that she couldn't recall a name to match this man's face; she had assumed she knew all her father's associates by this point. Perhaps he was a new acquaintance.

She once again offered the same false smile. "Many thanks, sir."

His chin dropped subtly when he smiled back, and she could almost believe his sentiments to be genuine. The right side of his lips tugged slightly higher than the left, its edges disappearing within a neatly trimmed beard. He extended a hand toward the dance floor in invitation. The quartet was taking possession of their instruments once more, the tune of a Kentucky waltz overtaking the hum of guest chatter and cricket wings.

"May I have this dance?" he asked.

What more harm could it do? Mr. Whitticomb was otherwise engaged at present and distraction was much preferred to witnessing him breathe his last. She had never been able to remove the sight of Linden's waxy expression from her nightmares. Even now, the image pushed its way to her attention.

"Are you new to town?" she asked the stranger. "I thought I knew everyone on the guest list."

"I arrived this afternoon. The name is Tobias Lark."

"A pleasure, Mr. Lark." She accepted his hand but instead thought of happier days with Linden. Her first husband had been a wonderful dancer and her debutante escort. Every day he lavished her with attention and praise. Such lovely dreams they had planned before the cholera stole them all away.

"This is such a charming celebration," Mr. Lark was saying as he turned her about the floor. He peered over her shoulder, taking in the ambiance rather than her. "All the receptions back home were frivolous affairs and rather exhausting. I much prefer this sort of intimacy."

Yes, she thought. *By wedding seven, the affairs do grow more intimate.* What she wouldn't have bartered to remove societal expectations and have a wedding with no more than her intended, their parish priest, Father Grier, and an otherwise empty church.

"Yes, thank you," she replied instead.

"Where has your husband planned for your wedding trip?"

"Why would you ask such a thing?"

He cornered the dance floor, her skirts lifting ever so slightly. He shrugged. "Curiosity."

Curious because he had no doubt heard every rumor and wanted to mock her with another honeymoon that would never be. For all intents and purposes, none of her marriages had been legitimate. Even after seven weddings, she had never once experienced a wedding night. Every man had fallen before they could consummate.

She offered a coy smile, as though she were any other bride embarrassed by his question. The heat in her cheeks was certainly as real as any other. "Mr. Whitticomb has business here to attend to through the summer. We plan to take a spin to Savannah when the weather cools."

He shook his head. "Charleston is much prettier in my opinion and not nearly so far."

"You've traveled there often?"

"I used to live there with my brothers."

"Are they still there?"

"One of them." His expression turned dour then, lips pressed in a tight line as his attention turned past her toward the darkened fields.

Around the party's edges, her father's servants stood at attention, in that place between the soft lantern glow and invisibility. Close enough to make out their presence, far enough to not be noticed unless they were needed. Mr. Lark seemed to examine them as they turned past and she wondered if he planned to make an offer to her father. The last time someone made an inquiry, Papa had been firm that no deal would be made. The labor and loyalty their servants provided was more valuable than any purchase price.

The stranger shifted his grip on her waist, turning her more quickly than the tempo of the song required. Even in the cool April evening, she felt the heat from his body warm her too thoroughly, his earthy scent mixing with imported flowers and the tartness of the hemp fields.

As they turned another corner of the floor, she caught Martha's eye, watching from where she served glasses of wine. Her delicate brunette twist was a match to her skin, although still several shades lighter than the muted black dress she wore. Her eyes flashed a warning. Mr. Lark was handsome and enticing and Sarah could get lost if she was not careful. Many mislaid years had taught her how, when it came to men, she should always be careful.

She wanted to abandon the dance, snatch Martha away, and run through her father's newly sprouted crop, far from the party's lantern lights. As children, the two girls had stolen through the fields at night, mud squishing between their toes, attempting to cover their laughter behind cupped hands. They would lay side-by-side in between the rows, their ears nearly touching, to count the stars and name each one. One for the people they lost, for the people they knew, for the families they planned to have someday.

"What'ya gonna name your babies, Miss Sarah?" Martha would ask. She always called her Miss Sarah, the same as the other slaves. Her father owned twenty field hands and three kitchen girls and they treated every one as well as they could. There was always plenty of food and clothing to go around; days off work for worship and leisure; and a full week of rest after a sickness or injury. Sarah had been told such accommodations were infrequent in the other northern slave states and unheard of on the southern plantations.

Ten-year-old Martha had come into their lives as the answer to a prayer. For eight years, Sarah's mother, Elda had tried to conceive a second child but never received another blessing. Despondent over her mother's anguish and longing for a sibling, Sarah begged her father for another little girl to fill the void. Back then, there was nothing he wouldn't grant her. So, one bright and sunny morning, they loaded in the wagon and went to the Fifth and Myrtle Market. Elda named their new addition Martha because it meant "pleasantness."

From that moment, Sarah considered Martha a sister even though they didn't share the same skin. Only a sister would be invited out to Sarah's special spot in the fields. Only a sister would be allowed to stare at the stars and dream the same dreams.

"What'ya gonna name your babies?" Martha had asked.

Sarah remembered the names she chose, each stitched on a sampler in her hope chest and which she hoped one day would go forgotten. Besides Martha, only Linden, Sarah's first husband, had known and approved of every one. She had wanted that life with him. The life of the white-washed farmhouse and the rounded belly, the baby nestled in her arms. It made no difference now what she wanted to name her babies. There would never be any babies to name.

The swell of violin strings brought another round of gentle applause. Sarah saw Mr. Whitticomb watching her from across the floor, ready to return to his rightful place. Face-to-face once again with reality.

She managed a perfect curtsy to match Mr. Lark's bow. As they righted, he offered her his elbow, looking to guide her hand into the crook of his arm and lead her off the dance floor. Although it was the social convention, it was not proper for a stranger to do while her husband looked on.

Unless he assumed her husband's presence to be immaterial.

But of course, he did. There was always another covetous man around the corner, one who didn't believe in curses, only padded pocketbooks.

"You insult me with your assumptions," she hissed. She yanked her hand from his and his smile wavered.

"My assumption was to lead you from the floor then hand you over to your husband. What is it I was supposed to assume?"

Perhaps he doesn't know, she thought, reining herself in before she made a scene. If so, he was the only person who didn't. She could suddenly hear the whispers all around them. Their accusations, their wonderments. She had an alibi for every one of her husbands' deaths, but somehow she remained responsible all the same. The sinister spinster. The unnatural beauty who not only broke but also stopped each beating heart.

A lady sniggered somewhere nearby, her words close enough to be whispered yet loud enough to sink right into Sarah's heart. "Already lining up the next while this one's still warm. Has she no shame?"

Mr. Lark removed himself another step, drawing a hand behind his back with a nod. "I see I have overstepped a boundary. I was unaware. My most gracious apologies."

The violin bows slid across their strings, swelling into another number, and her husband was there again, taking her in his arms in time to the melody. She looked for Mr. Lark, but he was already striding off the dance floor. The makeshift floorboards slightly buckled in spots where the nails had popped loose.

"Is everything well, my dear?" Mr. Whitticomb asked.

For the hundredth time that evening, she forced a smile and met his gaze. "Yes, of course. Everything is fine."

Jackson Wittcomb's hazel eyes were so very lovely. It really was such a shame he had to die.

2

Tobias stepped off the dance floor, sorely tempted to reach up and scratch his head at the bride's odd behavior. One minute she was heart-stopping smiles and the next she accused him of...what, exactly? An assumption? Clearly, she must be harboring an inner conflict he knew nothing about, even though he nursed his own inner conflicts often enough.

While she hadn't made him assume anything untoward, she certainly could make him want to. Between her golden curls and the touch of hazel within her striking green eyes, she could lead him anywhere.

No, not anywhere. *Harness the horses, Tobias.* He already had a path set and it led to Washington Territory. His time with her had been an innocent dance. It was a way to distract the other guests from noticing his brother, Garrett, taking mental inventory of the populace—and hopefully discovering the next recruit for their wagon party.

Garrett had wandered over to the refreshment table and was now speaking to a colored woman in a maid's outfit, no doubt one of the plantation servants. Garrett never could resist a pretty woman, no matter her station. It had earned him a fair share of their father's verbal—and physical—reprimands over his twenty-eight years and too many words of caution from all four of his brothers. Which could be why he continued to do it.

Tobias sighed. Right now, they should have been floating the Missouri River to their jumping-off point in Independence, Missouri if not for Garrett insisting they sidetrack through Hawthorn Ridge. It was always a no-win situation when his brother had a *feeling* about going somewhere. Garrett might be the next closest in age to Tobias's thirty years, but he was also the most hotheaded and likely to do some fool thing.

To appease Garrett, he had agreed to send their second youngest brother, twenty-six-year-old Jamison, ahead to the steamboat with the rest of the wagon party. Meanwhile, Tobias, Garrett, and their youngest brother, twenty-year-old Cade, continued to Hawthorn Ridge on horseback. Not being one for social situations, Cade had volunteered to keep watch over camp while his brothers searched for their latest recruit.

Tobias scanned the surrounding area again. Maybe he could locate their target on his own, if only he knew the tell-tale signs like Garrett did. Most of the guests were either dancing across the pine-plank floor or mingling along the perimeter. Dining tables, which had lined the space when they first arrived, were now being carried out by several servants, while others offered guests finger pastries on silver trays. Even without the substantial gardens of the Southern plantations, there were flowers in abundance, too many for this area in late April. Probably imported from the docks in St. Louis, shipping up on the steamboats from New Orleans. Tobias swiped a glass from a passing servant and a white iced cake, popping the entire cube into his mouth as he circled the edge of the dance floor.

So much finery. So much frippery. Even here, a thousand miles from Charleston, he was still suffocated by it. He couldn't wait to get to Washington Territory, where he hoped there wouldn't be a yard of lace or silver-topped cane to be found.

The bride was probably like all other plantation ladies, obsessed with herself, flawless with her rosy expression and delicate gloved hands. Never worked hard a day in her life or felt the sun break upon her beautiful face.

Yes, she was beautiful—stunning in blue—that much he would easily admit. Her husband had certainly found a proper jewel to parade before his friends. Their children would be the sapphires and rubies of Hawthorn Ridge.

Despite Tobias's own lavish upbringing, a life of luxury wasn't one he had ever aspired to. He did sometimes wonder, however, what it would be like to have a life so utterly dull as he imagined the bride and groom were bound to share. They were both ordinary and destined to lead ordinary lives. Tobias, on the other hand, had never had an ordinary life.

"You're doing it again," Garrett said, unexpectedly beside him, a glass of red wine in his right hand. Ten yards or so behind him, the maid handed another glass to the next guest, her lashes downturned.

Tobias had been so caught up in his own turn of thought—a common issue for him—he hadn't noticed when his brother appeared. "What do you mean?" he asked.

Garrett nodded to Tobias's hands where he held a collection of grass stems half-braided. His nervous twitch was in full force tonight. He hadn't remembered collecting the long prairie blades, his hands always eager to create even when he didn't tell them to do so. It made him more resourceful, able to build and whittle and manufacture in half the time it took other people, if they were able to construct them at all.

One summer back in Charleston, a rogue abolitionist snuck onto their plantation and burned down half the slave quarters. When their father threatened to sell the slaves to pay for the damages, Tobias took to the countryside, chopping timber by hand and building better quarters than before. He had help, of course, but he could haul and assemble one wall alone in the same time it took three men to finish the same.

It was the same as Garrett's knack for finding people, those *feelings* which guided him, often without solid intent. He didn't require a map or compass either; only his inner navigation. From Charleston to St. Louis, he had located forty-five wagons worth of folks who also saw Washington as an ideal refuge. Those hoping for a better life—slaves longing for freedom, families tired of injustice, men searching for companionship—the misbegotten, misunderstood, or just plain miserable. Forty-five wagons, yet never one soul who shared the Lark brothers' particular talents. Or at least none whose Gifts could be easily recognized.

It was how their father liked to refer to their unusual abilities: "Gifts." With a capital G, never lower-case, as though what they had could be reduced to a common noun. Gifts were the Lark family legacy, passed down from father to son, to show superiority to everyone else. Superior to women, superior to blacks, to Indians, and the low downtrodden families in Charleston's gutters. It was tripe which only Alonzo Lark believed, and it was a wonder any of his sons escaped his poisoned mind. It was only due to their mother's influence that they developed any principles at all, for their father had few in every way.

Of course, some brothers developed a stronger sense of morality than others. Jamison had chosen to study God's word while Garrett, on the other hand—

"I saw you dancing with the bride." Garrett interrupted. "You told me we weren't allowed to speak to anyone unless spoken to."

Distracted again. The grass braid in his hand was now a fully formed crown, long blades knotted tightly to act as gemstones. He crumbled it into a ball before shoving it in his jacket pocket. "Yes, a request you clearly ignored. I saw you not two minutes ago conversing with that servant." He pointed toward the maid in question.

"Yes, precisely. A servant. She is no danger to us."

"And the bride is?"

The beauty danced twenty yards away, her blue skirt swirling, her husband gazing upon her like she was the edge of magnificence. Garrett swallowed the rest of his drink, handed his glass to a servant in the shadows, and returned to his somber stance. "That's the Widow Walcott," he hissed. "They say she kills her husbands."

"*What?*"

"It's true. She's been cursed with six dead husbands, always widowed before the wedding night. People are placing bets on when this one will die."

That woman? A murderer? Although, it would account for some of her strange behavior. Tobias looked back at his brother. "Who told you this?"

"Practically everyone. Her servant confirmed it."

Could this woman be the aim of Garrett's Gift? Tobias wondered.

Six husbands dead wasn't particularly unusual, although it was a number higher than most. Men died all the time of hundreds of different ailments and young widows often remarried quickly. The Widow Walcott could have a knack for choosing clumsy husbands or those prone to illness, if not for one small detail. All of them died *before* the wedding night. A fact that didn't make much sense unless she was murdering them. But if everyone knew this, then why wasn't she in jail? And why go to the hassle of planning a wedding only to kill your husband after the ceremony? That wasn't even enough time to draw a new will or receive financial benefit upon his demise. Surely, any remaining funds would be channeled back to her husband's next of kin.

Unless...

The gears in his mind began turning as quickly as his fingers liked to tinker. What if she was actually...

"Oh, no, you don't," Garrett broke into his thoughts. He spun Tobias around so his back was to the dance floor and the bride. He gave his brother a shake. "We have to meet the wagon train in three days. We're only here to find our latest recruit and leave. *Not* to fall in love with a married woman."

"Lighten your load, Garrett. No one's falling in love here. It was only a dance."

"A dance with a side of your usual irrational hope. I know what you're thinking and as always, you're wrong."

Tobias strained a smile. "You cannot possibly know what I am thinking."

"You're wondering if she's Gifted."

Oh. Perhaps Garrett could tell what he was thinking.

"Tobias, you know women cannot carry the trait. Didn't father say that more than almost anything else?"

Their father had said it, many times. The tale of the shipwreck *Oblique* became the solitary way in which Alonzo Lark bonded with his sons. "Never forget that these Gifts belong to you and you alone," he told them. "There were others in the beginning, seven who survived the restless waves on the Northwestern seas. They were the first sons of the Gifted, granted spectacular abilities which changed their legacies forever. If not for stupidity and spite, they could have conquered the world. They thought too far beyond their strengths and, one by one, it led to their downfall. One-hundred-and-fifty years later, the Lark sons are all who remain."

Until the day he died, Alonzo Lark maintained his insistence that their family were the only Gifted still alive. Tobias had allowed him to live in his beliefs while ever hopeful that one day, they would find another like them. The day he could finally prove his father wrong. After all, he and his brothers were the only people alive who could argue with their father and win.

Outside of their family, no one thought of their father's persuasive Gift as anything unnatural. The Charleston populace assumed his influence stemmed from his charismatic personality. Despite drawing roots from a meager home, Father spoke as eloquently as a man drawn straight from the gentry. Whether he addressed a single man or an audience, they always listened and agreed. It was how he amassed his fortune. How he purchased Larksong Plantation at only twenty-two. How he acquired over a hundred slaves within the first two years of rice farming and another hundred in the more profitable cotton fields by the age of thirty. He asked and he was given. "Like Jesus," he would joke. It was blasphemy and no one laughed, especially not Jamison. Only their mother, for she had no other choice. She was merely a convenient way to pass along the Gifts to Alonzo's offspring under an eternal influence beyond her control.

The brothers each arrived two years apart, first Daniel, then Tobias, Garrett, Jamison, and six years later, Cade. Three stillborn girls followed, small and lovely, with cheeks like plump strawberries and velvet black eyelashes. Tobias had been twelve when the final sister was laid to rest in the family plot. He remembered hearing his father's words in front of everyone: "Three girls in the grave. You see what I have told you, Geraldine. It is a sign our line is complete. We will not try again."

He had turned to his sons, all in a line, hats in their hands. "Be mindful who you marry, my sons. Women cannot receive the Gift. They are inferior. Unworthy." He extended his hand to the quickly growing mound of dirt covering Tobias's youngest sister and smiled.

"Unworthy like this one was."

Their mother smiled too, drawn in by their father's words, lost in the effects of his Gift, but the boys were impervious to their father's charms. It was another result of their blessing. Apparently, you could not be harmed by others who carried the same.

Ten-year-old Garrett stepped forward then, slapped his hat on his head, and wound up, throwing a fist into his father's stomach. He was strong for a child, built tough and sturdy, but not enough to overcome their father. Alonzo quickly caught his breath, observed his son for a second, then struck the back of his hand across Garrett's face, so hard he stumbled into Jamison who accidentally drove two-year-old Cade onto the ground. The toddler began to cry, lifting his arms for his mother to hold him.

Their father would have none of it, however. "Leave him, Geraldine," he scolded as she reached for him. "If you coddle him, how will he learn?" With her same cloudy-eyed smile, she followed her husband back to the carriage, leaving Daniel to dry Cade's tears.

Their mother resided with them for six more years, until the summer of 1840 when Daniel found her hanging from the rafters in the plantation attic. Everyone knew she took her own life, but only the Lark brothers knew she had been persuaded to do so.

Tobias didn't believe in curses, but he didn't believe in coincidences either. If Tobias's Gift caused him to build without conscious appeal and Garrett's led them places without reason, why couldn't Sarah Walcott's Gift unwittingly prevent her from entering a state of married bliss? She hadn't meant to end her husbands' lives; it happened spontaneously without her command.

There were six other men on the *Oblique* besides their great-great-great-grandfather and they had never learned their names. Why couldn't one of them have been Sarah's ancestor?

Garrett continued to stare with that same exasperated expression. If Tobias pressed the issue, his brother would likely feed him a sleeping draught, hogtie him to his horse, and lead him away to Independence. Chances were Garrett was right and the Widow Walcott wasn't Gifted. Just like every other "suspicion" Tobias had about someone before, this one was also likely incorrect. But what if it wasn't?

"Garrett," he said slowly. "Please don't kill me, but I'm afraid I need another conversation with the bride."

3

Sarah heard Garrett's caution as she spun past in Mr. Whitticomb's arms. "That's the Widow Walcott. They say she kills her husbands."

Well, it appeared Mr. Tobias Lark truly hadn't known who she was or what she was capable of. He wasn't searching for wealth through marriage to her. Had he known the truth, he most assuredly wouldn't have asked her to dance. The dismay on his face was enough to confirm it. She would not be receiving Mr. Lark's attention again.

Nor should she desire it. She *didn't* desire it. She was married.

For now.

She had to get away from here. She had to stop this. All of it.

"I must go," she gasped. She spun away from Mr. Whitticomb, grasping her skirts above the damp grass, and fled toward the two-story whitewashed farmhouse. It wasn't much as far as plantations went; her grandfather's horse farm in Kentucky boasted a home nearly twice the size. However, its wide windows and green clapboard shutters were standard size for Hawthorn Ridge and had always been enough for their family of three. She threw open the rear servants' door, past the questioning looks of the two kitchen maids and their concerned statements of, "Miss Sarah? Ev'rythin' al'right?"

No, everything was not all right.

"Papa!" she called. She had seen him leave the celebration and head in this direction. He must be here.

She strode down the hall toward his office. "Papa! I must speak with you!"

She felt eyes at her back and whirled, but it was only Tildy, the eldest kitchen maid. "Landsakes, Miss Sarah. What is the commotion?"

"Tildy, I must find my father. He has to take Mr. Whitticomb and me to town right now."

She smiled. "Decided to 'eave' for ya weddin' trip tonight after all?"

"No." Sarah grasped the woman's plump shoulders. "Listen to me, Tildy. I need a divorce and I need it now. I cannot go through with this."

"Sarah." She whirled at her father's voice and pressed delicate fingers to her skull to stop it spinning. With her nerves on edge, she had consumed little more than a few bites of the wedding feast and the customary wine during Father Grier's blessing. The effects were now catching up.

Her father stood almost sentry in stance, shadowing his office doorway. His lips turned down beneath his bushy mustache, as peppered with grey as the hair upon his head. With a smattering of wrinkles stretching his face from brow to chin, he appeared ever so much older than he should have. The last ten years had taken nearly as much toll upon him as they had her. If not for his carefully tied cravat, the loose folds upon his neck would also be plain to see.

No matter what hardship these many years had brought him, she could tell with a sweep of his gaze that tonight would not ease their many sufferings. He would do the polite thing, the socially accepted action, as he had always done.

"Sarah," he said again, his voice low as he took her elbow and turned her into the main foyer. His eyes slid to Tildy, the maid's expression laced with confusion. "Back to the kitchen, Tildy. This is no matter of yours."

"Yes, sir." With eyes averted, she dipped her head and disappeared.

Redmond Walcott didn't once meet his daughter's gaze as he led her past the darkened parlor and across the diamond-tiled entryway. The hand not holding her elbow hostage came to rest on the entry door's brass knob. "You must return to your husband, Mrs. Whitticomb."

"No!" she shouted. "I must divorce him. There is no other sensible way about it."

Her father's chin did turn then, pegging her with dark annoyance. She swallowed and lessened her steam to a manageable tone. "With respect to you and to Mama, this marriage was a mistake. Mr. Whitticomb is a kind, intellectual sort. He will understand this choice to be in error. He does not deserve to be shackled to my curse—"

"Sarah Olivia Walcott," her father hissed. Quickly, he released the doorknob to cross himself. "You know we do not refer to such evil suggestions in this house."

"Then what should we call it, Papa? There is no other suitable name." When he did not immediately respond, she pressed on, offering him her most pleading affection. "Please, Papa. I promise I have committed no sin grave enough to earn this punishment. I don't know why this curse was forced upon me, all I know is it would be a mistake to allow it to continue." She was only sorry she hadn't strengthened her will sooner, when her father told her of Mr. Whitticomb's intentions. She should have refused louder and with more ferocity. She should have—

"It is too late to undo what has been done, my dear. Divorce is not an option for people like us. Isn't that correct, Elda?"

Sarah's mother strode down the central staircase, her hands folded upon her middle. Unlike her husband, Elda Walcott had barely seemed to age over her twenty-eight years of motherhood, but Sarah knew physical appearances only told a hint of the story. Despite corncob curls the same color as her daughter's and a slender waist pinched within deep green satin, inwardly her mother had suffered for decades. Losing one then another promising pregnancy until they finally brought Martha into their lives. But another house slave could never make up for the many years she missed with her own progeny, no matter how dearly she cared for her servant. Or how closely she held her only living child to her bosom.

Sarah raced to her mother, throwing her arms around her waist before she had fully met them in the foyer. "Mama," she cried. "Tell Papa we must go to town for a divorce. Tonight. You know it cannot wait."

Her mother pulled her in tight, rubbing a tender hand upon her daughter's back. Sarah sighed and leaned into her touch, closing her eyes. "Tell him, Mama."

A pause longer than the one before Sarah's latest, *I do*. She raised her head from her mother's chest. "Mama?"

But her mother wasn't looking at her. Her sights were somewhere else, not on her husband either, past even that. "Everything will be well, darling. After tonight."

"No, Mama, after tonight, Mr. Whitticomb will be dead. And if not tonight, then shortly after. Think of Linden..."

Her mother shook her head, attention finally returning to her daughter. Her expression was sympathetic, yet cold. Resolute. "Your father is right. This is your responsibility. We all hope Mr. Whitticomb doesn't meet his end, but if he does, you need to accept that this is still what you chose."

"You chose it for me! I refuse the weight of such decisions any longer." When she attempted to push past, her father held her back, one arm around her waist.

"We know this is difficult, but we've all had to make difficult decisions. What life can I give you as a spinster? I need grandchildren."

"To run your plantation when you're gone? Is that all this has ever been about, expanding your reach? You will inherit Grandfather's farm one day. Is that not enough?" She couldn't believe this turn of events. Tears leaked from her eyes and her voice died in her throat.

Her father's tone became gentler. "I will be honest with you, daughter; I do desire a name to write in my will, but this has never been purely about posterity. Your mother and I have always thought of you in our decisions. Your future. Your reputation. How you will be perceived in society. It reflects on us all. You will be here long after we are gone, hopefully with a legacy left untarnished. We must secure your future to secure our own.

"Sarah, this house, the farm, the slaves will be yours someday. I am eager to leave it to you. But how long could you tend it without a husband? What other means do you have to sustain this life?"

After all this time, how did they still not understand her? Her family had a rich history dating back to the Revolution and beyond, but she should have gladly given it all up the day she married her first husband. Linden Aspen had no practical endeavors to become an accounting officer like his father or a farmer like hers. He was willing to claim responsibility over her father's land only so Redmond Walcott would approve and they could remain together.

Linden had wanted to be a poet. Words flowed from his lips like the first cool breeze of a Missouri summer. He had inspired her, enticed her, and she encouraged his talent with every scratch of the pen. She regretted only her delay in rescuing his sheets of beauty before his father ripped them to shreds.

All too often, she imagined Linden's smile in her daydreams, his soft poems whispered in her ear while he caressed her hand and left her wanting more than was decent. She thought of the week before their wedding, together in his buggy, the steady *clop-clop* of horse hooves their serenade. "How content to simply be here with you," she had told him. She wrapped her arm through his as he held the reins aloft. "I feel richer now than with all the acres my father has promised us."

He looked down at her then, his hazel eyes covering her face from top to bottom. Taking her in with a question he seemed hesitant to mention. "What is it?" she asked.

"Would you want to go? We could do it together. Alone it isn't possible, but together...you said it yourself, we're richer with only each other than anything else."

She pulled her arm from his, truly meeting his gaze, wondering if he was serious. He couldn't possibly be. "Leave Hawthorn Ridge?"

He had spoken of it before, his desire to branch out on his own. Join the poets in Boston, but she always supposed it to be a flight of fancy. Like women leading the cavalry. She had never considered his dreams to be genuine.

He pulled up on the reins, drawing the horses to a stop right there on the dusty road. She could see the white boards of her father's house in the distance. One hand firmly on the reins, he took hers in his other. "Sarah, I would give you anything you asked for. If you say it's a dolt-headed fantasy, I'll pretend I never dreamed it. But first, just imagine." He pulled her into his side, pressing a kiss to her forehead. His words tangled in her hair. "You and me, in our own little place somewhere. It might not be pretty, but it will be ours. I'll write you poems every night. We'll drink wine from chipped glasses and cover our ears when the stray dogs bark in the street. Or perhaps we'll take one of those dogs in. We'll name it Jacque in honor of our horrible French neighbor whose swearing makes you blush."

She giggled. "Because he's such a mongrel."

He laughed back. "Exactly so." With one finger, he tilted her chin to meet his tender gaze. She knew he would give her so much, more than she ever asked for. He wasn't promising her a lifetime of ease, but he was promising that together even the difficult times wouldn't seem so trying.

She parted her lips and he lowered his, their touch featherlight beneath each tender caress. All too quickly, he backed away. Or had she? It was impossible to tell.

"It sounds wonderful, Linden..." She was unable to say more.

His nearly imperceptible statement followed. "But your answer is 'no.'" He took up the reins, clucking to the horses to begin again. His lips had fallen into a straight line.

"Linden, I...I am sorry." Her throat felt stuffed with cotton. It was hard to swallow. "I want to, but my parents...I'm their only child." She touched his arm, his muscles tense beneath her fingers. She had wounded him, but surely he must understand that a decision like this was impossible to make. Perhaps if her mother had passed on as his had, then it would be easier to leave it all behind.

"Please, Linden, you must believe me. I want to be with you more than anything. Think of your own father. He would be devastated to lose you."

"I do believe you, Sarah. I only wish I had my father's constancy the way your parents have yours."

Maybe that was the heart of her curse. The mistake which turned her life into a wasteland.

Now, in the shadow of the farmhouse stairs, she looked upon her father, straight and sensible. "I'm going to Boston, Papa. Tell Mr. Whitticomb I said 'Adieu.'"

She skirted her mother's dumbstruck stare and lifting her skirts, ran up the central staircase. She heard her parents shortly behind her, her father's fevered shouts, her mother's labored breaths squeaking with each step. "Sarah Olivia!" her father called. "You are not leaving this house without your husband, and certainly not for Boston. You will not become a Yankee."

She would. She must. She would save Mr. Whitticomb and break the circle of despair. She would go east as Linden had wanted. She would sip wine from chipped glasses and own an alley dog named Jacque. And she would write poems. Dozens and dozens. Every night until Linden's ghost finally forgave her.

4

Tobias, if we miss meeting the wagon train because you indulged in another delusion, I swear this time I will kill you."

Tobias continued toward the Walcotts' whitewashed farmhouse, refusing to make eye contact with his brother's sulking form. Garrett was truly so predictable. He could almost set his pocket watch to his brother's moodiness. "If I had a rice kernel for every time you threatened to end my life," he told him, "I would have my own plantation by now."

"I thought you didn't want your own plantation."

"I don't." He wanted his own town. But that was beside the point at the moment. They could be running out of time. If his theory was correct, they needed to find Sarah and explain about her Gift before her husband, like the others, met a grisly end. It would be the greatest discovery of their lives.

"Your Gift brought us here for a reason, Garrett. There is someone here we need. What if it's her?"

"Clearly, my Gift was wrong. I must be coming down with typhoid."

"Hogwash. You rarely fall ill unless it's your Gift causing the affliction." Every time Garrett was drawn someplace, he would be overcome with terrible headaches and queasiness. If he followed its trail, eventually the feelings would abate. If he didn't, however, his sickness could become unrelenting. "Do you feel ill now?" Tobias asked him.

Garrett frowned. "No. Haven't since we entered the party."

"See then, we're on the right track."

"I still don't believe it's the bride."

"Maybe it's the groom then. I could be wrong about her, but if I'm not, we can't simply wait for him to succumb with wine in hand. I reckon she isn't even aware she's causing it."

"My brother, every man's lord and savior," Garrett muttered. "You know, Father believed he was a god, too."

Tobias didn't justify his brother with a response. Garrett always liked to drive the knife in when he had no better excuses. "Come on. Let's get this over and done with."

He lifted the front door knocker.

"Can we at least swipe something valuable while we're here?" Garrett asked. Tobias paused mid-knock and stared over his shoulder at his brother who shrugged. "It's a good plan. You can talk to the doomed couple while I sneak into the parlor and find a trinket or two."

"For what possible purpose would we need to do that? Thanks to our inheritance, we have plenty of money."

"*Our* inheritance? Don't you mean Daniel's inheritance which he so generously granted us?"

"Garrett, I'm not arguing about this again with you. None of us liked the way it happened and that's why we left. Let Daniel deal with his problems, and we'll deal with ours." He punctuated his final words by slamming the brass knocker down.

He didn't like to spend too much time thinking about his eldest brother. Their father had left every asset to Daniel upon his death, leaving the others with nothing. Of course, Daniel gave them their fair share of the division, more than enough to make their way across the country, but he also gave away the one asset no one should own. Despite his brothers' objections, he sold off all the fields and nearly every slave along with them, keeping only those needed to run the Charleston townhouse. None of the Lark brothers liked slavery of course, but they had witnessed their father's callous attitude toward the enslaved. Without the brothers as overseers, those men, women, and children were likely to suffer far worse in the hands of a stranger.

It was a terrible way to treat other humans. No one should have a right to own someone else, to legally beat them and destroy families at will.

But slavery was a double-edged sword. The plantations needed manpower to provide supplies not only to the South but throughout the world. Slavery allowed them to deliver goods at a reasonable cost. If they had to pay their workers, they would be forced to raise production costs. Higher costs meant fewer purchasers. How had the newspapers always phrased it? *Slavery was the necessary evil of a sustained economy.* Cost expectations had been set. To backpedal now, even if morally right, could cause a nationwide economic collapse. The slaves would be free, yet left with nothing.

Still, Daniel hadn't listened. He didn't want to be a slave owner, simple as that, and legally the rest of them couldn't lift a finger to stop it.

Their eldest brother had always been different from the rest of them. He always beat to his own drum because he had to. Daniel wasn't Gifted. He had talents, of course, gifted with a lowercase g. An accomplished pianist, but he wouldn't be playing the halls. Highly intelligent, near the top of his class at university, but nothing extraordinary. He was well-liked, had plenty of friends, and the belles batted their fans at him, although he never entertained their affections past the ballroom. Daniel was no slouch, but neither would he build a schooner wagon in an afternoon as Tobias could.

As a result, he kept to himself for most of his life, only earning Father's respect by being the firstborn. Thankfully for him, their father wasn't one to reject tradition when it came to his heirs. No one in society knew about their special Gifts. It would raise more eyebrows at father than son if he refused to name Daniel his heir.

Tobias lifted the Walcotts' door knocker again. He could hear muffled voices on the other side and Garrett's not-so-subtle grumblings behind him. Maybe this was a poor decision and he should leave well enough alone. However, seconds later, the crash and subsequent glass shattering from within told him he shouldn't have hesitated.

Turning the knob proved fruitless—locked. Shoving against the door proved equally ineffective. Still, he did it again, banging at the panels and kicking them, while alternately shouting in the direction of the party for help. His actions garnered the attention of other wedding guests, many of whom now came running. As rumors swept on the breeze, it was barely minutes before the entire guest list moved with swiftness in their direction, the men at a run and the women, with their ridiculous hoops and dainty slippers, moving only slightly quicker than a sensible glide. A man could be dying and they worried about mussing their wardrobe.

"Why are we bothering with these people?" Garrett griped. "Even if we were sent here, none of them deserve to join our town." He leaned against the porch's corner pillar with arms folded, watching the commotion coming toward them. "Truly, look at them." The guests were chattering amongst themselves, some with apparent delight unsuccessfully hidden behind white gloves against their lips.

They're excited, Tobias realized. Eager to see how the Widow Walcott's latest husband had met his end. Afterward, they would settle up for bets won and likely place new wagers on when she would become engaged again. It was as barbaric as Christians ripped apart inside the Colosseum for sport. He could not be happier to say goodbye to this town.

A servant broke through the crowd, the same woman Garrett had noted as the bride's maid. She dipped between guests, eyes lowered in deference as she went, her expression one of the few carrying genuine concern. She paused before the brothers and held up a key. "Excuse me, sirs. I have come to grant you entrance."

Grant us *entrance?* This wasn't even their house. And what sort of house slave possessed a key to her master's home? The Larks' butler, Josiah had carried a key to Larksong Plantation, but he earned that trust over a lifetime of loyalty, over fifty years now. Outside their family, it was highly irregular.

The maid quickly unlocked the door, holding it wide for the crowd to rush past. Tobias was jostled along into the foyer where he met the sight of a lit twelve-candle chandelier, a flared staircase descending from the second floor, and at the bottom, the illumination of Julian Whitticomb's mangled body. Two crystal flutes lay shattered on the tile beside the remnants of a green glass wine bottle, its red liquid blending with that flowing from Mr. Whitticomb's temple upon the stair.

When a sob echoed from above, fifty pairs of eyes rose in unison. At the top of the staircase between her parents stood the Widow Walcott. Tears streamed down her mother's cheeks, Mrs. Walcott's face turned into her husband's shoulder. He wrapped one arm around his wife's back and his other around his daughter. The widow's eyes, however, focused on the body. There was no surprise behind them.

"You're right, Tobias," Garrett whispered. "Let's bring her with us. We won't have to worry about Indian raids and poisoned water. Her *Gift* can kill us instead."

⁂

Through her closed bedroom door, Sarah had heard Mr. Whitticomb tumble down the stairs as though watching it happen. Her hands reached out to grab him, the brief image of his hazel eyes staring up at her, wide as the Missouri River and full of terror. Then he fell backward and the world sped up again. His back hit the staircase with a sickening crack before rolling over itself down to the tile below. A second later, the crackle of shattered glass brought her senses back to reality. Back in her bedroom beside her parents and an open traveling bag.

The family rose as one, moving like ghosts themselves down the hallway to the central staircase. Her mother sobbed into her father's jacket, clutching at his lapels like her world was about to end. She supposed in some ways it was. For the seventh time, her daughter had not consummated a marriage. For the seventh time, there would be no grandchildren. No male heirs. As usual, all they had was a daughter who had failed them once again.

Sarah waited for the nervous shocks she felt all evening to transform into something more. A wail rose in her throat and lodged there, unwilling to emerge from between her lips. Tears and despair were elements of unexpected horror, but she felt neither. She had no attachment to Mr. Whitticomb past the ring on her finger and his death was certainly not unexpected. She had known it would occur since the day her father accepted his betrothal request.

If only she knew *why*. Why was this happening to *her*? She had only asked it every day for the last decade.

Mr. Whitticomb's left arm jutted away from his body at an unnatural angle, his legs tangled together upon the fifth and sixth stair. A slight trickle of red traced its way from behind his ear, weaving between the lines of white tile, aqueducts of Nile River red. One eye stared unblinkingly upward, the other half-closed as though in a lazy wink.

The foyer lay in chaos, party guests bumping together, straining for a view of her latest victim. Their chatter roared as suppositions tumbled over each other like rapids falling upon rocks. Dr. Humbull moved forward to press a hand to the fallen man's chest then his side, although he must have known there would be no purpose. Jackson Whitticomb, lovely man that he was, was also unmistakably dead.

"Sarah Walcott!" someone called. "What happened this time?"

Before she could even think to answer, another shouted, "Widow Walcott, how do you feel? Is it the same as all the others?"

"Oh, Ronald, it's number seven," a woman trilled. "Just ask it plain. Might there be a baby on the way?"

The polite way of asking if Sarah had finally bed one of her husbands, yet as rude as if she asked it outright.

Sarah's father gripped her waist and motioned her forward. "You must speak with them. There are certain to be reporters."

Yes, of course. There always were, ever since her fifth husband's death, the one in the duel. She would be a news story for the next week, then word would die down again for a few months. Then they would dredge it all up again when someone inevitably accused her of murder. Even with sound alibis, someone always threatened to throw her in jail. Nothing ever came of their claims, but it was horrific enough to know they believed her capable.

One more glance at Mr. Whitticomb's horrid figure and her breath caught, forcing her ribs against her corset stays. *Never again*, she thought. She had said it many times before, but this time she meant it. *Never again.*

The day after the funeral, she would be on the first stage for

Boston. She didn't care if her father did consider her a Yankee.

Her fingers finally found the banister and held on. She ordered her feet to move, to take a step, to do something. Martha lingered in the shadows beside the stairs, such empathy in her gaze. Sarah wanted to run to her dearest friend and embrace her. Martha would tell her she would be there no matter what, even if it wasn't hers to promise. They could run to the fields and cry together. Martha wouldn't make her take another husband. Martha would understand.

Sarah stepped down the stairs, her dress held an inch above the carpet runner so as not to reveal the barest bit of ankle or slipper. She would maintain some decorum if nothing else. As she paused on the stair above her husband's body, she allowed the crowd to edge in, everyone's eyes searching her expectantly. Two reporters stood front and center, their notebooks at the ready, pencil stubs between stained fingers. A hush fell, and that was when she noticed him watching from the back of the crowd.

It was the stranger she had danced with, the one who hadn't known her story at the time but knew now. She felt something pass over the man's gaze, more than curiosity, more than sympathy. There was a greater story he had yet to tell. The intensity of his attention chilled her, yet left her wishing to learn more.

Her father cleared his throat and she let her gaze fall back to the reporters. When she looked up again, Tobias Lark was gone.

5

The minute Sarah made eye contact, Tobias knew he and Garrett needed to be anywhere but there. They hadn't been invited, and should she choose to approach them at that moment, there would be numerous questions he didn't wish to answer. Possibly followed by a visit from the local sheriff.

They made away without incident, but his interest in Sarah Walcott wasn't through. Not by a long shot.

As soon as Cade saw them approach the camp, he shot up from beside the fire, tossing down the branch he had been using to tend the embers. Despite standing directly beside the fire, its light barely illuminated his charcoal brunette hair, so dark as to remind Tobias of the storm clouds his brother predicted. That was Cade's Gift—sensing weather patterns impossible for any man to foresee. For a plantation built on successful harvests, it had proved the most useful skill of all.

He folded his arms across his bare chest, his suspenders flat upon his shoulders like a pair of insufficient overalls. Even in the cool night air, he seemed unaffected. His shirt lay over a tree branch propped up near the fire, its material still damp and featuring a rather significant brown streak. He had likely received another mud clod to the chest while trying to pick a stone from his horse's hoof. Cade could read the weather like a book, but animals never had agreed much with him.

"You're alone," he called out as they rode into the clearing. "Didn't Garrett's Gift work this time?"

Tobias swung out of the saddle, his spurs clinking as he landed squarely. He flipped the reins over the mare's head and led her over to the trickle of a brook. "I think it did. He claims otherwise."

Garrett dropped to the ground beside Tobias. "Because you're delusional." Looping his mare's reins over a tree branch, he lifted his bedroll, untied the rope around it, and thwapped it hard on the ground. "Tobias wants to get married."

"I never said I was marrying her," Tobias told him.

"No, but you sure thought it awfully loud."

"Jumpin' jacks, who is this woman?" Cade asked. His jaw had fallen slack, a gaping dark hole in the flickering firelight.

"She's been widowed seven times," Garrett explained. "The latest time this very evening. The man fell straight down the stairs. Tobias thinks she's cursed." He released a harsh laugh and shook his head. "Oh, forgive me, that's not right, is it? No, he thinks she's *Gifted*."

"Again?" Cade asked, then immediately flushed, the red splotches on his cheeks visible even in the darkness. He turned to Tobias, bending down to adjust his boot unnecessarily. "I mean, why would you think so?"

"Because there isn't another good explanation."

"Murder's a good one," Garrett muttered.

Cade's head swung up, his eyes wide. "You want to marry a murderer?"

"No. She didn't murder anyone." He hoped. He squatted in front of his younger brother, offering him whatever assurances he could. He had to imagine this draw to Sarah was similar to the way Garrett felt when he was compelled toward finding a particular person, only without the headaches and nausea. Instead, he had stomach pains of a different sort, excitement marching through his insides.

"Cade, we were told women couldn't be Gifted, but what if it was because they could only be cursed instead? But curses can surely be broken. I believe her marrying another Gifted would do so."

"Father Corbin always said there was no such thing as curses. Not the kind you mean anyway."

"And most people would believe there's no such thing as what we can do. Yet here we are."

Tobias didn't believe in curses. At least, he never had before. He believed in miracles and works of God and unexpected blessings. And he supposed science too, drawing evidence to form a conclusion. If he was Gifted, what was there to prove Sarah wasn't? Two sides of the same Gift. What if that was what drew Garrett to her plantation tonight? What if meeting Sarah was providential rather than mere chance?

"We could use more land for the town," Cade admitted. "She could marry one of the other single men in the wagon party."

"No. It has to be me. That's the only way this will work. Otherwise, you've sent another poor fellow to his doom."

"How are you so certain you'll survive?"

"He's not," Garrett cut in with a snort. He had laid back upon his bedroll, one arm under his neck, an ankle propped upon his knee. "Tobias has let this lifelong quest go to his head once again. Remember when he claimed Debbie Martin was Gifted because she stitched a sampler in less than an hour? Or when Herbert Davis was Gifted because he magically discovered a needle in a rice paddy which we were all pretty certain he put there himself?"

"This is different," Tobias argued. "You know we haven't seen this type of Gift before, but maybe it's because we weren't looking. We assumed all Gifts were positive, but consider Father. He used his Gift time and again to extort and even murder—"

"You don't have proof of that."

"Why are you protecting him? His cruelty needs no defense." Tobias gave Garrett a long look to which neither he nor Cade made any further rebuttal. They were all well aware that their father had driven their mother to her death and likely found a way to take care of their sisters as well. None of them could prove it, but the inner knowledge of their father's treachery hung around them like thick mist in the morning twilight. Only since they departed Charleston had they finally felt it lessen.

He had to bring both his brothers into agreement.

"Garrett, please. Give this a chance. We've been wanting to find another Gifted all our lives and now one might be at our fingertips."

"We're not here for her. We already have our own troubles aplenty; we don't need hers. Besides, do any of those affluent snobs truly understand the quest for freedom? Did we?"

"We do now. We understand the price and we're here to recruit others who could help us."

Garrett finally rolled over fully, pegging Tobias with intimidation. In the firelight, his stare appeared even more hostile than usual. "Then let's take the slaves. I counted about seven at the wedding party and with a plantation of that size, there are likely others at the quarters. We offer them freedom in exchange for joining our group and helping build Larksong."

"So, they exchange loyalty to their master for loyalty to the town?" Cade cut in. "Isn't that just another kind of enslavement?"

Tobias and Garrett both stared at him, surprised at their brother's unexpected opinion on the matter. Usually, Cade kept his opinions to himself, especially when it came to quickly heated topics such as slavery. Don't address the issue in order to keep the peace. That had been his way ever since he attempted to feed a slave being starved as punishment and earned a punishment of his own. Cade had been only eight at the time, mere months after their mother passed. He had packed his britches full of rolls and honey from the breakfast table and scurried down to the whipping post.

There in the center of the slave quarters sat Kitch, only fifteen, still a kid himself really, his wrists bound to the eight-foot wooden post, sweat pouring down his back from the morning sun. In early June, the South Carolina heat was unrelenting. Moisture clung to one's skin and made each breath rough as sawdust. With the humidity came mosquitos in droves and those who forgot to draw the netting about their beds would suffer the consequences. Kitch's back was covered with their round raised bumps, red as welts and torturous to the touch. Tobias could only imagine how his night must have affected him. If he contracted malaria, itching would be the least of his worries.

When their father learned Cade fed the offending slave, he ordered his youngest son tied to the post instead and tithed ten lashes. When he was done, he cut Cade loose and left him in a heap on the ground. "Remember this," he said to the other brothers, "the slaves are not your friends or your playmates. They are workers. It is my job to dole out their punishments. It's yours to stay out of it."

That night, Jamison layered Cade's back with warm mashed rice poultices then fed him a tea of turmeric and ginger root he claimed would ease the sting. Unfortunately, their abilities were always diminished when used on another Gifted. Cade's pain lasted nearly a week, his slow eight-year-old cries bearing into each brother's soul when they mewled through the floorboards. By the time Cade recovered, Kitch had long since been removed from the plantation. By sale or death, they were never told.

Cade became quieter after that, more reserved, and less likely to spend time with others. To protect their remaining workers, he became an overseer, like the rest of them, as soon as he was able, but remained unsure of every decision he made. He worried his actions would release their father's anger and cause them or the slaves more trouble. He feared next time the lashes would never stop and he—or one of his brothers—would never recover.

The day they left home for the West, finally saying goodbye to Larksong Plantation, the brothers had paused along the drive. Despite their horrible childhoods, it had still been their home and a beautiful place to spend their formative years. Live Oaks lined the drive, their low arching branches draped in Spanish Moss. Framing the mansion's white stone staircase and high pillars, Azalea bushes flourished, their pink blossoms a breathtaking welcome for visitor and family alike. There had been happy memories there, times with their mother on the wide verandahs, sharing tea and conversation when their father was away. Even so, when the brothers paused along the plantation drive, Cade didn't offer the house so much as a glance.

"Don't you want a last look to remember it by?" Jamison had asked from atop his mare.

"Why would I want to remember anything about that place?" Cade said with vehemence. "Not one good thing happened to me there."

Now, Cade's eyes turned down to stare into the campfire, his shoulders curving forward into their usual meek posture. He had taken his moment and a moment was usually all they would receive from him.

Tobias nodded. "Cade's right. We don't have the money to legally purchase all the Walcotts' slaves and it seems risky freeing that many at once. We've only ever helped one or two escape before. Most of them don't trust our intentions, and we don't want them spilling our plans to Mr. Walcott, hoping for an improvement in their status."

Garrett shook his head. "I still like that plan better than bringing the widow along alone. If she really is cursed, I don't trust that your Gift will remove hers. We free those slaves or you can forget my cooperation."

"What if I can only gain a few? Would you take my side then?

"I'm not going to jump on board your quest for the Gifted, but I will agree to let her come with us, at least as far as Independence. Jamison should be there by now, readying the wagon train. Don't rush into anything stupid unless we at least have his approval. Fair?"

Tobias nodded, barely managing to rein in his excitement. He hadn't won Garrett's opinion, not by a longshot, but receiving this one acquisition was more than he usually received. Typically, Garrett just called him a dunderhead and walked away.

"Let me see what I can negotiate with Mr. Walcott. I don't think he'll give them all up, nor do we have the money, but I'll do my best."

"Good enough." With a grunt, Garrett flipped over to his other side. He tilted his chin to look back at his brother. "One more thing. We aren't telling Sarah yet about us being Gifted. If and when is another decision that needs to be made between all of us, not only you."

"Larksong is more important to Tobias than anyone," Cade said from where he lay on his bedroll. "He would never do anything to risk that. He'll find another way to ask her, won't you, Tobias?"

"Of course. I would never risk our town for the sake of a woman."

Turning away, he lowered himself to his own bedroll, resting his head on his folded arm and staring into the last glowing embers of the fire. He lay there for a long time thinking about their town, their family, and what he wanted from this life. He watched the stars blink through the branches above, winking like they knew his secret.

He had searched his entire life for another Gifted. If that's what Sarah was, he wouldn't let this opportunity slip through his fingers.

6

Church bells rang for the second time in two days, only this time a death knell. Jackson Whitticomb's coffin was carried down the stone steps on the shoulders of four men Sarah didn't know, perhaps cousins, perhaps friends. She and Mr. Whitticomb had never taken the time to learn much about one another. She had never felt the need to, knowing what she did.

Now, she clung tight to her mother's arm, both women clad head to toe in mourning black, although neither's dress retained the crisp edges of a fresh-made widow. Sarah's had long ago faded to dark grey in the summer's sun, her bonnet crinkled from tugging it against her face to block the mid-day rays. Thankfully, the day was pleasant enough with no need for fans and no rain to splash muck against their hemlines.

Her father stood on her other side, his back as rigid as the gate posts they walked through. His hand held his wife's elbow, his lips drawn as straight as his back. Probably contemplating how much he would need to pay out to Mr. Whitticomb's family and whether it was worth trying again.

She dearly hoped the answer was no. It was a hope which fell short every time.

"No more," she had told him after her sixth husband's death. "I'm not getting married again."

He merely took her hands and said, "I only ask you to try once more. Six is the devil's number, Sarah, but seven is the Lord's. Seven will succeed."

Clearly, Mr. Whitticomb had proven seven was not a perfect number after all.

Moist earth clumped atop the coffin one shovelful at a time, a thud for each beat of her rusted heart. She remained silent as the final shovelful was settled and the soil smoothed by the gravedigger's hand. Father Grier then prayed for Mr. Whitticomb's repose while the mourners bowed their heads above templed fingers. As their neighbors dispersed, common decency did as well, their whispers slithering around her like a snake's forked tongue.

In the storybooks, curses could be broken, but not hers. She had been prayed over, taken Holy Communion and confession with the regularity of a nun, and tried hard as she might to ensure her husbands' safety. Her sixth husband hired a guard to keep watch while he slept alone on their wedding night. He was the first to survive the night, but he did not survive the morning.

She saw her childhood friend, Bitsy, exit the cemetery with another group of Sarah's former friends. All five had shared their debutante year, laughed over gown fittings, and gossiped about the most handsome young men. Even fought over one or two. Now, they turned away without sentiment, as distant as the flowers on a papered wall.

Behind them, the mayor, Mr. Vaughn granted her a nod of sympathy—or was it pity? He too had considered her with favor once. At nearly thirty years her senior, the thought of being his bride had both sickened and delighted her. As Papa put it, Mr. Vaughn was "destined for the grave before fatherhood," yet Sarah imagined his age and position could afford her many grand and wondrous opportunities not available to her friends. Little did she know that her father's rejection had ultimately saved the mayor's life.

Mr. Vaughn swung up onto his horse at the same time another man's wrinkled hand came to rest on her waist, his lips bent to brush her cheek with scratchy whiskers. She peered up into the weathered face of Morris Aspen, her first father-in-law. Releasing her mother, she wrapped her arms around the man's dark coat, breathing in his honey scent. Nothing like his son, but it reminded her of warm summer days in their dining room, the windows open and the breeze fluttering the late Mrs. Aspen's lily curtains.

"Mr. Aspen," she managed. "How kind of you to come."

"I am always here for you, my dear." He held her a moment longer, then released her. He offered her mother a warm smile and squeezed her hand. "Elda, my condolences."

"Thank you, Morris. It is such a comfort to have someone understand."

"Of course."

If anyone understood their grief it was Mr. Aspen. The same cholera epidemic which stole his son had nearly claimed Sarah's life as well. On the evening after she and Linden wed, mere hours after speaking vows, she had become delirious and retired from the celebration to rest. Night had stolen her strength, but Linden remained by her bedside for three long days before he succumbed as well.

Cholera was a fierce enemy, whose wrath left no space for mercy. Linden died a hollow of a man, laying in a pool of his own filth. Never would she forget the stench of walking into that room after being told of his passing. The horror entered her nostrils and sent her heaving upon the rug before she even reached his bedside. Mr. Aspen had to lift her from the floor, carrying her to one of the empty bedrooms where she fell into a sleep steeped with nightmares. She hadn't seen Linden again until he was cleaned and prepared, lying in an open casket in the Aspens' front parlor. He was his father's only child.

Mr. Aspen now released her mother's hand to face Sarah, his expression swallowed within sharp wrinkles around his eyes and mouth. No laugh lines, yet he managed a slight smile. "Between old acquaintances, how are you, my dear?"

"It is so trying, Mr. Aspen," she whispered. "Trying to be hopeful."

"It is more trying if we are not," he told her. "We must believe someday we will gain back that which we lost...in one way or another. There is a day coming for you as well."

"Do you believe so?"

"I know so."

A cool breeze drew the rich scent of fresh-turned earth from beneath the cemetery's tallest tree. Bright shoots rose from every branch, green leaves intermingled with white and pink blossoms and a copper-breasted robin perched between its branches. A decade ago, Sarah and Linden had stood under this same tree together when his mother died. Her gloved hand had caressed his cheek as she kissed him so outlandishly. Her father had rebuked her, while Linden thought her spontaneity to be splendid.

A single tear traced its way down her cheek and she swiped it away with the back of her glove. A dark splotch appeared where the fabric met her skin. After all these years, shared grief was truly the only element binding her and Mr. Aspen together. She had little in common with him or he with her. They did not take tea or meals in one another's company, and there was never a desire to pursue matrimony as was sometimes done. They were two people on independent paths, both striding the boardwalk from opposite sides of the street. Occasionally, they glanced each other's way, but mostly, they walked life decidedly apart.

"I am sorry," she said softly. "I am sorry I took him from you."

"We cannot go back, Sarah." It was not forgiveness. It never would be.

A wind whipped up, sharp and unpleasant from the west, sweeping between the ladies' skirts and sending their curls into disarray. A single grey cloud darkened an otherwise clear horizon, visible between a break in the trees where the road flattened into the tall grass which bordered her father's fields. Sarah grasped her bonnet and squinted into the distance. They would need to press through the storm to reach home.

At her father's urging, they hurried to their waiting carriage. The two chestnuts snuffed their protest, metal harnesses jangling against the carriage shafts, their manes ruffled in the rising wind. "Hurry, Elda," her father said as he offered his wife a hand up into the open carriage, then extended his palm to Sarah.

She grasped his fingers and had lifted one slight boot onto the step before remembering to say a final farewell to Mr. Aspen. The wind stole the words from her lungs, however, when she saw two mounted figures silhouetted against the impending storm. Two men in styled overcoats, revolvers in their holsters, and hats low against their brows, their leather the same deep russet as the mares they rode. She would have cried "bandits" had the taller of the two not removed his hat to reveal sandy hair and a recognizable nod in her direction. Tobias Lark jutted his chin over his shoulder and jerked the reins, drawing his horse around and disappearing back into the brush. The dark-haired stranger at his side promptly followed.

She dropped her father's hand and stepped down from the carriage. "I would like to stay a while longer. To visit my husband and offer a prayer." When her father's mouth opened in protest, she threw her objection into the tossing wind. "I have had no opportunity to mourn him without an audience. I know we were not well acquainted, but I still feel his loss."

Especially since the divorce I requested—and you denied—may have saved him. She thought the words but allowed them to remain unspoken.

"In this weather?" Her father glanced again at the sky. Grey wisps had turned to clouds plump with moisture.

"It is Missouri weather, Papa. One knows how it can change in an instant. I would wager the storm will pass right on by, and my feet are not so sore from dancing that I cannot walk the distance."

"It is unwise," her mother said from inside the carriage. She patted the seat beside her.

Sarah took another step away, retreating toward the cemetery gate. "If I do not come home within the hour, send Sam with the carriage to make sure I haven't perished." It was not a humorous assessment and brought only dim silence save her own broken smile. If she indeed perished, would Linden's ghost transfer the curse to someone else? Her parents perhaps? Martha? Tildy or another of the maids? Who knew what happened when a person died unsettled? How far would it drive him to be at peace?

"I will bring her home," Mr. Aspen offered. He held his top hat between his hands while his sights considered her. He nodded. "We all need time for loneliness. Come to my home when you are through, and I will return you safely. Is this acceptable?" he asked her father.

Morris Aspen's red-brick estate was less than a third of the distance to her parents' farmhouse. With expressions equally

41

apprehensive, her parents consented. Her father stepped into the carriage and took the reins. First their carriage, then Mr. Aspen's clattered out of sight.

The wind held true, neither rising nor abating, threatening rain but none yet fell. Sarah waited a moment more with her back to the gravestones, drew in a breath of storm-kissed air, and for the first time in her adult life, lifted her skirts above her ankles.

Then she ran into the fields after Tobias Lark. As quickly as one in a crinoline and button-hooked heels could run.

7

Sarah swished through the high grass toward the dilapidated barn, her skirts sticking against brambles and collecting burs. The long blades bent and swayed with the wind, every so often concealing the narrow path made by the Larks' horses. Her skirt caught once again, this time on a tree sprout, its thin branch stuck out at an angle. She yanked at her skirt and tripped upon a dip in the hard earth, balancing herself seconds before falling flat into the brush.

Another wind gust hit her exposed face, knocking her bonnet back to hang by its ties around her neck. She tugged it back up and marched on until she reached the old barn, its roof sagging under years of neglect. What a place for a rendezvous. If the rain did come, she would return home afflicted with pneumonia and with much to explain to her parents.

Although the structure stood on the edge of her father's property, it had never been used by their family. Probably abandoned by another pioneer who failed to turn a profit and headed back east. The Walcotts could have torn it down—and would once their crops expanded farther—but for now, it was simply too laborious to remove.

One door hung at an angle while the other had completely rotted away, leaving only jagged pieces of its outside frame. She lifted her skirts through and allowed her eyes to adjust to the dim light. The stormy sky played down through the hollow rafters, threatening clouds passing by overhead. Wind whistled between holes in the wall chinking, but thankfully the boards stood solid enough for some protection from the elements. Across a dirt floor overtaken by weeds and clover, near several worn crates and old tools covered in grime, waited the object of her pursuit.

Tobias handed his horse's reins to his companion, his generous smile focused only on her. As he approached, the second man sunk farther behind their horses. She only caught the glimpse of a youthful face and muscular shoulders before he melded into the shadows, only his eyes and hat visible above the animal's withers.

She held up a hand, pausing Tobias when he was ten feet away. She pointed at the other man. "That isn't the same man you were with at the wedding."

"No," he consented. "My middle brother, Garrett, was with me then. This is my youngest brother, Cade."

Cade nodded and the creases around his eyes crinkled with a tight smile she couldn't see. "Pleasure to meet you, ma'am."

Sarah did not offer either man a smile in return. "If your brother told you anything about me, I'm not sure you should think so."

Cade's grip on the reins tightened and one of the mares shook her head in protest. He relaxed his grip. "There was some speculation between Garrett and I as to the wisdom of this meeting, ma'am."

She looked again to Tobias whose grin had lost much of its enthusiasm. "Let's get right to the purpose of our visit, Miss Walcott. My brothers and I have a matter of importance to discuss with you."

Her eyebrows raised, fingers clutched in her skirts for an easy exit. Well, it would not be easy. Running here in a five-petticoat crinoline had been difficult enough. Attempting an escape on foot when these strangers had the benefit of mounted pursuit, wouldn't be worth the try. She would probably just get trampled under hoof.

"If this matter involves your brothers," she asked, "then where is Garrett?"

"I asked him to watch over our camp. Cade's a little less...forceful when it comes to these sorts of dealings. Garrett has a tendency to speak his mind."

"Is that why your other brother stayed behind?"

"What other brother?"

"When we danced at the wedding, you told me one of your brothers was still in Charleston. Was it because of Garrett?"

He appeared impressed with the question. "A forward woman. We didn't see many of those back home." He gave her a nod of respect before turning serious again. "But no, it wasn't due to Garrett. He talks rough, fights sometimes, but he's never been cruel. You're safe around him. Our final brother, Jamison, is in Independence with the wagon party, readying for our departure."

Quickly, she added the sums in her head. Five brothers: Tobias, Garrett, Jamison, and Cade. Plus the one whose name hadn't been mentioned.

"Why did your brother remain in Charleston?"

"Dusty trails are not his preference. Now shall we get to the point before this storm drops a bucket on all of us?" As though to prove his point, another gust of wind penetrated the southern wall, causing the boards to creak with the strain.

Striding to his horse, he extracted a piece of parchment from the saddlebag, rubbing the mare's snout as he did so. He gestured to Sarah. "Come see."

Moving to the only crate that didn't seem like it would splinter in a slight breeze, he unfolded the parchment across its surface, then drew his revolver and placed it on top. The paper's edges flickered in the wind, gaps in the splintered roof lighting a map of the United States. Various points were labeled in small scratched handwriting. Thick charcoal X's lined the route from the coast of South Carolina up to Missouri.

Tobias pressed his index finger to Hawthorn Ridge then slid it across a vast emptiness to stop at the Pacific coast. "This is the path we're taking west to Washington Territory. Got a nice spot picked out north of the Columbia, right near the coast. Our town is nearly two hundred strong since leaving Charleston, but we sure could use a few more members. Every acre counts."

"You want me to join you?"

"If you are willing."

She followed the line he had drawn, moving her finger across the plains and mountains until it met with his. The farthest she had ever traveled was to St. Louis, a distance of only a few hundred miles. This length had to be thousands. Farther than she ever hoped to go and farther than anyone who knew her would want to travel. Farther even than Boston. She supposed she could write poetry and drink from chipped glasses anywhere, but would going west be the same as going east when it came to Linden's curse? Would it be enough?

"What would be required?" she asked. "I'm afraid I have very little to my own name."

Tobias took a breath and looked back at his brother. Cade didn't appear any more comfortable than he did. If possible, he seemed to withdraw even farther into the shadows.

"Here's the thing," Tobias said, drawing her attention away from his brother. He removed his hat and stared at it rather than her and his tone lost some of its confidence. "The government's land is only being offered to men. Women aren't eligible to claim it unless..." His eyes met hers again and she understood exactly what would be required to join their party.

He could not be serious.

"You want me to marry one of you?" He knew her reputation, the curse, what had happened before his very eyes. How could he even suggest such a thing?

She shifted away, but he placed his hand on top of hers before she could remove it from the crate top. His eyes held such horrible emotion, such pleading that she was suddenly reminded of Linden's brown-eyed gaze. He had held the same desperate look the day before he died, when he told her to continue on, to love again.

"Promise me, Sarah," he had whispered. "Promise me you won't give up."

She hadn't promised, hadn't wanted to believe those words were his last lucid moment with her. She had laughed instead. Actually laughed at her dying husband, the man she loved above all others. "I won't make a promise I won't need to keep," she told him. "I'm going to start packing the wedding dishes. I'll have Sam bring them to the house tomorrow. Everything will be perfect for your arrival."

His eyes still beseeched her, but he didn't say another word. She laced her fingers between his and pressed a kiss to his forehead. In the morning, he had passed on. Ten years and it could have been yesterday.

"Why not?" Tobias was saying. "You're beautiful, well-spoken, well-read I'm assuming? With a little instruction, you could be a hard worker. My brothers and I need hard workers."

"Those things do not matter when you have lost seven husbands. You saw what happened to Mr. Whitticomb. No man would risk his life that way unless he was insane. Are you insane, Mr. Lark?"

"I think I'm incredibly sane. I would like to think this is the most rational decision I've made yet."

"If this is rational to you, then you are insane. Find yourself an asylum, Mr. Lark. Please, excuse me." She yanked her hand away but he jumped to block her path. Each attempt she made to move around him was met with interference. Blast these too-large skirts! She could hide a city underneath them, but she couldn't slip through a doorway unhindered.

Tobias braced a hand on the cracked barn door and held the other palm out toward her. Part of her hoped the rest of the door would fall down and crush him.

"Miss Walcott, I know you are afraid because of what happened before, but I promise it won't be like the last time."

"How could you possibly promise such a thing? You don't know a hair about my situation."

There was a pause where Tobias and Cade looked at one another in a silent exchange. She couldn't decipher what was going through their minds, but she could understand the intention. Should they tell her the entire truth? Could she handle it?

Did she even *want* to know?

Finally, Cade spoke. "When you stay in a place too long, you accept that who you are is all you'll ever be, but Washington is unlike anything you've seen before. Mountains with snow caps, fields of lush wildflowers, mile upon mile never touched by man. The ocean's beauty stretches out like nothing you could imagine. In Charleston, our townhouse was not far from the ocean. It was a wondrous place, yet we have been told it pales in comparison to the Northwest territories."

How she would love to believe in such a place of beauty. Miles and miles of nothingness. To fly off to another world where no one knew her, where she didn't even know herself. Outside, the barn's planking seemed to creak a little less. Was it her imagination or had the winds actually faded? Perhaps she wouldn't be caught in the storm after all.

"Out west, you can be anyone you want," Cade continued. He stepped out from between the horses and his face now held a charming smile. "Women equal with men, whites with blacks. Larksong will be our town, where we make the rules we want. Everyone is welcome and no one will know or care about your past."

Her father might delight in having her far away where he didn't need to deal with her anymore. The whisperings would cease. He would certainly be happier if she didn't go north to "become a Yankee."

She couldn't marry either of them though. That was a chance she could never take again. If marriage was a condition, then she could never agree.

Deflect, she thought. Tobias clearly didn't mind that she had a terrible history with husbands. Providing an alternate excuse would be a better option.

She bit her lip and shook her head. "I could never leave without my maid, Martha."

"I will speak to your father. See if we can come to an agreement."

"The law doesn't allow him to free her and he would never sell her. He would never release any of them that way."

Her father might let Sarah leave, but he would never sell Martha. He might have purchased Martha to be her playmate, but she had grown into a fine servant. He needed her to tend the house. The more Sarah thought on it, the more she realized how much she didn't want to leave her dearest friend behind. It would be difficult to go to Boston without her, but impossible to imagine heading into the savage wilderness on her own.

She started as Tobias claimed her hand from against her stomach, unaware he had even approached. He held it between both of his, light enough to pull away if she desired, firm enough to engage her to stay. It was an intimate touch and far too forward for a stranger. She met his gaze slowly and wondered if he could see the confusion in her own.

"Miss Walcott," he said gently, "you must consider your own future now. There are other unmarried able-bodied men in our party. We've vetted each person properly, only the best have joined us, and one day you may be drawn to one of them. However..." He paused, looked again at his brother in another unspoken interaction. Mr. Aspen would expect her to return soon. Yet, she couldn't bring herself to tear her fingers from his grip.

"I have told you," she said, drawing his attention back. "I will never marry again."

"You will, Miss Walcott. And with the utmost respect, I would like to request that you marry me."

"To gain but some land? Surely, other women can fulfill that need without endangering your life."

"They can, certainly, but it is your rare gift which intrigues me more than anything else."

"Tobias!" Cade dropped the reins and was beside his brother, his hand gripping Tobias's upper arm. He pegged him with a harsh glance. "Tobias, we agreed. This is not the time."

"There is no other time!" he shot back. "We leave in mere hours. I know what Garrett said, but if we wait for Jamison's agreement, we've lost our only chance. Is that what you want?"

"I..." Cade began, then snapped his lips shut and turned away. He blinked hard. Had his brother actually driven him to tears?

When Tobias released her hands to tend to his brother in hushed tones, she removed herself several paces. She should turn and go. Leave them to their folly, let him find another wife who didn't carry the weight of death upon her shoulders. Tobias seemed a kind enough man, rather misguided in love, yet a nice enough fellow. There were plenty of flighty women who would ingest his prattle like cold spring water on a summer's day. They would admire his handsome features, his soulful eyes, and smart smile. When he had twirled her around the pine board floor, his touch had been gentle, his fingers on her waist featherlight. Later...after Mr. Whittcomb...he had met her gaze from across the room like he understood every thought inside her head. Like he knew exactly what to say if only they were alone.

They were alone now. Well, almost.

"Explain it to me," she said. Both men looked at her, thankfully with no tears on Cade's cheeks and simple astonishment on his elder brother's.

She folded her hands, five black-gloved fingers upon the others. "Whatever it is you must say, I promise to hold in confidence. I have no desire to give this town more opportunity to gossip on my behalf."

Five minutes later, however, she had thoroughly decided she shouldn't have asked. For Tobias Lark told her a tale so fanciful she couldn't dare believe it to be true. He explained how the brothers held special talents, inherited over a hundred years. His was the ability to build with incredible speed and accuracy, then he described building methods which hadn't yet been invented. That shouldn't even be physically possible.

The most irrational part of all was he claimed she was one of them! Her husbands' deaths were due to an unconscious Gift murdering them without her knowledge, and the only way to fix it was to marry another Gifted. Honestly, the man had completely lost his mind.

She looked to Cade for rationality, but he skulked backward, placing distance between them again. "What is your Gift then?" she asked him. "Shooting lightning from your fingertips?" His eyes darted in either direction, out the barn doors, and even up into the rafters. Honestly, who would be lurking there?

Finally, Cade shrugged. "Close. I can predict weather changes."

"If that's a Gift, then my father is Gifted too," she scoffed. "He falls ill with a headache any time the rain clouds form." He was probably suffering one at this very moment.

Tobias nodded. "If you're Gifted, then likely your father is too. Giftedness is in our blood."

"And my Gift is that I kill people?"

"Exactly, only I wouldn't be so macabre about it. We could call it unintentional mariticide."

If what he said was true, then her husbands had died by her hands. Not intentionally, but she was still responsible. Her. Not Linden.

"No," she said. "This is too much to be believed."

"It's true." Cade took a tentative step forward, one hand on his stomach and his expression green. "Show her, Tobias."

Tobias knelt before her then, finally allowing his intense gaze to fall as well. He plucked strands of grass and clover into a bundle, and she didn't consider the reason. She only debated why she wasn't running out the unguarded door. Flee to Mr. Aspen and insist he summon the sheriff.

From here, she could make out the faint path back to the road. It wasn't far. The sun was high, nearing noon and the lunch hour. Once on the boardwalk, she could get lost in the bustle of the main thoroughfare and be rid of these men and their crazy notions forever.

They *were* simply notions, weren't they? They couldn't honestly have some sort of strange abilities, nor could she. She couldn't be more of a freak of nature than she already was. Freaks were locked away or put on display. No, her husbands' deaths must be the product of coincidence or Linden's revenge.

Linden's revenge? Honestly, Sarah, listen to yourself. Is believing in ghostly vengeance any more reasonable than having a knack for unintended murder?

She lifted her hands, staring at them as she wondered if they would begin to emit some kind of magical glow. But no, they were only her same hands, fingers covered in black lace and a gorgeous ring of green and gold and white encircling her fourth finger.

Wait. A ring?

Braided and looped and more intricate than many rings of metal, the grass and clover he had plucked mixed with bits of golden flora she couldn't identify. Graceful and feminine unlike many of the garish engagement rings her friends delighted in. Everything about this creation was pure loveliness.

"It's so beautiful," she breathed. "How did you make something so delicate out of grass? And so quickly?" Tobias grinned up at her from where he still knelt upon the grass, one forearm draped upon his knee. She looked from him to the ring and back. "That's impossible."

"I told you, Sarah, we're Gifted. You're Gifted. You belong with us."

He rose from the ground and reached into his suit jacket, removing a wooden bird created from nothing more than sticks. Each twig bent over one another in perfect curves, beak to body swooped into a feathered tail, the lines more precise than any whittler could perform. No obvious twine, nails, or paste held it together, but there must be. It wasn't possible otherwise.

How many times had she said that in the last five minutes?

"A lark," he explained. "I made it the other night...after...well, just after."

"Yes, after," she whispered, her eyes on the bird. She had no desire to replay Mr. Whitticomb's horrid death behind her eyes yet again. It would haunt her dreams enough in the coming months. All her husbands' had.

She accepted the graceful lark, holding it in her cupped hands like it was a living breathing creature. She could touch it, feel it, see it with her own eyes. Every slant of every twig. Even if he hadn't made it, even if he stole it, someone had to have crafted it. Someone had accomplished something that simply should not be.

Everything in her life should not be.

He stepped toward his horse, taking the reins from Cade. "We leave for Independence this afternoon. Think about what I said, Miss Walcott. Think about where you belong."

With that, they were gone. She was left in a rickety barn with only a ring, a bird, and the grey heavens as they opened up upon her.

8

By the time she knocked on Mr. Aspen's door, the downpour had ceased, afternoon sunrays painting rainbows across the misty sky. He had shaken his head at her appearance, offered her a blanket to drape about her shoulders, and quietly directed his servants to ready the carriage. A little over an hour later, she now shivered in her parents' foyer, her skirts dripping upon the tile, while outside, lingering rain droplets trickled into puddles beneath the eaves.

"Landsakes, Miss Sarah," Tildy exclaimed. "Were's you caught in the storm?"

Sarah only nodded as she crossed the threshold into her parents' home. Mr. Aspen followed closely behind, his hat and shoulders only slightly damp, whereas she looked like a drowned puppy. She had caught the brunt of the storm on her walk back to his home, leaving her blonde curls plastered to her neck and dripping down her bodice. She had caused quite an inappropriate stir with her heels clacking down the boardwalk. Attempting to push damp tendrils out of her face while holding her skirts high was no simple matter and twice, she nearly tripped off the foot-high ledge into the muddy street.

From behind her father's closed office door rose the shuffle of desk chairs and footsteps across the hardwood. Two sets of footsteps. More visitors and her appearance as tussled as a kitten in a watering trough. There would be more stories flying about over dining tables tonight.

When the office door opened, a stranger was with Papa, the man's frock coat and trousers not nearly as polished, but still clean and with no sign of fallen hems or stray stitches. He had removed his hat to expose greased-back hair, the dark oil disguising its true shade. His straight lips and lack of greeting played rather formidably.

Her father faltered when he saw her standing there. "Sarah? Why are you so unkempt? And what is that?" He pointed to the wooden bird Tobias had given her.

She had forgotten she still carried it. Mr. Aspen had made no comment on it at any point. But there it was, wooden twigs firmly fixed between her palms, the woven ring braided around her fourth finger. Her father could see them too, which meant her conversation with Tobias hadn't been conjured by her own design. As she bounced along in Mr. Aspen's carriage with silence unending, she had allowed herself time to consider what took place in the barn and whether it was real. She couldn't explain how Mr. Lark crafted those items, but she couldn't believe it was as he claimed. What he had done didn't seem supernatural, yet it wasn't exactly natural either. Suspended somewhere between what was possible and what could be imagined.

"A gift from someone at the funeral. Unimportant." She slipped it, along with the braided ring, into the pocket bag tied beneath her skirt. She hoped the wood would not become waterlogged in the damp material. "I was caught in the storm, but see, I am here. No worse for the walking."

Her father strode to the foyer sidelight and looked at the clear sky through the rain-speckled pane. "So it appears. The water will be good for the crops." He seemed distracted and did not immediately turn, pausing to observe the exterior. "Perhaps you should go upstairs and change first. It is improper to receive a guest in such attire and I will not have you mussing the parlor upholstery."

This guest was for *her*? For the first time, she truly took in the stranger's appearance and realized he was likely little more than thirty. The perfect age for a twenty-eight-year-old widow. "Another husband?" she cried. "No, Papa, I can't—"

He held up a hand. "Silence, Sarah. It is not what you suppose."

She looked between her father and the latest in a long line of visitors over the past few days. "Then what is the reason for this call?"

54

Her mother entered the foyer, stopping within the doorway from the kitchen hall. She had changed from her ebony dress into a light green gown with a slender hoop more suitable for afternoon entertainment. After observing appropriate mourning traditions for ten years, was she now throwing societal expectations to the wind? Would her friends not find her behavior unsavory if they knew?

She offered Sarah a slight smile, but it contained little warmth. "There will be time enough to discuss after you change those dripping clothes. Martha is already upstairs readying your things."

"My things?"

"Yes. You're ah..." Her mother looked to her father as though silently asking for the right word. Finally, he turned.

"You're taking some time to convalesce, my dear."

"Convalesce? I'm not ill." She felt like her head had emptied, her brain fallen into her chest where her heart now thudded. Mr. Aspen lingered near the door, hands folded upon his cane as he took stock of the conversation. The visitor also eyed her as though an intervention would be required and his broad shoulders and thick muscles were happy to comply.

"This man is from Fulton's Asylum Number One. He's here to collect you."

She didn't know who spoke the words. It could have been her father, Mr. Aspen, or even her mother. It could have been Tildy who stood silently in the shadow of the kitchen door. Her brain wasn't comprehending male or female voices or to whom they belonged.

She felt her knees start to quake and suddenly she couldn't breathe. She needed to either move or crumple in a pile of rain-soaked petticoats and stifling black cotton right there on the foyer floor. "Water," she gasped. "I need water. I can't breathe."

"Wait here, gentlemen." Her father's hand was on her arm, quickly leading her down the hallway past her stricken mother and into the kitchen. The two servants paused in their dinner preparations and, upon seeing Sarah, rushed to assist. They each took one of her arms, lowering her into a chair at the squat table. At the same time, Tildy rushed in with a bucket of water from the pump, pouring some into a glass.

Sarah took it, her hands trembling as she swallowed the liquid down. It didn't help. She still felt like the stone floor was spinning up into the plaster ceiling.

"The asylum," she gasped. "I can't—you can't—I'm not..." She gulped the water until it was gone and pressed a hand to her forehead. She had always rolled her eyes at the girls who swooned for effect, but this time her affliction was no act.

Her father knelt before her, his hands pressing her crinoline down upon her knees. It now jutted out at extreme angles on either side, forming a crescent for her father to ease into. "Sarah, breathe, my dear. It is not as terrible as it seems."

She drew another shallow breath, her voice coming in spurts. "I'm not...a...a lunatic...Papa."

He shook his head. "I don't know what else to do. Our family is the dread of Hawthorn Ridge. Townsfolk placing bets on how long your husbands will live. Whispering even louder that you killed them."

"You know it isn't true."

"How can I know what to believe anymore? You've lost seven fiancés or husbands all before the wedding night. Perhaps you are murdering them and do not even remember."

"How could you think it? You were there when it happened." She felt her head lighten again. Tildy placed another glass of water in her hand and she drank it down.

"Sarah, we were only there for the last. I do not know what to think anymore."

Did he honestly find her capable? Was she capable? Was Tobias right?

No, it was Linden's doing. She could fix this.

She stood on shaky legs, moving her skirts out of her father's grip. She stared down at him, trying to regain her confidence. Her heart still fluttered, but at least she could breathe now. "You cannot send me there. If you must send me away, send me to Boston."

Her father reared back, stricken. He pushed to stand, towering over her once again. "That's twice now you've mentioned that devil place. You would further ruin your reputation—"

"Papa," she replied quietly. "My reputation is already ruined.

Linden's memory is holding me hostage. He wanted us to live in Boston. I will never be free of this curse unless I go." She turned to her mother who hovered just beyond her father's shoulder. "Mama, please don't let him. Please."

An emotion flitted across her mother's expression, something close to pity over her daughter's plight. She pursed her lips and turned to the kitchen maids, lined in a row near the stove. Their hands were folded against their waists and heads bowed, but they heard every word. Many of the townspeople thought the slaves too stupid to understand their masters' conversations or too ignorant to care. It was one of the reasons why it was illegal to teach a slave how to read or write. They had no need for the skill in their position and too much education would only confuse them. They would develop lofty goals far outside their station, only to be disappointed when they never achieved them. They were happiest when they were working hard. Or at least, that was what some folks thought.

Sarah knew all that was nonsense. Her parents knew it, too. While they had never initiated educational lessons with any of their servants, they had permitted Sarah to teach Martha how to read and write. In the discretion of her bedroom, she demonstrated the curve of each letter and how they stuck together to form words. It was their special secret concealed from all except her parents. They knew what could happen if they were discovered.

Slaves were capable of comprehending much more than they were given credit. It was why Sarah's mother now clicked her tongue and sent all three maids from the kitchen. She closed the door behind them and returned to Sarah's side, her expression void of any compassion.

"You embarrass yourself, darling, and you embarrass your father. At the asylum, you have a chance at a normal life. You will have work to do and a purpose. Companions with afflictions of their own and physicians who wish to cure them. In Boston, no one would lift a finger to help you."

Nor would they in this house. She could read between her mother's words. Her father had worked many years by the sweat of his brow and the break of his back to amass this plantation. Twenty-five servants, more than any other landowner in the county, certainly more than either of his brothers back in Kentucky with their fields of five and nine. If Sarah had been a son, she might have been forgiven for her eccentricities. After all, twenty-eight was not so old for a man to still plan a successful plantation, even without a wife. A twenty-eight-year-old woman, on the other hand, was well into her childbearing years. She was unlikely to produce the wealth of heirs a husband would want, even if she wasn't otherwise "afflicted."

"They will cure me there? At the asylum?" she asked. "They will stop this black mark I have upon me?"

"There are no guarantees, but they will try." Her mother's soft fingers reached out and grasped Sarah's, her eyes alight with tears, but also with hope. "Fulton is a fine institution. The superintendent seeks to give his patients a full life. Lush grounds to walk and new buildings painted white and clean. You are sure to find it as lovely as we did."

Sarah stared. "You've been there? When?"

"In December. The week after Christmas."

"December? I was already engaged to Mr. Whitticomb by then. You planned this even knowing I was to be married? You expected him to die?" She would be furious to discover it if she had not anticipated the same outcome.

"We prepared ourselves for the worst," her father explained. "Winter was coming and with it, possible illness. If illness did not take him, then any other number of ailments or accidents could and clearly did in the end. We had to consider every factor. At least I knew he wouldn't take his own life as Mr. Renfrew had done. I paid him handsomely to ensure he would stay true to his word."

A sharp rap interrupted from the hallway. Tildy announcing there was a visitor for Sarah's father.

"Another reporter?" he asked. "How far has this one come?"

"Not a reporter, sir. Just a man. Said he was interested in speakin' to ya about a purchase."

"Probably another suitor." He spoke over his shoulder on his way to the door. "Sarah, go upstairs and change. I expect you ready within the hour."

She went, for what else could she do? No young lady wished to be committed, but if there was a chance they could cure this wretched blackness on her soul, she had to try.

9

In the privacy of her bedroom, Sarah peeled off her wet gown, letting it puddle on the floor before stepping over the broad crinoline. Her thin bloomers twisted against her legs and now that she was settled and alone, she finally felt how her corset had chafed her skin during her rainy day sprint. She stood still as Martha silently unlaced the ties and removed the binding from around her chest, leaving her in nothing more than her chemise and undergarments.

Martha nodded. "Once you're freshened up, I'll take your wet things down for laundering. I've already packed your trunk there in the corner. I left out most of your fancy things, but I can certainly add them back in."

The trunk in question sat open near the Georgian-style writing desk. Two neat piles of folded garments peeked out from beneath the top insert which contained other daily accessories such as simple gloves and stockings. No jewelry or lace fans. No fancy hair combs. She wouldn't need those in Fulton. All her elegant gowns and slippers would remain behind in her chifforobe, waiting for her return.

If she returned. Without certainty of a cure, she would have no reason to.

"No, Martha. I won't need them."

"If you're certain."

"I am."

Her maid bent for the dress in a heap. "Martha?" Sarah called.

"Yes, Miss Sarah?"

"What would you do if you were in my position?"

Martha straightened, leaving the gown where it lay. She gave a small smile. "With respect, I will never be in your position."

No, that was true, she supposed. But weren't they still both women with hopes and dreams of what could be? They had spent many a night as children sharing exactly that. "But if you were?" she pressed.

Martha glanced from the puddled dress to the door and back to Sarah, still standing in her chemise and bloomers. "If I were in your position, Miss, I would find myself some clothes."

Sarah laughed then which caused Martha to laugh right along with her. She stepped forward to embrace her friend, her heart feeling lighter than it had in years. Perhaps finding proper clothing should be the worst of her troubles at the moment. Focus on what was right in front of her and leave the rest to itself. If her mother claimed the asylum could offer her a good life, then why shouldn't she trust it? Living there might not end the curse, but if she never married again—which she wouldn't—then the curse was as good as broken anyway. At least in Fulton, she would have a new start.

"I'm going to miss you, Martha."

Was it her imagination or did her friend's arms stiffen? There was a sheen over Martha's deep chocolate irises. "I as well, Miss Sarah. It will be lonely here without you."

"You'll still have Tildy and the other girls. And Mama and Papa, of course."

"Yes, miss, but—" She quickly looked away, down at Sarah's stomach rather than her eyes.

"What is it, Martha? Look at me."

Her friend slowly met her gaze again. "Your parents are kind to me and the other girls are too, but they aren't like you. You ask me what's the trouble and you care to know. You let me borrow your books. The other girls don't have none and couldn't read them if they did. I may be a servant, but the others know I'm different. Without you here, I don't have a place on either side." She smiled then. "But don't you worry about me. Let's get you ready."

Sarah nodded, feeling like she had encroached on a place she didn't belong. She had been married seven times and not once had

Martha ever expressed fear over her leaving. But likely, she had experienced these feelings every time. Sarah had never considered Martha might be lonely or misunderstood in her own home, especially since she had never planned to move far, only across Hawthorn Ridge. But this time was different. This time she was leaving and would not return. Likely, not even for holidays. That was how these sorts of institutions worked. You remained until you were cured or until you died. Her parents might have the option to visit, but a black woman would never be allowed inside their doors.

She swallowed hard. "Perhaps you're right."

Quickly, she faced away to exchange her damp undergarments for fresh ones. She clasped her simplest corset around her chest, then dipped her head and raised her arms, allowing Martha to lower a simple cotton mourning dress across her shoulders. It buttoned in front, easy for her to undo without a servant's assistance. No crinoline this time. Even the most slender was too grand for a place like Fulton. A single petticoat would have to do.

Seating herself before the dressing table, she allowed Martha to brush out her tangled curls in silence. Her friend took care not to cause pain as she fingered out each damp knot and eventually, the blonde locks fell loose again. Martha swept them up into a tight bun at the nape of Sarah's neck, then situated a black traveling bonnet atop. The hat's stiff brim curved around her face, leaving her chignon visible in back, but blinding her periphery. Placing the brush on the dressing table, Martha stepped out of Sarah's sight to gather her discarded wet garments. A second later something clattered to the hardwood.

Sarah twisted on the stool to see her friend lift Tobias's wooden lark from the floor, the mourning dress draped over Martha's opposite arm. With the commotion over her impending move to Fulton, she had forgotten the bird stored in her pocket bag. If Martha looked, she would find the braided grass ring as well. She didn't.

Rather, she crossed the room to set the bird on Sarah's dressing table and without a word, turned back for the door.

"Are you not going to ask where I got it?"

Martha paused. "I assumed you received it as a sympathy token.

You have others like it."

Sarah had received gifts after her husbands' deaths before, figurines made of porcelain or glass, but none of wood and none like this one. Martha had discarded the bird so quickly, she likely hadn't noticed the impossible craftsmanship, and Sarah shouldn't bring it to attention. She had promised the Larks she would make no mention of it.

Martha turned back for the door, but Sarah stopped her again before she could open it. "Wait." She snatched the pocket bag from her hands, turned it over, and let the braided ring fall into her open palm. Green and white and gold still entangled, slightly crumpled, but not too much worse for their travel in the bag.

This time, Martha did notice. Her eyes widened. "Did you make that? Out of...is that clover and goldweed?"

Ah, goldweed. So that's what the gold bits were.

Sarah held it out and Martha jostled the laundry in her arms to take the ring. She held it up to the window light. The storm long passed, sunlight now illuminated the edges of each flower. "This is...it's..."

"Without words," Sarah finished quietly.

Martha's eyes met hers. "Yes."

Sarah accepted the ring back and crossed to set it on the dressing table beside the lark. Outside the window, the yard was void of activity, all traces of the wedding stripped away by the servants while she slept. Sunlight glistened off the wet grass and highlighted several puddles on the dirt drive. Across the way, their stable hand, Sam led one of their mares out for a turn in the pasture, securing the gate behind her before wiping his palms on his thighs and heading back into the stable.

"He proposed to me," she said finally.

"Who?"

"The man who made this figure. He invited me to go out west with him and his brothers."

Think about what I said, Tobias told her. *Think about where you belong.*

Where I belong, she thought. She didn't know where that was, but it wasn't with him.

"You could go," Martha said. She hadn't moved from where she stood in the center of the room. "It would be better than the madhouse."

Sarah turned her back on the window. "You know what happens to men when they marry me. Mr. Whitticomb was a fine man, a lovely speaker, a talented dancer. I do believe he would have made a good husband. I could have prevented his death if I had only insisted on no more marriages."

She deserved to be confined to the asylum with only this wooden bird for company, to remind her of happier days and what could have been if only she hadn't been...well, her.

"They sing while they fly," Martha said then. She nodded to the bird. "Most birds only sing while perched, but the lark? They sing while they float on the breeze, happy to be free, happy knowing at least they are still alive."

Draping the mourning dress over the bed's footboard, she moved to lift the bird instead. She placed it in Sarah's palm, clenching her dark fingers around Sarah's pale ones. "You asked me what I would do if I were you. Well, I ain't free to sing like that, Miss Sarah, but you are. There are worse places to find yourself than under the attention of a handsome man. Especially one who would help you out of such trouble. No need to marry him if you don't want to. Make your own way instead."

She had considered it, hadn't she? Going west into the wide-open...but there was no way to claim the land without a husband.

Removing her hands from Martha's, she set the bird back on the dressing table and picked up her hairbrush instead. "Pack this. I may never see another social season, but that doesn't mean my hair must entice the rats for a stay."

A quick rap on the door punctuated the awkward ending to their conversation. When Martha answered, Sarah's mother rushed in. "Close the door, Martha. Quickly." Elda turned to her daughter. "Plans have changed, dearheart. You're not going to Fulton. Martha?" She swung back around. "Go pack your sack. You both need to run."

Martha didn't move. "But ma'am, this is my home. I do not wish to leave it."

"You must. Oh, Martha, I'm so sorry. Mr. Walcott's sold you."

The statement hung for the briefest moment before the truth of it slapped Sarah across the face. Her best friend sold? Her father had never sold one of their slaves before, much less one who had become so ingrained within their family.

She stumbled through her words. "Mama, how...how could he...? To whom? Why?"

"Your father didn't tell me his name, only that he offered a sum higher than four of our field hands combined. It was impossible to refuse such an offer."

Martha paled, stumbling, and Sarah grabbed her arm to help lower her to sit on the bed. It had been years since they sat together on her double-stitched quilt, ever since the night before her wedding to Linden. In any other house, it wouldn't be allowed. It might even earn Martha a lashing or two, but this wasn't any ordinary house and Sarah wasn't any ordinary woman.

She forced herself not to look at the wooden lark. If she was Gifted, why couldn't she possess a Gift which could fix this?

Her friend's hands trembled upon her worn skirt, her eyes focused on them rather than anywhere else. She had no choice but to run. A sum that high for a female slave was unusual and likely meant Martha wouldn't be working in the kitchen or as a lady's maid. It was said, albeit quietly, that Southern gentlemen sometimes purchased young black women, many still mere youths, to provide them with...intimate companionship. At thirty, Martha was older than most, but not so old and certainly still beautiful. She could serve her new master for decades. Sarah couldn't believe her father would do such injustice to a woman he had cared for like a second daughter.

"Martha," her mother said, "this is your only chance. I am granting you this freedom; unfortunately, I cannot grant it legally. You run, and I will deal with Mr. Walcott." She hugged her, which was unexpected, and Sarah watched Martha go stiff in her arms. "I have always loved you like a daughter. Thank you for all the years you gave me. Take care of Sarah now, you hear?" Martha nodded. "Good. Sarah will meet you at the kitchen door. Now pack quickly. Go."

As soon as Martha disappeared, her mother spun from the closed door. A lock of blonde hair had fallen against her neck. Her cheeks flushed scarlet, she began transferring clothing from Sarah's trunk into her lone carpet bag.

"Mama, wait. I thought you wanted me to go to Fulton. You told me they could cure me."

Her mother's hands stilled, clutching the sides of the bag. Another lock of hair broke loose, curling down across her shoulder. Sarah had never seen her mother with her hair down. She wondered if they would look more alike then and her mother more romantic. Sarah had never heard the story of her parents' marriage. She knew they lost many babies, and her mother cried often when Sarah was a child, but otherwise, she knew little.

"Darling, the asylum is but a bandage, not a balm. All you would have there is a life away from here. No one knows why you have lost so many husbands. I doubt anyone could ever explain it as more than the cruelest of luck."

"You do believe I'm cursed then?"

"A Catholic home does not believe in curses."

That reasoning was as good as saying "yes." Sarah's eyes filled with tears as she helped her mother pack the last of her belongings. More than half the trunk Martha packed now remained behind. She felt like her life was going up in smoke, those stars she had wished on in her childhood now blinking out one by one.

"Where are we to go?" she asked. "Ever since the new law, the slave catchers are everywhere." The Fugitive Slave Act said blacks could be captured and sold back to the South from anywhere. Even if they were legally free.

"Chances are still better in the North. You wanted to go to Boston. Why don't you begin there?" Her mother kissed her cheek then gently folded her arms around her daughter. She released a gasp. "Forgive me, dearheart."

Sarah clutched her mother, inhaled her sweet lavender soap and arsenic face powder. This moment had taken all the courage Elda Walcott had, and Sarah would never fault her for that. "You're already forgiven, Mama."

66

She grabbed the wooden lark and braided ring off the dressing table, snatched her bag from the bed, and raced down the back staircase. Martha waited at the door with her own bag in hand.

Her mother stood atop the stairs, strands of blonde fluttering in the breeze from the open door. She descended two steps as though she aimed to join them, then waved her hand forward. Her lips whispered a silent farewell.

If Sarah didn't leave now, she wouldn't have another chance. She would be set inside a carriage for the asylum and Martha...poor sweet Martha would face a far worse sentence.

A wind gust picked up as they raced into the hemp fields, high stepping through the saplings and crushing too many underfoot. Other workhands peppered across the fields, sowing the next rows of seed. A few briefly glanced her way, but seeing her with Martha, returned to their work. It was not unusual to see the two women together, only unusual for them to be running with traveling bags in hand. She had to hope they would say nothing to her father until the end of the day, after she and Martha had hours to slip away.

As they passed from the fields into the shadow of the trees, she clutched the lark tighter inside her palm. Eventually, the slave catchers might be sent after them. After all, Martha belonged to someone and it wasn't her. She had no papers to keep her friend safe. All those years stargazing together, and not once had she considered how dreams looked far different if your life was drawn on a deed of sale.

She knew what she needed to do, and it meant she would never see Boston.

"Forgive me, Linden," she whispered, but she didn't turn back.

By the time Sarah and Martha made it to the old barn, save for two sets of hoofprints, all traces of the Lark brothers had vanished. They followed the trail through the tall grass until it joined with the road, the tracks lost within hundreds of identical prints. Without knowing the brothers' current whereabouts, the only chance of locating them now was to travel west to Independence. Sarah had to hope she wouldn't arrive too late.

They kept to the trees and low-lying areas until the afternoon turned to night and the woods pitched so black, they could barely see. Then they worked their way back to the road and continued along by moonlight. No one should be on the road at night and hopefully, they would hear if the slave catchers were sent after them. They had to take advantage of the darkness.

Far above, the stars twinkled against the blue-black sky. This was a long way from how things had been with them when they were children. Now, there were miles of unfamiliar fields and the whisper of wind amongst the cicadas' whirr. Even her last wedding, mere days ago, seemed like another life. Sometimes, she wondered how much longer she would remember any aspect of Linden's face. She knew his eyes were brown, but was she remembering how they looked or just remembering what she knew to be true?

Another wave of guilt washed over her, her bag even heavier in her hand. She switched it to the other side but it did little to ease the burden.

She let their feet brush the earth for a few more strides before she said, "Martha?"

"Yes, Miss Sarah?"

"Are you sure you want to come with me? You're a free lady now. You could go anywhere, you know."

"Would you rather me go?"

"No! No, I wouldn't wish it at all. I'm glad you're here. I only want to be certain you want it, too."

"Want. It's a strange word. I stay here and your Pa might have the slave catchers after me. I go off on my own and who knows where I'll end up. I couldn't find the North any better than I could find the South. You've still been family to me, Miss Sarah. You've been kinder than anyone. You have been the closest to a friend that I've had."

She reached for Martha's free hand and squeezed. "We *are* friends. Heaven knows I don't want to do this alone either."

"Why didn't you go to Fulton?"

Of course, Martha didn't understand. She had been in her quarters when Sarah's mother explained how not even the asylum could work miracles on someone like her. When one was haunted or cursed, as she was, there was no easy way to escape it.

Her relationship with Linden—and his death—had been so personal. She had never really let loose her feelings to anyone after he died. There had been outbursts here and there, fits of tears late at night, and a few during the day. Curses at her father in his office and even more at herself in the silence of her mind. She missed Linden. Oh, how she missed him.

"I decided I would rather be more like you," she said. "To fly like the lark as it sings."

"My momma had a song like that. About flying away above the cotton plains, up and up to yonder land."

"Up North?"

"She never told me where it was." But the way she said it, so wistful, made Sarah believe her friend knew exactly what the song meant.

"Would you sing me a verse?"

Martha was silent a moment then finally said, "We should be quiet so we can hear if the slave catchers are coming."

Sarah nodded. She didn't try to ask again.

10

It was another two full days before they reached Independence, Missouri, a small town grand in diversity. From the obviously affluent to vagrants in worn sack coats and torn knickers, from white to black to the copper skin of Indians clothed in little more than animal hides. On the boardwalk outside the hotel, a tribal woman stood adorned in beads and bangles. A tiny infant slept sound in the cradleboard strapped against her back while his mother bartered away beautiful shawls with intricate designs.

Crossing the street was a feat of courage. If one could cross it safely, Sarah reckoned they should have no difficulty crossing the western plains. The road teemed in both directions with every sort of conveyance, from loaded-down wagons carrying families with multiple children, to single men on horseback with two saddlebags and a side satchel as their only belongings. Horses, mules, donkeys, oxen. Chickens running wild and feathers swirling. Dogs nipping at their owners' heels. And the noise! Ever so much more than Sarah had imagined.

Hawthorn Ridge's town center wasn't quiet; the clatter of carriage wheels and horse's hooves mixed with the echo of boot heels on the boardwalk and the din of conversation. But here it was near pandemonium. Brays and whinnies came from the livery stables and the congested streets made it impossible to talk without shouting. Metal triangles whapped from restaurant doors calling in customers to the mid-day meal. Two boys, no more than eight years old, ran straight across the path, nearly tripping Sarah clean into the dirt.

Leaping back, she instead almost bowled Martha over who was standing close behind.

How were they ever to find the Larks in such a mess? It could take weeks to locate them, by which time they would likely have moved on. The women had no food or water; they had spent the night sleeping under a bush and foraging for berries the next morning. She assumed the red rounds hadn't been poisonous, seeing as they were still alive. Thankfully, her mother had the forethought to pack Sarah a change purse, but without full access to her father's sums, the amount granted barely more than a few meals. By tomorrow, they wouldn't have even two cents to rub together, much less buy a way west with. If not for Martha, she would likely admit her foolishness and return home. She could suffer Linden's curse, but she wouldn't abandon Martha to the slave catchers.

"Stay close to me," she whispered. "Don't draw attention. Any one of these folks could turn us in if they suspect I stole you."

Martha nodded, dipping her chin and keeping a step behind as they wove toward the General Store. A young couple exited as they reached the entrance, each carrying two burlap sacks apiece and the man with another tied parcel tucked beneath his arm. Deep blonde hair peeked out from beneath his hat's broad brim, the skin upon his face crimson with a deep tan gone too far, a sure sign of someone not familiar with time in the sun. To the contrary, his wife's complexion was a lovely golden tan beneath her flowered bonnet and round silver spectacles. Her dark brunette hair swept back into a cinch with golden highlights and a smattering of umber freckles upon her nose.

As a lady, Sarah understood the implications of misplacing one's bonnet or umbrella in the noonday heat. If she had obtained freckles such as those, she would have been tossed from every circle even before her marriages made a debacle of her social standing. This woman's blemishes, however, provided her with a youthful softness, despite having to be several years past twenty.

"Pardon me," Sarah called. The couple turned their way, extending friendly smiles while hoisting their purchases.

Unable to tip his hat, the man nodded. "Good afternoon, ma'am. What can we do for you?"

"Forgive me, but I am trying to find a wagon party. The Lark brothers or perhaps the Larksong wagon train. I'm not certain what they are calling themselves."

Their expressions instantly brightened. They looked once at each other then back again. "Of course we know the Larks," he said. "We're in the same party as them. You and your friend planning to join us then? Ma'am." He nodded to Martha who was half-hidden behind Sarah, eyes resolutely focused on the soil. She remained silent.

What were the odds they would stumble upon the right party on their very first attempt? Were these people truly with the Larks or were they nothing as they appeared? Out to steal what little they had left? Suspicious of a lone white woman traveling with a lone black woman? Sarah couldn't believe divine providence would smile upon them after years of seemingly ignoring her prayers.

Slowly, she nodded.

"It is always a fine day to have more recruits on board," the man acknowledged. "I'm Oliver Shay and this is my wife, Coraline."

"Sarah Walcott and this is my..." How did she refer to Martha? Her friend? Her maid? Her servant? Her slave? She decided on simplicity. "This is Miss Martha Louis."

Martha nodded, knuckles white upon her bag.

Coraline's lips parted into a wide smile. She shuffled her purchases in her arms, attempting to extract a hand and offer it. Unable to do so, she dipped in a slight curtsy. "How delightful to meet new members. You must place your wagon right next to ours."

They had no wagon. They didn't even have a horse or a dollar with which to purchase one. They certainly couldn't stay in Tobias's wagon. That was indecent.

"Come," Oliver said. "Our party is grouped a ways out, on the edge of town. It's farther to the trailhead, but away from some of the bustle."

Bustle indeed. As they wove their way through the streets, it seemed the Shays knew nearly everyone and nearly everyone returned their esteem. Every way they turned, other pioneers called out greetings, asking questions or making plans. She noticed several wagon canvases had phrases painted in black or red such as

"Westward Bound" or "Washington or Bust!" One man stood on a wooden bucket with a brown-dipped rag in hand, in the midst of writing a large "B" on the side of the canvas. She could only wonder what that would spell. His name perhaps?

Beneath him, a girl hardly more than six clutched a rag doll, one wrinkled thumb in and out from between her teeth. She waved with her opposite hand. "Hey-ya, Mrs. Shay!"

Coraline wiggled her fingers back from beneath the burlap sacks. "Afternoon, Betty!"

Oh, Sarah thought. *Perhaps the man named the wagon after his daughter like sailors name ships after beautiful women.*

A few wagons down, a middle-aged woman packed jars of jam into a crate, a hammer and tacks upon its open lid. She looked up at the Shays' greeting and wiped the sweat from her brow. "It's a tart hot one today, Mrs. Shay."

"Indeed, it is, Mrs. Wilder. Best we're getting off before we're in the thick of it."

Across the row, a man about mid-forties looked up from where he lounged against his wagon wheel, eating beans from a tin bowl, legs stretched out and suspenders loosened. Beneath his worn hat, his skin lay darker than midnight, so deeply brown it held a slight blue sheen. And his lips so plump and pink as to defy that they belonged with the rest of him. Never had Sarah seen such a skin color in Hawthorn Ridge. Even the darkest of their servants were of a deep chocolate, the lightest ones closer to Martha's caramel hue. Beside the man crouched another colored woman about the same age, spooning beans into bowls for each of the five children seated around the small campfire. A colored family chatting with white folks and facing them full forward instead of at their feet. Except for moments of solitude with Martha, it was practically unheard of back home.

Oliver reached a hand down to grasp the other man's. "Afternoon, Levi. You and Mrs. Harper all supplied for the trip?"

Levi released his hand and picked up his spoon again. "There about. Got one or two things left to get settled, but we'll be in line with everyone come morning."

"Good, good. Coraline's been asking me if you had to sell your fiddle. Seems she's ready for more of those spirited tunes."

Coraline reddened. "I only told him I liked the music. You don't have to play on my account."

Levi chewed another bite of beans, swallowed, and gave a sly smile. "I'm happy to play for you, Mrs. Shay. As long as you agree to join my Marie in a song."

Tobias said their group accepted everyone, that there were no slaves in Larksong, but Sarah hadn't completely believed it before. These plantation brothers would completely defy Southern convention? Maybe there was more to them than she thought.

After a quick round of introductions and more promises of future musical entertainment, they continued on.

"Those Harpers," Oliver said as they cornered another wagon and out of earshot. "Fine folk, them. Used to work for the Larks back in Carolina. Some of the only ones left from before Alonzo Lark died."

"They were slaves then?" Sarah asked. She had assumed as much, but one did meet the occasional freeman. She had heard rumors there were even some colored folks who made their way into the St. Louis aristocracy.

"Sure. Whole family were. Them and Josiah. You're sure to meet him later on. He's likely up helping the brothers out. He's like a second father to those men. I spent plenty of time with both him and the Harpers when Jamison and I were planning things out back in Carolina. We're setting up a doctoring practice in Larksong." He waved a hand. "Enough talk. Let's drop these supplies off and we'll take you to Mr. Lark."

They headed toward a wagon at the end of the row, flaps tied at the back and big black letters across the canvas: "Larksong Library." An adolescent girl lay in the grassy shadows underneath the wagon bed, flat on her back with a book held open above her nose. She seemingly held no concern for the dust drifting over her by those passing by or the questionable number of insects that likely crawled upon her bare feet or up her gingham skirt.

"Alice Ann," Coraline called. She dropped her supply sacks at the foot of the wagon, startling the girl so she nearly dropped her book upon her face. "Come out here and meet our guests."

The girl wedged a finger between the book's pages, then closed it, and shimmied out from beneath the wagon. When she pulled herself upright, she stood an inch taller than Coraline, although her face looked several years younger, likely no more than seventeen. As expected, her front was coated in a fine layer of brown dust and her tanned complexion no lighter than Coraline's. A cinnamon-brown braid wrapped her crown, the strands' crimson highlights glinting like a halo in the afternoon sun.

"Hello there," she said. Her voice was melodious, her smile reaching the edges of her dusted cheeks. "I'm Alice Ann Owens. It's a pleasure."

"Sarah Walcott and this is Martha Louis."

"Alice Ann's my younger sister," Coraline explained. "Our papa went blind a few years back and insisted we see the world while we still could. Alice would have rather stayed, working on the family fishing boat, but Papa insisted. Mind you, I love the ocean too, but why a lady would want to work a grabber, I'll never know."

Alice Ann rolled her eyes. "Because it's exciting. I'd go out on the high seas if I could."

"Sailors only desire a lady for one thing, Alice Ann."

"Yes, yes, I know." She folded her hands piously upon her chest. "And my virtue is a gift I can only bestow once." She turned to Sarah. "I told Papa I would cut my hair and bind my chest. No one would know I'm a girl at all. Instead, I'm here while our older sister Mercy is home sitting around the house."

"She's a laundress," Coraline explained. "Takes in other folks' clothes and cleans them right there in the parlor. The lye sure stinks, and Mama helps sometimes, but it's difficult while caring for Papa too. Once he went blind, he couldn't work—"

"Cora," Oliver cut in gently. He had unloaded his supplies into the back of the wagon and now stood near. "Don't trouble yourself over it again."

Coraline adjusted her spectacles and gave him a soft smile. "You're right. Anxiety in the heart only depresses it."

"Good. Now, please stay here and pack the supplies with Alice Ann. I can take these ladies over. I need to see Jamison about our medicinal stock."

Sarah and Martha followed him down to the last row, where the mass of wagons opened into a grassy field dotted with trees and a single dirt road, two wheel ruts winding away over the landscape. With every wagon passed, she felt like an intruder. She knew Tobias had invited her, but he hadn't invited Martha. What if he threw her out? Sarah couldn't go west without her friend and she had nothing to offer to convince him to let her stay. She didn't even have a wagon of her own. And she couldn't promise him marriage either. At least not until they were settled in Larksong. Distance must be a stipulation of the agreement so she had time to figure a way out of it. If and when they reached Washington, she and Martha would sneak away one night and not return.

Tobias approached, shaking Oliver Shay's hand and asking him for the latest. Spurs clinked upon brown leather boots, their color a match to the worn hat upon his head. A new shadow of brown scruff lined his chin and jaw, providing a more serious composition than when last he and Sarah spoke. His revolver hung at his side with one hand on either hip, ready to move should the need arise. Confident and collected unlike her and Martha's mussed appearance. What a sight she must be. This wasn't at all the way she had hoped to approach the situation.

Oliver began to rattle on about the demeanor of the pioneers and which supplies he acquired that might be of use to the many as well as the few. Then he set in about Levi Harper and his promised fiddle strings. All the while, Tobias threw her slight glances. Was it her imagination or was he not surprised to see her? Had he truly been so confident she would change her mind and follow him? If she had other resources, she would be tempted to turn heel and abandon his invitation.

Finally, Oliver turned to them. "We discovered these lovely ladies round the General Store. They say you're expecting them."

"So, I was. Good day, ladies. So nice to see you again, Miss Walcott." Tobias gave a tip of his hat and a quick flick to the brim. An easy sile played across his lips. "Beautiful as always."

She wanted to laugh. Beautiful? Right now, she was about as

beautiful as a groundhog feet up in the sun. Somehow she managed to reply with a smile. "Yes, a pleasure, Mr. Lark."

"Seems all is in order," said Oliver. He stepped back in the direction he came. "I best be off to find Jamison. I will see you ladies on the trail." With a tip of his hat, he was gone and they were alone with Tobias who now grinned from ear to ear. Yes, he had certainly been that confident she would make an appearance.

"I heard you went to Boston, Miss Walcott."

"Heard from whom?"

He shrugged. "Here and there. What's in Boston?"

"Tea," she shot back. "I'm thirsty and I hear they have the best."

She felt the ground shift under her and he grabbed her elbow before she could fall flat. The heat and her rumbling stomach were taking their toll.

Directing her over to the nearest wagon—"Larksong Legacy" painted in red on either side—he ladled a dipper of water from one of two rain barrels attached to the rear corners. He handed it over and she swallowed several sips before handing it back. He then scooped it again and offered water to Martha. She immediately shook her head but he only pushed it in her direction again.

"You too. I imagine you haven't had much in days and the heat will only grow worse as we cross into summer. You need to start the journey right or it will be difficult to catch up later on."

Martha tentatively accepted the ladle and drank it down. She handed it back, eyes averted. "Thank you, sir."

"Tobias will do fine."

"With respect, I'd prefer to call you Mr. Lark."

"Whatever makes you comfortable, Miss..." Her eyes flicked up, not seeming to understand his pause, then lowered again. "Do you have a family name?" Tobias asked gently. "Or were you not given one?"

"No, sir. I was, sir. It's...it's Louis. Martha Louis." She looked lower, down to her shoes, their toes scuffed beyond reason.

"It's a pleasure, Miss Louis. Now, how about I show you to your wagon. You can leave your bags and then we'll scrounge you both up some sustenance." He offered Sarah his arm, but she didn't take it.

She had either misheard or was suffering from her rumbling stomach.

"You said we have a wagon?"

"Of course. It would be impolite for me to invite you, then not provide you with proper accommodations." He offered her his arm again. "Think of it as my way of wooing you."

"I'm not here to marry you. That isn't why I came."

He studied her a moment then looked back at Martha whose sights were still firmly placed upon her feet. He would find no ally there.

He reached for Sarah's hand and placed it through his arm. "If you insist."

11

Tobias hadn't been surprised by Sarah and Martha's arrival. Not in the slightest. Thanks to Garrett's Gift, he had known they were coming. What surprised him was his ability to maintain a composed demeanor when inside he was leaping with the excitement of a five-year-old.

For two days, he had practically held his breath with anticipation. Every time Garrett begrudgingly provided an update on the women's progress, Tobias expected they would turn back or head in another direction. Instead, they moved a little closer each day until they finally reached the Independence border. After that, Garrett refused to interfere in this "ridiculous escapade" anymore.

Tobias was simply grateful his brother had participated at all and even more thankful his Gift allowed him to track her. Their Gifts weren't supposed to influence another Gifted and until now, Garrett's hadn't located one. But perhaps that was part of Sarah's ability. It was most unusual already by her being a woman, possibly the only one of her kind. Maybe Garrett's Gift was enhancing with time. Tobias couldn't rule out any possibilities anymore.

Now that she was here with her slender arm through his, he had five months to earn her trust. Their last encounter had only convinced her of his instability; he needed to find a way to rectify that. When he first told her she was Gifted, she had looked at her palms as though some sort of light would radiate from them, but he knew they would always look like regular hands. No one could tell just by looking, which made it difficult to ever find another like them.

He shook off his thoughts as Jamison approached, calling Tobias's name. At twenty-six, his second youngest brother didn't have the typical appearance of either a doctor or a spiritual leader, yet he was both. He had nearly entered the priesthood after university; it was only family obligations and their eventual plans for Larksong which made him reconsider. After the Diocese refused the Larks' request for a permanent priest in Larksong, Jamison had gladly stepped into the role as best he could. Without ordination, he couldn't offer Mass, consecrate Eucharist, or baptize, but he could still speak feverishly of love and compassion. It was just as well; those bishops would never have accepted him in such western-wildcat attire and Tobias could not foresee his brother comfortable in a cassock.

Since leaving Charleston over a year ago, he had allowed his musket brown hair to grow out to his shoulders, now tied back with twine beneath his hat. The chain of their grandfather's nickel pocket-watch dangled against his black leather vest, his Colt revolver holstered at his hip. While Jamison never encouraged violence, it was an unfortunate circumstance of humanity's free will and folly to travel life unprepared.

When it came to injuries and illness, Jamison's Gift provided advanced insight into the most efficient remedies and the ability to perform complicated surgeries no other physician would dare attempt. He couldn't, however, lay hands and heal someone, no matter how many times he tried. Instead, he thanked the Lord for what Gifts he did have and used them well. "One cannot heal the body if one does not heal the soul," he always said. He was the kind of man who lived his faith, the rock that kept their family from tumbling headlong toward disaster.

Such as Tobias's relationship with Sarah. Last night, he had explained the entirety of their time in Hawthorn Ridge, including his intentions with the widow. Jamison listened politely, then explained in plain sense that he thought his brother's plans lacked some.

"Tobias," he said. "I know you desire to find another Gifted. I do too. But you're first and foremost the leader of Larksong. You're supposed to lead our town, not risk your life and theirs in the name of love and Giftedness."

Now, approaching his brother, Tobias saw the apprehension in his eyes and the instant understanding of who the two women were accompanying him. Jamison expressed nothing—he was supposed to remain constant for his flock—but Tobias had known him since he was born. He noticed all the ways his brother wore his emotions on his sleeve even when the average person could not tell.

"Oliver Shay was looking for you," Tobias said as they stopped a yard apart. A few paces over, Darcy Frendon glanced up from where she crouched, scrubbing soiled dishes in a tin tub. Wash water was shared amongst all the pioneers in each wagon circle then dumped in a trough for the horses to drink. When Tobias nodded, she quickly turned back to her work.

"I just saw him," Jamison was saying. "He's performing inventory of our herbal stores and mentioned you have some new recruits."

"Indeed. This here's Sarah Walcott and Martha Louis." He observed the slight narrowing in his brother's gaze when Sarah discretely removed her arm from his.

Thankfully, Jamison simply tipped his hat as he ought. "Afternoon, ladies. Pleasure to have you aboard."

"We thank you for your hospitality," Sarah replied with a slight curtsy. Martha nodded but said nothing, her eyes firmly rooted to the dirt beneath her feet.

Jamison cleared his throat. "Um, Tobias, I wanted to tell you we've been removed from tomorrow's departure. They're all full. But hold on now—" He placed a hand to his brother's shoulder. "Before you get riled, I've secured us another spot. It's this evening at half-past five."

"That'll only give us a couple hours of travel before we have to circle the wagons."

"I agree, but it doesn't waste another full day. We're already two weeks behind due to your detour to Hawthorn Ridge and our citizens are growing restless with the wait. They're afraid we'll leave too late and get stuck in the snow come fall. I'll admit, it's my worry as well."

"We have Cade to tell us when the weather's going to change."

"Yes. He can feel the snow coming, but he can't stop it. Knowledge doesn't change the risk of becoming trapped."

He was right. They couldn't afford to be stuck in the mountains when the weather turned cold. The majority of their party were from the southern states where snow was never a regular occurrence. Most of them hadn't even seen it, much less knew what precautions to take when it fell. Tobias could build shelters but even with his Gift, he could only raise so many so quickly. If a blizzard blew in, he would never have time to cover them all.

"Move the party into formation and be ready to leave by four. I'll address the wagon party and go over the guidelines. Give any doubters a last chance to turn back."

Jamison nodded. "Pleasure again, ladies," he said and with a tip of his hat, hustled off down the line.

Darcy Frendon was staring at them again, her washrag dripping into the bucket from her hand. "Best collect your husband and ready the wagon, Mrs. Frendon," Tobias told her. "You wouldn't want to be left behind. Come, ladies." He offered Sarah his arm again, but she pretended like she didn't notice the gesture, and he didn't feel like pushing the subject.

They followed him through a field beyond the wagons to where he had built theirs and hidden it within a copse of trees. Last night, he had laid on his bedroll underneath his own wagon, listening to the sound of Garrett's snores, the bullfrogs, and hundreds of other little tokens far distanced from his Charleston home. Sarah had been out there too, not so very far distanced, on her way to him. Sleeping under the stars just as he was. So close he wanted to leap onto his horse and ride to her, no matter how impulsive the action might be.

His fingers had twitched, antsy to move. He needed to fix something, but his Gift was worthless against the rough emotions needing fixing in his mind. He could build something new, however. He was good at building, so he had started with Sarah's wagon.

Once he began, the process pieced itself together in record time, even without the proper tools. His toolbox was in Jamison's wagon and he wasn't about to disturb his brothers at that hour. All he had was what was in his saddlebags: a knife, a hatchet, rope, his two hands, and advanced carpentry skills he could never fully explain. Only six hours later, however, Tobias stared at a fully built, a fully functioning prairie schooner, ready to blaze the trail. All its wooden skeleton needed was a canvas top and supplies stored inside, all of which were purchased come morning.

Sarah now stepped up to the schooner, walked around it, let her fingers trail the box, running her palm up the ribbing. Tree stumps peppered the area along with branches discarded from his work. She wound around them to the wagon's opposite side, her eyes roving over it in amazement, probably wondering how he could create something so large in so little time, with so few supplies, and no nails to hold it together.

He had solved that problem years ago. First, he learned how to create wooden nail pegs, then realized that if he fashioned the pieces with interlocking slots, pegs weren't even required. He would replace the wheel axles and line the wheels with metal the first chance he found some to work with. The journey would be rough and he didn't trust wood alone, no matter how much Gifted influence they might have.

"Did you build this?" Sarah asked.

"Yes. Last night."

"Last night? One night?"

He shrugged. "I told you I have a talent for building things."

"An incredible talent, Mr. Lark."

Martha stood to the side between two tree stumps, her jaw clenched. Otherwise, he reasoned it would have dropped to her chest. He wondered if she knew he was the one who held her purchase papers. He didn't want to ruin what could be his only chance at convincing them to join him and didn't wish Sarah or her closest friend's hostility during the entire five months and beyond. He would tell them when the time was right. Sure, he would. Or maybe not. Maybe he could keep the papers hidden and only take them out if they ended up with a slave catcher on their tails. It's not as though he planned to treat her as his property. The papers were for her protection only. She was free to do whatever she wanted, exactly like the rest of the wagon train.

"No," Sarah said. "It's too extravagant. I can't accept this."

"You can. You need your own place. You certainly can't ride with me and my brothers. That would be unseemly. And all the other wagons are full to the top."

"All we have are two carpet bags. It seems wasteful to have an entire wagon for so little."

"You have more. I've purchased everything you'll need."

Both women's lips did part then as Sarah opened the flap to reveal the wagon bed fully stocked. Crates of food, pounds of flour, lard, and tin pans for cooking. Extra country dresses and boots more suitable for walking, including a pair he felt would replace Martha's worn ones exceptionally well. They would travel near to twenty miles each day, most if not all of it on foot. Sarah might argue, but he knew slaves didn't receive garments nearly as nice as their masters, and plantation ladies hardly owned frocks suitable for a jaunt across the wilderness.

Garrett had called Tobias an imbecile when the General Store delivered everything that morning. He accused him of wasting money on a woman who was likely only going to get them into trouble.

She *was* going to be trouble; Tobias could feel it. But he also felt other emotions—stronger ones—a sense of chivalry and attachment he couldn't describe fully. At thirty years of age, he was ready to find a wife, but he would admit, this one had proved rather more complicated than he planned.

Sarah let the tent flap drop back into place. "I can't accept this, Mr. Lark."

"What about Miss Louis? I haven't heard her opinion." Both of them stared at Martha who retreated a step, eyes back on her boots. One hand rose to adjust her bonnet over her tight ebony braid.

"My opinion doesn't matter none," she said softly. "You made the wagon for Miss Sarah."

"I made the wagon for both of you. You're important here too, Miss Louis. You'll find your life has suddenly become very different than it once was. I value your opinion as much as I value Miss Walcott's."

He thought his kind words would have had the strength to raise Martha's sights, but her concentration remained fixedly downward. "I thank you for that, Mr. Lark, and I appreciate your thoughtful gift." It was a stock answer, something he expected a slave to say when given an opportunity by her master. He wanted her true opinion, however.

Was she here simply because Sarah asked her to come, or had she decided for herself? Given the choice, would she choose another path?

They were questions he would never receive an honest answer to if he asked. Martha didn't trust him and likely had trusted few people in her life. This situation would take time and delicacy and he was baffled as to how to handle it.

Therefore, he did all he could in that moment. He offered her a smile. "You are most welcome. Now, become acquainted with your new surroundings. I best retrieve your oxen."

He turned away, dipped behind the wagon, then moved off in the direction of their wagon party, hoping...hoping. It wasn't until he stepped out into the open sun, however, heat back upon his shoulders, that he heard Sarah's quick footsteps chase after him. She didn't hustle as he would have expected from someone like Alice Ann, and he could picture her holding her skirt high enough to allow motion, but not so high as to reveal a scandalous strip of stocking. *Plantation ladies*, he thought. This was a side of them he didn't miss.

He couldn't hide his grin as she grabbed his arm and attempted to whirl him to face her. He humored her by turning into her pull, so they stood but a foot away. When he met her attention, her frown reflected more gravity than her civilized tone expressed. "Mr. Lark, pardon me lest I seem ungrateful, but you have an entire wagon train to oversee. You can't be monopolized trying to win me over. It won't work."

"Miss Walcott, I will take care of every person in my party including you and your friend, and I do believe I can win you over with time. I think the entire community will win you over."

She sniffed. "They know about your magical powers then?"

He glanced around at the hustle of the wagon party several hundred feet away. Thankfully, he and Sarah stood on the outskirts, but still too near to speak in such rising tones. He stepped closer and dipped his chin, forcing hers up to catch his attention. He kept his voice level but low. "Our Gifts aren't magical. I can't snap my fingers and make a wagon appear; I have to build it, same as anyone else. I'm using my God-given talents, except I can do so quicker, better."

"Then, these people do know?"

"No. Except for you and Josiah and, of course, my brothers, no one knows. Josiah has been part of my family since before I was born. I would trust no one more to keep our secret."

"Yet, you trusted me?"

"Yes."

"Because you believe I share magical powers to murder my husbands without my knowledge and only you can save me?"

"As I said, they're not magical powers, but, yes, that is what I believe. You're still wearing the ring I gave you. A part of you has to believe I'm telling you the truth."

"It was too pretty to leave behind." She glanced at the braided ring, now having been moved to her bare right hand, and he took that stolen moment to watch her without notice. A plantation daughter out in the sun without gloves, with dust on her dress, and a tear in the hem. How beautiful to see her outside her sophisticated element. Although he could never deny he enjoyed her palatial sophistication, what he saw now was the realism he longed for.

He reached for her, but she avoided his touch, leaving his hands swinging back at his sides. He looped his thumbs around his suspenders instead. "You'll find these folks are good people, Miss Walcott. It was divine providence you met up with the Shays. Coraline is compassionate and will make a good friend. Her sister is immature but entertaining; you'll enjoy her company along the trail. And Oliver...well, he's in the doctoring business with my brother and is as caring as they come, but even he is not aware of all we can do. Humanity tends to reject what they don't understand. Was it any different in Hawthorn Ridge?"

He had seen how the guests at her wedding whispered their accusations. They were so quick to judge when they didn't even know, and her eyes still held some of the same hauntings now. He did not need to ask if she had betrayed them to anyone. She knew of the need to keep oneself a secret.

She removed herself another step. "We don't even know each other, Mr. Lark. Once you come to know me, truly know me past your assumptions, you might not want to marry me."

That's a fair acknowledgment, he thought. They didn't know much of anything about one another. Beyond their Gifts, they could be the worst matched couple in the world. It didn't mean he was willing to give up on this endeavor, but he was willing to temporarily curb his stampeding desires.

He thought he had removed every obstacle to her coming with them. She had needed Martha, so he made it happen. She didn't have a wagon or supplies, so he provided them. It appeared, however, what he truly needed was time and opportunity. Proximity would be his ally.

"A counter-proposal then. We take the next five months to become acquainted. If when we arrive in Larksong, you still don't believe you're Gifted, you're free to go your own way. I'll pay your fare back to Missouri, Boston, or anywhere else you want to go." He held out his hand. "One chance, Miss Walcott. That's all I ask. And you agree to keep the wagon."

He thought she would disagree...again. Then tentatively, she placed her hand in his. "Fair enough, Mr. Lark."

12

ere. Hold this while I hitch up the mules."

Sarah took the four-foot wooden switch Tobias handed her and watched while he bent to attach the two mules' neck yokes to the wooden beam—the tongue as he called it—which ran down to bolt into the front of the wagon. "What am I supposed to do with this?" she asked.

"You wanted to drive the wagon. Shouldn't you already know?" Even though his face was hidden behind his work, she heard the smile in his tone. He thought this amusing, finding the flaw in her request.

Originally, he had wanted her to use oxen like most of the other wagons in their party, but Sarah had no experience with the creatures. If she was going to be an equal part of the wagon train, she needed to be able to guide and care for her own animals. With her grandfather being a prized Kentucky breeder, she had plenty of experience with horses. She could saddle and ride them all the day long, likely even shoe them if it came to it. She had seen their stable hand, Sam perform the action enough to have the general idea of how it should be accomplished.

Unfortunately, Tobias claimed horses were high maintenance, in high demand, and easily stolen by bandits or Indians. The only horses in their party would be the ones the Larks brought with them from Charleston. In the end, they compromised on mules, although he claimed they weren't much better equipped to handle the journey than horses would be. Sarah told him everything would work out as it ought. So, here he was, hitching up two mules to the front of the schooner and she getting ready to lead them by slapping a stick over their behinds. Lovely.

"I do know what to do with it," she returned as he dropped the final peg into the wagon yoke and straightened. He folded his arms, waiting for the rest of her explanation. "Rather, I had hoped these wagons would come with reins."

"This isn't a standard wagon, Miss Walcott. It's a prairie schooner. No seat up front and no reins. No room to ride until we eat through some of our supplies. That goad stick is going to be your best friend for the next 2,000 miles." He leaned forward, his face inches from hers, those deep brown irises staring into hers. She felt her breath hitch right before he smiled and moved away. "You'll be in line between the Harpers and the Shays, two paces behind Cade and Josiah, and five behind me in the lead. You get into any trouble, you call to one of your neighbors and they'll pass word up to me."

"I can handle myself. I have Martha to help me."

"Wonderful. Then I suppose I'll see you at the group meeting."

"Meeting?" Sarah called after his retreating back. "What group meeting?"

But he was already gone, blended back in with the multitude of thousands. The mules stared at her from their ready positions and she held up the switch in what she hoped was a most threatening manner.

"Take care not to cross me, David and Solomon. I will find it in myself to use this."

"You named our mules after kings of Israel? How interesting."

Martha peeked out from the back of the wagon, tying her brown bonnet strings. She had freshened her dress into a new one of sky-blue calico with a tan apron, complete with small lace ruffles at the shoulders. The tiny yellow flowers in the dress's pattern brought out the hint of hazel in her brown eyes. Sarah had never seen her friend wear anything other than brown or black and the difference was astonishing.

"Why, Martha. That dress is lovely."

Her friend immediately looked away, a blush spreading into her cheeks although it was barely evident. "I know this one is a bit much for the trail—the color is bound to get mussed quickly—but I've never had something so beautiful. I had to see how it felt."

"And how does it feel?"

"I hesitate to say in case it doesn't last."

Oh, poor Martha. Every day Sarah realized more and more what her friend had been missing all these years. Life would be different for them both now. She would break her curse and Martha would find someone too. A young man who could make her happy with bumbling babies like Levi and Marie Harper. Her friend had dreamed of it once long ago in those star-studded hemp fields. No dream ran so far you could never get it back.

Like chipped wine glasses and poetry.

Oh no. Her heart stuttered in alarm. She had forgotten to bring a notebook for Linden's poetry.

"I need paper and pencils!" she cried. "We have to ask Mr. Lark for some coins for the General Store."

She spun away, switch still in hand, and Martha grasped her opposite wrist. Immediately, she dropped it. "Miss Sarah, it isn't the end of the world. We'll fetch some at the next stop."

"No, no. It must be now. I made a promise."

"A promise? Miss Sarah, I don't understand."

Of course, she wouldn't. She couldn't. Which would be more incredible for her to hear, that Sarah believed her late husband to be haunting her or that her current suitor believed her to be the cause? Neither of those would sit right. Not at all.

She raced back to the Shays' wagon and grasped Coraline's arm mid-shake of her apron. "Coraline, do you have a half-cent I could borrow? For the General Store? I need some writing effects."

"No need. Our wagon is full of things for reading and writing. Come, come." She folded back the wagon flap and rummaged through three different boxes before emerging with a stack of blank sheets tied with twine. A flat pencil was tucked within the bow. "I brought these for sending letters, but I'm happy to let you have them. I'll get some more at the next fort."

Alice Ann's head popped out from underneath the wagon, her book opened across her chest and feet still scandalously barefoot. "Please, Sarah, don't encourage her. My sister has plenty more; Oliver let her bring two full trunks worth just for her books."

"I haven't heard your complaints as you've continued to read those books," Coraline snipped back. "And nobody will be complaining when I open Larksong's first library."

"They will when we can't make it up the mountains and you refuse to lighten the load."

Two trunks? Sarah enjoyed reading too, but that seemed like a waste of valuable space even to her.

With a thank you for the paper, she tucked the satchel under her arm and left the sisters to quibble.

It was difficult to fathom how she had arrived at such a moment in her life, so far-reaching from the familiar, yet this *was* her life now. She may not have earned the provisions to begin this journey, but she would now earn her place in this wagon party for however long she was with them. Linden had always wanted to make a life through hard work and sacrifice, and now she would fulfill that dream.

She would do everything she could to make him proud.

13

By precisely half-past four in the afternoon, Tobias had settled every member of the Larksong wagon train into the first formation of the journey, two wagons across, twenty-two deep with his driving solo at the head. The positions would rotate back one position daily so that over the course of the month, everyone would equally experience the dust cloud famously associated with the rear positions. It also afforded him an opportunity to become further acquainted with each of the travelers, sorting out their individual strengths and weaknesses. Learning how their skills could best fit into their new community and most importantly, identifying any outliers with the potential to upend it.

At night, all forty-five wagons would circle up beside the trail, rounding the livestock at the center to protect them from thieves and keep their people safe. Animals and children alike were less likely to wander off if they had specific boundaries in which they were required to stay. It would be up to the Larks and their trusted seconds to trade off on watch, riding the perimeter with their sights set on the horizon.

Unfortunately, that meant Tobias would have little time to "become acquainted" with Sarah as promised. As the first of the Lark brothers born Gifted, it had always fallen on him to lead. Lead his brothers growing up, lead their wagon party, lead foolhardy missions to purchase slaves and rescue widows. Moving Larksong to Washington had been *his* dream, *his* mission. He had been encouraged by Josiah and Cade to take the first step, but the ingenuity had been wholly his.

He removed his pocket watch—4:35. He gripped the edge of the wagon frame and hoisted himself up on the rear wagon step, turning to look out over the sea of canvas covers. The travelers stood in the space between the two rows, packed together, faced forward in anticipation while their littlest ones ran haphazardly between the wagon wheels. He caught sight of Alice Ann tucked under her wagon bed as usual, one arm propped under her head while she read rather than engaging. That girl had an encyclopedic memory and dreams as wide as the western frontier. She would make a spectacular asset to their town...one day...when she finally grew into the woman she needed to be.

"Do you think they're ready?" Jamison asked from the ground below. Garrett and Cade stood directly beside him with Josiah and Levi close by. "They made it up from the South, but the frontier will be different. I don't think they know what they're heading toward."

"One in ten either die or turn back," Garrett said. He had mentioned this statistic before, but they still didn't like hearing it.

"We're not like most of the frontiersmen though," Tobias told him. "We have skills those other men didn't. We won't lose anyone, except maybe some cattle."

"It would still be helpful to get rid of the Widow Walcott before she kills us all."

"Why are you not a politician? Everything's always death with you." He hadn't intended to be so harsh, but that's the way it sounded and Garrett's expression made him know he heard it too.

Sarah met his stare from the next wagon back, Martha beside her. They had written "Free as a Lark" on their canvas cover and both their red-stained hands bore the evidence. Like the taint of her husbands' blood.

He shook his head, blinking to remove the image from his mind. Such thoughts had no place within his already crowded schooner. He wasn't going to die. Not at Sarah's hand.

A second later, Cade hopped up on the wagon to stand beside him. Together, they overlooked the wagon party, brimming with laughter and final farewells to the great state of Missouri.

"Look at your town, Tobias," Cade said. "It took us two years, but here we are." Two years since their father died and they decided to invest in the journey, one year since they last saw their childhood home. They would never return to this side of the country, never again step foot in a rice paddy—or see their brother Daniel again.

Tobias shoved that thought away, too, and imagined it rolling into the river down the opposite ridge. He should be glad never to see his selfish brother again, yet every time he thought of their final parting, he was washed in distress. As different as Daniel was from them, the Lark brothers belonged together. Tobias still didn't understand how their friendship became so fractured. Now he never would.

"You look like Moses," Cade said softly. "Taking your people to the promised land. All you need is a staff."

Tobias admired his little brother's upturned smirk. He remembered tussling his hair as a toddler, Cade's shrill laughter passing through every room of the house. Right up until the day a few biscuits and a pot of honey changed everything. It was good to see him joking again.

He grinned back. "I'll need a staff if I'm to defend us against hardheaded Pharaohs."

Below them, Garrett snorted. "Well, you did create plenty of commandments for us to follow. Those stone tablets too heavy to carry around yet?"

"Yeah, they are. Why don't you build me an ark to put them in?"

"Building's your gift, not mine."

"I think you'll enjoy the challenge." He slapped the brim of Garrett's hat, knocking it clean off the back and revealing a mess of dark curls. Glaring, his brother bent for it while Cade broke apart with laughter. Jamison's expression said it was time for serious matters, and it was, but hearing the sound of Cade's delight made Tobias want to knock Garrett's hat off every day for a year.

Cade lowered himself to the wagon step, legs dangling off the end as Tobias faced back to the crowd.

Lord, give me the right words to lead these people. Be the Aaron to my Moses.

"Town of Larksong," he began, "or I should say, the future

prosperous town of Larksong—" There was the general titter of low chuckles. "It is a beautiful day for us to begin this journey together. For some, it has been a year long coming. For others, the trail has just begun. I am honored to join you as your leader and hopeful that God will scatter His blessings on our path." Had he said that right? He had never been as eloquent as Jamison with faith speeches. He glanced at his brother who, thankfully, nodded his approval.

He could do this. Today was no different from the last two years.

"Before we leave, we must reiterate a few rules. Food will be prepared for all and shared by all. If you need to borrow a particular item, you may inquire of another circle, but please do not make this a habit. When meat supply draws low or when we are in fertile hunting grounds, we will stop to hunt. Sundays are for rest and religion. My brother, Jamison, will hold our service in the morning and the rest of the day is yours to do as you please. When I say rest, I mean rest from travel, not necessarily from work. Sundays are a fine day for laundry and boot shining. Sunday evenings we host a community social to thank the Lord for bringing us through the week and ask for guidance on the next. Monday through Saturday, wheels turn six to six.

"Hateful or violent actions or language will not be tolerated. All are welcome here, regardless of race, religion, or creed. There will be no tolerance to thieving, brawling, or other lewd behavior. Any actions which do not support this philosophy will be dealt with accordingly. Punishment for crimes will be discussed and voted upon.

"Most importantly, in Larksong we are equal. There are no masters or slaves. There may be leaders among us, but only because no society can survive without them. We must all work together to make our community thrive. When we arrive in Washington, we will vote on an official governmental system including a sheriff, deputies, and town bylaws. For now, my brothers—Garrett, Jamison, and Cade—along with Josiah and Mr. Levi Harper will share the responsibility of managing the wagon train and keeping the peace." Each man acknowledged their names as they were said, tipping their hats to the crowd in turn. "If you have a complaint, you bring it to one of us, understood?"

"I got a complaint!" The shout belonged to Antony Rigg, a wiry man with a pencil-thin mustache. He had joined them somewhere around Nashville with his spit of a wife and three children. He had had an opinion about everything ever since.

Tobias exhaled. "Yes, Mr. Rigg. What's on your mind?"

"You and your love for these two." He pointed to Josiah and Levi. "I ain't bowing down to no black man!"

A double negative, Tobias thought. *What spectacular grammar.* He had half a mind to reply with snark and acknowledge the man's comment actually meant the exact opposite of its intention. If he had been Garrett, he likely would have. A muscle worked in his brother's jaw even now.

Instead, Tobias replied with civility. "Mr. Rigg, I've known these two fellas a long time, for my entire life in fact. I trust them."

"What about her?" Antony pointed at Martha not more than two strides away. Then he quickly gestured to two additional colored families. "Or them? You known them your whole life too?"

"No. They were interviewed before we accepted them in."

The man laughed. "What's the need to interview if ya say ya trust 'em? By definition, that means they ain't as worthy as you makin' them out to be."

"Want me to belt him one?" Garrett growled. As much as Tobias would enjoy watching that—the man certainly had it coming—it wouldn't fit to start a brawl on the first day. He was trying to earn the people's trust, not break it.

He lowered a palm to Garrett's shoulder, gently holding him steady. "Mr. Rigg, you have me confused. You were well aware we had colored folks in our party when you joined up in Tennessee."

"Yeah, but 'till now they left me be. I didn't know they would want to lord over me."

"No one is lording over anyone." Tobias straightened, redirecting his words to the entire group. "These rules were developed by yourselves back in Charleston—or agreed to by those who joined at a later date. If anyone does not agree, then they can find another party to join up with. Thousands travel the trail at our bootheels." He shifted his attention back to Mr. Rigg, then to his wife standing beside him. The woman curled her shoulders, attempting to make herself appear smaller. She was embarrassed, but there was nothing he could do about that now.

It was then he saw Levi step out of line, a foot in front of the rest of them, fists curled at the end of each muscled arm. He and Tobias had worked side-by-side in the rice paddies back in Charleston; nearly twenty years, they tended the fields. He knew the strength it took to put in a twelve-hour day, day after day after month after year. Levi was not one to be reckoned with, especially now that he had his own mind and his own say. Away from Alonzo Lark's watchful eye, he had reason for a newfound conviction. If Levi jumped atop Mr. Rigg, Garrett would follow. They would be at the all-out mercy of the Independence sheriff, and both their community and Levi's family would suffer, possibly as far as the hanging tree.

Thankfully, it was Josiah who intervened. His shirt drew taut as years of hard-worked muscles contracted across his expansive chest and a tick worked in his peppered jaw. With limbs thick as plantation pillars and hands wide as horse hooves, he intimidated many. In truth, he was simply the gentler father the Lark brothers never had. It had been one of many miseries in Tobias's youth—watching a man over twice the size of Alonzo Lark simply stand back and take his master's verbal abuses.

"Levi," Josiah cautioned. The man turned an eye in his direction while keeping the other on Mr. Rigg. He wasn't surrendering, but at least he had been made to rethink his approach.

It was in Levi's pause—with the town clock chiming five—that another member of their community chose to raise a hand and his voice. Clinton Reed, with his close-trimmed beard and tangled curls so dark as to be edging black, made one imagine a pirate more than the cattle rancher he was. His daily walk was a borderline swagger, and Tobias suspected he used it to purposely clang his spurs extra loudly on the boardwalks. He had been one of the first to answer their advertisement in Charleston. With twenty head of cattle to his name, he had run clean out of room in the city to add more. His wife, Gabriella, stood beside him now, a slim brunette with sun-kissed skin and demure eyes, who never spoke, but always had a smile. If not for her modest presence, the Larks probably would have passed him over for a place in their group.

"Yah listen fellas," Clinton said, "I've got my own prejudices too, not going to say I don't. In fact, there are a few people I wouldn't mind putting in their place at the first opportunity. But for now, we have to ignore those whims." He wrapped an arm around his wife and pointed at Tobias. "I'm not thrilled about having such folks around either, but Mr. Lark knows how to lead a train. I reckon we should respect his judgment."

"Well, I won't let no blackie tell me what to do," Mr. Rigg shouted back. "You wouldn't either if ya knew your place. Come, Muriel."

And that was how their party became forty-four wagons instead of forty-five. In many ways, Tobias was surprised he and his brothers weren't the only ones left. They had taken a risk when they asked a group of Southerners to uproot their lives and their thoughts, knowing some might not be pliable. He had even thought about asking Josiah and Levi to step down to prevent incidents like the one they just witnessed. But if he did, then he wouldn't be him. He would be Alonzo Lark, a man with the respect of his workers only because his Gift persuaded them to do so.

Tearing himself away from the departing trundle of the Riggs' schooner, he cleared his throat. He wished he had a woodblock to whittle. His confidence would be stronger. "I want to assure every colored family, poor family, immigrant family...every widow and orphan...every person who has felt they didn't belong somewhere... you belong *here*. The truth is adversity will never leave us. Life will still be difficult once we reach Washington, but I promise you, it is the land of opportunity. My father was not a man worth admiring, but he did teach me one thing worth remembering: if you don't like how something's done, then change it. Starting today, your lives will change, but it's up to you to decide how they do."

Within the crowd, his eyes swept to Sarah, her hand now daringly folded inside of Martha's. There was so much he wanted to ask her, so much he didn't dare. At least not until the right time. He wanted to know everything about her. But she was still cautious of him, and Garrett would say Tobias should be equally wary.

Jamison stepped forward, inviting them to bow their heads while he offered a prayer for safety and abundance. His final line, "Be brave and steadfast for the Lord goes before us. He will never fail us or forsake us," was met with a resounding, "Amen!"

"Amen," Tobias whispered. He clapped his hands together. "Alright, fellas! Let's get this wagon train moving. I'd bet we're all about ready to kiss the past goodbye."

14

From Kansas to Nebraska, the eternal plains spread out before Sarah like a sea of golden waves, parted only by the deep wheel ruts their party followed. Sometimes the trail led two across, as they preferred to go; other times, the tracks spread as far as six to ten wagons wide. Already, they observed belongings left along the trail in an effort to lighten the load and signs of warning beside wooden grave markers: *"If the cholera doesn't get ya, the Indians will!"*

Cholera... She shuddered at the thought.

There were obvious places where other parties had circled to make camp, the grass within nearly stripped away by months of travelers' hungry oxen, sheep, and cattle. As much as the Larks hated to disturb more of the land, it was often necessary to claim a fresh space at night. Thankfully, game was plentiful for hunting and the streams ran cold and bountiful, allowing them to frequently fill their rain barrels and buckets between spring showers.

Each day, Sarah watched as Tobias's wagon moved farther and farther away, with his brothers' close behind, and she walking alongside Martha while their mules pulled the wagon. How she wished there was enough room for them to ride under the canvas cover! The dust clouds grew thicker as they moved back in the rotation, and after only four days, they had tied strips of Coraline's washrags over their faces. Sarah wasn't certain which was more stifling, dust in her nostrils or the warm material over her mouth and nose, which left her faint and nauseated. It certainly did nothing to ease her ability to speak with Martha, and conversation was the only way to replace boredom and ignore her tired blistered feet.

By Sunday, she was ever so grateful to sit at church service, sit during meals, and sit in her wagon writing while everyone else engaged in social niceties. She often chuckled at the humor of it all. Back in Hawthorn Ridge, her parents would never have allowed her to hide in her bedroom while a function occurred downstairs. Prior to Linden's death, she wouldn't have wanted to. She had enjoyed parading his handsome physique past all her friends to watch their covetous expressions. Dancing with him and accepting his arm along the boardwalk after Mass on Sundays. Which was the singular reason it startled her when Tobias requested they do the same after prayer service each week. Their agreed upon "getting-to-know-you" time.

Of course, she could never tell him that walking together reminded her of Linden. He would likely say her first marriage was ten years ago and it was high time she moved on. Heaven knew how often she had heard that same sentiment from her friends back home. She couldn't even use the excuse that her feet were horribly worn, although they were. In only a few weeks, she had already walked through her first pair of shoes. Tobias had packed several pairs of new boots for her, ones which appeared far sturdier than those she brought, but she refused to wear them. She wouldn't give him the satisfaction. If she mentioned how her feet hurt, he would summon Jamison to tend her and start quacking about their Gifts again.

So instead, she walked the wheel ruts with him every Sunday and insisted one of his trusted seconds join them as a chaperone.

"A chaperone?" he griped when she made the non-negotiable stipulation. "I'm thirty. I think I've passed the need for a chaperone."

"I insist we retain propriety," she calmly replied.

"Fine," he muttered. "Persnickety plantation ladies," and Cade, who had been elected first chaperone, simply laughed.

She knew there wasn't a genuine need for an escort, but she wasn't about to offer him any sort of leverage to charm his way into her affections. For that was exactly what she feared if they were left alone. She would admit she found him attractive, and there was no harm in that. Many men were pleasing to the eye. In honesty, she found all of the Lark brothers handsome. Unlike his brothers, however, Tobias wanted her to open her soul, share her world, and make him a part of it. Even with his brother there, he had no qualms bringing up marriage or children—he wanted seven, which surprisingly, was exactly what she had always wanted, too.

She needed to dampen her emotions, stop paying him or anyone so much mind. She enjoyed Martha, Marie, Coraline, and Alice Ann's company and gladly engaged them in the evenings, but even with their helpful handiwork, her own domestic skills continued to lag behind. Meals charred under her watch, pots boiled over. Repaired seams tore out again within days of mending and she had always thought herself a talented stitcher! She supposed embroidery and crochet were not much service when it came to the actual construction of one's garments. Even though Coraline provided ample instruction, she still felt it was a hopeless cause. Tobias witnessed her atrocities, yet she knew it would never turn him from pursuit. Not so long as he believed her to be Gifted.

One morning after breakfast, the sun not even licking the horizon, she made a fiasco of hitching up the mules to the wagon. Normally, she had assistance from Tobias, Oliver Shay, or Martha, but that particular morning, all three were summoned away. She figured now was the perfect opportunity to complete the task herself and demonstrate that she indeed had some skill. Yet only a few minutes in and her left fingers tangled in the harness straps while her right attempted to maneuver the heavy yoke over the second mule's shoulder. The animal huffed and stomped its hoof, telling her in no uncertain terms what it thought of her. If it kept that up, she would probably get trampled.

Garrett, of all people, had been the one to rescue her. He lifted the yoke from her grip with one hand and shifted his body so she was forced back against the wagon. He glared at her as he attempted to settle the mules enough to re-situate the yoke. "Tobias said you had experience with mules."

"Horses," she corrected. "My grandfather was a prized Kentucky breeder."

"Hmm, well, if this is any indication of your usefulness, you will quickly end up a liability, likely killing yourself or someone else.

Leaving you behind would have been more gracious to us all, and I'm looking forward to hearing my brother admit I was the first to say it." His tone was simple, direct, no nonsense. Exactly how she would have imagined given her brief observations of him and the stories fed to her by Tobias. This, however, was the first time he had bothered to extend her a word.

Sending her back to her family would probably be the kindest mercy for everyone. She had no aptitude for anything out here except caring for the mules and even that was proving more difficult than anticipated. There was little future for her back in Missouri except for a lifetime labeled as a "lunatic" and separation from her dearest friend.

"You need to trust your brother more," she told him.

He peered down at her, his fingers still maneuvering the yoke into place against the mules. "I do trust him. It's you I don't trust."

It was more than a lack of trust. She could see it in his eyes and the way his back muscles contracted as he turned into his work. He hated her as much as those in Hawthorn Ridge who had called one of the Widow Walcott's husbands "son," "nephew," or "friend". Garrett didn't believe she was Gifted. He probably slept with one eye open and a finger on the trigger, ready to pounce the moment she turned on Tobias.

"I won't hurt your brother, Mr. Lark. As long as I remain unmarried, I'm not a danger to anyone here, except perhaps myself."

"There's no way for a woman to claim land out west unless she's married. I know Tobias told you that."

"He did, but I still don't aim to marry him."

He released the mules and faced her, one hand running over the weeks' worth of growth upon his jaw. "My brother thinks you're Gifted, but you're not. You can't change my mind when it comes to that. So, you had better find another way to prove your worth before we reach Washington, or else find another town to keep your company."

She nodded and watched him saunter back to his own wagon, hitching up the oxen with ease. She went to the back of hers, retrieved her paper and pencil, and sat on the wagon step, waiting for the right words to come. Linden's words.

The next wagon back, Martha played a hand clapping game with the Harpers' second youngest, Aphid. Their sing-song voices floated toward her like chimes in the kitchen window. As a child, she had sat on her parents' kitchen table and watched as the servants did the baking for the next week, the sweet scent of yeast and flour plumping loaves in the stone oven. Martha would pound the dough and let Sarah take the smallest taste for herself. The raw dough was always icky, but she tried it every time, hoping it might improve as Martha's skills did too. Later, she learned that was simply how the dough was always going to be. It wouldn't taste good without going through the fire.

She placed pencil tip to paper.

Today the sun shines brighter, tomorrow the larks, they flew
Today I live in loneliness, tomorrow, I'll have you.

She read over the words again then again. Awful. She looked up and saw Oliver Shay return to his wagon, black physician's bag in hand, greeting his wife with a gentle smile. He handed her the bag and she placed it in the wagon bed, filling his now empty hand with a tin cup of steaming coffee. It was probably darkest black and utterly bitter, but he sipped it as though he found it pleasurable.

To have a marriage like that... To have more than a few hours with her husband... What she wouldn't give.

Drawing herself up into the wagon bed, Sarah closed the canvas flaps around her, and crushed the poem into her palm. Her closed fist found her lips and she moaned silently into it, anguished sobs tracing down her cheeks in the way she had grown so accustomed. In the way that no one would hear.

Tobias didn't know what to make of Sarah's behavior. If Garrett's Gift had sent them to collect her, it certainly wasn't because it thought she would make a good asset to their party. While she seemed skilled enough in caring for the mules, everything else she did was without polish. She fretted too much over her hair pins and nearly lost herself when her bonnet blew away, leaving her flawless skin sun-exposed for more than ten minutes. She was behaving like all the other fussy plantation ladies with too many layers of petticoats and no capability for simple domestic tasks.

In the evenings, he observed her from across the camp circle as she attempted to make meals, Martha and Coraline always intervening before she burnt everything to bits. Most evenings, she chatted with Martha or the Shays, sometimes the Harpers, but every other time, she had her attention fixed on a packet of papers, scribbling upon them furiously. He wondered what she was writing and if it was any good. Probably diary entries. Plenty of the other ladies and even some of the men documented what occurred each day. Even if it was as mundane as, "Traveled 12 miles, saw a herd of buffalo, worried about the Indians." Although, if her inner thoughts were anything compared to the concern she held for her outward appearance, her diary probably held an itemized list of complaints against him and the rest of their group.

At least on Sundays after prayer service, she accepted his arm for a walk together down the trail. One hour out, one hour back. There they would engage in the promised "getting-to-know-you" time, although most of their conversations revolved around plantation crops, Kentucky horses, and Southern society. It was all very surface level, safe and structured, exactly as he would expect if he were courting an actual Southern belle. But what choice did he have when she insisted on bringing one of his brothers as a chaperone? For almighty sakes, he was well past the need for such formality.

He was willing to step the dance though. Every twenty-two days, her wagon would align with his and they would spend an entire day— fifteen to twenty miles—side by side. The front of the line was nearly free from dust and he had not yet encountered a trail mate willing to spend an unmasked day in silence.

The rest of the wagon train seemed to have settled into the routine of breakfast, walk, luncheon, walk, supper and sleep then do it again. There had been few disputes they weren't able to settle and every morning, they rose before dawn without complaint. Every head bowed while Jamison read the daily Bible verse and each pair of lips said, "Amen."

He knew their easy days wouldn't last, especially when they traveled out of the plains and into the mountains. The people would grow weary of the endless days and at some point, food would likely be lacking. Even with his Gift, he couldn't strike water from a rock. If Moses couldn't keep the Israelites from complaining and molding idols, what luck was he to have?

15

D inner was burnt...again.

"Here, let me see to that." Coraline nudged Sarah away from the blackened bean pot, a rancid odor marring the otherwise edible food in Marie's pots one fire over. They always preferred to stoke a double campfire side-by-side rather than two distanced. It made preparations for their eight-wagon circle much easier when they were able to work together. But despite that, and being assigned some of the easiest culinary tasks, Sarah's skills remained utterly and completely hopeless.

Martha, meanwhile, had the far easier task of tending to the Harper children. The youngest, Quint, sat upon her hip, Aphid tugging at her skirt while she supervised the older ones, Jonah, Marilee, and Reeslie, who chopped potatoes, skin and all falling right into the pot. The children had taken a shining to Martha on their first night out and practically clung to her every evening since. Marie didn't need to explain her gratitude; it was evident in her relaxed posture and laugh. On particularly arduous days, once she handed their care off to Martha, she returned to the campfire a new lady. Sarah wondered if all parenting was so trying and if all parents wanted to rid themselves of their children at one point or another. She had always imagined she would dote and love on her children as her parents had doted on her all through her younger years. It wasn't until after her many marriages that tensions began to form.

"See, this is where you went wrong," Coraline was saying. She went to the rain barrels, returning with a ladle of water, which she added to the pot. Vigorous stirring, however, only made the beans clump further. She pressed her lips together. "Hmm, well, perhaps we can add more herbs. I believe Oliver has some in his stores."

She headed off to find her husband while Sarah stirred the pot, allowing her mind and her eyes to wander about the wagon circle. Tonight, Tobias dined with McKinleys, seated amongst the couple and their four children, ages two through nine. As the wagon master, he was invited to other wagons several nights each week. His absence meant she had more time without his smothering nature; although, too often she found herself watching him anyway and taking note of his interactions with the other pioneers. He cared more about each individual than she had ever seen anyone in Hawthorn Ridge care about another. Whatever their need, he found a way to make it so, whether he fulfilled the request himself or delegated it to one of his brothers. Yet, despite it all, he always spared a moment to offer her a smile and a few warm words—a sweet "goodnight" and the promise of tomorrow—even if she made no effort to return them. The next day would see him do it once again, without fail, without complaint. He was like the Gift he claimed to have, something crafted in such a way no one knew how it could stay together.

"You gonna keep that man waitin' forever?" Marie asked, her lips curved with a secret smile.

Sarah felt her cheeks redden under the other woman's scrutiny and quickly looked away. "Which man?" she asked, a comment that elicited the same reaction as every other time she said it.

Marie propped a hand on her hip and the metal spoon across her arm. One dark eyebrow raised. "Mmm-hmm. You know the one."

"We all know the one," Coraline laughed as she walked back into the circle, one hand clutching a bunch of green leaves. She ripped them into thin strips and dropped them into Sarah's bean mess.

"She'd better make it soon," Alice Ann called. "She can burn Mr. Lark's supper instead of mine." The girl was under the wagon again, her nose stuck in a book, bare feet crossed at the ankles. A week ago, she had given up on keeping her hair manageable and it now lay in two frizzy braids on either side of her neck. Coraline certainly wouldn't need to worry about her sister getting herself into any trouble with men. Between her coarse appearance and her ongoing interest in becoming a fisherwoman, Alice Ann would be lucky if any man placed an interest before spinsterhood.

Coraline rolled her eyes at her sister. "You know, Alice Ann Owens, instead of complaining about your food being burnt, maybe you could cook it yourself."

"I'd be glad to once we get some fish."

"And just where do you expect to find fish in the middle of the plains?"

"I dunno. Isn't there a pond around here or something?"

"I don't know and I'm not about to wander off searching for one. That's a good way to find yourself attacked by Indians."

Alice Ann finally lowered her book. "Then let me go hunting with the men. I already showed Cade what a good shot I am. I bet I'd catch more than all of them combined."

"You heard Garrett yesterday. We've got plenty of meat to last. Too much and it'll spoil."

"Then it sounds like we've come to an impasse." Alice Ann raised her book again and the discussion was over.

Coraline shook her head and went back to stirring Sarah's pot, which they both knew was beyond repair. She exhaled, blowing loose strands of brunette hair against her cheeks.

"Why do you allow her to speak to you like that?" Sarah asked softly. Marie watched their friend's reaction as well, likely wanting to jump in with her own mothering advice. It was bound to be different though, raising a seventeen-year-old sister rather than a young child. Alice Ann was practically a woman and an unruly one at that.

Coraline removed the bean pot from the fire and sat it in the dirt. She lifted the first tin bowl and began dishing out the blackened char. "She's my baby sister. We'd always been friends before; Mama and Papa were the ones to discipline. She listened to them. Since coming out here, they've expected me to stand in their place and I'm only six years older. Alice Ann doesn't want things to have changed and neither do I. She wants me to be the friend she had, not the parent I've become."

"Land, Mrs. Shay," Marie exclaimed. "She needs a momma and if you're all she's got, then you're what she's got. Life ain't easy, but we gotta do it."

"It isn't that simple." She glanced at Alice Ann's bare feet sticking out from under the wagon and lowered her voice. "I stole her from a life she loved. She had the ocean and Papa's boat and even though many were unlikely to happen, she had dreams to cling to. Now, she's forced to be here with me in an impossible situation. One that will only grow worse."

Sarah reached over and stole the spoon from her friend's hand. She ladled a helping of beans and handed it to her. "Tobias believes our troubles will be better in Washington. He said we'll be near the ocean. That should brighten your sister."

Coraline simply shrugged and turned back to supper preparations. Soon after, the men returned from their tasks, settling themselves down within their families and the opportunity for feminine discussion was lost.

Everyone joined around the fire together, eating as one. Oliver beside Coraline beside Marie beside Levi. Martha hustled the children back to their parents, then took her place beside Sarah and across from Jamison, Josiah, and Cade. Dialogue flowed freely between them, discussing the day's path and concerns for the coming one. After over a month, Sarah had finally gotten used to the strangeness of having the white and colored folks sitting together, stoking the same fire, eating the same meals. It wasn't that she thought they shouldn't, but after so many years, it was difficult to step into such a different way of living.

Back in Hawthorn Ridge, she had never experienced this side of their servants' lives. She hadn't been allowed in the slave quarters; it would have caused tongues to wag even more than they already did. Martha lived with the female servants in the farmhouse attic and ate her meals in the kitchen. It was only after joining the Larks that Sarah realized how similar their conversations must have been to her own. Sometimes their inflections and word choices were unfamiliar, but they still laughed at the same sorts of jokes and commiserated over many of the same troubles she did. The heat, stubborn mules, and the confusing ways of men, to name a few.

It was in the eventual decline of silverware against tin that the first soft spiritual emerged, its melody slow at first then gaining strength as it released from Josiah's expansive chest. At nearly seven feet tall, he appeared a fortress unto himself, one she could never imagine being a slave to anyone. But he was contemplative in a way too, despite his breadth. He didn't speak often, but beneath his peppered beard and greying hair, his smile was always kind. She could see why the Larks considered him a second father, or perhaps more accurately, a grandfather. She found it unfair that the man had never had any children of his own, nor did he even have a last name. She wondered when that decision had been made. Some slaves took their master's surname when they were freed, but not this man. He had always been Josiah and he still was simply that.

His deep bass rolled over the campfire like the words he sang about, rumbling low in his chest. *"Ole Satan is a busy ole man; he rolls stones in my way. Mass' Jesus is my bosom friend; he roll 'em out o' my way."*

Levi picked up his fiddle for the refrain and pretty soon nearby families were wandering over to join in the song.

"O come, go wit me. O come, go wit me. O come, go wit me. Walkin' in de heaven I roam."

Surprising to Sarah, it was Oliver who joined in with the next verse of the spiritual, his voice blending with that of the other colored families. *"I did not come here myself, pray Lord, It was my Lord who brought me here. And I really do believe I'm a child of God, A-walkin' in the heaven I roam."*

After another round, the song ended and Levi laid his fiddle across his knee, "Where'd you learn of the spirituals, Mr. Shay?" he asked.

Oliver rubbed his neck and glanced at Coraline. He reddened as though he had erred by singing, but she only nodded in encouragement. "Our servant," he said softly. "Her name was Kandeh."

"You owned slaves then?" Sarah asked. It didn't surprise her; he was from the South after all.

Then Oliver shook his head. "No. Most of the folks I knew didn't. It was those mighty plantations like the Larks which carried the majority of the slaves for the entire South. Kandeh was a slave, but not with us. She escaped from one of those big places with her daughter, Sokey. We found her hiding in our cellar trying to escape a terrible thunderstorm. I thought my papa for sure would send her out, not want to get mixed up with the slave catchers. Or maybe turn her in for a reward. But instead, he invited her to stay. He didn't own her, so he couldn't free her, and there was no room for quarters outside of ours. We lived in the city, you see. He made up a space in the attic for the two of them and paid her a wage for years, until she earned enough to buy her and her daughter's freedom. This was years ago, before the laws prohibited it. I often wonder what happened to those women. If they stayed safe."

There was a moment of silence, a hollow surrounded by the chatter of the other wagons and the bray of livestock at its center. The fire popped, sparks shooting only to dim before singing shoes and skirts. To Sarah, it felt like an acknowledgment of mourning, a feeling she knew all too well. Oliver would never know what happened to that woman and her child. He would never see them again. In some ways, it was almost the same as if they had died.

"They were grateful," Levi told him. He watched as his children ran past, laughing and pushing each other as children do. They had abandoned their empty plates without asking for permission, yet neither he nor Marie reprimanded them for it.

"Do you think they were?" Oliver asked. "All my life I've always wondered."

"Well, some of our kind, they think we should hate the white folk for purchasin' us and hate even more the ones trying to be our saviors. Truth is there's only one Savior and men like you is just trying to do what's right. The law ain't fair and it ain't easy, and it certainly won'ta be changin' overnight. It's taken two hundred years to get here, long before you's were even thoughts in your mommas' minds. Hatin' you for something beyond your reckoning ain't deserved."

He reminded Sarah of her third husband, Mr. Benton. He had been a nice man with an outlook that seemed to match Levi's. He made her laugh and despite their age difference, she enjoyed his company. Nine years difference was not truly so many compared to some marriages.

Levi began another hymn and this one she knew: "The Red Sea's Dangers Now are Past." They had sung it at the prayer service the first night out and a few times since. The tune was slow and would have seemed somber, if not for its hopeful words.

"The Red Sea's dangers now are past; Clad in white robes, come, let us taste the Lamb's most royal feast; And sing a hymn of praise to Christ our King."

Josiah added his bass to Levi's baritone followed by Jamison at his side. Garrett paused between his rounds, watching from horseback behind them. Cade joined in, settling himself beside Alice Ann who had emerged from beneath the wagon, her book for once closed in her lap. Finally, Oliver's alto met theirs in a harmony reserved for church choirs, the type to leave one misty-eyed and clutching the hymnal to their chest.

"O true celestial sacrifice! By thee hell's power vanquished lies; Relentless Death unlocks his chains, and life eternal man regains."

Why couldn't she write poetry like hymns, whose words fell so easily from these men's lips? Linden would have been able to compose like them. She, however, was left with nothing but crumpled sheets, the same ones she threw in the fire night after night.

"That we forever may possess, this joyful paschal happiness; From death of sin, O Jesus, free, those that are born again of thee."

She swallowed hard, wanting to join in, but once again feeling like an imposter. Many of these folks had been together since Charleston, some had even grown up together like the Larks and Josiah and the Harpers. They were more than simply traveling companions or servant to master; so many of them were friends, even family. Josiah and Levi were here, not because they were purchased, but because they wanted to be. They trusted the Larks and the Larks trusted them. She had never had comradery with any of their servants, except for Martha. In the end, she hadn't even been able to trust her own parents. Not even herself.

The song came to a close and Levi raised his fiddle, launching into a lively melody that encouraged several couples to leap into a square dance between the campfires. Oliver and Coraline immediately joined in the fun and Cade extended an invitation to Alice Ann, gently tugging her book from her fingers to place it in the wagon. She smiled at him shyly and Sarah wondered if perhaps there might be hope of romantic interest for the wild girl after all.

Young love, she thought, wistful. To be concerned about something so innocent was rather the luxury.

One of the Harper children—adorable six-year-old Reeslie—ran up with two clover crowns in hand, her toddling little brother, Quint, right behind. She held them out to Sarah and Martha, her face alight and one tooth missing from her smile. "For you!" she declared. "Princess Martha and Princess Sarah! Please bow for your corneration."

"Coronation," Marie corrected with a laugh and a shake of her head.

"I said that, Mama!" She pegged her mother with a stare. "Corneration." With a huff, she turned back to the ladies. "Please bow."

In turn, first Martha then Sarah tilted their heads so the child could crown them as princesses of the evening. The woven crowns were nothing like the ring Tobias had crafted for her, which somehow still lay miraculously intact upon her finger. These were as one would expect a child's creation to be: clumsy, uneven, and already bits of white clover rained down as the crown was jiggled upon her curls. She was glad she had chosen to remove her bonnet in the evenings now; otherwise, she was certain Reeslie would have placed the crown atop it.

"Do you have any siblings?" the little girl asked Sarah.

"No. I wasn't blessed with anyone except Martha."

"I had a sister," Martha said. "Her name was Roma. She was a few years older than I."

Sarah stared. Martha, her Martha, had a sister? She gaped at her friend picking her meal's last burnt bits onto her fork and forcing them into her mouth. She stood with her empty plate, but Sarah touched her wrist before she fully extracted herself from the ground. "You have a sister?" she gasped. "Why did you never tell me?"

Martha pegged her with those soft brown irises, the same from the last twenty years together. "You never asked."

16

Except for a simple, "Yes, Miss Sarah," or "No, Miss Sarah, or "I don't think so, Miss Sarah," Martha had stolen herself into silence. When Sarah approached her over a tub of dirty breakfast dishes, apologizing for her oversight the night before, Martha replied with, "It is no matter, Miss Sarah."

Sarah was starting to hate the way Martha called her, "Miss Sarah," with an edge of spittle like it was being driven as an insult. She knew she had made a mistake, but surely Martha wouldn't hold it against her forever. She could do better. Today, she would begin learning about Martha's past like she should have long ago.

After packing the breakfast dishes away, they yoked the mules to the wagon in silence. Since her confrontation with Garrett, they had become a proficient team, able to settle the animals in no time flat. Once that was completed, Sarah would take up the goad stick and Martha would grab their bonnets from the wagon, always handing Sarah hers before placing her own. This morning, however, she emerged from the wagon with her bonnet strings already tied.

She held Sarah's black bonnet out to her. "Best put it on, Miss Sarah. The sun's bound to be hot."

Sarah stared at the bonnet but didn't take it. She didn't have to be a well-bred woman to understand the thinly laced insult toward her untanned and flawless complexion. She covered Martha's hands with her own, only the bonnet's stiff fabric between their skin.

"Tell me about your family," she said.

Martha's eyes immediately shifted to her shoes.

"Martha, look at me."

Her friend's sight finally rose and her expression made Sarah wish to retreat more than a step. There was a hard edge there, wholly unexpected. Usually, Martha allowed unpleasant circumstances to roll off her back with a shrug and a smile, but today there was genuine offense in her gaze. The two women had never quarreled before, even as young girls, and it was not a situation Sarah reveled in.

"Martha," she breathed. "I am truly sorry. I should have known."

"It is no matter, Miss Sarah. I had a sister and now I don't. Parents and a little brother too. Lemuel was seven then. He was still at the market when your Pa brought me home."

She had sent her young brother to do the marketing? Sarah thought in confusion a half-second before foolishly realizing which market Martha meant—the slave market. Martha, Roma, and Lemuel had been there together and then auctioned off one by one. Separated.

Sarah still remembered that day at the Fifth and Myrtle Market. They went all the way to St. Louis to bring Martha home. They could have gone elsewhere, but like gifting a new toy, Father wanted to find his eight-year-old daughter the best. She stood between her parents as slave after slave was paraded past and bid upon. Men, women, children. Even infants, snatched up by an elderly matron in a feathered hat and too many cascading petticoats. She remembered the mothers screaming as their babies were torn from their arms and placed into the matron's, then handed off to a manservant and carried away.

Sarah tugged on her father's jacket, alarmed at the scene spread before her. "Papa, what is she gonna do with those babies? Will she hurt them?"

Papa bent down and met her eyes with his gentlest assurance. "No, my dear. I know it seems frightening, but it is simply the way of things. Like an orphanage. Children whose parents can't care for them properly. Fret not, Sarah, the babies are so young they won't remember any of this."

She was much older—older than she liked to admit—before she realized "the way of things" was not as neatly tied as her hair ribbons had been. She had been so happy to have a friend, almost like a sister, that she skipped off for the buggy, practically dragging Martha behind her. Of course, Martha's name wasn't Martha at the time. Slave owners often changed their slaves' names and her new friend didn't come with one. So, Elda Walcott selected "Martha Louis" for its pleasant meaning and for the city where she was found. They never once spoke about that day again.

Until now.

From two wagons back, Garrett watched them, his eyes dark with judgment and not bothering to conceal it. Last night after his rounds, he had taken Martha aside. They spoke in hushed whispers until most were in their bedrolls and the campfires dimmed to soft embers. From her own bedroll, Sarah watched as he silently kissed Martha's knuckles and bid her goodnight. Even Garrett, for all his rough edges, had found an alliance where she could not.

Martha now stood with eyes on her new black boots, rather than her usual pair of hand-me-downs. As a housemaid, she always had nicer things than the field hands, but never anything as nice as Sarah wore. She wasn't allowed to attend social events or even grace the parlor for tea with Sarah's friends. Growing up they played together in the fields and laughed under the covers late at night, but their sisterhood remained tethered to the farm and no farther. Martha wasn't allowed to eat at the family table and when Sarah went into town, her name was never mentioned. There had always been a disconnect between them; only she had never noticed.

Maybe her curse wasn't Linden's doing after all. Maybe it *was* her sins and the sins of her parents which brought this upon her. Maybe she did deserve it after all.

"Martha, I—"

Then Garrett was there, forcing them apart, one elbow propped back on the square edge of the wagon bed. He angled himself toward Martha, half his back blocking Sarah from her friend's attention. "Excuse me, Miss Louis. I wondered if you'd care to join me today?"

Martha's eyes instantly alighted. "Morning, Mr. Lark. Join you for what, if you don't mind my asking?"

"For walking. Jamison's been called away to assist with a case of the ill stomachs in the Queller wagon and it gets right lonely walking twenty miles by myself." He rubbed the dark stubble on his chin, a patch sticking lopsided where his shave missed the mark. "Unless the Widow Walcott needs another chaperone. She is in lead with Tobias today. That's twenty miles of potentially unscrupulous behavior."

Martha's eyes shot to her then, quicker than Sarah could have imagined. "Do you need a chaperone, Miss Sarah?" Her tone was agreeable enough, but her expression was not. She had no desire to remain.

Sarah wanted her to though. She didn't wish to be left alone for a full day with Tobias when she was in such an emotional upheaval. She was barely holding back tears yet still had to be prepared to lead two mules across twenty miles of prairie. She didn't have the luxuries she had once, to fall across her comfortable bed and weep until she had nothing left to give. She didn't even have a bedroom to go to or a door to lock.

She wanted Martha to stay so they could fix this. She was fast becoming friends with the Shays, but Martha was the one she came here for. They were like sisters even if there had been an illusion about it before yesterday.

But even sisters sometimes needed their distance.

With a pleasant smile, she took her bonnet from Martha's grip and folded it over her pinned bun. She slipped the bonnet strings around to tie under her chin. "If you would prefer the company of Mr. Lark today, I shall be fine on my own. If the wagon drops an axle, Tobias will be able to assist me."

"Good." Garrett swung an arm around Martha's shoulders, leading her away before Sarah could so much as stutter. "Better get your feet to moving, Widow Walcott," he flipped over his shoulder. "My brother waits for no man...or woman."

Not once did Martha turn back.

17

Bright sunshine and warm breezes greeted Tobias throughout the morning. Twice, he removed his hat just to feel the glorious day upon his face. The oxen were familiar with the day-to-day process by now and needed little encouragement except for a quick prod to change direction. Luckily, the thousands of settlers gone before them ensured an easily identifiable trail, leaving their party in good spirits. Except for Jamison, called away to assist with the Queller sickness, they had no needs to attend to today.

Well, save for one.

Sarah's wagon had finally rounded back to the front of the line, side-by-side with his. This was the first time they were without his brothers—without anyone—and he had been determined to ask all the personal questions he hadn't had a chance to before. She, otherwise, seemed determined to ignore him. She focused on the trail ahead, the wind in her face and lack of dust in her eyes. It was truly the most substantial blessing of being the lead wagon. No need for face coverings and one could breathe clean air to their heart's content. Yet he would gladly be covered in grit every day if it meant gleaning even one meaningful response from this woman.

Failing to maintain attention to his steps, he stumbled into a wheel rut and tripped against the side of his wagon, pulling his foot away seconds before the wheel crushed it. *Pay attention, Lark*, he scolded himself. *You bust your foot and then what kind of leader will you be? You can't mend broken bones like you mend a fence.* And Jamison's assistance would only be adequate at best. The entire world of medicine was taking up space in his brain and none of it worked on his Gifted brothers.

Tobias stepped back into pace, a full ten feet away from his wagon and ten feet closer to Sarah. She was staring at him now. "Are you hurt?" she asked. It sounded like she might legitimately be concerned.

"No, ma'am. How are you doing today?" Good gravy, that sounded stiff even to his ears.

She paused a beat. "Would you like an honest response, Mr. Lark?"

He nodded silently while wanting to scream, "Yes! For once, please answer one of my questions with some emotion!"

She took a few steps closer and her mules instinctively side-stepped in the same direction. She swatted David and Solomon to move them back into line.

"I'm afraid I've been better. I'm beginning to understand that friendships are more complicated than I always supposed." She gave an ironic sniff. "That must sound like a ridiculous revelation from the woman who has had nothing but complicated relationships."

Behind them, one hundred and eighty wagon wheels creaked in procession, the rumble providing cover to their conversation. "Was there an incident? Has one of the men been forward with you?"

"More forward than you?" She laughed and he liked seeing her smile again. There seemed to be too little of it. She waved away his concern. "Never worry. No one's proposed marriage except you."

"Then what is the trouble?"

Her expression turned serious again, and she fiddled with the goad stick in her hands. After almost a month, she was still wearing the ring he gave her.

"It seems like the entire wagon train sees you as a leader and a friend. Josiah and Levi would follow you to the ends of the earth, even though they were your slaves. How did you get them to trust you? Walk on water?"

"No, I certainly can't do that, although my father probably thought he could." And never, *never*, would he be like his father.

Sarah watched him for an answer while he watched the trail. He wasn't walking it alone, and he supposed, for that at least, he should be thankful.

"Trust isn't like a Gift. It isn't something you inherit. You have to earn it. And you should only give yours to those who do." *Even when you earn it, that isn't a guarantee you will keep it*, he thought. Daniel had Tobias's trust once and now he didn't, while their father never earned it at all. Not once had that man shown he deserved anything but disdain.

"It took a lifetime to create the bond I have with Josiah and Levi. Levi's only a few years older so we grew up working together, playing together, holding conversations in the slave quarters when father wasn't watching. He asked me once if he could spend the night in the house when father was away, just to see what it was like. I wanted to let him. I would have if it wasn't for the other servants. We had hundreds of slaves. I couldn't allow them all in the house, and if I let Levi, he could fall out of favor with the others. Lose their respect by earning mine. I'd heard of uprisings on other plantations. Slaves killing other slaves, setting fire to the crops. That wasn't something I could risk."

"Maybe you should have helped the slaves revolt. Shown them you were on their side. That you understood."

She made everything sound so easy. Reducing complicated Southern politics down to what he'd like to do versus what he must. Freedom was never that simple.

"It doesn't matter now. All the slaves are long gone. Josiah and the Harpers are the only ones left, as much as I hoped to bring the others."

"Why didn't you?"

"It wasn't my choice to make. The slaves were Daniel's inheritance. The house, the land, everything. Daniel didn't like the concept of slavery, and had no real interest in farming, so he sold everything except the townhouse and a handful of servants. In the end, we all received our fair share of the profits, and he didn't fight me on keeping Josiah and the Harpers, but I knew after that day I would never see him again. Daniel isn't Gifted. I guess I should have always known that eventually we'd part ways and not look back."

When she didn't respond right away, he thought perhaps he had reached the end of her willingness. Truth be told, he was surprised he had managed to come this far. He didn't want to press her to explain more, even though it was eating him inside not knowing why she had asked. How could he earn *her* trust if he constantly bombarded her with breached borders?

Up ahead their next stop, Fort Kearney, came into view. It had come upon them quicker than he anticipated. He had waited twenty-two days to spend one whole day with Sarah and now they would only have an hour more together, likely less.

"Do you think you'll ever forgive Daniel?" she finally asked. "After everything he did, how could you?"

Why did she have to bring that up? After two years apart, he didn't think on his brother with the red-filled vision of those first months after their father's death, but neither did he recall it with fondness. The memories were simply there, lingering in his backward thoughts, occasionally floating around to the forefront only to be bobbed back again like a cork on a line. His feelings didn't exactly equate to forgiveness; he doubted he could actually say those words if he stood in front of his eldest brother right now. "*I forgive you, Daniel.*" But he didn't want to start his new town—and hopefully someday a marriage—with resentment festering.

"It's more of an acceptance with Daniel," he said at last. "That someday I will be able to forgive him."

She nodded and they fell back into silence while the chatter of their trail mates began to trill louder behind them. As they edged closer to the fort—more a fenced-in series of log cabins than an official government building—their excitement grew and lists were made. They would have an opportunity to purchase or barter for supplies and replenish food stores. He had also heard rumors that other pioneers left the latest travel recommendations about which paths were growing treacherous and bandits to be on the watch for. Jamison's worries would probably prove to be right. They needed to lead these people straight or they could fall victim to any number of calamities. He would make sure to check his knives and hatchets, as well as his lumber, twine, and nails. He couldn't be caught out on the prairie with a broken wagon and nothing but waving wheat to fix it. Of course, he could still fix it with wheat given a desperate need, but why tax his Gift unnecessarily?

"Will you or Martha have any purchase needs when we reach Fort Kearney?" he asked.

"I think you've provided more than plenty, but I would like to post a letter to my mother. She helped Martha and me, and I want her to know we're safe." She turned to look at him, her face half-veiled in her bonnet's shadow. "Or do you think it unwise?"

"I think..." He paused, trying to express an emotion she couldn't understand with both her parents still living and loving her. An image of his mother approached unbidden, dark hair tucked behind her ears, curls against her shoulders as she kissed him goodnight one final time. He swallowed and tried again. "I think if my mother were alive, I would probably write her every day."

Sarah smiled and he knew he had said the right thing. The words would put her mind at ease, at least for the moment.

The truth was, however, he wouldn't have written a single letter to his mother.

Because if Geraldine Lark were still alive, he never would have left.

June 1852
Fort Kearney, Nebraska

Dearest Mama,

I hope this letter finds you and Papa well. Martha and I are safe and on our way to Washington Territory. A kind group has invited us to join their town, a life so different from ours, it is difficult to describe. Never have I seen so many sorts of folk working and enjoying one another's company without restraint. Someday, I hope Martha and I may too feel this sense of belonging.

I am sorry I cannot provide the grandchildren you long for, I am sorry for not being the daughter you wanted, and I am sorry for taking Martha from you. Desperation leads us to do what we may not otherwise. I know you only wished to help me.

Be good to the servants, grant them their freedom when you can. Perhaps it is better to make a small fortune with a few hired hands than to have a grand life on the work of slaves. I am not sure what I believe yet, but I hope to find it in Washington.

Do take care.

All my love,
Your daughter, Sarah

P.S. I am also writing poetry and cooking my own meals, even if most of them turn out much overdone. I pray that does not horrify you too much.

18

nother broken wagon wheel. Honestly, Tobias was sick and tired of these rotten roads, if one could even call them that. For as much as he was glad to be rid of the trifles of civilization, he missed bricked streets and raised boardwalks. Unfortunately, the trail wasn't apt to get any better and once they reached their claim in Washington, there would be no roads at all.

After propping up the front left corner of the Pryors' wagon bed with a barrel, he pried the wooden wheel away from the axle. It had cracked when the wagon dipped down into a puddle that, as it turned out, was much deeper than anticipated. The trail had narrowed to single-file a few miles before, waist-high prairie grass rising on one side and the Platte River banking the other, with no way to avoid the collision. The wheel lurched into the hole with a splash and a sickening crunch, busting three spokes clean off and leaving the rim beneath in tatters. The Pryors didn't have another wheel to spare, nor was Tobias eager to use his lumber stores yet.

He slung the offensive wheel over his shoulder, marching to where Jamison sat nursing seven-year-old Marta Green's swollen fingers. She had smashed them in the door to their wagon's under compartment and the red digits now lay in a bowl of water while Jamison mixed together some concoction with his mortar and pestle. Tobias had no interest in what the sickening substance was or how his brother made it. It would work and that's really what mattered.

"James," he called. "I've got to chop some wood for a new wheel. Can you watch the camp?"

Jamison glanced up from his work, eyes heavy and rimmed red with fatigue. Before Marta, he had fixed another boy's broken leg, splinted it up good and tight with a method Tobias had never seen any doctor besides his brother make work. But he knew it would and the patient would be healed and walking in less than half the time of a normal person. Even Oliver Shay had been impressed.

He turned back to his patient, slathering the green ooze across Marta's knuckles. "Take Garrett with you. There are Indians about. I've seen two tribes on the horizon already."

"I've seen them too, but I don't think they'll be a bother. Remember what the soldiers told us at Fort Kearney? As long as we pass straight through but don't settle, they shouldn't mind."

"Shouldn't and won't are different words. Is your revolver loaded?"

"Always is."

"And your rifle?"

"Jamison, why don't you call in the cavalry to escort me? I'm chopping a tree down and crafting a wheel, not inciting war. I'll be fine."

"Take Garrett. Speaking of the devil, here he comes now." He nodded to where Garrett was riding up fast, not attempting too hard to avoid those in his way and who now leapt aside lest they be trampled.

By twenty-eight years old, Garrett should have cast this careless wild streak to the woods. Being a trusted second should have made him step into his new boots with responsibility. Yet he continued to exasperate with frustrating regularity. The only reason he still held any sort of rank was that Tobias, Jamison, and Cade didn't want to lose yet another brother.

"Exactly who I needed to see," Tobias called out as Garrett swung down from the saddle. "Jamison's making me take an escort out to find wood for a broken wheel. I'm tired of arguing today so I thought you could—"

"Not now," Garrett interrupted. "We need to devise a search party."

"For what purpose?"

"The Morrow girl is missing. She wandered into the grass, and her parents are about to run in after her."

"So, use your talents and go find her."

Garrett waved his hand over the endless grass. "If she's lost in that and I go alone, how am I going to explain how I found her so easily? Don't forget your mind, Tobias. We need a search party so it makes more sense when I stumble across her."

"Or," Tobias countered, "you could go out on your own and be a miracle worker."

"Nah, I'll leave the miracles to Jamison."

Jamison tied off a stretch of checkered fabric around Marta's hand and gave her a smile. "There you are, Miss Green. I bet by tomorrow you'll be good as new. Off to your Mama now. Don't dally." He took the bowl in both hands and stood, watching Marta scamper off. "You need to watch your talk, Garrett. You run your mouth in front of the wrong folks and you'll only bring us trouble. I worried about those folks not understanding the trials ahead, but I think maybe it was us who didn't know."

"More proverbs from the preacher," Garrett muttered. "That girl was no more than five. Who's she going to tell who will actually believe her?" He flicked a finger against the bowl in his brother's hands and the metal released a merry ring. "Now, get rid of that mess and help me round up Josiah and Levi. Tobias, if you could find Clinton Reed; I spoke with him this morning and he seems to have a good handle on the landscape. Should make the search more convincing."

"Very well. I suppose this wheel can wait another hour." *More delays*, Tobias grimaced. Maybe Jamison was right and they were the foolish ones.

Garrett and Jamison rode toward the front of the line and Tobias headed in the other direction, weaving between wagons until he reached the center where Clinton Reed's cattle usually settled. He was with them now, trying to keep them corralled, but their movements appeared erratic. They would shuffle in one direction, then the next, the sound of muffled hoofbeats second only to their soulful moos.

Tobias reached out to run a hand over one's back only to receive the wary eye. "Hey, Reed," he called. "What's got them all antsy?"

Clinton pushed his hat farther on his head and cracked his thumb knuckle against his hip. "Darn cows don't like this place and neither do I. Either they don't care for the grass, or they don't care for the river, or maybe it's the look of the clouds movin' across the sky, but they've been turning the whites of their eyes at me since we stopped."

Turning to the west, Tobias noticed darkening clouds over the late afternoon sun. Or maybe the clouds were blocking the sun, making it seem later than it was. The air didn't smell like rain; there was hardly a breeze to speak of. Calm.

Too calm? Nah, the cattle probably just didn't care for being cooped up in such a confined space.

He promised Reed they would be on the move again soon. There was a missing child to tend to and a broken wagon wheel, then they would be on their way.

"Who've you got looking for the kid?" Clinton asked.

"Garrett's rounding up some folks now. We sure could use your help."

"Can't. I take my eyes off these cattle and they'll be gone across the grass before I can jump the next ditch in the path. My sympathies are with the child, but my urgency is to my steers. You understand, of course."

"Of course." Tobias believed people were more important than livestock, but to a man with no heirs, a reclusive wife, and a livelihood that depended on the welfare of his cattle, it was easy to understand why Clinton thought how he did.

Rather than fight a path through the herd, Tobias turned back the way he had come. Mr. Pryor called out as he passed back by their wagon and dropped the broken wheel to the ground. "I thought you were fixing it. This still looks broken."

"That's because it is broken. We have a more important situation at the moment, a missing child. Your wheel will get fixed in due time."

"Oh," Mr. Pryor mumbled. He ran a thumb across his mustache. "Anything I can do?"

"Garrett's rounding a search party in the front of the line. If you head up there, he'll tell you. Much appreciated, Mr. Pryor."

He kept moving, alerting each wagon as he went with several more men hustling away to help. When he passed by the Shays, he was surprised to see Cade leaning against the wagon speaking in hushed whispers with Alice Ann. What was going on with that boy lately? He had never shown an interest in a woman before, or rarely, and now he'd turned attention on the most unladylike of the bunch. Not a day went by that she didn't talk about her marvelous fish-mongering dreams, and she must have misplaced the last of her stockings because he hadn't seen them on her for weeks. She must have heels of iron to not suffer from the many miles.

"Tobias!" Cade called as his brother approached. He hurried over, Alice Ann close behind. "I need to speak to you."

"I need to speak to you, too. There's a child missing and we need help finding her."

Cade stepped closer, tilting his chin to whisper nearly right into Tobias's ear. "That's really Garrett's specialty. What good would I be?"

"As good as anyone else." Tobias glanced at Alice Ann and left it at that. "What did you need to tell me?"

"There's a storm coming. We should lash everything down and camp until it passes. Likely by tomorrow."

Tobias considered the way Clinton Reed's animals were behaving and what the rancher had said. He glanced again at the darkening in the distance. It did seem like a storm was drawing closer, yet he couldn't justify stopping any longer than they needed to. They had already lost hours thanks to the Pryors' broken wagon wheel—which still wasn't repaired—and would lose more time by searching for the lost child. Which, he gruffed inwardly, if he could only send Garrett out alone, it would save more than half the time of rounding up a party.

"It's only mid-day," he told Cade. "I don't want to camp yet, especially on such a narrow path. If another party comes up behind us, we'll have to move to allow them passage. How large is the storm?"

"I can't tell. These feelings are unfamiliar, but we're also in unfamiliar territory." He scuffed his neck, running a hand around to his nearly smooth chin. "It isn't like anything we've seen back in Charleston. I don't like it, Tobias, not knowing what we're up against."

Tobias let his next dismissive remark go unspoken as Garrett rode up, pulling to a halt beside them, his horse's hooves padding the ground where he stood.

"I have a group ready to go," he said. "What's the delay?"

"Cade's nervous about the approaching storm."

Garrett full-on snorted. "You're such a crybaby, Cade. We've had rainstorms before and we'll have them again. If we stop for every drop of rain, we won't make it to Washington before winter and we'll be stuck in the snowcaps. It's time to grow up and use your Gift for something useful. Now hurry up."

He pulled his horse around and cantered off before either of them could reply. Tobias could tell his smarting remark had hit its target though. Cade folded his arms over his chest and watched his brother's departing form, eyes already brimming. Alice Ann cast him the same concerned glance Tobias was sure his own face reflected, although she said nothing, assurance or otherwise. Of their family, Cade had always been the most sensitive. Garrett was especially hard on him, and Tobias suspected every dig only drove another hole in Cade's already fragile confidence.

A wind whipped up, strong and unexpected, the smell of rain on its crest. With every second, the sky darkened a bit more. Maybe Cade was right about this being different than the others, and they would quickly learn exactly how limited their Gifts could be.

"Tell me more about this storm," he asked. "What do you think we're facing?"

Cade shook his head. He tried to turn away but was blocked by Alice Ann on one side and a wall of prairie grass on the other. The blades swayed as high as the wagon beds, while the clouds seemed to lower, a sinister breath enveloping the three within them. His eyes held such misery, his complexion tinging on the now hazy yellow-green of the sky above. "I'm sorry, Tobias. I can't. My Gift...it isn't...I don't...I have to go."

"But Cade, we have a child to find."

"Garrett will find her. He always does. You don't need me for that."

"Cade..."

Alice Ann reached out a hand, took a step forward, and Cade mirrored her movement in the opposite direction. He pushed past, backing down the trail with both hands extended. "Leave me alone, Miss Owens. I need to be alone." Then he turned, running toward the back of the wagon train, dodging around folks as they tied down their wagon flaps and secured their belongings. Oxen stomped and snorted, and he only barely managed to leap away and avoid being knocked clean down by one of Clinton Reed's cattle. Turning, he bumped into the Lennons' wagon which doubled as a four-chicken coup. They squawked and fluttered with the disturbance, tossing feathers into the air. With an apology to Mr. Lennon, Cade darted between two wagons and disappeared.

Tobias placed a hand on Alice Ann's trembling shoulder so she couldn't see how rattled he was himself. He didn't have time to go after Cade and console him; he had to help with the search party. No one knew about Garrett's unusual Gift and it would be worse for them all if Tobias, as the wagon master, appeared to not care whether the child was found or not. He knew she would be, but the rest of the train didn't. And judging by that sky, they didn't have much time to search and return safely themselves.

"Return to your wagon, Miss Owens," he told Alice Ann. He had to raise his voice against the commotion. "Help your sister secure the flaps and remain inside until the storm passes." Her eyes narrowed, prepared to argue, when the grass whipped sideways, cutting Tobias across the face. A burning sting traced its way down his cheek and he bit back a lash of profanity.

He let go of her shoulder to touch the tender spot. "To your wagon, Miss Owens," he repeated and this time, she complied.

"Mr. Lark!" another voice called.

He audibly groaned. "What the devil does someone need now?" he snapped before he turned to acknowledge the owner of the voice.

Sarah's face appeared from between her wagon flaps with both brows raised at his hostile tone, a paper and pencil clutched between her fingers. The wind threatened to steal them from her grip and her eyes went to the sky, the clouds swirling lower. They needed to find that child and get under cover before the worst of it set in. It would take infinitely longer if he had another item to attend to.

He gave a silent curse as she pocketed her paper and pencil in her apron front and flipped her skirts over the wagon bed. She came alongside him, her skirts whipping to and fro with the wind. "Where are the men going?" she asked. "Have you looked at the sky? We need to get to a cellar."

He scowled at her. "Where do you suggest I find a cellar in the middle of the Nebraska plains?"

"There must be a house around here somewhere. Surely this isn't complete wilderness? What about help from the Indians? I've seen them appear from time to time."

He exhaled loudly, a breath lost in the rising wind. "A child is missing, Miss Walcott. We must find her. There is no one else to come to our aid and certainly no cellars. I suggest you return to your wagon."

"I want to help with the search."

"We have it handled. Please return to your wagon."

"But..." She paused, turned, looked to the west. A rumble sounded in the distance followed thereafter by a click upon wood. Then another and another growing in rapid succession. A small piece of ice landed at their feet.

Tobias grabbed her shoulders, pushing her back against the wagon at the same moment a shower of hail pelted down upon them. He threw his arms over her head to protect her from the worst of it, covering her even as he felt the sting upon his own shoulders and back. She pressed herself against his chest and under different circumstances, he would have relished the way her grip tightened upon his open jacket.

He grunted as a particularly large piece of hail struck his shoulder and his hat vanished, blown into the heavens. He dipped his head on instinct, trying to save himself from the gravelly ice which struck him now. He caught a glimpse of Coraline and Alice Ann crouched in the front of their wagon bed, attempting to settle their oxen while their hair whipped in their eyes and ice scattered across the hard soil.

Their oxen snuffled and snorted still attached to the yoke, rustling the wagon forward then back, as they tried to move out of line but couldn't. Their choices were to run into the river or through the plains and either option seemed enough to widen their eyes and halt their paces.

Of course, the exception could always be counted on in such a situation. Farther back, Tobias watched as first one, then a second, and a third wagon's lead oxen trampled out of line. The first wagon aimed left into the plain, cutting a line of broken grass behind the runaway. Enough room for the next two wagons to follow and leave their passengers stranded behind.

A fourth and fifth wagon veered opposite them and directly for the river. The fourth wagon's owner charged after them, but stopped at the water's edge when he realized his oxen would not. The wagon went in, waterline up to the bed, supplies floating downstream as the oxen bellowed, snorted foam, and then slowly went under. At the final moment, another man and woman leaped from the wagon bed into the river, drawing arm over arm until fellow pioneers' hands yanked them from the water. Thankfully, the fifth wagon's oxen halted before they entered more than wheel deep, allowing their owner to lead them back up the embankment.

Seeing their opening, ten head of Clinton Reed's cattle charged forward through the grass, fanning out across the prairie toward the darkening sky. They didn't know where to go, all they knew was the river would offer no safety. It turned out, however, the prairie would be equally unkind.

Thick clouds churned into an ominous green soup, like that of the herbal ointment Jamison had placed on Marta's swollen hands. For a moment, the air seemed to still, then it swirled again, faster than before. A dark funnel descended from its center like a great cluster of birds, yet so close together he could not decipher one from the next. From deep within that darkness, a solemn whistle emitted, long and low. Terror found a new place inside him as he thought of his family still out on the prairie searching. Garrett, Jamison, Josiah, Oliver, Levi, and Cade...the last had gone in the opposite direction. What of the child lost in the grass? Would they all be swept away?

Holding tight to Tobias, Sarah watched the tornado claim its place upon the prairie. Being from rural Missouri, she was no stranger to green skies and cellar visits, but it was always a precautionary measure. Never had there been a storm like this.

It descended like a dream, similar to when she witnessed Jackson Whitticomb's death within her imaginings. Except for this time, she was living it before her eyes, a dark howling monster devouring everything in its path. She saw Tobias's lips form the word, "Move!" right before he tugged her down and shoved her underneath the wagon. Together, they rolled into its center while the bed thrashed violently above them.

Would those meager bits of wood and canvas be enough to protect them? Despite the metal wheel rims, there was not a single nail or latch holding it together. Tobias claimed to be Gifted, said he had a knack for building that far surpassed the average man. She did not want to find him failing when the wagon broke to bits.

From her limited vantage point, there was only grass before them and the trail beneath them with no way to see where the tornado was headed. Bits of grass and twigs rained down, the larger pieces slicing into the wagon cover above. With every shred of the canvas, she expected them to race straight through all her belongings and the wagon bed to strike them down where they lay.

Where was Martha? After over three weeks, they still weren't speaking. Most days after hitching the wagon, she traveled with the Harpers or alongside Garrett, close enough for Sarah to glance, but still a thousand miles away in spirit. Today she had been with the Harpers, little Quint asleep upon her chest at luncheon. Where was she now? Was she safe?

Above them, the wagon continued to rattle, a clatter of crates and dishes and all the thoughtful supplies Tobias had purchased. Linden's poems were tucked safely inside the under compartment and would continue to be as long as the entire wagon wasn't sucked into the storm. She pressed a hand to her apron pocket where her latest poem lay hidden against her middle.

Across the many plains I fly, alone, my love, and lost.

My breath, my breath comes quickly now, pulled forth at such a cost.

She felt Tobias's hand slip into hers, drawing her tighter against him. Her skirt blew up her shins, exposing her stockings and the mud-stained underside of her petticoat. She couldn't do a thing about her state though, nor did she even think twice about the indecency. Brown boots ran past splattering mud and she buried her face in his shoulder, not wanting to watch whatever happened.

At such a cost.

Was entertaining a man's mere acquaintance enough to set off Linden's rage? Would he kill Tobias without her ever needing to marry him?

Please, she begged whoever would listen. *Please.* Her bonnet flew off then, the ties whipping painfully against her face as it soared out from under the wagon. Up into the dirty swirl, a little patch of black against the deadly yellow sky.

Her hair needed no more encouragement. It broke free of its pins, blonde masses tangled about her cheeks, her ears, her throat. Blinding her to what occurred before her very eyes. Screams sounded nearby. Was *that* Martha? Coraline? Alice Ann? Marie or one of the Harper children? Had they been torn straight out of their mother's arms?

It was terrible enough to think she had wrought such a fate upon Tobias, but it seemed their entire wagon party would be taken along with him. All because of her foolishness. Because she had chosen her comfortable life over Linden's dreams.

But as it turned out, such devastation was not meant to be. At least not that day.

The storm was over as quickly as it had begun. The wind ceased and the prairies stilled and Sarah was left holding Tobias's hand between their still-beating hearts.

19

Tobias crawled out from under the wagon, bracing himself for all manner of carnage. He gripped Sarah's hand and expected them to be the only two people standing there in a sea of destruction, wagons, belongings—and bodies—scattered within folded prairie grass.

But when he looked over the line of wagons, every single one remained intact. A few were battered, a little worse for wear. Three or four had even lost all or part of their canvas coverings. It appeared their party had survived the storm relatively unscathed. There were certain to be injuries, he expected. Even animals gone missing or killed. Those he could deal with as long as every *person* was still alive.

They walked the line together, checking on each wagon in turn, Sarah tending to the women and children while he spoke with the men and took stock of lost supplies. They had been beyond blessed, all things considered. They hadn't lost anyone and no one was too terribly injured. All of their animals were accounted for minus a few chickens, several of Clinton Reed's cattle, and the oxen which had rushed the river. Only one wagon had been lost to the river with a few other personal items either lost to the prairie or fallen in the current and swept away. Nothing that couldn't be replaced at the next fort or repaired by one of their party. Injuries had been confined to minor scrapes and bruises, the occasional gash which required stitching, and one broken arm. Most amazing of all was that Garrett had both located the missing child unharmed and found a low-lying ditch for the search party to scamper into for protection. What were the odds of such a place in the middle of the prairie? God only knew.

It was cause for celebration and they would have one to be sure, just as soon as everything was put back together.

For the rest of the day and late into the evening, the families tended to their recovery. Jamison and Oliver bound wound after wound while Levi, Garrett, and Clinton rode the prairie in an attempt to locate even one of the missing animals. Meanwhile Tobias, with help from Cade and Josiah, fixed wheel after axle after yoke after canvas cover without stopping, even when his finger joints stiffened and he wanted to drop into the dirt. He had never been so thankful to finally reattach the Pryors' wagon wheel seven hours after he first attempted the repair.

Wiping sweat and dirt from his face with an equally soiled handkerchief, he trudged down to the river in hopes of washing a little more thoroughly before supper. He could already distinguish the crackle of campfires and the deep stench of burning buffalo chips.

As he neared the river, he saw Cade hunched on the bank, elbows on his knees and his familiar dark curls clenched between his fingers. Josiah's broad form squatted beside him, one hand on the younger man's shoulder, speaking in indistinguishable whispers. At the sound of Tobias's approach, Cade gave only a moment's pause before he pushed up from the bank and ran toward camp without a word. On instinct, Tobias moved to follow, but Josiah was already there, gently holding him back.

"Let him go. He needs a moment to himself. He's feelin' guilty 'bout the storm and all."

"It wasn't his fault. He told me he had a bad feeling, and I dismissed it. He should be blaming me if anybody."

"Weren't nobody's fault," Josiah assured him. "Without Cade's Gift, you would've figured it was nothin' but another summer storm."

"We have his Gift though, and I ignored it. We could have ended up in far worse shape than we were."

"Without your brother's warning, you may have been. Or without stopping to fix the Pryors' broken wheel. Or without that youngin' getting lost. There was a reason we was stopped and ya need to start listening to the signs."

Jamison would agree there were no coincidences, only opportunities God used to nudge them in the right direction. He believed in signs the same as Josiah. While Tobias...well, he certainly believed the Lord had a plan, but he doubted whether humanity was allowed knowledge into its inner workings. How was one to know if something was a sign or if it just was what it was?

Josiah lifted his hand from Tobias's shoulder. The whites of his eyes were yellowed in the moonlight but still contained a sparkle. "I'll let you get down to the water. You're starting to stink."

Tobias rolled his eyes. This conversation was clearly over. "No more than you. When was the last time you bathed?"

"When did we leave Charleston?"

"Umm, over a year ago."

"Hmm, seems I do need a bath then." He gave a loud guffaw and without one move toward the water, strode back in the direction of the wagons, his laughter carrying all the way. Tobias hoped Josiah had been ribbing him over his bathing schedule. He honestly hadn't stunk that bad.

Still, it had been months since any of them experienced anything close to a proper washing. Wiping one's face, neck, and arms with a handkerchief wet from the rain barrel or standing in a cool morning drizzle fully clothed did not constitute proper hygiene where he came from.

Casting a cursory glance and finding no one about—and his stomach rumbling with the rise of rabbit meat sizzling on the open fires—he unbuttoned his vest, then his shirt, flinging both to the ground in a pile. Next came his boots and stockings, two large holes worn through either heel where the repair stitches had broken once again. He would need to darn those. To maintain modesty, should anyone wander by, he left his trousers on and waded into the river.

The water was colder—and grittier—than expected, but despite its murkiness, was still more delightful than anything he had experienced in weeks. Remaining close to the bank so as not to be swept off, he floated back, allowing his body to extend atop the water, its gentle lapping sending his hair floating against his cheeks. His sandy locks had grown longer since leaving Missouri, down past his ears now and nearly touching the nape of his neck. They still didn't compare with Jamison's, which now fell past his shoulders and were in dire need of a trim.

He allowed his legs to drop back beneath him until his toes found the muddy river bottom. Then he splashed water across his arms and torso, scrubbing—and sometimes scraping—off weeks' worth of grime. A cut on his arm stung as his fingers passed over it, a wound he wasn't even aware of until now. Likely the morning would only find him with more aches and pains and having to move on without complaint. Dipping beneath the water, he combed his fingers through his hair once more before he buoyed back to the surface and sputtered.

Well, rake him over rice, he wasn't alone.

From ten feet up the bank, Sarah's wide eyes grazed down his half-naked form, no doubt assuming the half beneath the water was also undressed. Quickly, she spun her back to him. "Apologies. Supper is nearly ready, and I was sent to find you."

Nearly ready? He had been down here longer than he thought. He rose from the river, water sluicing from his limbs as he stepped onto the bank and collected his clothes. They were dirty, but for modesty's sake, would have to do for now. He drew his shirt on, buttoning it across his torso, then added the vest over it. He was glad Sarah couldn't watch his every movement and yet wondered if her watching would have at all influenced her answer to his proposal.

"You can look now," he said. Slowly, she turned, her chin first peeking over her shoulder, then the rest of her followed. "Why did they send you to find me? Trying to save another meal from destruction?"

She frowned. "You are positively presumptuous."

"And also, I assume correct. Yes?" He raised an eyebrow and she folded her arms in a huff.

"No. Martha went to tend to Garrett, so I figured you probably hadn't given a thought to your own welfare either." She gestured to his wounded cheek. "Seems I was right." He touched his fingertips to his cheek and winced at the tender cut oozing a liquid wet and warm. All his river scrubbing must have broken it open again. Who knew grass had the ability to provide such infliction?

"Martha's tending to Garrett?" he asked. "Is he injured?"

"Not much. A few cuts and scrapes, same as you, and men are terrible attending to themselves." He could now see she held a rag and one of Jamison's glass medicinal bottles, a dark substance in residence beneath the cork stopper. She gestured again with the rag to his cheek. "May I? We don't want it to get infected."

He nodded and found a dry space away from the mud of the riverbank. He tugged his boots on as she knelt beside him, so close the edge of her skirt brushed his knee. The black fabric was coated with mud splatter from the storm, a dark line of grime wet against the hem and likely soaking through the front where she now knelt beside him. Her hair was mussed, bonnet gone, her wind-swept golden locks long and loose about her shoulders. While she examined his cheek, he could examine her dark eyelashes, fluttering with every blink. So close he could peer directly into those perilous green eyes. Perilous indeed. If she wasn't Gifted...

Then she pressed the washrag to his cheek and rubbed the wound like she was scrubbing the kitchen floor, causing him to grit his teeth and forget all about her allure. He pushed her hand away. "Good gravy, are you trying to rub my skin right off my skull? That is not how you tend a wound."

"Well, you'll need to excuse me, but I've never needed to tend a wound before. When one of the servants was injured, they either tended it themselves or we called the doctor. When I was injured— which was rare—I had the house servants to attend me."

"Martha then?"

"Usually." Averting her gaze, she unstoppered the bottle and dipped a finger into the goop. She tapped upward along the wound, far gentler this time. "It looks like you might need a stitch or two on this cut," she told him. She spread another layer of ointment across his cheek and he forced himself not to wince. He probably would have to stitch it up when he returned to the wagon. It didn't seem deep, but he couldn't chance having it break open every time he smiled or shouted, and in a wagon train, there were plenty of opportunities for shouting.

He pushed himself to his feet and offered his free hand down to help her stand. "I'll close it up when I get back."

"You're going to stick yourself with a needle? Why don't you ask Jamison to care for it?"

"Jamison won't be able to help me."

"Why not? I thought he was an extraordinarily Gifted physician."

Nice blunder, Lark. Although Jamison could stitch up anyone non-Gifted without leaving a scar, those skills didn't extend to his brothers. Early on, they had learned to minister to their own scrapes and scars. If Sarah was Gifted, in a dire situation, Jamison wouldn't be able to help her either. Tobias didn't want her to worry about that, on top of everything else.

"Jamison's already run ragged helping the others. He'll tell me to fix myself up and he's right. When things settle, you should ask him or Dr. Shay to teach you a few basic techniques. It's good to have some skills when you're faced with the unexpected."

"Could you teach me?" she asked.

"Me?"

"If it wouldn't be too large a bother. I know our wagons don't align most days and you're always busy with one trial or another."

He stared at her but her expression wasn't revealing anything. What was her motivation behind asking him specifically? Coraline must know far more medicinal cares, being the wife of a doctor. Even Alice Ann had probably been taught a thing or two. And hadn't Sarah said Martha always played caregiver back in Hawthorn Ridge? Why would she not go to her over anyone?

Dash it all. She had asked *him*. Who cared the motivation?

He offered her his arm and, thanks be, she accepted it. He grinned. "Of course, Miss Walcott. Ask me anything you wish to know."

20

Just when Sarah thought the mindless trail of dirt, heat, and flies had extinguished any excitement over surviving the tornado, the land opened up to the sight of Fort Laramie.

Although more substantial than Fort Kearney, Fort Laramie still wasn't much to behold. Before leaving Missouri, she had never seen a military fortress, but she always imagined them to be similar to those discussed in her renaissance history studies—a grand impressive structure. Instead, these were several wooden buildings with a high-flying United States flag at the center and surrounded by a tall wooden fence. There were no stone battlements and no turrets with archers at the ready. A muddy channel ran along one side which, she supposed, could serve as a moat.

As their wagons rolled closer, a thousand dark specks moving near the fort turned into recognizable impressions. Pioneers and prairie schooners camped outside the walls, smoke from campfires rising from within their circles, and the raucous sounds of livestock huddled together at their centers. On the fort's opposite side, Indian teepees dotted the landscape, their wooden framework poking through painted animal hides. While most of the native women tended near their homes, the men mingled amongst the pioneers and even entered the fort, assumedly trading as they had in Independence, Missouri. Their decorated costumes continued to amaze her both for their bold colors and beadwork detail as well as lack of modesty. How cool it must feel without a petticoat or stocking to be seen and most without shade for their faces! Their skin was already a creamy reddish-brown;

perhaps there was no worry of a sun-scorched complexion when one was so naturally tanned. If the thought wasn't so scandalous, after these many long months in the sun, Sarah felt even she might like to try it.

Farther across the prairie, a lazy herd of bison mellowed along, their wooly brown coats in the process of molting, revealing the lighter hides underneath. Bison had crossed their trail before, although never successfully hunted. With firewood becoming scarcer, they had started collecting buffalo chips for kindling. She would forever recall the pungent smell of each hard chip landing in the campfire, and their journey was not nearly over.

Once the wagons were circled and Sunday prayer service said, luncheon prepared and eaten, and the men returned from the fort with supplies, it was finally an opportunity to celebrate. They had traveled nearly halfway without any fatalities, despite gravestone after gravestone telling a different tale for so many. Two births had already occurred, with another three darlings on the way. They had managed river crossings, Indian sightings, and hunting trips without incident. What struggles they had encountered, they managed to overcome with teamwork and respect. Despite the unusual way she first joined them, Sarah felt that remaining in Larksong might be a possibility after all.

On one end of the wagon circle, far from the cattle hooves, Levi organized a mismatched frontier orchestra, ready to lead their wagon party in celebration. He tuned his fiddle one peg at a time, the harsh sounds joining two banjos, a harmonica, and a rain barrel repurposed into a rather impressive drum beat. They then stoked up a jig she had never heard and immediately, folks were on their feet and swinging one another about. None of their frivolity would be accepted in the ballrooms of Hawthorn Ridge.

Turning away, she climbed into her wagon and drew the flaps. The closed canvas made the interior warm with stale air and she instantly wished she could wear a lighter color than her mourning attire. At least today she had removed a layer of petticoats and selected a dress with short sleeves. If they were traveling all day on the trail, it would be impractical, but on Sundays, she was allowed to relax a little and feel the breeze on her bare arms. She giggled to herself as she withdrew her poetry papers from their secret space.

For all the world alights / And all is still

A mockingbird / A mockingbird

Truly awful. Maybe she should focus more time on practical skills and work on her poetry craft later.

The canvas flaps drew open, a rush of cool air hitting her ankles. Coraline lifted a boot onto the wagon step and flipped her legs into the bed beside Sarah. "I saw you scurry in here," she accused. "Why aren't you outside dancing?"

"I'm still in mourning."

"Oh, biscuits, that's no reason. I know it's convention, but we're hundreds of miles from any city of influence. You need to come join the merriment. Even Alice Ann has relinquished her books for one afternoon. Honestly, what else are you doing in here? It's too hot to be napping."

It *was* too hot, and the dance did sound enjoyable. Music swelled outside the canvas covering, and Sarah imagined herself being swung around from fellow to fellow and finally landing on Tobias... No, she must stop thinking that way. Her focus needed to fulfill long overdue regrets. Linden was the key to everything.

"I don't care much for dancing," she lied. "I would rather write poetry."

"Oh, how wonderful! I am pleased my paper was helpful. May I read it?" Coraline pushed her spectacles higher on her nose and attempted to peer at the papers in Sarah's lap, but she folded them over and hid them in her skirt.

"I'm not very skilled, I'm afraid."

"That's no problem if you enjoy it. You do enjoy it, don't you?"

"Not particularly."

"Then why ever are you doing it?"

Yes, why? How could she explain the reasoning without sounding like she belonged in the asylum her father wanted to send her to?

"My first husband, Linden," she said at last. "He adored poetry. He had dreams of us running away together and living impoverished in Boston. He would write; I would care for our children. We were going to have a scraggly dog." She laughed. "It sounds foolish to you, I'm sure. Me caring for home and hearth when I can't bake a biscuit or sew on a button? How would I ever keep children or a dog alive?"

"You would learn. You're learning now, however slowly that may be. It's a way of living you've never needed to know. It takes adjustment. It did for me too when we first set out. I was used to living with my family on the ocean. We ate fish nearly every night and now I haven't tasted it in months. I was used to being someone's daughter, and then suddenly, I was married and leaving for a place entirely unknown."

"But you do want to be here?"

"I do." Coraline offered her a long gaze, brown eyes blinking from behind metal frames. "It seems to me maybe you need to stop living someone else's dreams and start following your own. What do you want?"

Sarah was silent, Linden's poems clutched between her fingers. She hadn't dreamed about anything for herself in so long that no dream felt like it could ever become reality. "I don't know," she said truthfully. "I've lost so much that very few dreams are worth considering anymore."

"Well, you haven't lost everything and you never will. Remember that. Even in our darkest hour, we still have the Lord to guide us. That's why He gave us the sun and the stars."

God, she thought. He was too silent for her and the stars never spoke. A worthless gift like the one Tobias believed she had.

"Come out and dance with us," Coraline urged. "I know you have some new gowns. I saw Mr. Lark the day he selected the fabric."

"*Tobias* made them?"

"Sure. He stitched them in record time. I simply do not know how the man manages it all."

There had been mere days between leaving Hawthorn Ridge and her arrival in Independence. How would he have had time to craft five dresses and a wagon, while also caring for an entire wagon party?

But of course. She felt foolish the moment she thought it. His Gift must extend to almost anything he built with his hands. Logically, he would be a skilled tailor as well as a carpenter.

146

"My suggestion would be the yellow," Coraline said. "It will emphasize your pretty blonde hair and glow in the sun. Perfect for new beginnings and Mr. Lark is certain to find you stunning."

She didn't really want him to find her stunning, did she? It didn't seem like it would matter. He granted her equal attention no matter what she wore or how soiled her appearance.

If a man found her enticing of his own accord, that was something she couldn't help, but she didn't want to present herself as though inviting such attention. As lovely as the yellow was and as much as she would like to remember her youthful self again, she knew it wasn't sensible.

"I'll come out," she agreed, "but I'm wearing black and I'm not dancing."

"Close enough!" Coraline grabbed her hand, and Sarah barely had time to stuff her poems into her apron pocket before she was dragged out of the wagon. Her friend ran into the throngs of dancers while she remained to the side, bare hands folded demurely upon her middle. How unladylike to attend a social function without gloves. Heaven have mercy, she even forgot to grab her bonnet before she left the wagon.

As she moved to fetch it, she caught sight of Garrett on horseback, taking a turn around the exterior perimeter. He held his rifle across his lap and a revolver in his side holster, head swiveling as he spied outward. His vigilance surprised her. Everything had seemed rather safe when they arrived, especially with the soldiers in the nearby fort. The Indians hadn't appeared overly hostile either, at least from her vantage point.

"Festivity is when folks lower their guard. That's when Indians and thieves make their move."

She startled at the rough voice, turning as Clinton Reed stepped from between two wagons. He nodded, two fingers on his hat brim in greeting. He watched Garrett sway behind another wagon before he spoke again. "Thieves'll steal in when we're not watching. We've got a long road ahead of us and we can't afford to lose any of our supplies. So's the Larks are taking turns at watch. I'd be with them if they trusted me yet." He gave a grim smile. "I know I don't look the part of a pleasant fellow, Miss Walcott, but I assure you, I do try. Even if I trimmed my hair, shaved my beard, and handed my gun off to God Himself, I'd still be me underneath it all. It's tough for a man to suddenly find himself learning to live another way."

"You preach to the choir with that sentiment, Mr. Reed." She smiled, discretely sliding her hands within her bonnet's folds so he wouldn't note her gloveless impropriety. "How is your wife adjusting to frontier life?" She had hardly seen the woman since leaving Independence. Gabriella spent all her time in or near the wagon and never spoke to anyone. *Because of her nervous disposition*, her husband told them. If Mr. Reed was having a difficult time on the trail, how his wife must suffer doubly so.

Mr. Reed shook his head. "I'm sorry to say she is adjusting poorly. The dust makes it difficult for her to breathe. It seems she'll remain in the wagon until we reach Washington. I've heard the northwest water can cure all ails."

"Is that true?"

"It is what they say." He stared at her with hazel eyes so desperate she finally had to glance away. She recognized herself there and it wasn't a sight she liked to linger on.

Mr. Reed cleared his throat. "Apologies, Miss Walcott. You've made me remember I've left my wife long enough. Excuse me."

The moment he departed, she exhaled, fighting to catch her breath and not think about what Mr. Reed had said. She couldn't indulge in the belief that there might be more than one way to break her curse or she would seek answers forever, never trusting any outcome.

Settling her bonnet, she tied the strings under her chin and returned to watch the dancing. Oliver spun Coraline round and round, both of them bright and smiling. Coraline leaned in to say something with a laugh, and he reciprocated her amusement.

After another turn, Levi set down his fiddle and grabbed his wife's hand, swinging Marie into the next dance, the two of them seemingly as delighted as the Shays. Even Martha accepted the hand of first Avery, then Wallace, and finally Benjamin, all three former Tennessee slaves and attractive young men. Her gaze caught Sarah's as she spun by, but only for the briefest instant before she turned away again.

Sarah missed her friend. She missed lying awake on their bedrolls, whispering when they couldn't sleep despite the day's exertions. Discussing where they would live in Washington and what type of house they would have, even though neither rightly knew whose land they would be allowed to settle on. They didn't have the skills to tend their own crops, so likely they would need to make their way in town somehow. It was a daunting consideration made less so by having a partner to help accomplish it. Especially when that partner was one of her dearest friends. Now Martha slept nearer the Harpers, claiming to help care for the children, but the silent truth spoke louder than her words. Would Martha ever forgive her?

"You seem mighty lost in thought, there, Miss Sarah."

She jumped, the force sending her bonnet backward. Quickly, she tugged it back up and tucked her stray curls inside. She glanced at the mountain of a man who now leaned against the wagon bed with a ray of concern in his gaze. She and Josiah had never stood so near and she now realized how tall he must be, for she craned her neck and still came up short.

She wasn't sure how to respond to his question. This was the first time he or any of the former male slaves had engaged her and she wasn't used to speaking freely with them. She had never gone into the fields back home and rarely into the stable unless Sam was tacking up her mare for a ride. Even then, conversations were often limited to "Yes, miss" or "No, miss."

Josiah must have interpreted her hesitation as a social faux pas rather than uncertainty because he stuck out one meaty hand and grinned. "Might sorry, miss. It's rude of me to engage ya without introductions. Name's Josiah."

"Sarah Walcott." Slowly, she placed her small hand in his thick one. Never would she have expected such a gesture from a servant in Hawthorn Ridge. There were calluses on every pad of his fingers, but his grip was gentle. He gave her fingers a slight squeeze and quickly released them.

He smiled. "The cure for a bad bit of thought is a happy line of dance. You shoulda be out there."

"I'm not much for dancing. Miss Louis may be willing, however."

"She's your traveling companion? Martha, is it?"

"Yes." Although the phrase *traveling companion* made her envision old ladies who hired girls to read them dull novels and select fabrics from the seamstress. If the girl was lucky, she might receive a special holiday down South or if truly blessed, a chance abroad, but most wasted away discussing ailments and detailing nurses on sleep schedules. She could only imagine the grimace on Martha's face if Sarah told her.

She bit her lip, allowing her teeth to worry once across before she spoke again. "Josiah, if it is not too impolite, might you tell me why you do not use your family name?" The minute she asked, even she knew it was too impolite. Her parents would have accompanied her question with a stern reprimand post-query.

He hooked his thumbs through his suspenders with a light snap. "My family's been servin' the Larks since the days their greats grandpa Lark played mate on the *Oblique*. Few survived when she wrecked, and those who did returned changed men. My granpap stuck to the only one of 'em Larks who came back. If we had ever had a family name, it died with him."

How troubling. She had carried eight surnames in her lifetime, while this man never had one. Was he content to not know? He didn't offer, and she had the good sense this time not to ask.

A cheer went up from the dancers followed by the zing of a single fiddle string. They both turned to the commotion but had missed its cause. "Family ain't always the people we born with, Miss Sarah," Josiah continued. "It's those we choose to stand by. When them boys asked me to join 'em, I coulda gone anywhere. They gave me the choice. But I need them boys as much as they need me. Likely more. They're the only ones who can get me the life I need."

"They must mean a lot to you."

"Indeed, they do."

In the pause, they listened to strings thrum and harmonicas twang back into melody, palms tapping a new dance beat on the side of the rain barrel. She watched as each of the Lark brothers, minus Garrett out on rounds, stepped through the dance, grasping hands with the lady across and twirling her around to take the hand of the next dancer. Jamison and Cade and then finally Tobias.

The sunlight glinted off his silver vest and strands of sandy hair curled from under his hat brim, trailing down his neck. He was ever so distinct; she had noticed it even the night they met. His wasn't a beauty like many of the men she knew, especially after having weathered months on the trail. His attractiveness was more subdued, natural, a rugged feeling that he could not only provide for her financially and socially, but care for all her needs, wants, and fears as well. He wasn't afraid to find dirt on his hands, to build a life himself instead of merely hiring someone to build it for him.

A knot tightened in her center, drawing out until it turned uncomfortable. Martha swung by again, her hands in Benjamin's. He was six or seven wagons back in line, not in their circle, but they had crossed paths at Fort Kearney. He seemed nice enough. She hadn't ever considered Martha leaving her, but in all likelihood, she would marry someday. If Martha was gone and Sarah couldn't marry again...

"Do you have a schoolmarm assigned?" she asked Josiah.

He peered at her curiously. "Not officially, no. Planned to leave the early schoolin' up tos the families."

"I'll do it. You need an unmarried woman to teach, and I've had the very best education. Thoroughly schooled in reading, writing, arithmetic, and cultural studies. And ladies' lessons of course. One of the finest at finishing school. Will you place a reference for me with Mr. Lark? It seems you have his ear."

"His ear?" He chuckled. "I've known Tobias since he was head high to a rice patty. Not sure how much listenin' he's been doin'. He's coming this way though; why don't you ask him yurself?"

Sure enough, Tobias had abandoned the square and now sidled in their direction.

"Josiah," he called, "just the man I was searching for. Have you been showing Miss Walcott a fine afternoon?"

"Yes'ir, a right decent talk. She asked to be schoolmarm. Says she's the finest at finishing school. Makes her qualified to teach the youngins."

Tobias gave an amused smile. "Well, Miss Finest at Finishing School, it's time to make my rounds. Ready for our Sunday walk?"

21

You're not going to ask me to dance?"

Was it his imagination or did Tobias detect a hint of disappointment in Sarah's tone? He, however, contained his smirk. "You're still in mourning and social custom dictates that dancing isn't appropriate for a grieving widow. Also, if you had desired to dance, you would have worn some color. Your dreary ensemble does not invite anyone to extend a lead."

"Yet so far, I have been thoroughly bothered by Mrs. Shay, Mr. Reed, Josiah, and now you. So, it would appear my intentions are not striking true."

"Or maybe after months on the trail, we don't care about ballroom etiquette anymore."

He had to admit, at least to himself, that he was disappointed she still wore black every day. He had painstakingly chosen colorful fabrics especially for her and stitched them with the knowledge that someday soon he would see her in them. His thoughts often turned to the exquisite blue ballgown from her wedding, but over two months had passed since, and not once had she indulged. He thought surely once the temperatures started to rise, she would come to her senses. Yet she had not.

Frivolous plantation ladies and their ridiculous traditions. Even a thousand miles from a ballroom or garden party, they felt the need to maintain them.

Thankfully, when he offered Sarah his arm, she slipped hers through without a fight. After the tornado and their subsequent conversation by the river, it seemed their situation might be warming to something resembling friendship. She no longer behaved as though their walks were purely out of obligation and he even saw her edge a smile during each stroll. Despite those strides, she still wouldn't entertain being Gifted, however, forcing him to consider a new stance on the subject. She didn't need to believe she was Gifted, so long as eventually, she believed she was no longer cursed. Unfortunately, that was a tactic he wasn't exactly sure how to approach.

He turned to Josiah. "Best fetch your hat. We're strolling the perimeter and it's a warm one out of the shade."

Josiah ran a hand over his tight peppered curls. "Sorry, Tobias, I's got things to do. 'Fraid you're on your own today."

"Things? What things?"

"Important things. Keep me busy 'till supper."

"I think you're full of hot air."

Josiah gestured out with both hands toward the rolling land. "All around us is full of hot air. Woulda call the land a liar, too?" He raised a brow.

It was good to see Josiah relaxed and joking after years under Alonzo Lark's rigid thumb. Tobias rolled his eyes at the jest, but his smile wasn't easily hidden.

"Oh, go then to your important 'things.'"

Josiah hustled away, raising a hand to Levi and the other band members in a distinctly non-important-things fashion and Sarah stuttered, "Are we to be walking alone then?" Her fingers tensed on Tobias's arm, and he sensed he had only seconds to save the situation.

He slipped his opposite hand atop hers. "We've been alone before. The day I showed you the wagon for the first time, the evening you tended my wound by the river, and every time our wagons ran side by side for an entire day. There's an entire wagon train not fifty feet away and a fort full of soldiers up the ridge. Plus the neighboring pioneers and the Indians too. If you don't trust me with all that to run to, I've clearly done something very wrong with my life."

She stared at his hand covering hers. "You make a fair point."

"Then shall we walk?"

With her nod, she let him lead her between two wagons and along the exterior perimeter. There were volumes she wasn't saying, and he wished to ply the words from her pursed lips. He could pester her until hopefully she spoke, or he could demand it which would destroy the amicable agreement they had established. Forcing one's voice wasn't the way they had arranged their walks to this point.

He decided to swing the subject to something safer. "Why do you want to be the schoolmarm?"

Her grip relaxed upon his arm. "As an unmarried woman, I can't claim my own land, and I need a place to live when we reach Washington. Being the schoolmarm provides a roof to sleep under and a wage to care for myself. I know I can't cook or perform most domestic tasks too well, but I am knowledgeable. Life in the wilderness isn't any place to find proper book learning, and I think my experience could make a genuine difference to these children."

"Well, I'll be, there can be more to plantation ladies than lace and suggestive fan waves."

His jest plied a small smile of her own. "In truth, I would love a fan to shoo the insects away and cool this everlasting heat. I miss my comfortable bed and servants to draw my bath. And the walking! Never in my life have I walked so terribly far. I fear my feet will never be right again." She looked up at him. "I must sound awfully selfish."

"No, you sound realistic. It's a hard life out here and will be still when we reach Washington. I can't say I wouldn't want a down-feather mattress and a pair of new boots either. To sit in the parlor and challenge Jamison to a game of checkers would be a delight. I've never been handy at cards, and it seems that's the only game we have out here."

"I miss Papa's bookshelves. And proper tea. Made on a stove not over a campfire."

He smiled. "I miss tea too. Josiah's coffee always turns out a little too gritty. Despite your complaints, I think you will make a fine schoolmarm."

He knew allowing her to become the town teacher was almost the same as admitting defeat in his attempt to woo her. Teachers were always unmarried; everyone knew that. In some places, it was even illegal to hire a married woman for the position and once an unmarried teacher married, she was immediately required to resign. The belief was that a woman's first duty was to her husband and her home. If she was forced to divide her devotion between her family and her students, she would lose her focus and her family would suffer.

Tobias agreed there were few greater positions for a woman than that of wife and mother, but he wasn't certain he believed a woman could not accomplish more. He thought of his own mother, chained to her duty as Alonzo Lark's wife, forced to bend to his every whim and lose herself in the process. Until the day she died, Tobias could not recall if his mother had any interests outside of those his father placed upon her or if she had dreams beyond Larksong Plantation. The books she read were what her husband chose, the women she took tea with were the ones Alonzo approved. How would it have happened if her parents encouraged her to pursue her own longings from the first? Would she have still married Alonzo? Would Tobias have even been born to ask the question?

Alonzo Lark never needed Geraldine. Any bride would have sufficed so long as her mind was pliable. So long as she was like everyone else. So long as she wasn't Gifted. And Tobias should have seen the warning signs long before he did. Before Geraldine Lark hung from the attic rafters and time was lost.

"Oh, look!" Sarah cried, pulling him back from his reflection. She pointed upward where the moon hung in a perfect crescent. "I adore seeing the moon out in the daytime, don't you? Something beautiful where it shouldn't be." For another minute, they stood staring up together, that small sliver of white pasted against the blue sky. He wondered if anyone besides God would ever discover the mysteries of the firmament above.

"Martha and I used to tell stories about the stars," Sarah told him. "We would make wishes on them like they were flower petals."

"Did any of them come true?"

"Not yet." She tugged on his arm to continue the pace, tossing a greeting at nosy Darcy Frendon as the older woman craned her neck around her wagon.

"Our family tutor was interested in astronomy, too," Tobias said

155

once they passed. "He had a telescope and would point out all the constellations. Every one had a legend to go with it. Us brothers liked to pretend those stories belonged to us instead. They were always better than whatever life Father had us tethered to.

"I attended university—high marks—but it was really Josiah who gave us a proper education. The servants never went to school, but sometimes it seemed they knew far more than we did. Except for Cade. He's got more of our mother in him than any of us—her kindness and her sensitivities. While my father...well, shall we say that none of us wanted any part of him."

"My father always meant the best for me." Her voice broke and she coughed to cover her stumble. "But he didn't know how to handle my...situation...anymore. I didn't know how to, either. He thought an asylum could cure the darkness inside me, and I wish he had been right."

Grief and guilt had a way of tearing a person up inside. He would know. Tobias believed well of his own father once and long ago, exactly as she believed her father truly had her best intentions at heart. It might be true in Redmond Walcott's eyes, but Tobias couldn't imagine ever locking his child away. No matter how hopeless the situation might seem.

"If you believed the asylum could help, why did you run away?" he asked.

"Father sold Martha, and Mama heard she was being sent south. We'd heard such awful things about how slaves are treated down there. I couldn't let them take her."

"If she hadn't been sold, would you have stayed?" he asked gently. "Gone to the asylum?"

"Likely I would have."

Was now the best time to tell her that it was his influence which brought her here? If not for his last-minute deal with Redmond Walcott, Sarah would have never joined their wagon train. She hadn't decided to come west because she wanted to, but because she wanted to save her friend. Hers was a truly compassionate decision unlike Tobias's which had been purely selfish. He had desired her to join them for himself alone, to prove he was right and his father was wrong, to show that female Gifted existed whether she wanted to live that life or not.

It didn't change how he felt about her. With every step along the trail and every conversation, he grew more attached to her presence. It was only the motives behind that emotion which he questioned. Was he falling in love with her or her Giftedness? What if she wasn't like them after all? What if her husbands' deaths were all a matter of coincidence? Would he still love her if she could offer him nothing more than her shattered heart and a handful of death certificates? He wanted to believe he would. He needed to prove it to her. Prove it to himself. Once he did, then he would tell her he had purchased Martha.

"Would you tell me about your husbands?" he asked. Her chin quirked up, one tan brow rising with it, suspicion in her emerald eyes.

"Why do you want to know about them?"

"They're an important part of who you are. You're standing here because of them. I'd like to know the ghosts I'm fighting for your hand."

She jerked to a stop and the motion, combined with her arm through his, caused him to trip a step and let go. He pivoted only to have his vision filled with her shaken expression. "How...how did you know?"

"Know? About what?"

Her right hand found her bonnet strings, one finger tugging them away from her chin as though they strangled her. With a gentle touch to her shoulder, he directed her into the shade of the nearest wagon where she removed her bonnet and let wisps of hair fly free about her face, others stuck with sweat to the back of her neck.

"How did you know Linden's haunting me?" she asked. "I haven't told anyone that." She fisted the bonnet to her heart. "Can you read minds, too?"

"What? No, of course not. Who's Linden?" Honestly, what was happening? Someone was haunting her?

She stared at him another heartbeat before her breathing finally seemed to return to normal. "Linden Aspen was my first husband. I thought...when you said...I assumed you must have discovered the truth about him. Or guessed. As I said from the beginning, I'm not Gifted. Linden asked things of me when he was alive that I refused, and now he's cursed me."

"What sorts of things?" His mind had fallen into a seriously disturbed chasm, and he was now imagining all manner of terrible requests. What sordid secrets had he opened with his questions?

Retying her bonnet strings, she slipped her arm back through his and walked on, leaving him no choice but to follow her lead. "Linden was a dreamer, not like his father at all. He wanted a run-down tenement rather than a plantation. We would own little, but be rich in happiness. It was me who couldn't give up what I had. I told him I wouldn't leave my family, and he chose to stay in a life he didn't want rather than lose me. His ghost has made me answer for my selfishness ever since."

Tobias couldn't put words to his initial thoughts. This must have been how it felt for her when he initially told her she was Gifted. Being haunted was nearly as impossible to believe...but not quite as much. What clouded his senses more was that she thought she should have *wanted* to live in poverty. He had seen the dilapidated establishments in Charleston and passed men sitting cross-legged beside the gutter, a torn hat in one hand and holes in their shoes. He had dropped coins into those hats and tossed fresh apples to them from his carriage. He didn't think Sarah was being unreasonable for wanting a husband who would offer her more than scraps on the street. Linden had been unreasonable for expecting it.

"How did he die?"

"Cholera. A wave swept through Hawthorn Ridge even before the epidemic in '48. I fell ill on our wedding night, and then he caught it, too. He died a few days later. We were lucky none of our wedding guests suffered likewise."

Thankfully, the Larks had never suffered the disease and their wagon train had so far been spared it, despite stories from other parties up and down the trail. The awful ailment resulted in diarrhea which could dehydrate one to death within a day, sometimes even hours. He thought of having to not only endure the disease himself but then watch one of his brothers silently slip away in the length of a

Mass. He couldn't even imagine the agony she must have gone through.

They waved a friendly greeting to Mrs. Higgins who was scrubbing and polishing her husband's shoes as she did every Sunday. A pointless endeavor given the level of daily dust, but it did provide some sense of normalcy. Beyond her wagon, Mr. Pryor's banjo twanged out a solo hymn, Levi's fiddle no longer heard. Marie must have caught him and forced a dance. Or one of the children had jumped on his toes and made him totter.

"I know you must find me senseless," Sarah said once they were alone again. "It's why I didn't tell you before. Ghost stories are for dark parlors, not real life."

"You're only as senseless as I was when I said you were Gifted."

"Completely, then?" she smiled. "You remind me of him sometimes. You want to escape that life, too. You don't see color on anyone's skin, you only see the person. You were meant to be Larksong's leader."

"Sometimes I wonder." The sun was falling lower, its powerful orb casting the world in crimson. He twisted his wrist to clasp her fingers, raising them lightly to his lips before returning them to the crook of his arm. "'Arise, my beloved, my beautiful one, and come. For see, the winter is past, the rains are over and gone. The flowers appear on the earth, the time of pruning the vines has come, and the song of the dove is heard in our land.'"

"That was...beautiful," she breathed, "and far better than the poems I've attempted. Linden was the true poet. I suppose that is another trait you have in common."

"It would delight me to claim ownership; however, the author was actually King Solomon. I believe you named one of your mules after him."

"That's in the Bible?" she gaped. "But it's so romantic."

"It is. God delights in romance when it's the right kind of romance." He looked down at the amazement in her eyes which then filled his own. He hadn't initially said the verse to romance her; he had wanted to bring her comfort, to show her how to retain hope.

"Sarah, I know you probably believe I only chose you because you're Gifted, and you wouldn't be wrong. But I've also since learned that you're intelligent, resourceful, kind, and caring. You're beautiful even covered in trail dust, and your smile lights even the most tornadic winds. You can't cook, but you try, and you're a true friend to Coraline and especially Martha. What you did for her was beyond the usual borders of friendship. I've seen how you include her in your life, and how your own has changed along with it. You may think Linden has cursed you, but maybe he has given you a new way of thinking. 'Let me see you, let me hear your voice, for your voice is sweet, and you are lovely.'"

"Another Bible verse?" Her question was barely a whisper.

"Yes, ma'am. I'm not as pious as Jamison, but there are a few dozen I know rather well."

"And you chose to memorize the love verses? Did you always plan to use those to entice a lady?"

"Well, I certainly wasn't memorizing them to recite to my horses." He smiled and she smiled and then they laughed together. It felt like a window had opened, allowing in a cool breeze where there had been but stale heat before. It wasn't a door; he couldn't walk through yet, but an open window was better than a glass pane.

He could hear the music dying down and the clatter of the other pioneers setting campfires and pulling plates and pans for that evening's supper. She would have to assist, and he would need to find his brothers for evening remarks, but their walk had been such that he lamented its ending. For the first time, they had spoken in true intimacy rather than the stilted conversation of chaperoned courtship. When they were back on the trail, she might decide to have one of his brothers join them again and all their progress would be lost.

"Would you care to join me for a quick drink before supper?" he asked. "There's one bottle of Carolina wine that didn't get destroyed in the storm."

She surprised him again when she smiled, her gaze meeting his own. "I believe I would. But only one glass. I won't have you ply me into marrying you."

He laughed. "I wouldn't think of it."

Rushing off to his wagon, he returned with the wine bottle in one hand and two wine glasses in the other, both with chipped rims, but otherwise unscathed. "Sorry for their damaged state. It appears I didn't pack them as well as I believed." He poured the bitter blend and held one glass out to her, but she shook her head, her complexion paled.

"For-forgive me, Mr. Lark. I...I'm afraid I must go."

"What's the matter?"

"It's nothing, honestly. We have a long day of travel tomorrow and I need to assist with supper."

She turned away at the same time he moved toward her, and her shoulder nicked the wine glass, knocking it from his hand and shattering on the ground. Maroon liquid splattered across his chest and dripped upon her hem where she stared at the mess in horror.

"It's only a little wine, Miss Walcott. Our clothes are far worse off from all the dust and mud. After all the brown, I don't mind some color."

Snatching the second empty wine glass from his hand, she turned and ran.

Sarah stumbled up the step into her wagon, drawing the canvas closed and praying Tobias wouldn't follow her. She observed the crimson stain on her skirt while she imagined the wine splotches on Tobias's chest behind her eyelids. Like a knife stabbing him between the ribs or Mr. Whitticomb tumbling down the stairs. The duel that blew a hole in Mr. Fillmore's neck. Mr. Inman hanging from the lower branches of the tallest maple.

Chipped wine glasses without Linden. He was sending her a clear message not to cross him or she would lose Tobias too. Every time she was near him, when he spoke with such passion as he did today, she started to feel more pieces of her heart edge themselves back into place. But she couldn't. She shouldn't.

You may think Linden has cursed you, but maybe he has given you a new way of thinking. 'Let me see you, let me hear your voice, for your voice is sweet, and you are lovely.'

She wrapped the wine glass in a handkerchief and stashed it in the corner of the under compartment. Then she picked up her pencil and paper once again.

She must remain steadfast for Tobias's sake.

For his sake and hers.

22

JULY 1852
WYOMING

The dance was the last bit of merriment Tobias—or any of them—would see for a while. After Fort Laramie, their party began the treacherous ascent up the Rocky Mountains, plagued with hot days and cold nights. The weather changes gave Cade frequent vertigo, although they couldn't explain to the rest of the pioneers what brought on his discomfort. As they passed grave after grave, everyone whispered how the youngest Lark would be next. When they encountered a torrential thunderstorm that left the oxen high-stepping across flooded paths and Cade vomiting between ankle-deep rain puddles, Tobias knew he needed to intervene.

"I'm fine," Cade argued, even as rain poured off the brim of his hat and past a face paler than sun-bleached sheets. "It's only a storm. Storms are my specialty."

Tobias shook his head. "Your 'specialty' is no good if you die of dehydration. Go lie in the wagon, drink some water, and for pity's sake, rest."

"There's no room in the wagon."

"Then have Josiah move a crate into my wagon. This is not a request, Cade." Rainwater seeped through a tear in Tobias's boot seam, one he wasn't even aware of, the sensation cold and annoying. As was the riled expression on his younger brother's face. *To be twenty again*, he thought. He would never choose to go back to that age, but he would sell his best boots for a day's rest alone.

The storms rolled on for three days straight, morning, noon, and night. The trail eventually became so thick with mud soup that the wheels began to slip. Rope was hauled out and secured, heaving the schooners up the steepest hills by a combination of animal strength and human power.

By the fourth day of the deluge, Tobias felt more like Noah than Moses and was plum exhausted. He had fixed so many wagons, he could barely keep his eyes open as they walked the trail. He, like nearly everyone else, was coated in mud practically head to toe and the animals were not much better off. Slop caked them from their hooves to their flanks. He even considered foregoing a meal just to gain an extra hour's sleep.

But no, he couldn't. He didn't have the freedom to simply disappear like Cade could. There was always someone who needed something. Someone always came looking.

A crash of thunder shattered the sky, and he thought he heard a scream sound within it. He turned his ear but continued walking, waiting for the thunder to diminish. At first, all he could distinguish was the ever-present rain pattering off the wagon canvas and his hat, the steady *plip-plip-plip-plip* as each drop landed one on top of the last. He forced his hearing past the usual sounds and registered a horrific screech, one so inhuman he was certain it must be. Then wailing came, screams of anguish from halfway back in line. Calls passed slowly forward as the rest of the train shared the command to halt.

Tobias moved to settle his own oxen, a task not easily accomplished on the slick path. Their hooves slipped haphazardly as they attempted to stop the wagon's momentum. Eventually, the wheels fell silent, leaving the oxen squelching in place.

Goad stick still in hand, he ran—rather slid and fell into the mud, slathering his front with a fresh layer of muck—toward the middle of the train. A crowd had formed and he pushed between them, a sick sensation growing ever stronger as the wails grew more prominent. He could now distinguish the tortured sound as belonging to Mrs. Tull and the corresponding shouts of, "Away, away, have you no decency?" were those of her husband.

Heaven and the Lord above, where were their children? They had seven, from the age of thirteen to the young babe still in her womb.

Jamison shoved past, knocking against Darcy Frendon who held all ten fingers to her mouth rounded in a silent "o." His passing opened a gap in the bystanders, allowing Tobias to angle his way in until he discovered the Tull children, all on their knees in a row. Beside them, their parents cradled a toddler in their arms, a broken and bloody vision nearly indistinguishable.

Their two-year-old son, Ephram.

Beneath the toddler's shirt, his thin frame folded in awkwardly. Tobias didn't know much about medicine, but he knew enough to guess every rib had been broken inward.

"Back in the wagons!" he shouted. "No one comes near." He felt he might be sick.

Mrs. Tull continued to moan, rain rushing over her crumpled form, her son's legs still lying limp beneath the wagon. *The wheels*, Tobias realized. The child must have fallen and been crushed beneath them. Even in the best circumstances, it took time to halt a prairie schooner. In the rain and the mud, it would have been impossible to stop in time.

Jamison dropped to his knees to feel for a pulse, knowing he would find none. It had all happened too quickly. No one—not even the Gifted—could have saved that little boy's life. As a result, his parents would probably blame themselves for the rest of theirs. Tobias was supposed to be their leader, but no guidance could ever fix this.

They buried Ephram within the hour. Tobias crafted a child-sized coffin and a wooden cross with rolled engravings along the edges, the boy's name and dates upon the front. The moist ground was easy to dig although heavy to move and Tobias felt even *his* muscles begin to burn with the many shovelfuls. Then, at last, the grave was dug and the coffin placed inside it, the mud piled on top, and the grave marker hammered into the turned soil at the child's head.

"Ephram!" Mrs. Tull wailed, limp within her husband's arms, the man's own eyes leaking more than his share of emotion. He clutched his wife's hand atop her rounded belly, the assurance of a new life never enough to replace the one they lost. Beside them, the other five siblings stood solemn, the oldest with arms wrapped around the two youngest. Tobias remembered his own mother laying to rest each of his three stillborn sisters. Their father had refused to allow them to name the babies. After all, they were only girls, who likely died because of their lack of Giftedness. Not worthy to grow to womanhood. Not worthy to grow at all.

He folded his arms and dipped his chin, his eyes closed while he listened to Jamison pray for Ephram's soul and the family left behind. Funerals were never for the dead; they were always for the living. To provide closure, a reasoning. Their mother's burial had been sparsely attended, only a simple service with the brothers and their father in the family cemetery. Not even allowed to have a Christian funeral, as she had taken her own life. Suicide, according to the Church, was a direct ticket to hell.

"Show me the verse!" Tobias had shouted at Jamison. He threw his Bible at his brother so hard, it later left an angled bruise on Jamison's shoulder. "You believe in God Almighty. So, you tell me where it says our mother is damned for all eternity. You know she didn't do it, James. You know this wasn't her!"

"I know." But he never could give Tobias an answer to his question.

Sixteen-year-old Garrett had a more suitable solution than flipping pages. Taking a verse out of the Book of Matthew, he decided to flip tables instead. He broke every single candle in the church sanctuary, leaving their wax dripping across the tiled floor and down the sides of the statues. He screamed at Father Corbin, but it did no good. All it resulted in was Garrett being banned from the church. Then he went home and threw a knock right at their father's face, laying him out flat across his office floor. When Alonzo came to, he locked Garrett in the attic for two days without food, water, or company. Only the sight of their mother's cut noose still hanging from the ceiling.

That was the day Tobias realized he couldn't turn the other cheek anymore.

Suddenly, a hand was on his shoulder, stirring him from his thoughts. Jamison's expression held such agony that Tobias felt like he stood before a looking glass. Except for the Tulls still beside Ephram's grave, the other mourners had returned to their wagons.

"They've decided to stay behind," Jamison told him. He glanced over his shoulder at the couple. "They're heading back east in the morning."

Tobias nodded. "Did we do the right thing in bringing these people out here? Or are we just leading them all to their deaths?"

"You mean like Father did to Mother? I know you were remembering it." He paused. "I was too."

Tobias didn't say because he didn't want to know. He knew what he had organized wasn't the same as what their father had done. He didn't have that sort of persuasion nor would he ever want it. Still, he had charmed them, offered them hope of a better life, an escape, freedom—whatever he needed to call it to convince them to come. He had offered a promise to the Tull family, too, and it fell to the wayside like extra weight tossed beside the trail.

Jamison's advice was typical, yet sound. "Trust in the Lord with all your heart," he quoted, "and on your own intelligence rely not. In all your ways be mindful of Him, and He will make straight your paths."

Clearly, his own intelligence wasn't getting him very far. If their Gifts were wrought by God, he wished he knew why those Gifts couldn't fix so many of the worst troubles they faced. He supposed he could trust that the Lord had a plan; Jamison certainly believed it.

He only wished God would provide a straighter path.

23

The entire wagon train applauded, hooted, and hollered when Independence Rock came into sight one week later. Even Sarah breathed a little easier, knowing they had finally made it halfway with only three weeks delay. To avoid the winter snowstorms, most pioneers tried to arrive at this point by July fourth, but between the tornado, incessant rainstorms, illness, and poor road conditions, the Larksong community had celebrated Independence Day on the trail and with little fanfare.

Now, however, at the sight of the 136-foot-tall Independence Rock, its wide back stretched like a giant turtle shell beside the Sweetwater River, they found an extra burst of speed, hustling their animals along a breadth faster. It wasn't the first rock formation they had seen, but the others they had traveled past with only a glance. This time, they would climb to the top with thousands of others, carving their names into "The Great Registry of the Desert." Leaving their permanent mark. Turning back now would take as long as pressing forward.

Sarah ushered David and Solomon to their place in the camp circle before retrieving some feed and offering it to them from her open palm. They gobbled it up instantly and likewise when she placed a bucket of water under each of their noses. She laughed at their antics, glad they were not suffering from respiratory ailments like many of the others' oxen. She decided she was glad, after all, to have selected mules to accompany her on this journey. They had proved good company and she could hitch them to a buggy once in Washington. She would need to get to and from places on her own, buying supplies from the general store (once there was one) and visiting children's families as the schoolmarm.

Once the mules had their fill, she hung the feed bucket back on the wagon peg and wiped her hands on her apron. She took a drink of water from the rain barrel and made sure her bonnet strings were tight in preparation for the journey up the rock. She would find the Shays and see if they planned to join the excursion.

However, it wasn't the Shays whom she found first, but Martha exiting the Harpers' wagon, tying a fresh apron around her waist. When their eyes met, they both halted their progression, lips parted slightly in equal awkwardness. No one else was about. Sarah couldn't imagine the littlest Harper children would be climbing to the top, but wherever they were, they weren't nearby.

"Hello," she managed.

Martha's eyes dropped to her feet. "Hello."

"Have you been well?"

"Illness has stayed away." Her friend's eyes raised an inch. "How have you been, Miss Sarah?"

To tell the truth? This was the first they had spoken in well over a month, the first time Martha had acknowledged Sarah's presence outside of formalities within the wagon circle. She didn't want to broach a subject that could lead them back to silence, but there was no other way to fix this than to simply fix it.

The emotion came tumbling from her lips then, tears leaking from her eyes in bold swells. She tugged her sleeve cuff into her fist, swiping it across the wetness lacing her cheeks. She couldn't help it. "I have missed you," she blurted. "You were always my sister, Martha, and I never realized it should have been any way than what it was. Please, please, will you ever forgive me?"

She couldn't bring herself to meet Martha's expression or silence the tears that fell between her fingers. If she did and found rejection, she didn't think she could bear it.

"It's been a week since Ephram Tull died," Martha said. It wasn't what Sarah expected, and she coughed mid-sob, her tears somehow lessening. She rubbed at her eyes and at last, opened them. Martha was watching her with considerable compassion, her brown irises deep with an understanding Sarah couldn't comprehend.

"Remember the boy who fell under the wagon wheels? Ephram Tull?"

"I remember." Of course, she remembered. How could she ever forget the sight of the child's twisted body or the unnatural wail released from his mother's lips?

Martha's eyes moistened, although not a single tear fell. She blinked once slowly. "I've thought about him almost every hour since. Every time I hold one of the Harper children, I think how it could have been them. In weather like that, roads so slick, those wagons couldn't have stopped for nobody. It could have been any of us. It could have been you."

Sarah felt her tears swell again, both from relief and regret. Although she hadn't explicitly said it, Martha still cared about her. But was caring for someone's welfare enough to overcome two decades of past hurts?

She reached for Martha's hands, gripping them hard between her own. "I'm sorry I never asked about your family before. I never took the time to know you as I should have. But I can start today. Please, Martha, I want to know."

Her friend's eyes found the ground once more. "It isn't a happy story."

"I still want to hear it."

"Then we should speak alone."

Hand in hand, they returned to their wagon and climbed inside, drawing the canvas. Martha sat atop two stacked flour sacks while Sarah settled herself beside their dress crate, her knees tucked up carefully under her skirts. Perspiration immediately clung to her skin in the enclosed space, the sun against the canvas forcing them to roll their sleeves and remove their bonnets. There was something cathartic about sweating in such an uncomfortable situation, being forced to sit in the unpleasantness and face it together.

"I don't remember much of my family anymore," Martha began. "Only names and faces blurry in my memory. Roma, Lemuel, and I all went to the stockyard together. She was twelve, he was seven, and I, as you remember, was ten. We huddled together in a dark storehouse for days with twenty other children until we were ushered on a train. I didn't know it was the market we were headed for, but that's where we were going. Bound together hand to hand and foot to foot as the car jangled and swayed. They sold Roma first, and then a few hours later, it was my turn. I had to leave Lemuel behind, no matter how much he cried.

"I don't remember the auction block or meeting your family. I felt like I was inside a nightmare. I didn't want to be there. I wanted to be with Roma and Lemuel. Even on that market floor covered in filth and huddled together, I would have rather been with them than apart.

"From a young age, I had known we would be separated. We saw slaves disappear all the time and, eventually, new ones would replace them. No one spoke much of it, but we knew where they went. The day they took us, my ma and pa were working the fields. They would have returned to find us gone."

Sarah gasped, her hand rising to her lips. To be ripped from your family was terrible, but to be taken without any chance to say goodbye? She had at least been given a choice. She had the opportunity to tell her mother goodbye, to embrace her one last time. Despite the circumstances of their departure, she still wished she had been able to have the same farewell with her father. At least, she could still write to him. Martha had no such option.

"Martha, I..." she began, but every condolence seemed inadequate.

Her friend was staring at her skirt now, rather than Sarah. She ran a crease of the brown and white flowered fabric between her thumb and forefinger, another of the new dresses Tobias had designed. "I remember those first few years when I hated everything, even myself. I questioned why my parents had me or Roma or Lemuel when they knew we would be gone one day. I remember you saying we would be sisters, but I had a sister and she looked like me, not you. It was Tildy who dragged me out crying from the closet under the stairs and told me I had to try. 'It'sa hard, child,' she said, 'but we all been where you standin'. And you haveta try.'

"I knew it wouldn't be the same, but you surprised me by being so kind. To you, dark skin and light weren't an important thing to notice." She gave a sad smile. "I thought you were the most stupid girl

I ever met."

She had been. Foolishly so. Looking back on all she had learned over these past few months on the trail, she couldn't believe how naïve she had been. Hawthorn Ridge had truly been a veil, and she had hidden behind it spectacularly.

"I was," Sarah admitted. "You would think after seven husbands, I would be more knowledgeable about life."

She was surprised when Martha shifted off the flour bags to the wagon bed, so they sat knee-to-knee. Martha's hand was in hers again, her ring's white clover blossoms standing out against her friend's caramel skin. Like when they were little girls sharing secrets on Sarah's bedroom floor.

"Miss Sarah, I was going to be sold eventually. I thank the Lord every day that He didn't send me to worse places."

"I'm thankful you were there all those years," Sarah replied softly. "Through every husband, I knew I wasn't completely alone. I can't imagine doing this without you."

"You've managed fine with that handsome Mr. Lark always doting on you. Free wagon, free supplies, sharing special moments out on the trail..." Martha gave a shy smile. "Wish there was someone like that for me."

"What about Garrett? Seems you've been spending as much time with him as I have Tobias. I see you offering him looks when he's not paying attention."

"Don't be so daft. He's plenty to look at, that's for sure. Has a pleasant voice when he speaks. But we come from different sides of the river. He was a slave owner and I'm a slave."

"Not anymore and he's not an owner either. Things are different out here."

Martha shook her head, eyes once more on their clasped fingers. "I can't, Miss Sarah. When I leap, I want it to be with someone like me. I want my babies to look like I do."

It was reasonable. She would want the same. Although, something inside her twitched, wondering. Out here the same rules didn't apply. If in Larksong all were truly welcome, then none of those societal expectations applied. If not for the curse, she would entertain the notion of another marriage. What if she found a colored man who met every need except his skin? Would she entertain his affections if he offered?

"The Larks must know everyone in the South. After we're settled, maybe we could find your family. We'll grant them their freedom too."

Any ease in Martha's expression died in that moment. "I'm a runaway slave, Miss Sarah. There might be summons all throughout the South by now, seeking me back. For now, I'm at peace being on our way to a fine new life, both of us free at last." She squeezed Sarah's hand. "And you can be at peace knowing all is right again between us."

At the top of Independence Rock, amid the many other pioneers, Sarah and Martha gazed out at God's beauty in amazement. The land stretched on forever, sandy and golden and green all at once. Empty and yet full of life, the sun casting an array of hope over all it washed. Sarah could see their wagon train far below and the dotted line of strangers' wagons parading off into the western horizon. They were so small in the grand scheme of life, so insignificant, yet to each other they played a role greater than all of it.

"We would never have seen this if we stayed in Missouri," she said softly.

"No," Martha agreed. The sun's golden glow bathed her skin like amber glass. "Nothing in Missouri is like this."

Carefully, Sarah carved her name into the stone, one etching at a time, fragments dusting her fingers. She held the knife out to Martha. "You could use your own name," she offered. "Instead of the one my mother gave you. You could change it back."

Martha hesitated but a second before she began to carve an M. "I think I'll keep it. The last time I shared that name with someone, it only found me trouble. I'd like to have one thing that's mine and no one else's."

A few more scratches and it was finished. Their permanent mark on the new frontier: *Sarah W & Martha L 1852.*

Making peace with Martha seemed to bring the entire world into a new rosy outlook. Suddenly, Sarah again noticed the smiles of her fellow pioneers. Coraline and Oliver's hearty greetings as they passed arm in arm. Alice Ann's wave, her nose stuck in its usual literary residence. Levi's nod and Marie's "Good day," as she stirred soup upon the fire. Optimism was everywhere when only hours before, negativity hung like a shroud.

It seemed strange to acknowledge, but she actually had friends on this trail, something she never imagined with a past such as hers. Perhaps she should begin to open herself up more, offer friendship to the lonely as others had offered it to her.

"I'm going to invite the Reeds to supper tonight," she told Martha. "Poor Gabriella has barely left her wagon since Independence." Likely, she could use the company, even if they sat in silence.

"You go on ahead," Martha told her. "I should get to helping Marie. Besides, Mr. Reed doesn't seem to like me much."

"Why? What did he say?"

"Nothing particular. He just has a little too much of the South still stuck in him."

"Oh, I see." She remembered Clinton Reed's comments in Independence about having to put his prejudices aside for the sake of the wagon train. Hopefully, with time, he could turn his opinions as others had.

After checking the Reeds' wagon and finding it unoccupied, then rounding the camp circles and coming up short, Josiah motioned her down to Sweetwater River, where he had last spotted Clinton heading. Certain enough, she found Mr. Reed alone on the riverbank, splashing water upon his face and wiping a wet bandana across his neck. He wrung the rag out into the water and stood, startling when he spied her approaching.

"Why afternoon, Miss Walcott. Didn't hear you there." He adjusted his hat back on his head and tipped the brim. "Did you have a chance to go up the rock?"

"Good afternoon, Mr. Reed. I just returned. Incredible to see so many names all together. New ones are added year after year, and they'll all be there forever. Generations from now, folks will know what we've done."

"Yeah," he snuffed. "That's why I didn't put my name on it. This is but my passing through point to where I belong. No reason to leave my mark."

It seemed morose, but she supposed she could understand it. She had been rather negative about things, too, until today.

"I was pleased to see your wife has left the wagon. Does that mean she's feeling better? We would like to invite you both to our circle for supper."

He gave her a hard stare. "What do you mean, Gabriella's left the wagon?"

"I stopped by for a visit, just now. She wasn't there."

Without a word, he strode past her, mud flicking up with each stride. He made a straight line back to his wagon with Sarah quick on his heels. She had to lift her skirt with both hands to keep up with his longer stride and arrived panting for breath.

He hopped into the wagon bed, letting the flaps close behind him. She could hear him rummage through supplies, every so often letting out a curse hardly appropriate for a lady's ears. A few minutes later, he opened the flap and stared down at her, stricken.

"She's gone," he muttered. He raised a hand to his eyes and released a low groan. "How could she leave?"

24

abriella Reed had vanished. Or at least, that's what Garrett's Gift seemed to imply. He couldn't get a feeling on her whereabouts and didn't know where to begin looking. So Tobias insisted they simply search everywhere.

They would devise a good old-fashioned search party as would be done for any other disappearance. Like they did when the Morrows' daughter went missing on the day of the tornado. Except for this time, they would legitimately need every man's skills at their best.

Some of Gabriella's belongings were gone, but not all. Two dresses and underthings, jerky and fruit, a knife, and her small daguerreotype of her parents. She had taken only the necessities, implying she packed only what she could carry and left at her first opportunity. There would be few better chances to flee than with nearly everyone at Independence Rock.

As for where she was headed when she left, one man's guess was as good as the next.

With so many other wagon parties scattered around Independence Rock, the search quickly grew tedious. Eventually, Tobias devised four teams, one to head in each cardinal direction. Cade and Josiah to the north, Oliver and Levi east, Clinton and Garrett south, and Tobias and Jamison west. They traveled two miles, inquiring within every visible wagon party, but still no luck. It was time to spread their search.

Tobias took Garrett aside. "We need to go farther. I know you couldn't sense her here, but maybe she's moved on from the area. We separate, go ten miles in each direction, and ask everyone. We still don't know if she made it away safely. It's possible she was overtaken by Indians or encountered a wild animal."

His brother pounded his fist into his hand. "If she was anywhere nearby, I would be able to send us in the right direction. How can she be nowhere? And don't you dare tell me it's because you think she's Gifted, too."

Even though he didn't truly believe it, he had considered it for half a minute. But now wasn't the time to bring up that age-old argument again.

"Garrett, we all have limitations on our abilities. I can't make carpentry supplies appear out of nowhere, Jamison can't place his hand on a wound and heal like an apostle. Sometimes, as with the tornado, Cade can't correctly predict the weather. There had to be a time when your Gift found its limit as well. Maybe it's the type of rock here that's blocking you from searching farther away. Maybe your Gift can't find someone if they're hurt or dead. You've never tried to find a corpse. Maybe you can't. Things have already happened we can't account for."

"But—"

"Garrett, take heart. We're going to find her."

Except they didn't find her. They headed out in teams of two, each spreading like wheel spokes with Independence Rock at their center. They searched high and low, beneath trees and up within, asking every party they came across and cautiously, several Indian tribes as well. Thankfully, the natives responded to their inquiries without hostility, although their responses were in their tribal tongue and thoroughly unhelpful.

It worried him that Garrett was unable to find Gabriella. His brother had never experienced trouble with his Gift before. Was it a case of the landscape blocking his abilities or perhaps too many people gathered in one place? Were their Gifts locked onto Charleston and the farther away they traveled, the more they would lose? For perhaps the only time in his life, he wished his father were there. If anyone would have the information they needed, it would be him.

The search teams trickled back into camp one by one, each shaking their heads dismally as they arrived. No one needed words to express the truth. Wherever Gabriella Reed was, she wouldn't be found by them.

It was the miserable duty of Tobias as wagon master to deliver the news to Clinton that they would be moving on in the morning. As he approached the man's wagon, he saw him sitting beside the campfire, tossing clumps of dirt into the flames. He looked up as Tobias sat down. "It's over, isn't it?"

Tobias gave a slow nod and Clinton exhaled, staring back into the flames. "I figured. Guess I always knew she would go eventually. Just hadn't figured it would be so soon and without even a final word." He gave a low chuckle. "I always like to have the final word."

"Interesting sentiment. Were you and Mrs. Reed having trouble then?"

"Nah, she didn't do nothing. It was all my doing. I hate it when plans change, don't you?" He tossed another clump of dirt into the fire and Tobias nodded, unclear whether he needed to worry.

"Listen, Clint. We all do things we're not proud of. Maybe you drove her away, maybe not. What I need to know is if I can keep you on this train with us. Were you good to your wife? You never hit her or made her feel less than?"

"Never. Not once. That's the truth. I've done my share of misdeeds, but striking a lady isn't one."

"Good. And can you promise you mean no harm to me, my brothers, or anyone else with us?"

"I want to make it to Washington, same as you. I think we're better working together than against."

"Me, too." Tobias rose, offering his sympathies from across the firelight. What if it had been Sarah who ran? Marie from Levi or Coraline from Oliver? Any of them would be devastated and would always question why.

"I'm sorry for your loss, Mr. Reed. If you need anything at all, all you have to do is ask."

"Thank you, Mr. Lark. I'll hold you to that."

Tobias returned to his wagon with head held high and his usual confident stride, extending assurances to anyone who asked about the missing woman. *Did he fear Indians would attack their camp?* No, of course not. *Did he think wild animals had torn her to bits?* Unlikely. Their children were safe to sleep. *What about bandits? Had they captured her for their own carnal means?* No, he would reply, he didn't think they had anything to worry about.

When the truth was, they always had something to worry about.

He dropped in the dirt behind his wagon, removing his hat and bunching it between clenched fingers. He rubbed away tears of frustration before they could emerge and reveal to the entire train he didn't have a clue what he was doing.

Oliver Shay limped by, one hand pressed to the side of his thigh as he went, a deep grimace curling his features. His breath hissed through his teeth with every step. Another perfect example of how Tobias didn't have time to worry about his own inadequacies when another problem was always around the corner.

"Shay," he called out. "What happened?"

Oliver glanced over, trying for a smile and failing. "Tripped in a prairie dog hole while out on the search. Went down hard and took a rock straight to my thigh. Stitched it up fine, but it still hurts something fierce." He gave a dry chuckle. "It's rather an embarrassment when the doctor needs a doctor, huh?"

"We all fall down sometimes, Shay. Even doctors. What's important is that we get back up." He spoke as much to Oliver as to himself. He couldn't let his shortcomings leave him sitting in the dirt.

His friend's expression softened, and was he imagining it, or were Oliver's eyes moistening over? The hardships of the trail must be overwhelming him more than he let on.

"Thank you, Tobias. It has been an honor traveling with you. You are going to do wonderful things for these people."

"I hope so, Shay. God be with us, I hope so."

Oliver started to shuffle on, but Tobias called out to him. "It *is* only a minor wound, right?"

Oliver smiled. "Of course. I'll be back up in no time."

25

O liver Shay lived barely two days before he left this world
forever.

The night he died, Sarah knelt near the fire, preparing
another horrible meal when he wandered into their circle. He bent
low, placed a hand to Jamison's shoulder, and said, "I've finished
tending to a few folks suffering from heatstroke. They'll be all right.
Also, I changed the bandages on Andrew McClary's arm. The wound's
healing and should be clear within a few days. I also—"

Without warning, he doubled over. His body landed in a tangle
across Jamison's lap, his eyes rolling closed and head limp. Coraline
and Alice Ann immediately dropped the pans they held, raw squirrel
meat scattering into the dirt as they hurried to Oliver's side.

With swift practiced movements, Jamison maneuvered him onto
his back and pulled up each eyelid to examine his irises. His lips drew
tight as his fingers slid to the side of Oliver's neck.

"He's flushed, pupils dilated, pulse weak. Whatever this is, it isn't
good."

"You mean you don't know?" Sarah asked. "Aren't you supposed to
be—" Jamison shot her a warning look before she could finish her
question with the truth. She had meant to say *Gifted*, but settled for,
"a doctor?"

"His symptoms could be related to several ailments. I need more
information."

"Oliver!" Coraline cried. She shook his shoulder but was only
rewarded with an incoherent mumble. Oliver's words slurred beyond

recognition. "What happened?" she cried. "What's wrong?" It took another mumble and another shake before his eyes fluttered back open.

Oliver's hand immediately pressed to his thigh, hissing through his teeth. "Sn...ake...bite."

"What did you say?" Jamison shot back.

Sarah had never seen him so angry. Calling for a knife, he sliced through Oliver's pant leg and reared back at the sight, all of his frustration turning to horror. "Oh, Lord in heaven, have mercy."

Oliver's entire leg had swollen, the immediate area around the double-pronged bite tinged grey, and the skin around that a bright red. Darker maroon streaks stretched out from it in every direction. It was impossible to tell where they ended as they continued beyond either end of his torn pant leg.

"This didn't just happen," Jamison accused.

"No."

Oliver then admitted he was set upon while searching for Gabriella Reed at Independence Rock. The supposed prairie dog hole he tripped in had likely been a snake den and the reptile's lunge so quick, he hadn't time to react. He had known immediately there was no hope due to the bite's location. A hand or foot could have been amputated. A thigh though, as high up as it was...there was nothing to be done.

"Why didn't you tell me?" Jamison shouted. "I could have fixed it!"

Jamison never shouted. He never had the hopeless frustration in his eyes that he did now. Oliver Shay lay slumped across his lap, sweat dripping down his brow, and his friend was full-on yelling at him.

Oliver didn't seem affected though. He gave a wry smile. "How could you? You're a doctor, same as me. You know I'm a dead man."

"I could have done...something." There were tears on Jamison's cheeks and he closed his eyes, turning away. His hand gripped Oliver's shoulder. "Shay," he breathed. "You're such a fool."

Perhaps there really was no cure—Sarah didn't know—but if Jamison was truly Gifted, there might have been. Now it was too late.

The funeral was quiet and solemn. No one could help but

remember Ephram Tull's tragic death only a week ago. They all noticed the grave markers along the trail, becoming more frequent with each passing day. Animal carcasses piled up, meat rotting in the sun. Whispers went through the party like those Sarah still heard from her husbands' funerals. What was the cause? Who would be next? Once again, she wondered if everywhere she went, tragedy was sure to follow.

Stones were placed in Oliver's pockets and a threadbare blanket wrapped around his body, tied tight at neck, waist, and ankles. The Harper children collected wildflowers to tuck in the rope bindings, offering beauty the adults weren't able to find. A few yards off the trail, they buried him, now one of many wooden crosses other pioneers would see along the way. Just as was done for Ephram Tull, they placed rocks atop the body, then buried it, hoping to deter scavengers. Sarah didn't want to imagine some hungry wolf using their friend as its next meal.

Coraline stood beside her, their arms threaded together. Alice Ann's head rested against her sister's shoulder and Martha remained close to Sarah's opposite arm, their fingers clasped. Coraline said nothing, did nothing, didn't even cry. She stared at her husband's grave in silence and Sarah remembered when she lost Linden, the absolute numbness of the funeral followed by the worst emotional pain of her life. Months of walking in emptiness, tears that flooded her nights until she felt she would drown in them. No one could fix the grief; they could only stand with you in it.

Tobias scattered the last of the dirt and tipped the shovel into the hard soil beside it, hands folded on the handle. He nodded to Jamison to begin the prayer.

When his brother spoke, he never once looked up at those gathered. "For our brother, Oliver. A son, husband, friend, and physician. He cared for all he knew and all those know he is with the Father."

There was a soft round of "Amens," the sign of the cross, and the group dispersed. Sarah met Tobias's gaze for a moment before she turned away and followed Coraline.

Tobias and Jamison were the last to depart Oliver Shay's gravesite, standing side by side, neither wanting to walk away and leave their friend behind. Tobias knew it was harder for his brother than for him. Oliver had been Jamison's business partner for two years. He quickly fit into their family, and when he asked Jamison whether he thought Coraline Owens would make a good match, Jamison heartily approved. His brother hadn't only lost a business partner but a friend, and one who under any normal circumstances, he could have protected.

"I should have been able to save him," Jamison said. "Oliver thought there was no natural cure for it, and he was right, but I could have saved him. If he had told me immediately, I could have drawn the poison. At worst, if he told me later that day, we could have taken his leg at the hip and had you craft him a new one. We both know it would have been better than any peg leg made in the South. We had the power to fix this, but we couldn't because we never told him about our Gifts. Maybe we should tell everyone."

"James, you know we can't do that."

"Tobias, they think we're failing them, and I think they're right. You asked me before if we're leading these people to their deaths. I didn't think so then but now...I'm not so sure."

"We can't tell them," he said again, even while he wanted to say the opposite. He wanted to be done with the secrecy, yet at the same time, it was better when people didn't know. He told Sarah, after all, and she didn't seem to fully accept it. "Either they wouldn't understand, they would be envious, or they'd begin placing demands we can't fulfill. We've functioned as we are for this long and we'll keep on as we've been. It's an unfortunate turn, what happened to Shay, but the guilt has to be his to bear, not yours. He could have said something. If he had, you would have fixed him up and taught him a new skill in the process. He would have assumed you were a talented doctor, which you are even without your Gift."

"Am I? Even with my Gift, I doubt how much ability I have."

Some days Tobias also wondered if they had magnified their Gifts in their minds. That their talents were the result of good blood and the story of the shipwreck was something his father invented to exaggerate their family's legacy once again. Abilities that surpassed the average man, but nothing more spectacular than that. It was only the severity of their father's actions which made him doubt that theory. Their mother's death convinced him of it.

He swung an arm around Jamison's shoulders to lead him from Oliver's grave. Slowly, they put one foot in front of the next, making their way back to the wagon circle. "We're not all-powerful, Jamison. We can't fix everything."

"You're right. Only the Lord giveth and the Lord taketh away, but I need some time to understand why." Then he shrugged out of Tobias's hold and headed back to the wagon train, where traces of firewood and smoking bison returned on the wind.

26

After Oliver Shay's funeral, five more families turned back, even though they were already past halfway. Their worries were clear: if the doctor couldn't keep himself alive, what hope remained for the rest of them? Two of the unmarried men planned to branch off for the California Trail at Fort Hall and three more families would too, making their way for Sacramento or San Francisco, perhaps even farther south. At least there, they would find an established city with a port of call. If their luck ran dry, they could purchase passage back east rather than risk death on the trail again.

The next month brought only dry dusty trails and eerie silence among the Larksong wagon party. Drought followed them with little rain to fill the barrels or wash their filthy clothes. Even the shallow playa lakes seemed tainted. The heat was only made worse by burning cow chips to save their scant kindling stores. She longed for a spritz of rosewater from the opal glass bottle upon her vanity, anything to remove the pungent odor from her nostrils.

Instead, she slept on the rough ground night after night, usually rolling upon a rock or twig in her efforts to find relief. Her neck remained stiff and her shoes had worn out again. Thankfully, she discovered another pair within an abandoned wagon along the side of the trail. As she slipped them on, she chose not to speculate on why their owner left a half-empty wagon behind. The shoes' soles were horribly worn, but at least they were without holes, able to keep dirt and pebbles out of her stockings.

Among the abandoned also lay a cast-iron stove and a lovely

mahogany dining table with scrollwork carved right into its limbs. She pictured its extravagance in her new house by the sea, the one Tobias liked to mention, overlooking the rolling waves on one side and the forest on the other, miles of green rising into the mountains. When she closed her eyes, the scene appeared as beautiful as the commissioned paintings in her parents' parlor. Then she opened them to the Idaho landscape where summer's hot breath seared her skin and she still cooked abysmal meals over a fire she couldn't even light without assistance.

The abandoned shoes only lasted a week. Which meant one Thursday evening, she was scavenging through her wagon for more suitable footwear. When she finally located the slim brown boots, they were the right fit, the right style...everything to her exact measurements. In those boots, every mile walked wasn't quite as harsh and blistered as before. They were the most comfortable shoes she had ever owned and tears spilled over, thinking of how long she had begrudged Tobias's generosity.

Not only had he built her and Martha a wagon, sewn them dresses, and purchased them supplies to last a journey, but he had also offered a new way of living. Before they met, her options had been another tragic marriage or an asylum. Martha's future held only endless days of servitude. Life on the trail wasn't as easy as afternoon tea, but despite the struggles, it was much preferred over what could have been.

The next Sunday saw Tobias tackling wagon train duties, forcing him to cancel their usual afternoon walk. Sarah tried to stifle her disappointment. She had grown used to their time together. Moreso, she now anticipated it. On a trail lined with surprises, it was comforting to have one element of stability.

With their wagon numbers dwindling, Coraline lost in her grief, and the rest of the pioneers struggling to keep positive about anything, she needed that constancy right now. Back in Hawthorn Ridge—in her old life—there were schedules to adhere to, so many of her days perfectly planned around community events and social calls. Breakfast at eight, luncheon at one, tea with her mother at precisely three o'clock every afternoon. Supper between seven and nine depending on if they ate as a family or had been summoned away on invitation. Mass always at nine a.m. on Sunday morning. Her mother took friendly visits in their parlor on Wednesday afternoons, the other days traveling to different society ladies to exchange false pleasantries and the latest gossip. Often, gossip about her.

There were no such schedules on the frontier. While they typically adhered to start and end times on the trail and lunch taken at high noon, whatever happened in between was anyone's guess. One day could be no-nonsense travel, the next a broken wagon wheel and a tornado threw everything off its axis.

Even without Tobias, Sarah needed to take that walk, if for no other reason than her own ease of mind.

Donning an apron in a weak attempt to keep more dust off her Sunday dress, she tied her bonnet strings and slipped a kitchen knife in her front apron pocket. She doubted she would come across anyone of ill intent, but one couldn't be too cautious.

She set out on the eastward trail, keeping to land already familiar. Her footsteps tapped upon the hardened earth, dirt sweeping over her hemline with each movement. Along the side of the trail, brief clusters of wilted grass bowed over, their thin reeds begging the sun to offer relief. Today's skies were clear, as they always were these days, with nowhere for the sun to go except to remain where it was.

"You really shouldn't be out here alone."

Startled by the rough statement, she tripped into a rut, reaching for the knife in her pocket while trying to keep her balance and failing at both. Her palm closed around the blade rather than the handle, a scorch of pain shooting up her wrist along with the immediate flow of blood.

Garrett caught her arms before she fell headlong into the dirt. He lifted her back onto her feet and reached for her hand. "Let me see that."

"I'm fine." She stepped away, curling her fingers over the wound, an action which disguised nothing. If anything, it made everything worse. She reached for the hem of her apron, intending to press it against the wound and stifle the flow, but Garrett's handkerchief was there first. He pressed the cotton, surprisingly cleaner than she would have expected, to the wound, then curled her fingers back around the fabric. He lifted her hand so it was level with her chest. "It doesn't seem worse than superficial, but keep your hand above your heart. It'll help to lessen the blood. Why were you carrying a knife anyway?"

"For protection."

His eyebrow raised with the corner of his lips. He gave a chuckle. "It didn't work."

"Thank you for your assistance. I will see you back at camp." She stepped around him and continued walking eastward down the trail. Her hand throbbed, but she wasn't about to give Garrett the satisfaction of belittling her continued incompetence.

"Where are you going?" he called after her. "Get back to camp."

"This is the time I take a walk, every Sunday. I need to take this walk."

"Where's Tobias?"

"Busy."

"It isn't safe for a woman alone. Especially injured."

She paused, tilting her chin enough to look at him without turning fully. "What concern is it of yours? You don't like me and you've made your opinion on my presence quite clear."

His eyes narrowed. "My brother wouldn't be pleased. He gave you everything you need for this journey. You have an obligation to him to remain safe."

Since when had Garrett cared about her relationship with Tobias or what she owed him? She opened her mouth to rebut his statement when he held up a hand. "Shhh. Before you speak again, consider this. If you get yourself killed on my watch, my brother will blame me. At least, let me walk with you."

She turned to face him fully. "You trust me enough to do that?"

"No, but you don't exactly trust me either, now do you?"

"No."

"Very well. Let's go. Keep that hand up." He offered his arm and she slipped her non-injured hand into the crook of his elbow. Her other hand pressed against her chest, the handkerchief soiled in red, although the bloodstain had traveled no farther. The ache remained, but it seemed the wound was indeed superficial as Garrett had suggested.

They walked for perhaps another quarter of a mile, the sun's warmth soaking through her dark dress and sending sweat down her back and thighs. His proximity did nothing to help matters, waves of heat washing from his side into hers, sweat visible upon his jaw and brow. He didn't look at her, sights set on the horizon, humidity floating above its edge.

"I don't know why he chose you to come along," he said finally.

"Excuse me?"

"Miss Louis, I understand. She's skilled in about every area a woman can be and has intelligence you don't find too often, in women and men alike. She should be here, but you? I can't figure it out. What does Tobias see in you?"

Was there a reason he would even find acceptable? There was the obvious reason of her Giftedness, then the lesser known reasons Tobias had admitted the night of the town dance.

Her kindness, her caring, how he adored her smile, and her friendship with Martha. The way his voice sounded when he said, *"Let me see you, let me hear your voice, for your voice is sweet, and you are lovely."* She repeated that verse to herself nearly every night. Every one of those reasons she held dear and were reasons Garrett would only scoff at. She would rather keep them treasured and untarnished.

"Tobias believes my curse is also my Gift," she told him. "My husbands' deaths are an unconscious ability that will only be solved when I marry someone who is like myself. Also Gifted."

Garrett snorted. He looked down at her with one eyebrow raised so high it disappeared beneath his hat brim. "Did Jamison write that excuse for you? It sounds like an encyclopedic answer." He shook his head, swiping misplaced hair behind his left ear. He readjusted his hat and nudged her arm tighter against his.

"You need to stop indulging Tobias's fantasies. He's always had these delusions that he's going to find Gifted people. Back in Charleston, he had a *suspicion* at least once or twice a year. I'll let you in on the real secret though—they don't exist. He's going to look forever and never find a single one. It's my Gift to find people. If they were out there, don't you think I would have found one by now?"

"Tobias told me that your Gifts don't work on each other, so no, I don't think you would have."

He frowned, turning his attention back to the trail. "Regardless, I think we would have stumbled across someone by this point. I reckon all the other sailors' kin are long dead or maybe the originals never made it off the *Oblique*. Heck, my father might have murdered them, so he could be the last and greatest Gifted. Sounds like something he would do."

Murdered, she thought. *Just like Tobias said their mother and sisters were.* Who had this father of theirs been to destroy so many lives with a single Gift? Not so different from her she supposed, but intent was everything. She had never wanted to kill her husbands.

"Listen, Miss Walcott," Garrett sighed. "He's decent folk, my brother, but misguided. I know you've had a bad way of it with all the dead husbands and the asylum threat, but that's no excuse to lose your senses. I would caution you, when my brother gives his mind to a cause, he's determined to see it though."

"That sounds admirable."

"From a certain perspective, it is. From another, it's the symptom of a madman. Take the story of Romeo and Juliet for example. Some ladies would consider a handsome man outside their window a romantic notion. Others would view it as the sign of something sinister. Honestly, Romeo breaks into her father's party then climbs over her wall to obsessively fixate on her. I don't care if their families were rivals or not, no father will give you his daughter if you're creeping in the bushes."

Sarah had to admit, Garrett actually made a good point. She had never considered the Romeo and Juliet story from that perspective. Put that way, the whole relationship did sound insane. Was she?

"If you think he's mad and you think I'm mad, then could our union not be a fitting end to the madness?"

Garrett stopped walking. There in the middle of a dusty nothingness, he looked back over his shoulder from where they came. The wagons were barely visible, their once-white canvas tops now tanned against the golden landscape. "Sarah," he said slowly. "You should never place too much belief in other people. In the end, they are more likely to disappoint than impress you."

"Then who do *you* believe in, Garrett? God?"

"Myself."

"That seems lonely."

He turned her back toward camp, one step moving forward after the other. "Lonely? Nah. I have what I need and people when I need them. I don't have reason to be lonely." His jaw clenched tight, brokering an end to the conversation.

The man with the Gift to find people didn't believe there was anyone even worth finding, let alone worth trusting. The irony was apparent and so was the lie within his words. Life had hardened Garrett and while Sarah didn't doubt that he was as tough as he let on, she also didn't think he was completely without hope. He said he wasn't lonely, but she knew what loneliness was. She knew how it felt to be a solitary weed in a field full of flowers, a mule surrounded by well-bred mares. Misunderstood, unwanted, unloved. Convincing herself it was better to live in loneliness than to suffer another heartbreak.

Washington was not Boston. It didn't contain any of the things Linden had planned. Her wagon compartment was lined with poetry and she had the chipped wine glass still stored, but she wasn't close to creating the life he had wanted.

Because this is not his life, said a voice, subtle yet coherent. *It is yours. What will you make of it?*

Only one thought came to mind, the one she could only admit in the whispers of her mind. That she never wanted to leave Tobias's side. She wanted to remain here, working with him, sharing her thoughts, her *life*, with the man who, try as she had to fight it, she had grown to love. For the first time since Linden, her heart had opened again. This dream Tobias had of Larksong, she wanted it to be her dream too.

Questions about her curse still abounded, fear over the wisdom of pursuing such a life, but the more she considered a way outside of sorrow's path, the more she wanted to believe one existed.

Everyone was broken, even if their cracks were carefully plastered and painted over. Even a stitched sampler looked messy on the inside.

Garrett was wrong. Everyone—even the Gifted—needed someone to believe in.

27

AUGUST 1852
IDAHO

Tobias felt fifty years old instead of thirty. The crick in his neck had lasted for three days and attempts to rub out the muscles only left the skin red and rough. He wanted to sleep for days, but when he dropped onto his bedroll each night, the ground seemed firmer than the last. Everything had this constant dull throb he could never quite move past. He didn't want to build another rotten thing, no matter how easy it might be to do so.

He should stop whining; he was the wagon master, after all. All of his brothers were out of sorts. Between sickness, broken bones, and other ailments, Jamison was dead tired from caring for everyone while trying not to manage it too quickly. People were starting to question his ability to find the perfect remedy. No doctor was that skilled. When Tobias told him to attribute some of it to luck or to ease off, Jamison flat out yelled at him.

"I'm trying, Tobias," he shouted. "But I can't stand watching people suffer for no reason. And neither should you." Then he stormed off to find Garrett and probably rail on him for who-knew-what.

Garrett never had overcome his inability to find Gabriella Reed. "It doesn't make sense," he griped time and again. Then he would choose a random person in their party to locate simply to prove he still could. It always worked and Garrett always sulked afterward. There was simply no pleasing him either way.

As for Cade...well, Cade worried Tobias the most.

That night, as he returned from his rounds, he stumbled upon his brother and Alice Ann sidled up in the shadows of his wagon, their backs against one wheel and Cade's arm wrapping Alice Ann's waist. They were speaking close, practically cheek-to-cheek, with her thin figure nestled into his side. Although nothing appeared untoward, who could say what might have occurred prior to his return?

What was he going to do about this? Alice Ann wasn't exactly the type of well-mannered lady he would choose for his youngest brother. She could be rather turbulent, and Cade was a heartfelt romantic. While Tobias could handle his own feelings not being reciprocated, Cade would wither under such rejection. If there was an attraction between them, he hoped it moved both ways and if not, that Cade could come to his senses about it soon.

When he cleared his throat, they both jumped, shooting to their feet like they were caught canoodling under the wagon rather than sitting beside it. Alice Ann, however, sported a sassy grin quite the opposite of Cade's red-faced embarrassment.

"He-Hey, Tobias," he stuttered. "Beautiful night, isn't it?" He glanced at Alice Ann and shuffled another step to the side.

"It is a nice night," Tobias agreed. "Think it will stay that way?"

"No indication to suggest otherwise." Cade peered up at the sky. "Oh, look, the moon. Appears to be nearing full."

Tobias wanted to laugh at the awkwardness of it all, but didn't. If Garrett had been there, Cade would have received a ribbing his middle brother would never let him live down.

"Suppose I should head back," Alice Ann said. "Thanks for a pleasant evening." She stood on toe to kiss Cade's cheek then with a smile and a wink, skipped off to her own wagon. Cade waited until she disappeared to exhale.

He could barely glance at his brother. "I can explain this."

"Doesn't seem like it needs explanation. You've got your eye on Alice Ann, and she's stringing you along."

"It isn't like that, honest. If anything, I'm stringing her. Maybe there are two strings." He scuffed his boot in the dirt, lifting a low cloud around their ankles. "She's sure pretty, but she's only seventeen."

Tobias wanted to ask what his point was; Cade was only twenty. Instead, he said, "You're not the type to lead a lady without expectation. Truth is, you're not the type to lead any lady, but especially not that type of lady."

"Who says I'm not? You don't even know me, Tobias."

Tobias stepped back, losing his voice with the realization. He *didn't* know his brother. To him, Cade was still the eighteen-year-old kid they let tag along from Charleston. For all he knew, that boy could be completely different from the man who stood before him.

"I'm sorry, Cade. I've been so busy planning Larksong, I apparently missed you growing up."

Cade shrugged. "I'm used to it. You're the leader. You have important things to do.

"I'm also your brother and the oldest, now that Daniel's gone. I have a responsibility to you."

"Tobias, I don't want another father. I didn't even want the one we had. I can care for myself."

Tobias hoped that was true, but given recent history, he feared Cade's words were more likely false. Well, all the words except not wanting the father they had. That was truer than true.

"I'm not lonely," Cade continued, "if that's why you think I'm sparking with Alice Ann. And it isn't because she's the only girl who's shown me a fancy. There have been others."

"Why then?"

His brother shrugged again, but at last, his expression softened. "She's different." His eyes lit up. "She can shoot a revolver dead shot. I've never met a girl who could do that."

"Yeah, me neither." He understood his brother's affection for the unusual. Wanting to find someone whom others quirked their eyebrows at and called a little off the mark. Wasn't that his initial draw to Sarah?

"Mr. Reed says Alice Ann reminds him of the gold diggers he met in San Francisco."

That caught Tobias's ear. "Clint's from out west? He told me he was from Carolina."

"He was...originally. He served on a clipper ship for a while then stopped off in California and just kind of stayed there. Had a lot of fun he told me—" Cade grinned sheepishly. "A *lot* of fun."

Tobias rolled his eyes. "I can only imagine."

"California was no place to find a decent wife so he went back South and married. Figured he'd stay there, but your offer was too good to pass up. Who doesn't want a free 320 acres to do with whatever he pleases?"

"At least that part matches with what he told me. Guess I'd be shy to admit to a sordid past too if I wanted to join our train. I did sell it as the perfect society." Tobias glanced outward. "Turns out my grand vision isn't so perfect after all."

For a few minutes, they stood in silence, shoulder-to-shoulder, folded arms to folded arms, and stared out into the night. Across the vastness lay only darkness, the moon not enough to light the unknown. Above, the stars twinkled in their usual constellations, never changing, only moving with the seasons.

"Maybe Reed should have a greater say in developing the town," Cade suggested.

Tobias raised an eyebrow.

"Just listen, Tobias. He's been out there in the world, traveling, seeing things. He's seen men shot and fought in the street. Been drunk more than his fair share, spent the night with prostitutes, and—"

"If you're trying to convince me, this isn't it."

"My point is, we stayed on the plantation most of our lives except for fancy parties and trips to the townhouse. What do we know about maintaining life out here?"

Tobias still was leery. "Yes, Reed is more worldly, but perhaps a little too much so. Scuffles and prostitutes? Not exactly the ideal for a trusted second."

"I'm not ideal either. Some days I feel like running from my own shadow. During the tornado, I hid. When Ephram got busted by the wagon wheels, I threw up. I'm not like the rest of you. I have no courage." He glanced back into the wagon circle where bedrolls dotted the area around and under the wagons. "I think you should find someone else to take my place."

Tobias wished he knew a way to help his brother overcome his insecurities. Cade had been barely eight when their mother died in such a horrifying way. He grew up with his only remaining parent being someone to fear, who never once told his youngest son he loved him, but rather berated him at every turn. Who had literally whipped him into silence. The rest of them had been able to stand up to their father at one time or another, but never Cade. Cade *was* afraid of his own shadow and hid behind it rather than experience parts of life he deserved.

Tobias wasn't ready to give up on him as a potential leader of Larksong. Someday his brother would have to rise to the occasion, but he would never force him to become someone he didn't wish to be.

28

Ha ow many more are we losing?"

Tobias glanced between the men—Jamison, Garrett, Josiah, Levi—each a trusted second, each waiting on him for direction. None apparently willing to provide an answer to his question. Behind them, the dingy outline of Fort Hall's once-white exterior wall stood out in stark contrast to its log-hewn interior buildings. Leather boots and moccasins passed by in both directions amid the chatter of pioneers, Indians, and United States soldiers. The hustle of another day he wished would pass quickly.

He gripped the open map and traced the remaining miles with his eyes. They only had to travel from Fort Hall to the Dalles and then north into Washington until they reached the claim site. Compared to how far they had already come, there wasn't much to go; however, their group dwindled by the day. Once the wagons in question split for California, they would be left with only twenty-two, less than half their original number. He supposed he should be grateful most had departed of their own volition rather than in their graves.

Was every wagon master this bone-weary? He just wanted to arrive already. To sink his bare toes into the waters of the Pacific coast and breathe the salt-soaked air, one of the few pleasant reminders of his hometown. He couldn't wait to build a house of his own, furniture to place inside it, and have, God-willing, a wife to share it with. The day the last nail was in place, he would sit for a solid three days straight, watch the waves break, and enjoy whatever passed for tea and food in the northwest. When all was said and done, maybe he would light his wagon on fire. Let it go up in a blaze of glory. He would walk everywhere and only purchase what he could carry.

"How many?" he asked again.

"Seven," Levi admitted.

"*Seven*? Last word was we were only losing five."

"Ned and Terrance, the Pryors, Cooks, and Hardings were already plannin' to go," Levi said. "But then the Duvalls and Moores heard 'em talking about California and now they can't gets it outta their heads."

"That may be partly my fault," Clinton Reed spoke up, and Tobias wanted to punch him in the teeth. He was only in attendance because Cade sent the rancher in his place. Apparently, his brother had been serious when he said he wanted out of the decision-making and also apparently serious when he suggested Clinton as a replacement. Even though the man hadn't done anything lewd while part of the train, his past indiscretions left Tobias with a bitter taste upon his tongue. Clinton hadn't earned the right to be a leader, yet Cade wedged him in where he didn't belong.

Judging from Garrett's scowl and Levi's raised eyebrows, they owned some reservations as well.

"What did you do?" Jamison asked. He was the only one without a hint of opinion in his expression.

"I told them about my cousin out in San Francisco. Took to the rush of '49 and came home richer than Midas." Reed drew a glass vial from his vest's watch pocket. Inside held a small golden nugget. "He gave me this before I left Charleston. For luck. Told me to cash it in once we got to Washington, use it to help build the ranch. Glad now I never told Gabriella about it."

Jamison leaned in. "It looks real enough."

"I'll be the judge." Without asking, Garrett reached across and swiped the vial from Clinton's hand. As the sun sparkled off the stone, it jingled inside the glass, almost seeming to hold a life all its own. Garrett's eyes widened as he held it up to the sky and Tobias found he was holding his breath as much as the rest of them.

"I think it is real," he murmured. "There's something unusual about it. Where did you say your cousin found this?"

"Somewhere in San Francisco. Could have been anywhere though. He claimed at one point men were sweeping gold dust off the streets."

Garrett's eyes met Clinton's. "Off the street? Is that so?"

With an aggressive exhale, Tobias snatched the vial and shoved it back at Clinton's chest. The man barely bobbled it into his fist without dropping it to the ground. "Put that away," he ordered. "Don't bring it back out until we reach Washington."

Clinton slipped it into his pocket. "Understood, Mr. Lark."

"It's a sore thing to have more of our numbers leave us," Tobias told them. "They're on the search for gold, and it's likely a one in a hundred chance they'll draw a vein. Let them do as they wish; we will continue as we planned. I met a colonel here who suggested we sell or leave anything of lesser value to lighten the load. He claims the trail grows even more treacherous later on and it's wise not to haul more weight than we need. I agree. No sense seeing it left to ruin on the trail."

"Not sure how much we'll have to leave," Levi said. His fingers slicked over his dark beard, smoothing the whiskers against his chin while he pondered. "I know of at least two families who are running low on the essentials. Another few who could make do, but need a little more. None of 'em have money to hold over though."

"Then we'll have to provide them with what they need." It would cut into their already dangerously depleting funds, but what else could they do? The goal was to keep their town self-sufficient. They needed townspeople to have a town.

"Clint, can I see that nugget again?" Garrett asked. He stepped closer, hand outstretched like he would take it whether the man offered or not.

Reed placed a hand over his pocket. "Your brother asked me to keep it away."

"Since when does my brother make the rules?"

Clinton's eyes flashed between Garrett to Tobias and back again. "Since...since I thought, always."

When his brother took another step forward, Tobias stuck an arm out, letting it bump against his chest. Garrett's eyes held Clinton's pocket with a dangerous gleam.

Reed eased backward. "It's only a small piece. Nothing worth causing a fuss over. I said I'd use it for the town, didn't I?"

Garrett only pressed closer. "Yeah, you sure did." His fingers rolled into a fist at his side. "Now, hand it over."

"Garrett!" Jamison's hand latched onto his brother's, yanking him back hard. Garrett toppled square into Jamison then to his knees in the dirt. He pressed a hand to his chest, breathing hard, his opposite palm pressed flat to the ground.

What was wrong with him today? Tobias had seen him upset, seen him throw punches and tantrums and destroy property, but this was plain odd, even for Garrett. He had never been obsessed with money, save his heated opinions on Daniel's distribution of their inheritance. Then again, they always had enough to go around. Could it be that the first time they experienced something short of well-off, he couldn't handle the pressure?

What was their family coming to?

Still on his knees, Garrett's palms rose to either temple, his eyes squeezed shut as though in pain. Perhaps a headache like the one which drew them to Hawthorn Ridge those many months ago? It had found Sarah then, the first Gifted they ever discovered outside themselves. Could he have found another?

Tobias knelt beside his brother. "Is it happening again?" he whispered. "Is there someone we need to find here?" Like the other forts they visited, this one wasn't large. It shouldn't be too difficult to locate a target.

Garrett shook his head. "Tell Clint to leave."

"Why?"

"Just do it!"

Tobias turned, but Clinton Reed was already moving away. At the entrance gate, he paused, directly in the way of those entering and exiting and causing a general traffic impairment. There was no doubting the nervousness in his expression. He knew he had set some battle in motion with his gold nugget, and he didn't want the blame pegged on him any more than it was.

But if his gold ultimately led them to another Gifted, Tobias would shake that man's hand instead. He wouldn't tell him why, but he would shake it all the same.

The sound of vomit expulsion turned him back to Garrett's side. Hunched over, his brother retched into the dirt until nothing remained except dry heaves. Within a few minutes, a circle of bystanders had formed, an armed soldier pushing his way through at their center.

"Anything the trouble here?" the man asked. He held his rifle across his chest, hands steady on the stock and ready to move if needed. He narrowed his gaze at Garrett. "We do not allow intemperance at Fort Hall."

"He isn't drunk," Jamison quickly interjected. "He's ill."

The soldier retreated a step. When he waved to the onlookers, they flew like chickens. No one wanted to catch one of the foul diseases plaguing the trail. But how do you explain that Giftedness wasn't caught like cholera or dysentery?

"Get him out of here," the soldier growled. His grip tightened on his weapon. "And see that your party moves out within the hour."

"I'm a doctor," Jamison said. "I assure you he isn't contagious. It's nothing more than a migraine."

"A *what*?"

Migraine wasn't a new term, but information reached the western settlements far slower than their eastern counterparts. The glare which pegged them sat on a face not much older than Cade. If this soldier had been raised on the frontier, he very well might not know the word.

"You may be more familiar with the term megrim," Jamison explained. "A severe headache which can also result in sour stomach."

Tobias nearly laughed at the inaccurate simplicity of his explanation. As a child, Garrett had spent days curled in his bed, the draperies drawn to darkness while he cried from pain, an empty bowl on his bedside table for the moments he could no longer stomach. The headaches manifested even years before his Gift, or at least before they recognized the connection. Garrett was almost twenty before Jamison discovered the official term in some hundred-year-old British encyclopedia and started piecing it all together. The next few years were spent pouring over numerous university medical journals only to attempt treatments that barely eased his brother's pain.

"A headache?" the soldier now scoffed. "I can name a dozen other ailments that cause the same reaction. Now get him out of here, before you earn yourselves a night in the garrison and I ship your colored folk back to the southern markets."

Garrett jumped to his feet, causing the soldier to shoulder his weapon. He swayed on the spot but managed to remain upright. "How dare you!" he shouted. "Those men are decent folk!" He stepped straight into the weapon's path, blocking the way to their former servants. "Go ahead and arrest me because I ain't moving!"

"Garrett, stop!" Tobias shouted, but he might as well have spoken to the endless suffering of the overland trails. The soldier slammed his rifle into his brother's shin, dropping Garrett to the ground in a groaning puddle, the stench of his vomit mixing with horse manure and the sweat of a hundred men.

With the prospect of some action, those onlookers previously ushered away now returned. Their shouts and jeers accused Garrett of anything from being a blackie-lover to a plague upon humanity. They wanted him locked up, they wanted him thrown out. Someone even demanded a lynching, which by God's good hand, led the soldier to bark orders for "everyone away!"

As their brother was shoved through the doorway of the nearest building, Jamison yanked Tobias in the opposite direction. Josiah and Levi were already ten steps ahead, on their way to the open gate and their wagon circle beyond. It appeared the soldier didn't care to fight anyone but the man who used him as a verbal spittoon.

"We'll come back," Jamison said. "We won't leave until they release him. Right now, we need to make sure the rest of the wagons are protected."

29

As requested, their wagon party moved on within the hour, relocating about a mile west of Fort Hall. They would remain there an additional night before continuing on the trail.

Tobias, Jamison, and Cade traveled back to the fort alone, but it was Clinton Reed's gold nugget that ultimately bailed Garrett out of the garrison. Jamison hadn't wanted to accept it when Clinton first offered, but Tobias thought it only fair since that stupid nugget started the tussle in the first place.

When they handed it to the soldier sitting sentry outside the jail, his eyes widened. "Don't ya reckon how much this is worth?"

"I have a fair guess, yeah." With their inheritance funds ever dwindling and more hard times certain to fall, that gold nugget would have brought a generous income.

With the clank of metal against metal, the iron bars slid open. Garrett's tempered gaze met theirs, a nasty bruise purpling the area where cheek met jawbone. He must have gotten into it with the guard after they left. Leave it to Garrett to make enemies after he had already been defeated. And it appeared he was still in a sultry mood when they arrived.

Rising from the wooden bench that doubled as a cot, he attempted to exit, but Jamison grabbed his arm, launching him back into the cell. Garrett's fingers curled at his sides, unkempt locks falling across his eyes as he tried to sidestep them again. There would be nothing for it. Tobias and Jamison each seized an arm and wrestled him back to sit on the cot between them. "Hold your horses there, Garrett.

Before we leave, we have a little talking to do."

"*Now*? Can't we do this at the wagon?"

"Can you offer us a minute?" Tobias asked the guard.

The soldier shrugged. "You've already paid. Not my concern if you *want* to stay in jail. I'll wait outside." With a twirl of the keyring around his finger, he stepped out the garrison's front door and closed it with a jolt.

"Aren't we leaving?" Garrett expounded. He tried to stand again to no avail.

"Sure," Tobias said. "After we talk about what happened to you this afternoon. Cade, get in here and guard the door."

Cade still stood outside the cell, casting anxious glances between Garrett and the guard's back visible outside the window. "Maybe we should leave?" he suggested. "We can talk at the wagon."

With a sigh, Tobias rose from the cot, striking out an arm to drag his youngest brother to the cell door. He pushed Cade inside and slid the bars closed again, turning his own back to the metal. Ignoring Cade's protest, he met Garrett's scowl. "Well, where are they?"

"Who?"

"Whoever you're being drawn to. Your demonstration with the guard...that was a devil of an affliction. I'm assuming this is an unusual case." He longed to point out how such a strong reaction could only mean the location of another Gifted, but Garrett still didn't agree with his original hypothesis about Sarah's Giftedness. "Tell us where they are, Garrett."

His brother only ground his jaw and didn't answer.

"Just tell us," Jamison pressed. "If you don't, he'll keep us here all night."

"How can I tell you what I don't even understand? I've never had a feeling like this...my Gift has never asked me to go so far—"

"Far?" Cade asked. "How far do you have to go?"

Garrett looked from Jamison to Tobias then peered at Cade from under heavy lids. "San Francisco."

"*What*?" Cade scurried backward until his spine hit the cell bars with a clang. He reached behind him and clutched the rungs, his complexion draining like a corpse. "No," he breathed. "You are not going to California."

Garrett wrenched upright and this time Jamison let him. He approached with caution, but when he tried to rest a palm upon Cade's shoulder, his brother spun out of reach. He backed into the opposite corner, visibly trembling. "Garrett," he whispered. "You can't. We don't have Daniel anymore and we...we promised we would stay together."

"I know, Cade, and I'm sorry, but I can't ignore this feeling. I can't explain it...when I touched the gold, my brain started screaming for relief, while also demanding I follow. It didn't show me an exact location, but Clinton said the gold came from San Francisco, so I think that's where I need to go."

"You *think*?" Jamison asked. "Isn't the essence of your Gift that you *know* where people are?"

"I've never been asked to travel this far. I'm sure I'll gain a better map as I get closer. We don't know what could happen if I ignore my Gift for too long. What if I don't go and it kills me?"

Cade opened his mouth, but it was Tobias who spoke. "It won't kill you."

"How do you know?"

"I'm the leader and I know." He knew Garrett hated when he claimed leadership in order to place demands, and it embarrassed him to even play such a card. "Something about this doesn't feel right," he continued. "Why would you be called a thousand miles away when you never have before?"

"Who knows? Maybe my Gift is growing stronger. Isn't that a good thing?" When no one answered, Garrett scowled. His hands fell to either hip, his holster empty after his arrest. "Y'all are throwing a fit over nothing. I'm coming back."

"Are you? If one of us leaves, how do you know our Gifts will still work without you here? What if we lose them so far apart? I'm not sure our town will survive without Jamison to heal or me to keep the wagons rolling."

"I couldn't find Clint's wife while we were all together. If we're losing our Gifts, it seems they'll be lost with or without me." He shook his head. "We've been without Daniel for over a year. Even being ungifted, maybe he was the key that held ours together. We haven't been able to keep people from leaving or dying anyway. Maybe losing these talents altogether wouldn't be the worst thing in the world." He shook his head again.

Garrett might be relieved to lose his Gift, what with the migraines and the sickness he had to endure, but Tobias didn't want to face that possibility for his own abilities. He had never physically suffered like his brother, but it would still take a toll if the ease with which he built suddenly vanished. To craft at the sluggish pace of a normal man after a lifetime of rapid creation? He couldn't even fathom it.

Situated on opposite sides of the cell, it felt like they stood on opposite sides of the world, each brother taking his own corner, his own stance. The already warm air seemed to rise by twenty degrees. Then thirty. Sweat rolled across Tobias's forehead until he was forced to wipe it away.

He looked to Jamison for assistance. No lecture, no sermon, nothing? There had to be a Bible verse applicable to brothers leaving brothers. The prodigal son, perhaps? Was that the right story? Something about being your brother's keeper? Every verse squashed together in his brain until he wasn't sure he had even read the Bible.

"We need you to tend your land," Tobias reasoned in one last-ditch effort. "We can't claim it for you."

"What if I mine a fortune in gold?" Garrett said. "I'll bring back a bundle and improve the town."

"There won't be land ready for you though. What if the government isn't giving any more away when you arrive?"

"As I said, if I'm lucky, I'll make a fortune and can buy as much land as I want."

"Things could happen to you out there on your own."

"Things could happen to me here, too. You're offering all those other people freedom." He met his brothers' eyes one by one. "Please, for once, offer some of it to me."

Garrett didn't even wait for dawn. Within mere hours of his

liberation, he had his wagon packed and oxen yoked, ready to move out. Tobias sent him off with an extra supply of flour, bacon, jerky, and plenty of tools, wood, and bullets. He strapped a second rain barrel to the back of the wagon and offered him an extra water sling. It was more than Garrett would need and would lessen Tobias's guilt enough to let him go.

It also helped to learn he wasn't going alone.

"You're not leaving, too!" Cade shouted when Josiah announced he was joining Garrett in the Golden City. Cade ripped the bedroll out of the burly man's arms and threw it into the wagon bed. "I won't let you!"

"Come now, Cade, m' boy." Josiah stared down at him, a hand falling to rest on either of Cade's shoulders like he always had when Cade was a boy. "We'll be-a back before ya know it. Keep ta smilin'. Show your lady you a grown man."

Cade didn't smile and he didn't look at Alice Ann either. She stood mere feet away beside her sister, near Sarah and Martha and Marie, too. Marie didn't hold back her tears, choosing to lose them within her apron. Her children crowded around Josiah's legs, scrambling for hugs until the older man was forced to release his youngest "son" and turn their way.

Josiah had been there the day they were all born. He had been a stalwart source of guidance for the Harpers and the Larks alike. More a father than Alonzo Lark ever was. How could his presence simply disappear?

Garrett claimed the opportunity to stick his hand out in Cade's direction. "Take care of yourself, eh?" he said with a smile. "I want letters, and you're gonna tell me all the stuff Tobias says not to mention."

Cade made no move to return the gesture. He stared at his brother's open palm. "I'll tell you when you come back, so stay alive, all right?"

"That's a promise."

Without another word, Cade returned to his wagon and climbed inside. From here out, he would have to manage the oxen without help, his wagon much emptier now that Josiah's supply share had been transferred to Garrett's. Maybe Cade would ask Alice Ann to walk with him during the day. Despite Tobias's misgivings over their childish romance, she would have better luck at Cade's side than anyone else.

Garrett reached for each of his friends and family members around the circle. He claimed it wasn't goodbye forever, but it sure felt that way. No one knew what temptations San Francisco held or how long he would be there. What if he found a wife and decided to stay forever? What if a mine collapsed on both him and Josiah and word was never returned to Larksong? Jamison prayed over both of them with a smile, but it felt reminiscent of the many funerals Tobias had attended in his life. Eulogies spoken while the bodies were still warm.

He shook Josiah's hand, then Garrett's, before finally handing over Josiah's purchase papers. His brother slipped them into his saddlebag as though the transaction were happening with someone else. "Don't find too much trouble," Tobias said low. "I've heard stories about California."

"I've heard them too," Garrett replied. "Clinton talks a lot."

"Too much."

"Maybe you should watch out for *him*."

Tobias managed a chuckle. "Yeah, maybe. Be careful?"

Garrett grinned wide. "When am I not?" With a final wave, he took up the goad stick and prodded the oxen into movement. Josiah joined his stride and then they were gone, vanished into the blue-grey twilight of a day still struggling to end.

"We'll rest another day here," Tobias told Jamison. "Resupply what we need and head out early the next."

"Are you sure? We're already weeks behind schedule and I know how you feel about losing more time."

Tobias waited another beat, focused on the darkening California Trail. "Yeah, I'm sure."

30

Ominous clouds rolled in for most of the following day, making it nearly dark as night. *Good*, Tobias thought. He could be alone and no one would find him for once. He could scream or curse and no one would say, "Tobias, calm down," or "Tobias, leaders don't show weakness," or "Tobias, don't you know other people are suffering? Now go fix another broken wagon wheel."

Half a mile from the wagon circle, he tied his mare to a lone tree, its branches as forlorn and barren as the rest of the landscape. With his back to the trunk, he sat in silence until the sun sank and the stars appeared. This wasn't how it was supposed to be. Garrett was supposed to be with them. All four brothers creating a perfect world together. Though if Tobias searched his heart, he knew it never would be perfect, even if Garrett had stayed. They were still only four parts of a five-piece unit.

Even with their constant disagreements, Daniel should have been a part of this. Gifted or not, Larksong was his legacy, too, and Tobias missed him. He hadn't admitted it to himself until he watched their middle brother trot away to California.

Would they all be divided in the end? Jamison would likely stay, but Cade was only a breath away from a hysterical breakdown, even though he would never say so.

An owl hooted as it glided overhead and some animal skittered across the dirt. A mouse maybe; its tracks didn't sound large, but there were other creatures to harm him if they chose. Wolves, snapping turtles, and snakes. He thought of Oliver and his grief flowed anew.

"It's the shortest sentence in the Bible," Jamison would say. "'*And Jesus wept.*' Even the Lord grieved when His friend died, and He knew Lazarus would rise again."

So, that was what Tobias did. He cradled himself on his side against the ground, knees drawn into his chest, and had never been more thankful to be alone.

The next morning, he woke to hoofbeats approaching rapidly. The first rays of light poked from behind the mountains, though not so bright as to discourage bandits on the hunt for unsuspecting travelers. He sprung from the ground, hand ready on his revolver until he saw the rider appear through the morning mist. Sarah rode astride Jamison's mare, her body pressed low over the horse's neck as she urged the animal on. Blonde hair floated about her face, the strands glinting where the barest daylight broke through the shadows. Ten feet away, she pulled up on the reins and in quick succession, lifted them over the horse's head and swung down from the saddle. She led the mare forward, the combination of hoofbeats and her swishing skirts a surprising addition to nature's symphony.

"Let me guess," he said. "My brothers sent you to find me again?"

Her fingers twisted in the leather reins. "No. This time I volunteered."

"Why?"

As the sun tipped the horizon, a stream of gold passed over them both, illuminating her green irises' hazel flecks with a gilded edge. Sympathy passed through her green-eyed gaze, the only person from an entire wagon train not willing to leave their leader to his loneliness. "Because I think I understand you better now. It's the same as me. Our pasts haunt us. How do we deal with something we can never escape from?"

"Are we to speak of Linden's curse again?"

"No. I only want you to know I'm here."

He scuffed his palms over his face. When he lowered them, Sarah was staring at the scar on his forearm, visible with his sleeves rolled to the elbows. The gash had faded over time to three intersecting white lines, but their memory held a familiar pain.

"One of the unfortunate side effects of being Alonzo Lark's son," he told her. "You never earned love with my father, only scars." For Garrett, Cade, and him, the scars were visible. Jamison had one which healed over on its own, probably with assistance from his Gift. Daniel always pandered to their father, avoiding the brunt of his physical anger, but Tobias knew his eldest brother held scars on the inside, drawn where no one could see.

He rolled both sleeves down and buttoned them at the cuffs. "I'm sure your father would have never done anything like this to you, Miss Walcott. For whatever it's worth, I do believe he made mistakes, but he wanted the best for you."

She shook her head. "I'm sorry for what your father did to you."

"He was a right heathen, my father. Why bother with God when he thought himself better? If it didn't fit his plan, his way of thinking, then it was to be discarded or destroyed. No one said no to my father, except for his no-good sons."

Bending, he tugged up the hem of his trouser leg, pushing down his stocking to reveal a scar the length of his calf. The bright white line constricted with the pulse of his leg muscles, taking him right back to the day it happened. "This was from the night I helped my mother's maid, Lilith, escape. She was with child and wouldn't say by whom. All we knew was the affair hadn't been approved by my father. Heck, we reckoned the man might *be* my father. She had confided her fears to Marie, who told Levi, who then told me. When my father learned she was gone, he didn't ask who was responsible. Somehow, he knew. He caught my leg with a fire poker when I walked into breakfast the next morning. It took seventeen stitches to close up."

Tobias dropped his trouser leg but remained where he knelt. He pressed a palm to the hard auburn soil and let the grit rub against his skin. He wouldn't reveal the rest of his scars: the one on his collarbone or near his hip from his days out in the rice paddies. He could have spoken for hours about the ways Larksong Plantation had maimed him, but what would that achieve? His father was dead and it was all over and done with now. They were on their way to build a new Larksong and there wouldn't be any scars in that place.

"What of your mother?" Sarah asked softly. "You never told me how she died."

He dug his fingers into the earth, filling his palm and sifting the granules out again. "My father's Gift, of course. He convinced her what she had was what she wanted...until he convinced her that it wasn't. Even though us brothers promised to save her, in the end, our Gifts were powerless to help. Do you know how hard it is for everyone to believe your mother ended her own life and only you know she didn't?"

He finally lifted his eyes and sunlight glittered within Sarah's unshed tears. He rose. "Apologies, that was more than you needed to know about your wagon leader."

"I don't mind." She looked down at her shoes, scuffed black boots poking out from beneath her tattered hem. She probably needed some new ones. Now that was something he could fix. The hem too.

"I'm sorry about your mother," she said, "and Garrett. Daniel too. I'm sorry you couldn't make things right with your father before he died."

"Good gravy, you make me sound pathetic. Between all the mourning and self-pity, it's a wonder our entire wagon train hasn't driven straight down a mountain."

"You're allowed to grieve, Tobias."

"How do you grieve for something you should have stopped? My Gift is to fix things. I couldn't fix that though."

"People aren't wagons, Tobias. Sometimes they can't be fixed." She reached out and gently lifted his hand from where it propped upon his hip. Their fingers laced together on instinct, as though they belonged in that position. Suspended between them, he could make out the braided ring still around her fourth finger. Why hadn't she moved it? And why was she suddenly standing so close as she was? To comfort him? He didn't want that type of comfort.

Or rather he wanted it, but not when he knew where it would lead—nowhere.

He released her hand. "I withdraw my marriage proposal. I should never have tried to force you. I tried to manipulate the situation to make something happen which clearly shouldn't."

Her fingertips went to her throat. "You're...surrendering? But I thought—"

"Don't let someone else decide your life for you, Miss Walcott. Garrett didn't really want to be a part of this either. He came because we're brothers and brothers stick together, but I talked him into it. Well, me and Cade and Jamison. Now he's gone anyway without the goodbye it should have been. It's no different with you. I should have never made you stay."

"You didn't. I stayed because I wanted to. For Linden, for Martha. I couldn't leave her on her own."

"What about for you?"

"It seems selfish."

"That's how people are, aren't they? We're all selfish people pretending to care about one another. Then we see something pretty as gold dust and we lunge after it without a care for anyone else."

"You're not like that."

"No?"

"No."

Her emerald eyes held his. She drew a step closer. Two more and they would practically be toe-to-toe. "Do you believe I'm Gifted?" she asked.

"I've said from the beginning that I do."

"Yes, but do you really and truly believe it?"

He sighed, pushed the hair out of his eyes which only made the sun shine brighter. Right into the corner of his vision, forming halos around Sarah's features and blinding him to all else. "I do, but a Gift has to be freely given. It cannot be stolen or coerced. I'm sorry for trying to work everything to my advantage."

Another step. "But you believe with certainty our marriage will break my curse?"

With certainty? No, of course not. There was plenty of doubt. Especially now, witness to the hope in her eyes, thinking how this could be the tipping moment. There could be one final chance to convince her to stay with him. But he couldn't lie to her. He couldn't make promises in order to keep her. She had to hear the truth.

"No," he admitted. "I'm not certain. As a matter of fact, I doubt almost everything I do these days. But as Jamison would say, that's what faith is. Believing without knowing for sure."

"I never thought of it like that before." She bit her bottom lip, worrying her teeth against the supple skin. He would have liked to kiss her in that moment, tell her how much he cared about her, how he never wanted her to leave. He could imagine the simplicity of such a moment, the two of them beneath the glow of an Idaho sunrise, the mountains at their back and mist across the valley. A moment of splendor.

Then Jamison's mare nuzzled her shoulder and he stepped away. "We should head back to camp. Have some breakfast before we move out." Turning, he flipped the reins over his own horse's neck and gripped the saddle. His boot reached the stirrup when she called out to him.

"Tobias!"

Her fingers gripped his arm and his foot dropped back. Her chin tilted up to meet his stare. "If I asked, would you still marry me? I...I'd like to have the faith you do."

"It's yours." He wasn't going to question. He wasn't going to ask. Without a word, his hand tucked her waist. His lips melded to hers. And wonder of wonders, she let him.

Sarah shouldn't have said yes. She had a history with husbands and it was a bad one. But Tobias—sweet, kind, loving Tobias Lark—was different than all the other men who passed through her life. He could build a wagon overnight and he could heal her cursed soul. In the light of a new day, armed with his faith, it finally made sense.

Even when you weren't cursed, you could have the other half of your heart stolen in an instant. Whether from cholera or a snake bite, they were still lost to you. What was life without being able to tell the people you loved that you loved them? Far too long she had allowed fear to drive her, rather than believing in anything. Tobias was willing to risk his life to show her what faith could mean.

Which was why less than an hour later, they stood beneath that same barren tree—the very definition of her life—and promised to love and cherish each other with everything they had, for as long as they had. Even dressed in the most joyful gown of goldenrod, fashioned by her husband's own hands, Sarah still trembled with every breath. "I do," felt like a death sentence as she said it, yet she still did.

"It will be all right," Tobias whispered. His hand cupped hers and squeezed tight. "I promise." He couldn't promise that, but she trusted him anyway. If he was still alive tomorrow, then she would believe anything he said for the rest of her life.

"Let us pray together for this couple," Jamison said, and hands pressed upon them from every angle. Cade and Martha, Coraline and Alice Ann, Levi and Marie. Their family, still gripped with grief over Oliver, Garrett, and Josiah's missing presence, yet asking God to grant happiness upon this moment. Heads bowed and eyes closed, including Tobias. Sarah lingered on his reverent expression, the strong angle of his jaw, the dark beard upon his face, unkempt from weeks of neglect. His sandy hair curled against his neck. Severely handsome from every angle and made more so by his willingness to risk death to be with her. Her chest constricted. She was not deserving of this sort of paradise.

Jamison rested his hands upon both of theirs. "Blessed are you, O God of our fathers; praised be your name forever and ever. You made Adam and you gave him his wife Eve to be his help and support, and from these two the human race descended. You said, 'It is not good for the man to be alone; let us make him a partner like himself.' Now, Lord, your child, Tobias, takes this wife of his, Sarah, not because of desire but for a noble purpose. Call down your mercy on him and on her, and allow them to live together to a happy old age. Amen."

Not once since her third husband had Father Grier prayed for her marriage to have a long and happy life. He had always known what she did. That a happy old age was not in the dealings.

Tears welled behind her closed lids. She prayed and prayed—oh how she prayed!—that this time, they would receive God's favor.

31

Other than those few at the wedding, they kept the occasion quiet. Tobias and Sarah spent the day in separate wagons and ate meals like nothing out of the ordinary had transpired. Although neither voiced it, they were both wondering what the night would hold. It was better to not announce the news if their worst fears were realized.

All through supper, Tobias watched his new bride from across the campfire. For once, he had received no meal invitations and had no other needs to attend to. He suspected his unoccupied schedule was Jamison's doing, and for that he was grateful. He still wondered at the ease with which he had convinced his brother to marry them.

"Do you love her?" Jamison asked when Tobias approached him and made the request.

"I do."

"Have you considered the risks? That she isn't Gifted and you're walking into a trap?"

"I have. Have you considered that even if she isn't Gifted, she also isn't cursed? All this could be a coincidence."

Jamison slapped him with a look that clearly said, "Seven times? Some coincidence," then told Tobias to round up their family members and meet him back at the tree. They would hold the ceremony and be on their way before the rest of the train suspected anything was out of sorts.

Marrying Sarah had been one of the best and also the most agonizing moments of Tobias's life. This was what he wanted since the moment he set eyes on her, yet now that it was here, he couldn't keep himself from wondering if it was the right decision after all.

Have faith, Tobias. You must have faith.

Easier said than done.

When Sarah caught him watching her from across the fire, he offered a knowing smile. He loved how it made her blush, her lashes fluttering as she turned back to her food. The yellow dress he stitched for her was as exquisite on as he had hoped it would be with each draw of the needle. All evening the other pioneers flooded her with compliments on its beauty although none knew why she chose to leave mourning months early. They assumed hazards of the trail had finally encouraged her to seek new apparel rather than don the same dirty layers with tattered hems. Only those few at the wedding knew the truth.

He stood then, dunked his plate in the washtub, and strode to Sarah's side. Bending low, he whispered, "I'll see you after my rounds. Meet me at my wagon."

With less than a smile, she reached for his hand, but then drew back, darting to see if anyone noticed the gesture. The chatter around the campfire continued without pause. Martha sat at her side observing their interaction, although she studied her tin bowl as though she didn't.

"We have to tell them sometime," he murmured.

"We will." This time she did take his hand. "I'm afraid."

He squeezed her fingers, brushing his thumb over the white clover blossoms of her ring. "I know. So am I."

Come back to me, her eyes silently begged.

"I'll be back soon." Wishing he didn't have to let go, he left her to her supper and set off to find his horse. He would take first watch.

He traveled the perimeter, keeping an eye to the distance and an ear to the inner circle, all the while trying not to dwell on the night to come. Confidence had been his companion these many months, but now his hands shook against the reins, the spurs upon his boots jingling within the stirrups. Heat flared inside his chest and grew hotter by the minute. He was going to die tonight, wasn't he? *Oh, God,* he prayed, *what have I done?*

With blind direction, he steered his horse into the darkest night. Faster and faster they charged along the line of wagon circles, down the trail, and past two more parties making camp. He made a wide berth around Fort Hall and continued into the barren stretch of land between the trail and who only knew what. He wanted to climb the mountains, reach the sky, and stop himself from being sick. It was only a few hours to midnight and he was married to Sarah Walcott, the seven-time wedding night death knell.

Encountering the trickle of a stream, he fell from his horse and onto his knees beside it. As he splashed water on his face, he wondered if it would be enough to drown him accidentally. Would his horse throw him on the way back? Did tribal warriors lay in wait to scalp him and leave his body for the wild? What if the animals found him first? They could drag his bones to a cave and no one would ever know. If he made it through tonight, would he still retain this paralyzing fear for all the days to come?

Have faith.

He rose from the water, sitting back in the dirt and letting the night sweep over him. The cool breeze, the sound of nature's steady rhythm, and the gurgle of water washing stones smooth beneath their crests. Even within all the movement of the wild, there was a stillness, a hidden peace if he could let it sink into his soul.

Jamison's final words at their wedding came back to him then. *Your child, Tobias, takes this wife of his, Sarah, not because of desire but for a noble purpose. Call down your mercy on him and on her, and allow them to live together to a happy old age. Amen.*

He felt his breathing slow, the heat in his middle diminish, but not quite disappear.

"Faith," he repeated. "Faith is believing what I am not certain of."

His horse released a thorough whinny, reminding him she was still there. He smiled up at her. "You're right, girl. I haven't died yet. God willing, maybe I won't tonight."

Reframing his courage, he swung back into the saddle and kicked the mare's flanks, heading back to Sarah and hopefully a long and happy life.

By the time Tobias's horse disappeared into the night, Sarah was so full of terror, she felt like she was going to faint, vomit, or both. Then she did retch, twice, right behind her wagon. She stood beside the mess, alone in the dark, hands trembling and breath running fast. She didn't want to leave this spot. She could walk away to find Tobias poisoned or shot or having stumbled and hit his head on a wagon wheel just so. It was three hours to midnight and most of the camp was asleep or nearly there. What if bandits attacked or a bear or—

Martha appeared beside her. "What're you doing out here?" she asked as though she couldn't see the vomit-strewn ground and didn't know her perilous marriage situation. "Everyone's settling down for the night. Shouldn't you be with Mr. Lark?"

Sarah shook her head, along with everything else. Inside she was running, but her feet wouldn't move. "Tobias hasn't returned from his rounds."

"He was probably detained by another wagon and caught in discussion. You know how the train keeps him busy."

"On his wedding night?" Sarah choked. "What man wants to converse when he has a woman waiting in his wagon?"

Martha silenced. She had nothing to say because Sarah was right. Surprisingly, the acknowledgment helped. She felt her fear plateau, then the tremors in her limbs subside. "He's dead." She was surprised she managed the words.

"You don't know that."

"You didn't deny my statement, Martha, only that it isn't yet confirmed."

"Mr. Lark is a strong man."

"I'm afraid this sort of strength is a gift no man can possess." She had hoped her faith—and his—would save him, but no man could outrun the devil on his heels. It mattered not whether it was a Gift or Linden's curse which killed Tobias in the end, the result remained the same.

A cool breeze drove between the wagons, raising goosebumps on her skin. She looked in the direction it headed, but there was nothing to see. No specter of her dead husbands waiting in the distance. No Linden whispering, "You should have listened."

She wrapped her arms around herself, but Martha was there with a shawl instead, arranging the black and red knit upon her shoulders. She tied a knot upon Sarah's breastbone with a smile. "There, Miss Sarah. Something to keep you warm."

She fingered the soft material. "This is lovely. It looks like my mother's."

"It is your mother's," Martha said. Her eyes found her clasped fingers. "I had seen it hanging in her wardrobe, and sometimes when the missus was out, I would take it out to feel the silks between my fingers. I have nothing of my own mother and I...I wanted something to remember her by."

"Oh, Martha." Sarah reached out and drew her friend in close. She felt her emotions slipping again at the thought of what was to come, the pain the future days would hold. "I've been so selfish. Even if Tobias were to live, where would that leave you? Unable to request a land claim and no husband of your own. Just like Coraline." She held Martha tight, filling her expression with the determination she knew she must feel. "I'm so tired of feeling desperation at all hours, like I must keep my life at a distance. I promise you I will never marry again. I will never leave you."

Martha studied her. "This situation is not new, Miss Sarah. You have already lost seven husbands, and promised up and down many times that you would not take another. What did Mr. Lark say to convince you this time was to be any different?"

"You believe it will be different?"

"I believe in your heart, you must believe it too, otherwise you wouldn't of put that man's life at risk. You hold more affection in your eyes than I've seen since Linden. You are not so selfish as to condemn a man you actually love." Martha's eyes said she was serious. She believed there might be something different this time, even though she had no idea what that difference could be.

It will be all right, Tobias told her at their wedding. *I promise.*

When Martha took her hands, they weren't empty this time. Her friend slipped a golden band into her palm, small, fragile, and unadorned in any way, but Sarah would know it anywhere. She had worn it when she was but a young girl of eighteen, when she pledged her life to the only other man she had truly loved. Then watched him die with her banded hand in his.

One year later, her father had taken it in exchange for an engagement to Mr. Quint. She mourned its disappearance through her next three husbands, before her heart hardened to save itself.

"Did you steal this too?" she asked.

Martha's cheeks pinked. "Yes. I figured at some point you would need a reminder that there was a time when you were very loved and loved someone in return. Linden may be gone, but his spirit has never left you, and I think you've been searching for him ever since."

Promise me, Sarah, Linden whispered the day he died. His smile filled her mind. *Promise me you won't give up.* How she had adored him and he cherished her. She would have gladly died in his place.

Her friend's eyes turned toward the sky where the stars twinkled out their song. *The lark sings while it flies, happy to be free.* Martha turned back to Sarah with a sad smile. "Now it is your wedding night. Dead or alive, you must find your husband."

32

Tobias returned to a silent wagon circle. He settled his mare, then tiptoed around the sleeping bodies leading to his wagon. Martha was near to the Harpers' girls, little Aphid on one side and Reeslie on the other, both snuggled close. Coraline and Alice Ann lay beneath their wagon, a book still propped upon the younger woman's chest where she had attempted to read by the dying firelight. Levi rode through the darkness on his rounds, keeping watch. When Tobias tipped his hat to his friend, he received the same in return along with Levi's salacious grin.

After the wedding, he and Jamison had helped Tobias rearrange the wagon bed so that for once, there would be ample sleeping room. Spending his wedding night on the ground in sight of everyone was not how he wished to spend it, especially if it was the last one he had.

With a deep breath and an even longer exhale, he stepped up to his wagon, pausing to say a quick prayer. He repeated Jamison's words at the wedding. *For a noble purpose and to a happy old age.*

You can do this, Tobias.

When he opened the flap, he found Sarah curled in the corner, blankets balled between her fists, still clothed in her golden wedding gown. When her gaze lifted, tear stains streaked her cheeks and his heart shattered to know it was fear for him which caused her anguish.

Quietly, he climbed into the wagon and tied the flaps closed once again. Darkness enveloped them save the barest glow of moonlight through the canvas. He offered her his outstretched arms. "Sarah," he whispered. "I'm here."

She needed no persuasion. Her arms flung around his neck, drawing him in until they knelt chest-to-chest, cheek-to-cheek, her thin frame wrapped tight within the comfort of his arms. Her golden curls spilled across his shoulders. "Martha told me to find you, but I couldn't. If you were dead, I didn't want to know. I was so afraid."

"So was I," he admitted. "I doubted everything I told you until I thought it would be better to outrun it."

"Then why did you come back?"

"I realized that even if I died tonight, it would be worth it to have every last second with you."

She drew back then. Her hand found his watch pocket and withdrew the timepiece, then opened it. She held it up to the moonlight.

"What time is it?" he asked. When she said nothing, he repeated the question. "Sarah? What time is it? What's the matter?"

With agonizing slowness, she turned the open watch so he could see the hands, both pointed for heaven. Midnight.

The watch clattered to the wagon boards, dragged along by its chain as his lips claimed hers, and all too quickly buttons found their loops empty. Suspenders loosened, stockings discarded. His fingers caught between blonde tangles, grasping strands without a pin to find.

"I love you," she whispered. "As though I've never loved anyone else." *As though Linden's ghost doesn't stand between us*, he thought but could never say it. He had survived. None else mattered.

"Have you ever been with anyone else?" she asked quietly, almost like a church mouse trying to hide from the congregation. Her timidity made him smile.

"No." He took each of her palms and kissed them softly. "I've never loved anyone like I'm about to love you."

Together they tossed and danced and tangled in a night of miracles. Decades of pain and distrust and heartache being offered up for the sake of one beautiful treasure. Worth more than any gold nugget, more than any town. It was the life he wanted until the last sun had set.

This was better than being Gifted. This...this was perfection.

Even after Tobias's breath grew restful in slumber, Sarah lay awake, waiting. Their wedding night had been a blessed experience, a series of spectacular moments filled with grace and joy and dare she say it without blushing, ecstasy? No, she couldn't even *think* about it without blushing. She felt heat spring to her cheeks and her muscles ache within her.

Tobias's every touch had been gentle, beckoning her on in a way no man ever had. Not even Linden. She wanted to remain in those arms forever, never leave the safety of this wagon. For outside those canvas flaps, the real world awaited. A dusty trail full of adversity. Perhaps if she never went to sleep, then morning would never come. They would never have to leave this pocket of grace God had wrapped around them.

If she didn't sleep then maybe...

Sarah woke with her heart pounding, her fingers entwined between Tobias's, squeezing them like she expected to extract lemonade. Either he did not notice, did not mind, or could not respond because he was... She squeezed her eyes shut, not wanting to know. Pretending was so much easier.

"You're too beautiful to be so tense."

Her eyes popped open to find him on his side next to her, his head propped upon one arm, the rise and fall of his chest in steady rhythm. The sun hadn't yet broken outside the canvas cover, but even in the near dark, she could make out the lines of his tender expression and felt the warmth beneath his fingertips as they slipped along her bare waist to pull her close against him.

She lifted her own fingers to trace directly over his heart. She could feel the hum of life inside and smiled, tears sliding unbidden down her cheeks. "You're alive," she whispered. She wrapped her arms around him and pressed her forehead to his chest. "You're here and you're alive. I thought I would have to dig a grave for you beside the trail. I thought...so very many things."

"Rest easy, my love. I have no intention of ever leaving you."

Thank you, Lord, she thought. *At last, I can find peace.*

Her husband pressed his lips against her skin, one tender caress into another, and for the first time in ten years, she was no longer afraid.

33

They reached the Snake River crossing on the third Tuesday of September, a bright day with cool winds to greet them. For two nights, they camped along its bank, awaiting their turn much as they had at the previous crossings. Although there were fewer wagons to contend with—so many had turned back, fallen behind, or perished—hundreds of pioneers still congregated at various points. Over the course of the days, they filled their rain barrels, washed clothes and themselves, and tended to tasks long overdue. Native tribes camped on both sides of the embankment, willing to barter supplies or offer their services as ferrymen or trail guides. At night, the white glow of firelight flickered behind their teepee skins and Tobias and Sarah lay awake listening to tribal drum beats in time to the rhythm of their hearts.

In all his thirty years, Tobias reckoned that right now, even exhausted, often hungry, and usually filthy, might be the happiest he'd ever been.

The morning before their turn at the crossing, he and Sarah exchanged a secret smile while they stored their bedrolls and their gaze lingered long after she finally joined the women at the fire. He could stand there like a fool all day watching her and get nothing accomplished. He was more than half-tempted to let the wagons move out without them. They would catch up...eventually.

Ignoring the wagon master duties he should really attend to and the great number of observers, he waited until she broke eye contact, then gripped her apron strings and spun her into his chest. Both hands moved to her jawline, drawing their lips together for a solid minute, only to be parted by the purr of catcalls and hollers. He distinctly heard Levi chortle, "Hey, no more babes on the trail! I got enough for the both of us!" and Sarah prettily hid her face against his shoulder. With one finger, he tipped her chin up and brushed another soft kiss upon her rose-tinted blush.

"They've known for weeks now," he smiled. "Are you embarrassed to be seen with me, Mrs. Lark?"

"I'm embarrassed to be carrying on in front of everyone."

"I'd bet you never carried on in front of anyone before."

"In front of respectable company, surely not."

"Respectable, you say?" His fingers moved to the back of her neck, tucked snug beneath her bonnet. "Every one of your dress hems is horribly frayed and you haven't worn a petticoat since our wedding. And where are your hairpins, my lady?" He let his fingers trail the length of her loose curls, coming to rest upon her hip. "I must say, it seems like any respectable company has been left long behind us."

She smiled. "I thought you were supposed to fix things. It seems you've broken me beyond repair." Then she lifted on toe and kissed him once more, dancing quickly out of his grip before he could reach for her again.

Sarah contented herself with staying close to Marie and Coraline throughout the day. The poor widow was so out of sorts after losing her husband, and the guilt of marrying so soon after sank deeper with every glance at her friend's despair. Especially after she and Tobias had carried on in front of everyone the way they did. She should be more sensitive to her friend's feelings. She knew, after all, the loss of a beloved husband along with the loss of many who were not. Even if Coraline and Oliver had not been as enthralled with one another as it always appeared—of which she had no basis for judgment—he had still been chosen as her partner. Without him to offer her a home, Coraline must be fearful for her future. Lately, it seemed the only one who could break her from her sullen mood was Marie and her maternal encouragement.

The rush of river water played accompaniment while the three women rinsed the day's dishes in the Snake River, the slap of washrags upon tin offering a rhythm to work by. Up and down the bank others did the same, mostly strangers and all at a distance. There was an understanding by this point on the trail that the wagon parties would remain separate. It took a pocketbook to embark on the way west, but fortitude to survive it. Most no longer wanted to share supplies or worse, have them stolen. Proximity only invited false sympathy and resulting disaster.

Marie was the first to add words to the river's melody. "Cora, honey?" she asked. "You mind passing me another tin?"

Without preamble, Coraline handed her another bowl from the supper stack and continued scrubbing the same one she had handled since they began. Marie and Sarah exchanged a troubled glance and Sarah bit her lip in a silent, *What can we do?*

Marie dunked the bowl into the river, swirling the water round and round. She kept her sights on Coraline as her washrag took a lazy circle about the tin. "Have ya thought about what you're gonna do in Larksong?" she asked. "Now that Sarah here's married to Mr. Lark, they'll need a schoolmarm. Seems like you'd be takin' for the job, what with all those books you haul around."

Even after discarding so many other provisions on the side of the trail, bartering others, and leaving several at Fort Hall, Coraline's book trunks had remained. Alice Ann read the same volumes for the fifth time, still flipping the pages as though they held secrets she missed the last time around. Coraline, however, read less and less as the trail wore on. After Oliver died, she nearly stopped altogether.

"What a wonderful idea," Sarah agreed, her washrag flipping droplets across their skirts. "I bet you've read every book to exhaustion. The children could learn much and you would still have the marm's house to live in."

Coraline considered her, her eyes sunken purple rings behind her spectacles. "Reading books isn't the same as teaching them, and Alice Ann has asked to be closer to the shore." Her focus turned again to the tin in her hands. "I won't be without. Jamison has offered us space on his claim."

"You're to share a home with Jamison?" Sarah couldn't keep the astonishment from her voice. Alice Ann was of age, but she was still impressionable.

Coraline's cheeks colored. "Not at all. He'll build on one side of the claim and Alice Ann and I will build upon the other. He will register the claim, but we will control our part. I had thought perhaps Martha would accept the schoolmarm position. Marie, your children do adore her."

Marie craned her neck to peek up the hill between the wagons. Martha played a skipping game with all five of the little ones, trying to pull Quint off her leg while Aphid tugged upon her hand. Her lips released a scold while even at a distance, it was clear she embraced every moment.

"Has she said anything?" Marie asked. "I would trust her 'till His kingdom's come, but she's never mentioned teachin' in her plans."

"I suppose it's because she never had plans before," Sarah said softly. "Now she does."

"We've got the whole wide world open to us..." Marie chuckled. "Never knew how big it was before."

Tin clattered as Coraline grabbed the stack of clean dishes and stood. "I'll get these back and stored before we head out." Then she was up the embankment and past Martha who returned a jerky wave, young Quint having managed to climb up to her shoulders. She swung him around, tickling his stomach severely while the child cawed.

Sarah could imagine her and Martha both married with babies of their own running across the farmyard. Their husbands with the older tots upon their shoulders while the women rocked their littlest ones beneath a beautiful colonnade. The ocean was the artwork outside their doors and a cool breeze taking away every care.

"Your husband did a good thing," Marie told her, "by purchasing your friend."

The front porch vision exploded behind her eyes. "Purchase?" Sarah stuttered. "Tobias didn't purchase her."

Marie's brow crinkled. "Oh lands, I'ma sorry. I only assumed...you see Levi told me it was Mr. Lark's idea to recruit other colored folks, not just those from our plantation. Has papers on everyone, so ya see why I assumed your friend...can you think of the cost it musta been to do it legal?"

A cost beyond reckoning, she thought. Her mother's words came back to her like a slap. *"He offered a sum higher than four of our field hands combined. It was impossible to refuse such an offer."* Few men would have been able to afford that kind of payment...unless they had a recent inheritance payout.

Quickly, she swiped the final dish dry and placed it atop the pile. "I think we should return to camp. We don't want them to leave without us."

Marie caught her elbow halfway up the hill. Her brown irises squinted, the crinkles at their edges formed by more than morning sunlight. "I didn't mean to upset ya," she said. "Mr. Lark's your husband, so if he says he ain't bought Martha, I must be wrong."

Sarah patted the woman's hand with a sturdy smile. "Don't give it a thought, truly. I'm not troubled by it, so you shouldn't be either."

They headed up the hill to re-pack the wagons, but when Martha asked Sarah if she needed help with the doing, she politely shooed her back to the Harpers. She needed to be alone to consider. She had told Marie she wasn't bothered by the news of her husband's financial dealings, but how could one not be?

As Tobias helped her tend the oxen, she watched his every move. Given the upturn of his lips and each helpful gesture, she wondered if Marie was mistaken. With the respect he garnered from the train, it had to be a misunderstanding. Maybe he told that story so they felt no reason to fear the slave catchers. Josiah and the Harpers had served them in Charleston, so it made sense he might still possess their papers. But not the others, not Martha.

She waited until he moved off to help Mr. Reed with the cattle, then with trembling fingers, peeled back the canvas flaps and slipped inside. Her eyes slid the width of the small space, wondering where he would keep important documents. He wouldn't want them to be stumbled upon, but would need easy access in case he required them at a moment's notice. When a slave catcher arrived to repossess a slave, there could be only minutes before that person was stolen away. After that, there were no assurances he or she would ever be found again.

It turned out the papers were in the very first place she looked, almost as though he didn't mind their discovery. Settled right underneath the rice barrel lid lay thirty-two sheets folded into a tight packet and secured with rawhide cord. She shimmied the cord until she could slip the papers out and unfold them. On the top, purchased first, were papers for Levi, Marie, and all five of their children. Those indicated an exchange of hands, slaves passed from brother to brother at no cost. What followed were all those she wasn't as well acquainted with: couples, full families, a few individual men purchased along the way. Benjamin, Avery, and Wallace were all accounted for, verification of their time in Tennessee.

As she neared the bottom of the stack, she found her emotions at war between hope and terror. Hopeful that perhaps Martha was the exception and she wouldn't find her name. Terrified because she knew she would.

It practically screamed at her from the last parchment. *This bill of sale grants one Mr. Tobias Lark with the purchase of a slave girl Martha Louis.* Redmond Walcott's signature scrawled the bottom followed by the date, *April 24, 1852.* When Sarah read the amount paid, she almost fainted at the cost. Her mother hadn't lied. Her husband purchased Martha for an amount only a rice empire heir could afford.

Tobias spouted freedom for all, but his kindness was two-faced. Offering freedom on one day, holding it hostage on the other.

That was how he would build his town. Curating supporters, making sure they were loyal, and if they proved not to be, holding freedom over their heads like Damocles' sword. She supposed she was no different now. There wasn't an official license yet, but they had half a dozen witnesses to their wedding and made the announcement to the entire train only days later. She was as bound to him as his slaves were.

What was she going to do?

Commotion circled the wagon like a clock hand ticking down the seconds. Chatter of her wagon mates without a care. Didn't they realize the ramifications these documents held? The Harpers' came from the Larks' plantation, so they must. Perhaps they didn't mind. Maybe they enjoyed their station, as she had believed about her father's slaves. Or perhaps it was simply better than the alternative unknowns.

Redmond Walcott had always treated his servants well and had given them all they needed. Exactly as Tobias did for the men, women, and children he purchased for Larksong. For Martha and Sarah, he even provided a wagon and every supply they required. She had found his generosity astounding, yet admirable. Now, his actions took a new and bitter taste. Back in Hawthorn Ridge, Martha had pretended to be content, while inside, she was never fulfilled. Her newfound freedom had garnered her courage, but could she ever be truly sound if she knew what Tobias had done?

Sarah heard him calling her from outside the canvas. Footsteps drew closer. He would find her with the purchase papers and he would know what she discovered about him. She should wrap them up and shove them back in the rice. Forget she ever saw them and he would never worry over her lost confidence. Her mind ordered her to hide, yet her body didn't move. She couldn't even cry despite wishing to quite badly.

A sudden coolness indicated the canvas had been withdrawn. The clatter from outside grew louder, yet Tobias froze in silence, visible out of the corner of her eye. His fingers clutched the wagon flap, his hat brim casting a diagonal shadow across his expression. He glanced once behind him before lifting himself into the wagon and closing the flaps again behind.

"Sarah," he breathed. He crouched beside her, half seated on stacked burlap sacks. "What are you doing?"

Only her eyes lifted. "You purchased Martha."

He didn't hesitate. He didn't stumble. She could tell in an instant that his defense was well prepared, likely thought on for weeks since the wedding, if not since the moment he met her. "You wouldn't come west with us if Martha was left behind. You said it right out when we met after the funeral."

"So, you purchased her like she was property?"

"Isn't that what you did?" Tobias asked.

"I did nothing of the sort! Martha is my friend."

"Now she is, but at one time your father purchased her first."

"It isn't the same at all. I never had any siblings, so Father—"

"Bought you one? Why didn't he adopt a child instead? Orphanages exist for exactly that."

"I..." Her father wouldn't have even considered an orphanage. A waif in their home would have caused more clucking tongues than social acceptance. "That wasn't an option for us."

He shook his head, removed his hat, and hung it on his knee. He swept his hair back behind his ears with an exhale. "Sarah, I love you and so I hope you'll forgive me for keeping this from you. As far as these people are concerned, I freed them. They each want a new life for themselves, their family, and this country. They agree things are not headed in the right direction and that slavery is an injustice. The colored folks should work alongside us, not for us. That's something your father didn't understand."

"He did. He worked in the fields alongside our servants every day."

"They may have brought in the harvest together, but who reaped the true benefits of the labor? Not his servants. They belonged to you and were not free to do as they wished. They could not make a living wage except for that which you provided. They could not take their belongings and their kin and leave as my family has chosen to do. They may have been cared for, but they were still trapped. That is where your father and I differ."

"You still can't purchase people and expect them to follow you," Sarah countered.

"In order to move across the country, they have to be owned by someone and their owner must have the legal papers. I promise this is all only to keep up a presence, to abide by the law which we know is corrupt."

"You say they are free, but what will happen if they leave? Will you remain true to your word? Or will you bring them back due to the papers which hold them captive? You say we are equal but are we only worthwhile in so far as we make Larksong thrive? Controlling others to create one man's perfect paradise?"

He sat back against the sacks, appearing stricken. "Even with purchase papers, if they choose to leave, I'll let them. Just as I was willing to let you. Please believe I would burn those papers in an instant if I thought it would make a difference."

He covered her hand with his own. "Sarah, I need you to trust me. As my wife, you're going to be a leader of Larksong, too. The people will look to you for guidance, and we need to be united in our advice. I promise—"

"Tobias!" A shout rang from beyond the wagon, strong and insistent.

"Ignore it," he told her. "Let my brothers handle it."

"Are you sure?" The call came again, closer and more urgent. She didn't want him to leave in the middle of this conversation, but if the town needed him...*Sarah*, she scolded herself, *isn't this the very point you were trying to make? That the town always comes first? Now here he is, choosing you over them, and you're shoving him away?*

The shouts turned in their direction, perhaps only fifty feet away...then forty...thirty...

Tobias sighed. "It's Reed. I'll send him to find Jamison." He squeezed her hand. "Wait here."

He yanked open the wagon flap and as expected, Clinton Reed raced toward them, a cloud of dust around his ankles and thoroughly harried in his pursuit. However, he was not alone. A crowd gathered in his wake, growing larger with each step until seemingly the entire town followed at his heels. Not a one seemed pleased with the approach.

This wasn't a usual request. Not at all.

Sarah gripped Tobias's arm. "What do they want?"

"I don't know." He turned and with fear swimming in both their eyes, held her gaze. "I promise everything will be well."

"How can you promise—" she began, but he was already stepping from the wagon box and reaching to help her down beside him.

"What's wrong, Clint?"

Mr. Reed thumbed over his shoulder. "That man. He says he's here for your wife."

"What?" A stranger rode a roan mare through the center of the commotion, approaching without haste yet his posture assured of business of a serious nature. Stern eyes peered from underneath his hat brim, a revolver at either hip, and spurs clinking with each clip of his horse's hooves. The silver star on his chest, while dingy and dented, gave a clear announcement of his occupation.

Tobias's arm protectively circled Sarah's waist. "Clint, who is that?"

Mr. Reed swallowed. "Deputy of Hawthorn Ridge. Your wife's wanted, Mr. Lark...for murder."

34

Murder? No, that was impossible.

Tobias held Sarah within the protective circle of his grasp, keeping both eyes on the stranger while his free hand instinctively hovered upon the revolver at his hip. As the man rode closer, one train member after another pointed him to their location. Tobias felt as though they were back in the Walcotts' foyer with Jackson Whitticomb's dead body at the bottom of the stairs and every accusing eye turning in Sarah's direction. Even Clinton appeared wary and he had seen the seedy underbelly of San Francisco.

The deputy halted in front of them. "Miss Walcott?"

Sarah gave a weak nod and Tobias drew her closer, staring the stranger down. "She's Mrs. Lark now and my wife. What need do you have with her?"

"Mr. Lark, I'd suggest you leave her to me." He drew a rolled parchment from his jacket and opened it to face Tobias...and the crowd quickly forming around them. Martha and Coraline appeared as he accepted the sketch with shaking fingers, the ladies' twin gasps enough to assure him what he viewed was real.

A primitive sketch stared back from the paper. The eyes were too narrow and the hair too dark, but blonde was a difficult element to capture in lead. Even with its inaccuracies, the woman in the drawing was clearly indicative of his wife. Above her picture scrawled the words: *Wanted for Murder. Reward—*

He crumpled the paper in his fist. "What is this?" he managed. The words felt like raw rice clogging his throat.

"I was commissioned by the sheriff of Hawthorn Ridge to return this woman to the Jefferson City jailhouse where she will await trial. She's certainly put me through the paces to find her."

"It isn't true!" Sarah cried. She gripped Tobias's arm, her thin nails upon his skin like pinpricks against frozen fingers, that's how numb he felt.

"This can't be," he managed. "She's been with me for months. We would have known if she killed anyone and, more importantly, there's no basis. Our party is based on mutual need. Sharing among the people. She had everything she needed and no need to cause ruin."

"I ain't concerned with what's been goin' on since she joined you," said the deputy. "This here warrant's for ten years of misdeeds. She killed her husbands. Every last one of them." He sniffed. "I guess 'cept for you."

"Where's your proof?"

"Got it right here. Signed testimony from the families." From the man's saddlebag, a leather packet was handed over and beneath the ties, handwritten testimonies by the dozen accusing Sarah of horrific crimes. From poisoning her first husband, Linden, to shoving Jackson Whitticomb down the stairs.

A statement signed by Morris Aspen rested halfway through the stack. Linden's father, if Tobias remembered the surname correctly. Mr. Aspen had been at the Walcotts' the day he went to purchase Martha. He said he was waiting to escort Sarah on a trip. Mr. Walcott mentioned how time away would help his daughter's unfortunate situation. Then she disappeared, along with her maid, and Tobias was dismissed before he could acquire additional explanation.

Sarah later told him her father's "time away" meant the asylum, but that could have also been a deal her father bargained with the police. Life in the asylum rather than see his daughter suffer imprisonment or worse, execution, for mass murder. She wouldn't be the first wealthy woman to earn such a dispensation.

"It's a lie, Tobias," Sarah whispered. Her voice was a mere breath against his neck. "You told me I was Gifted. You told me I was like you."

He returned the testimonies to the packet and looped the clasp. What was he supposed to believe? He could accept that her Gift killed her husbands without her knowledge, but it turned his blood cold to hear she was willingly responsible. Neither Gifted nor cursed, but wicked.

When he looked down, all he could see was a wave of golden curls spilling from beneath her bonnet. When he looked up, it was them and the deputy at the center of a hundred faces.

"Did you do it?" someone yelled. It sounded like Darcy Frendon, but he couldn't be certain.

"No!" Sarah turned to face the crowd, but her arms stayed strong about him. He was glad for it. When she let go, he would have to as well.

"I have been married seven times," she said, "and it's true they all died. Not because I murdered them, but because I'm cursed."

"So, death follows you. That's what you're telling us?" That time Tobias was sure he heard Darcy Frendon. "Are you the reason that little boy, Ephram, died?"

"What about Oliver Shay?" another voice called. "Left us short a physician! Get her out of here! Send her away before the curse befalls all of us."

"Enough!" Jamison pushed into their midst, positioning himself between Tobias and the deputy. He turned a circle, pegging each of their members in turn. "Curses? Banishment? You are the rotten ones. There is no such thing as curses."

"Did the Lord not strike down Egypt with locusts and boils?" Benjamin asked.

"Those were plagues, not curses."

"Perhaps a different name for the same punishment. She owns slaves, too. Even still she owns one!"

"Martha is not my slave," Sarah said, but a cacophony of arguments surrounded her words, suffocating them with their demands. Martha reached for her, but Coraline pulled her from the throngs with a simple clasp of her wrist and a shake of her head.

With every breath, the accusations grew more hideous. They said she was a witch whose spells protected only the Larks and herself. A

239

love potion on Tobias for how else could he be so blind to her deceit? She was responsible for all their troubles. Had Gabriella Reed truly left or had she been murdered too? Her body left for the coyotes to carry off? The crowd pressed closer until Tobias had Sarah backed against the wagon, sheltering her body with his own.

"Throw her out, or we'll mutiny!" Darcy demanded, then silence.

What was he to do?

Maybe she had murdered them and couldn't remember. Or maybe she did and was lying. Maybe she did deserve to be locked away. The world might be safer if she was. It all rested on his shoulders.

The night they met, he had questioned her motives, questioned what financial benefit she would receive, questioned everything...until the possibility of Giftedness overwhelmed all else. It hadn't been only him; at one point or another, all three of his brothers had expressed their concerns. Tobias was the leader of a wagon train; he didn't want to believe he had been duped and especially by someone he otherwise loved beyond cognition. Perhaps that was the true source of his err— he *did* love her beyond all rational thought. The real question was, how much did she love him?

"You know women can't be Gifted, Tobias." His father's words. *"How many times did I have to tell you and here's the proof?"*

The testimonies burned in his hands, physical proof of his wife's guilt. How much more did he need to finally come to terms with what he should have always accepted?

Jamison grabbed his arm. "You're their leader, Tobias. Say something! You're not going to let them take her, are you?" His brother's hazel eyes examined him like he was the villain of it all.

Maybe he was.

As much as he loved his wife, loved his family, loved Larksong, he saw no solution in sight. The people were rebelling. They didn't trust him anymore. If he stood by Sarah, they would leave. He couldn't send her to her doom, but he couldn't destroy their dreams of Larksong either. He was the leader, but he couldn't be the one to make this decision.

He handed the packet of testimonies back to the deputy and met Sarah's eyes. He wished he hadn't. "Forgive me?" he begged even while knowing her answer should be "*never*."

"Tobias..." Her word was a mere breath, a movement of lips more than an audible sound.

Turning out of his brothers' grips, Tobias shouldered through the crowd, untied his horse's reins, and galloped away before Jamison could shout the final breath of his name.

"Tobias!"

Sarah felt the world bend as her husband left her to an accusation so horrible, she couldn't fathom the consequences. They wouldn't possibly jail her for this, would they? No sane judge would. She would swing for this crime and no one would blink an eye or think the word *injustice*.

"My brother is a coward!" Jamison hollered after him before rounding on Cade. "And you didn't help!"

It was cowardice, but would she have done differently? Would she have believed her? Likely not. Not with such a wealth of evidence to the opposite. If her husband thought her a murderer, he also no longer believed her to be Gifted. It was the irony of ironies that his survival these last weeks had finally sparked her belief that she actually was. Without the promise of their entangled talents, there was nothing holding them together.

"Don't lose faith," Jamison assured her. He took her hands as the deputy wrapped rope thrice around them, knotting the end against her wrists. Jamison gave her fingers a firm squeeze that made her wish they belonged to his brother. "I'll make Tobias see reason. We'll set you free."

Martha nodded, fresh tears wetting her cheeks. "Bring me with you. I can swear your innocence."

Oh, her brave friend. How she wished she didn't have to be alone in this. Now they both were.

The smile she provided was marred by the ache in her chest. "Martha, you have been the sister of my heart since I was eight. I will always adore your spirit. But you know they will never hold merit to a colored woman's words. If I am committed, you will be, too." Unable to provide a proper embrace, she leaned her shoulder against Martha's. "Go to Washington. Have the freedom you know you deserve."

"Please, let me come with you. You are my sister. I can't give you up."

Sarah stepped away without meeting her friend's eyes again. As she turned to the deputy, she raised her bound wrists, her chin held high even though it quivered. He grabbed her arm and shoved her toward his horse.

She searched the rough terrain for some glance of Tobias, but all she saw were hundreds of other wagon trains moving toward the riverbank. Their dust trails peppered amongst the path, waiting for their chance at the new life she would now turn away from.

"Tobias let me go, Martha. It's best if you do too."

35

A grunt escaped Tobias's throat as he thrust his hands back into the scrub and yanked another pile of undergrowth and leaves into his chest. The roots came with them this time, the plains' golden dust flouring his legs like the bottom of a kitchen pan. He grabbed his hatchet again and swung, chopping the branches into fine twigs easy for bending into his desired form. Exactly as he had curved the skeleton of Sarah's wagon. Board by board, carefully, tenderly...with all the promise of tomorrow.

The structure before him wasn't careful or tender and it wasn't hopeful. It was a crooked beast of gnarled wood and twisted roots fifteen feet aloft. It didn't have definition. Just ugly and weathered like he felt inside.

Bending at the knees, he hefted a section against his chest and moved it to the other side of his creation. Then he grabbed the hatchet again and hacked at the wood until his arms throbbed. Sweat rolled down his spine even though he could have crafted as easily without effort. When he was constructing, he had the strength to move with ease...unless he chose not to embrace his Gift as designed. Right now, he wanted this task to be as difficult as the one he left behind.

When he first brought the idea of Larksong to his brothers, the idea had seemed so simple and he supposed it was. Simple in theory, impossible in practice.

They had curated their residents, each chosen by their individual skills, all with positive recommendations and merits to their names.

As carefully as they had been chosen, however, from the first step out of Independence, nothing went the way it should. Although he could fix wagon wheels, they still broke. Too many people had died. Oxen starved, cattle drowned on river crossings, pitiful rabbits and squirrels became the only hunt available for a week. Tobias wavered between loathing Daniel for staying in Charleston and wishing he was back there with him. Daniel had no Gifts, but right now it felt like he was the best off of them.

Tobias grabbed a board and slammed it against his creation, wood striking wood with a thunderclap across the clearing. Drawing his hatchet, he drew four slits through the board, the exact space needed to loop a slender branch around each and attach it in place. With a final swing, he lodged the hatchet blade into the side of the new addition.

"You about done there?"

Thirty feet away, Jamison sat atop his horse, wrists crossed at the horn. What kind of protector was Tobias to not hear a horse approach until it was thirty feet away? If he had been on watch and his brother was a bandit, he would be dead and the entire wagon party ravaged.

"What are you doing out here?" he grunted.

Jamison didn't approach or swing down from the saddle as expected. He pursed his lips, a low hum escaping his throat while his eyes cast to the wooden object of Tobias's frustrations. "Why, of all things, did your Gift take you back to Charleston and craft our family's Live Oak?"

"Our oak? No. This is just humbug, something thrown together and collided."

Jamison nodded to the structure. "Look again."

Tobias let his eyes roam up to the farthest reaches. A curved trunk formed from twisted branches, lashed together with braids of grass. Those rose to outstretched arms, waving in the wind. Leaves scattered amongst them, somehow having survived his emotional upheaval, and from the barren branches, thin silks of prairie grass waved like the delicate green moss so common to the Southern states.

Even with its crude form, his craftsmanship was clearly reminiscent of the great oak tree which stood outside their plantation house in Charleston. With gnarled branches that enticed one in the sunshine and threatened after dark. Where he climbed as a boy with his brothers and stood under imagining the world beyond his father's clutches.

He knew how he had made it, but why? Why this memory?

He placed his hand on the tree's trunk and closed his eyes. The breeze filtered through the branches in the hollow way wind moves in the winter, clacking empty twigs together in the highest boughs. He thought of home and the beautiful oak-lined plantation drive, the path where guests arrived in oiled black carriages, horse hooves prancing over packed earth. From high in their branches, he watched his father's acquaintances arrive, and as he grew, he hid behind the largest trunks to observe each invited belle step from her carriage. One dainty slippered foot, then a flash of petticoat, and finally the young lady's face. He dreamed of the day he would stand with his intended beneath the largest oak, its picturesque olive moss floating while moonlight glinted through the stars above. Women adored those sorts of romantic moments, especially when a proposal meant love, not merely a financially advantageous contract.

He had never wavered in his desire for love as a precursor to marriage, even though his father hadn't deemed it necessary. Tobias saw how his father ordered his mother like one of their servants and she happily obeyed, the glaze across her expression revealing how she could not release herself from her husband's pull.

Early on, the brothers agreed. Once they were old enough, they would steal her far away from Alonzo Lark's villainous persuasions. Finally, show her what good could come from a legacy that had, until then, only kept her hostage.

But they were ignorant children then. Their mother died and in time, Tobias walked dozens of women under the plantation oaks. Loneliness became a cloak, his grief clutched inside, and none of those potential brides ever earned his trust or his vast promises for a shared future. Not until Sarah.

Jamison's voice emerged from beside him. "It isn't our fault Mother died. You understand that, right?"

"But we didn't save her. We made an oath, Jamison."

"You were twelve. I was eight. Cade was a toddler. None of us would have been able to save her. You can save Sarah though." He paused, took a breath like he thought Tobias would belt him if he spoke again, but then did so anyway. "You don't believe she did what they say. Neither do I."

Tobias opened his eyes and whirled on his brother. Jamison took a step back as he moved forward. "There was a mountain of evidence against her, James. Do you think all of those people lied? Did the deputy ride a thousand miles for nothing? Why would he do that?"

"Do you honestly think God led Garrett to her for no purpose? You need to ask yourself if she lied to you, or if you want to believe she did so you can keep Larksong intact. Trying to create a perfect world isn't going to bring Mother back."

"Larksong was never about a perfect world. It's about creating a place that's right and just and fair."

"Right and just and fair, you say? Three things Mother never had with Father. She was never happy, so you think you can't be, either. Not unless you're with someone like you."

"I'm afraid I'll hurt her. If she's Gifted, I can't turn my ability on her. She'll never suffer as mother did."

There it was. The truth and horrible way of it. He would rather lose her than do what his father did.

"There are more ways we can hurt someone than by using our Gifts," Jamison scolded. He was slipping into his pastoral voice and didn't even recognize it, but Tobias did.

"Stop lecturing me over how we can hurt people. I well know."

"Then stop using your Gift as a bushel to hide behind. To not live the life God made you for. Maybe there are no Gifted women. Tell me why that matters. We really might be the last ones left from that ship, but it doesn't change how we treat people. I know the evidence is against her, but do you really believe Sarah would murder with intent?"

"One doesn't have to be Gifted in order to kill." Tobias felt the rough bark of the tree beneath his fingertips, heard the rustle of the leaves above and his vision swam in swirls of color.

"If I go after her, the people will abandon us like Garrett did. Like

Daniel. A town isn't made of three brothers. What good is building a new life if we have no one to share it with?"

"Exactly. You deserve someone to share it with. Search your heart and answer me true. Do you believe she's guilty?"

"I don't know."

"I think you do. Remember this?"

Tobias found Sarah's wooden lark being placed into his open palm. The twigs bent together to form wings up to a beak open in song. Still as beautiful as the day he made it for her.

"You believe Sarah's innocent," Jamison told him. "As innocent as Mother ever was, and your heart deserves to know for sure."

36

For an hour, they bounced along the rough terrain, Sarah barely able to keep her balance and unable—also unwilling—to grip the deputy's arm for support. Her wrists stung where the rope met her skin and the saddle's rough leather jabbed through her skirt to pinch her thighs. Whenever the deputy shifted his weight, his legs pressed flush against hers, his chest firm against her spine. His constant presence curdled her stomach. Would they ride the entire way back to Missouri like this? Could one travel such a distance merely on horseback?

As the sun's orb swung lower overhead, devastation crept in like a bandit at a wagon circle. The people of Hawthorn Ridge had finally brought Linden's vengeance upon her. She hadn't fulfilled his goals, hadn't picked up her poetry once since marrying Tobias. Hadn't even thought on it until now. The tiny tenement he dreamed of had turned into a wood-planked home overlooking the sea; her babies with a beautiful life rather than the hardships she would have endured with him. Hardships she should have accepted. Although it appeared Tobias's Gift had indeed broken hers, Linden's ghost still lingered between them, as though he walked beside her every step of the trail. He let Tobias live, but he never forgot her husband stood in another man's place.

No, she didn't blame Tobias, didn't hate him. Not for this, not for the slave papers, nor any of it. She couldn't. She loved him and all she could do was be thankful he still lived. He would be well without her.

He would find a noble wife, a frontier woman with knowledge

beyond plantation ballrooms and stitched samplers. Someone he could share a life with to a ripe old age, surrounded by his brothers and their wives and multitudes of babies. God had in the strangest way answered all their prayers today. Larksong would grow and thrive and become the beautiful town Tobias always dreamed of. She would go to prison where marriage wasn't allowed or to the asylum her father had originally planned on. Or worse. Yet, in any outcome, at last, the curse would be broken.

Judging by the sun's position, the hour neared eight in the evening when they turned off the main trail, following a single set of wheel tracks and oxen hoof prints. The light fell low against the dirt road, casting everything in a deep crimson haze. Coupled with the silence of twilight, it set her senses on edge as an eerie feeling pricked her skin.

"Only a little farther," the deputy told her, the first words from his lips since their departure an hour ago.

She looked back, but the main trail blended into the purpled landscape, any prairie schooners now dark pricks against the sky. The Larks would be dousing campfires and unrolling bedding. Tomorrow, Coraline, Marie, and Martha would find one fewer pair of hands to help with breakfast, however incompetent those hands could be.

A sharp jab to her side brought her back around. The deputy veered the reins left and she raised her still-bound hands to shield her eyes, squinting against the setting sun. An open wagon appeared in the glow, smaller than most prairie schooners, with a single horse tied beside it. A man rose from the nearby campfire, his form a silhouette within the horizon's burning glow. He strode toward them, finally stepping into the wagon's shadow.

Her breath caught. "*Mr. Aspen?*"

Morris Aspen reached for her, his narrow fingers fitting her waist to ease her down from the saddle. His hair and beard were longer and greyer than the last time she saw him, his clothes filthy and frayed, presumably after months upon the trail. This time, there was no smile, no friendly embrace, no warm words of condolence. Every feature hardened, eyes narrowed, lips drawn tight, the ends turned into a scowl. Had her father sent him to assist the deputy? Redmond Walcott wouldn't be able to leave his plantation to chase after her, not with planting and harvest at hand. Of course, he would send his trusted second in his place. She couldn't expect Mr. Aspen to be pleased after such an arduous journey, especially if made in that rather inadequate wagon. How had they even managed to catch up to her?

Her feet hit the dirt, the feel of solid ground nearly buckling her legs from beneath her. On instinct, her bound fingers scrambled for Mr. Aspen's sleeve to steady herself, but it was only seconds that he allowed its use. He reached for a square leather satchel at his hip and lifting the flap, removed a thick sum of cash, bound with twine in both directions. He held it out to the deputy; however, when the other man grasped the edge, he did not immediately let go.

"Do you still have the testimonies?" Morris asked.

The deputy withdrew the damaging papers from his saddlebag and handed them over. "Worked exactly as you predicted. A few questioned the claims but were easily overrun. No one wanted a murderess in their party."

"Excellent. My appreciation..." Mr. Aspen's brows raised. "...and your silence?"

The man yanked the money away. "For this sum, I'll take it to my grave."

Sarah stared blankly between them as the money was stored in the deputy's saddlebag. Her father-in-law was behind her arrest? What nightmare was she living in? He knew she was innocent!

Mr. Aspen's scowl twisted upward into a hollow smile as they watched the deputy mount his horse and quickly disappear back through the brush. The sun's final rays dipped behind the horizon, leaving only the campfire's warm glow flickering upon their expressions.

Mr. Aspen tucked the testimonies into his satchel. "It's easy to find a mercenary out in these parts. Everyone is so uncivilized. I'm pleased to see he found you in one piece."

"A mer-mercenary?" She stumbled over the word. "Mr. Aspen, what have you done?"

"Done? Only what I needed to do. The police would do nothing when you disappeared. They determined after so many husbands dead, you must have taken your own life. They dismissed the case, but then your letter arrived from Fort Kearney. We knew where you had been and where you were headed. Still, the police refused to help. Your father entrusted me to bring you home by whatever means necessary."

A spark of hope lit in her middle. This was a misunderstanding. That's all it was. Mr. Aspen could return her to Tobias and explain everything. The testimonies were forged and now she had a witness to declare her innocence. "I'm sorry you went to so much trouble, but you must take me back to my wagon party." She extended her wrists for him to untie.

Mr. Aspen maintained the same hard-set expression. "I'm afraid I cannot do that."

"Untie me or take me back?"

"Either. I will release your bonds once I am assured you won't run. Are you hungry?" He motioned to the pan sizzling upon the fire. For the first time, Sarah acknowledged the scent of cooked squirrel and felt her stomach rumble. Although she had eaten supper, this meal was cooked over wood without any buffalo chips in sight.

It would only help her to be polite. "I would like some, thank you."

She sat beside the fire and watched as he scooped some stew onto her plate along with a hard crust of bread. He drew his canteen and poured water into a tin cup, helping her sip from the edge. The cool moisture soothed her dust-scratched throat.

Accepting the spoon he handed her, she awkwardly scooped the stew to her lips. A few drops spilled upon her skirt, lost in the endless dust already accumulated there. The squirrel was delicious, incredibly tender considering its method of preparation. Despite his investment in servants, all those years as a widower had taught Mr. Aspen decent culinary skills.

He sopped up his meal with the crusted bread, his attention never once sliding from her face. The rough creases on his neck and brow turned dark in the firelight and she wondered when the years had become apparent. Why agree to come himself? Why had her father not hired someone from the start? It seemed simpler than entrusting the task to a man whose farthest western reach was Kansas City and who had a servant polish his shoes every Friday evening. Look what the frontier had done to him. Never had she seen him so disheveled, nor would she have suspected him capable of false murder testimonies and mercenaries for hire. If Linden could only see his father now...

"You don't belong out here," he said. "In this mess with savages at every turn. You are a lady with an inheritance awaiting you. A plantation with servants and an easy life. You will not be forced to marry again; your father has already promised it."

"Then you do not believe me a murderer?"

His lips raised in a half-smile. "No."

"And Papa does not intend to send me to the asylum? He will allow me to remain in my own home?"

"That is your father's intention."

She could have a new relationship with her parents, one built without unfair expectations. No more risk of lives destroyed. The townsfolk would still call her Widow Walcott, they would still whisper, but her own family would embrace her in totality, curses and all. She did miss her parents, but she feared her heart said goodbye long ago.

She set her spoon in the tin and shook her head. "I don't belong in that life anymore. I don't want it."

"But you want *this*?" His arms swung in both directions, indicating what they both knew lay beyond the darkness. She stared into the fire and focused on the crackle, a reminder of every time her life burned a little more trapped in Hawthorn Ridge.

"The plantation life is built on slaves and daughters alike being sold off to the highest bidder. For profit or an alliance, either way, freedom is traded. Anything different becomes another way to divide and alienate. In Washington, we will stand shoulder-to-shoulder as equals. As much as I love you and my parents both, I do not think you could handle the woman I've become." She paused, inhaled, glanced at Mr. Aspen because she knew her words would likely upset him. "Most importantly, I refuse to leave Martha or my husband."

"Your *husband*?" He gripped his spoon with a powerful fist. "Who have you married now?"

"A lovely man. We married three weeks ago and he believes he has broken the curse. His reasons sounded so fantastical at first, but I think he was the key to everything." Her eyes implored him to understand. "Not since your son have I felt such content."

"You unruly harridan," Mr. Aspen spit, such that spittle hissed into the flames. He sprang to his feet and his tin bowl clattered to the ground, the remains of his stew darkening the dirt while he glared down at her. "For ten years, you told me you regretted the day Linden died, that you wished you could turn back the clock and return him to life. Now you tell me he can so easily be replaced? You would give up your life, your parents, and Linden's memory for this rebel who believes all men are created equal?"

She felt herself lean away involuntarily, but did not waver in her words. "All men *are* created equal. My brother-in-law preached on it once. 'Neither Jew nor Greek, neither slave nor free, not male and female; for you are all one in Christ Jesus.'"

Mr. Aspen stared at her like she had lost her mind. Although the Walcotts were a Catholic household, although they attended Mass every Sunday without fail, never had they discussed the Lord so openly. Her parents, like Mr. Aspen, likely believed she couldn't quote the Bible at all. And six months ago, they would have been correct.

Much had altered since then, not only her, but her faith. Through the Larks, she had found so much more than freedom and a broken curse. She also learned a new way of living and she would not give that up now.

"I loved your son, Mr. Aspen," she said gently. "I still love him and wish he were with us. I am allowed to wish for those things, yet find a way past them. It has been ten years and eight husbands. Is it not time for me to have back an ounce of the happiness Linden once gave me?" She had been overcome with guilt for so long that maybe it was time to relinquish that guilt to the One who made her. She would never hear Linden say he forgave her, but she finally believed she could be forgiven.

Mr. Aspen stepped toward her, rage in every movement, fingers fisted at his sides. "No. You do not deserve it. You deserve to live in that regret, to have your happiness stolen as you stole the life from my son. Your cholera killed him and I'm determined to make you remember every day."

"Please," she begged. "We have been friends for many years. Except for you, no one cared for your son more than I, but it is time you let this bitterness go. Before it destroys your soul."

"My soul? Consider your own, my girl, before you aim to save mine." Quick as a weevil devours grain, he snatched her arm and dragged her to her feet. Her bowl spilled across her skirt and he kicked it away, bouncing against the rocky ground. He grabbed her chin and forced it to face him, his own mere inches away.

"I tried to convince you with kindness, but in lieu of that, I will use force. You are coming home with me. You will either rot for an eternity in prison or be convicted to the asylum. You will have everything you love stolen from you, for that is what you did to me the day you killed my son. I might have murdered your husbands, but never forget it was your hand which writ their sentence."

There was nothing after that.

No sound.

No speech.

For an instant of time, there was simply silence.

Then a monstrous roar ravaged her ears and he gripped her arms, still bound together, a smirk of satisfaction layered beneath cold-eyed repugnance. She longed to faint and forget what had occurred. She held her breath, but too soon her body betrayed her will, and air released in a rush. Her chest rose and fell and tightened, her heart raced and burned within.

Emotions tumbled inside, each one pressing to escape more forcefully than the last. Fury. Grief. Relief. Pain. How could the same man who fathered Linden's kindness also murder six innocent men? How could he place blame for his son's death solely on her control? On the edge of death herself, she had done all she could do to save him.

Because of this man, for ten years she had drowned in hopelessness. She couldn't have saved Linden, but perhaps her second marriage would have been successful after all. She would never know now, all because of one man's grief-induced mania. He had robbed six men of their lives, ruined their futures and their families, and destroyed hers in the process. He had wrought deceit and vengeance and everyone believed it without question. Even Tobias.

Morris Aspen would not steal her happiness. Not anymore.

Even if it took her final breath to stop him.

Clasping her fingers, she swung her bound fists upward, slamming them into his nose. With a yell, his grip loosened and she dashed toward the darkness. He was back in an instant, his arms around her from behind, lifting her heartily from her feet and carrying her toward the wagon. She kicked his shins, determined to drive him to the ground then shove him, beat him, steal his revolver if she could. He dropped her in a heap and this time when she leaped again, he was ready. He seized her arm and with a twist behind her back, jabbed his revolver into her spine.

"I would prefer not to kill you," he growled, "but I will."

"I'm not worth the moral struggle," she gasped. "Leave me out here alone. Without food or a proper shelter, chances are I'll die before too long anyway. I'm not worth this fight."

"You're not." His eyes moved above her head into the shadows. Waited a beat before drawing his expression into a self-satisfied grin. "But I suspect he might be."

Fifty feet away, horse and rider emerged from the shadows one foot at a time, the firelight revealing Tobias's outstretched revolver before it revealed his face. "Mr. Aspen!" he shouted. "Let her go!"

The pistol moved to her temple. "I assume you're the latest in her line of husbands?"

Tobias appeared confused. "I am. Now, let her go and we can all walk away from this."

"Not all of us will walk away, I'm afraid. My son is but one example. You, I'm afraid, will be another."

Why wasn't Tobias moving? Did he have others waiting in the darkness? Maybe his brothers or Levi, but he wouldn't have placed them in danger. Besides, no matter their proximity, by the time they rushed in, it would be too late. "Run, Tobias!" she screamed. "He'll kill you! Run!"

Instead, he offered her a tight smile. "It will be all right, Sarah. Didn't I promise you?"

He had, but how could he have accounted for this? He hadn't believed her. He had left her. Did he believe her now? Had he heard everything that had been said? Was he watching from the shadows?

She must believe he had a plan. A little faith was all she needed.

Slowly, she nodded. "You did."

Never taking his eyes off her, he dropped from the saddle into a crouch, placing his gun in the dirt beneath him. Finally, he looked up at his opponent. "Please, let her go."

"How polite." Mr. Aspen leaned in, his breath moist against her cheek, so close she could only see his chin. "I hope you're keeping count, Miss Walcott."

Then his revolver slid forward and a single shot reverberated through the clearing.

"That's eight."

37

That's eight, Miss Walcott."

Sarah screamed amid Morris Aspen's laughter as the bullet streamed through the left side of her husband's chest. The darkness and distance concealed its exact entrance position, whether higher in the shoulder or closer to the heart. He landed with one leg underneath him, both hands grasping at his chest, eyes wide while he stared at the inked sky above.

With all her strength, she struggled against Mr. Aspen's solid grip, unable to care if he shot her too. "Tobias!" she cried. "Tobias!"

Shallow groans emanated from between her husband's lips as blood oozed from his wound, half his shirt now stained with it. "Oh God, do something!" she cried. What would the Lord do? He hadn't stopped the bullet; what purpose would He have for saving them now?

Faith, Sarah, have faith!

Mr. Aspen pushed her forward, then shoved her to her knees beside her husband. "See this?" he spat. "You did this."

"No," she gasped. "You did."

He shook her arm, the force jostling her entire body. He holstered his revolver and squatted beside her. "This. Is. Your. Doing." One venomous word slithered after the last. "Your. Fault. Without you, my son would be alive and this man would go on to live a full life, likely with another wife and children of his own. You brought this sorrow upon him and upon yourself."

She couldn't speak. What does one even say to such evil?

"I am not an unjust man, Sarah. You know this is fair punishment; however, I will allow you a final moment to say your goodbyes." With the draw of a knife from his boot, he cut her bonds and paced back to the fire.

Sobs drove forth as she stared at Tobias's barely blinking eyes, his chest heaving erratically as she pressed her palm flat against the open wound. The bullet had lodged higher in his shoulder, but warm crimson still spilled from beneath her fingertips.

We'll break the curse, Sarah.

The curse was indeed broken, but not because of them. How cruel. How twisted.

Why, Lord, she asked silently. *Why would you allow him to survive this long only to steal him from me now? Why would you allow a man like Mr. Aspen to be overcome by the devil's inclinations? To murder men whose only crime was to have married me?*

Tobias's breaths grew ragged, his sides unnaturally drawn, lips parting as he gasped against the agony.

It is not over, my child.

But it was over. Her husband was dying beneath her hands. She pressed harder to stop the bleeding, but his back arched with her touch, his fingers now white-knuckled against his side. "Tobias," she cried, desperate for him to hear her. "You said you were the only one who could survive the curse. You said everything would be all right."

"I'm sorry," he gasped. "I was wrong." His brown eyes flicked to her face once before they closed.

"Tobias?" She shook his shoulder. "Tobias!"

She whipped around so quickly, the world tilted sideways before righting itself again. She glared at Mr. Aspen where he lounged beside the fire, ankles crossed like they were old acquaintances in her parents' parlor. But they weren't. They never would be again.

"How could you?" she shouted. "I was your daughter! You were supposed to love me!"

Mr. Aspen shrugged. Both shoulders raised and then lowered beneath an expression of utter apathy. "You were supposed to love my son."

"I did! But I love Tobias too!"

In a blind rage, she reached for her husband's revolver. She had never fired a gun, but she was certain she could figure it out. She swung the barrel around, aimed. Morris simply stared right back, the fire flickering in his gaze, daring her to complete the task. He didn't think she had the gumption. He still believed her to be a lady raised on cumbersome crinolines and dainty gloves. She who, before the west, had ridden horses, but never mucked a stable or gotten on her knees to pluck a stone from beneath one's hoof. Her aim remained still, her sights never wavering. Tobias's blood stained her hands and she couldn't allow that crime to go unpunished.

When the shot sounded, the explosion of it startled her. Morris Aspen's lips parted in silent surprise before he crumpled upon himself. His hand clutched his chest mere seconds, before everything went still. He never even spoke a word.

Tobias's revolver remained cold in her hands, the chambers fully loaded. She hadn't fired. Hadn't taken the chance.

"Mrs. Lark?"

She spun the revolver toward the voice, aiming with intent until she caught sight of Clinton Reed's left hand up in surrender and the other pointing his revolver at the ground, still smoking. Rock crunched underfoot as he moved forward to nudge Mr. Aspen's body with his boot. Satisfied, he holstered his weapon and returned to Sarah's side.

"Are you hurt?" he asked. She shook her head and glanced at Tobias. He hadn't moved.

"I was too late," Clinton said. "I followed him...I thought it best to keep a distance...but I was too late."

At that moment, she couldn't dwell over the weight of Mr. Reed's actions or inactions. Why he had followed or why he spared her from ending Morris Aspen's life. She must be grateful that he had.

For Tobias's sake, she needed to maintain perspective.

"Help me lift him into the wagon. We have to stop the bleeding and get him back to Jamison." She could only pray the minimal doctoring skills Tobias taught her would be enough.

She laid one hand on her husband's cheek, the other to his wound, warm and sticky beneath her fingers. His lids fluttered open and she stared into his muddy eyes, uncertain if they could even recognize her. "You cannot die today, my love. You have too much left to build."

38

When the bullet slammed into Tobias's shoulder, he hit the ground, skidding into the dirt and spraying grit behind him. Fire raced through his body, pulsating with a horrifying heat. He ground his teeth, but still couldn't contain the moan of agony that escaped his lips. His left hand fisted against his side while his right dug into the cool earth. His fingers curled around the rocks and weeds beneath him, while his back arched, trying to relieve his body of incredible pain.

He was dying. Living couldn't possibly feel this way. Or was it worse because of his Gift? Did the Gifted always suffer an excruciating death?

He screamed, his eyes sliding closed, the sound echoing inside his skull. He didn't know if anyone else was even there. All he knew was this agony, ripping his limbs, slicing him open. How long until he died? Would it be soon? *Please*, he prayed, *let it be soon*.

An explosion shattered the empty air. A gunshot or his brain crumbling? The world imploding? Was that what happened when a Gifted died? He would be responsible for the disintegration of the universe?

Ridiculous. His father died and many other Larks before him and the Earth continued right on as expected.

Tobias! He opened his eyes and a face appeared surrounded by a glowing halo. *You cannot die today, my love. You have too much left to build.* Hands on his face, the only thing holding him anchored to this life. The pain, he couldn't...it wouldn't stop. It wouldn't stop. It wouldn't...

His eyes shot open, even though he hadn't closed them. *Help him*, he heard a voice say. He was pretty sure she shouted, but to his ears, it appeared muffled and far, far away. *Please!*

I can't, came another, this time male, strained. *My Gift can't save him when he's Gifted too.*

The hands left his face, the beautiful halo lifting to look past him. *You went to medical school. You trained with Oliver Shay. Don't use your Gift, use your brain as God intended!*

It isn't that easy!

It is! Stop letting your Gift control you, Jamison. Aren't you always telling us how God made us for more than this life? This is what you're made for. Please, save him.

A firmer hand pressed against Tobias's wound, bearing down, shooting another race of fire straight down the bullet wound to his core. Why were they trying to kill him? He threw his hands out and one of them gripped another man's fingers. They squeezed. *I'm here, Tobias.*

Jamison. It was his brother's hand upon his wound, even though they both knew it was futile. Jamison couldn't save him, but he would pretend to try for Sarah's sake.

Sarah. That was who belonged to the halo. He had wanted more time.

He laughed. Maybe his wife was cursed after all.

Sarah knew the end was near. As much blood as there was, it had to be. With her own hands pressed tight to the wound, she had managed to stifle the flow long enough for Mr. Reed to drive them back to the wagon party, although Tobias never woke, despite the occasional outcry. Now that Jamison had taken over ministrations, however, blood flowed anew.

His hands were covered with it, his fingers desperately searching for the bullet which quickly stole the life from her husband's body. To afford Jamison focus, she tried to keep the few remaining Larksong residents away, but another rainstorm blew in with a vengeance, torrents breaking upon them, and she decided perhaps it was better to face her husband's death amongst friends than to face it alone.

Only a handful remained of their original party: the Larks, the Harpers, Clinton of course, Martha, Coraline, and Alice Ann. All else had abandoned the group the minute they learned Tobias chased after his murderous wife.

Martha and Coraline knelt in the mud beside her, rain-drenched, bone-chilled, and trembling. Sarah squeezed their fingers until her own went numb, but they didn't complain or move away. Martha rested her head on Sarah's shoulder and began to sing what sounded like a lullaby. She didn't know if it came from her mother or Martha's or if the words were an invention of her friend's imagination. They soothed what little could be soothed and she was grateful.

With Tobias's next shriek, Cade turned and ran. Alice Ann followed. No one went after them. Every person deserved to grieve in their own way.

As her eighth husband's breath grew more ragged, as the light slowly left his eyes...as his distance between this life and the next shortened, Sarah clung to Martha's song and prayed.

39

At long last, the bullet was removed and the wound closed—by Sarah's own needle no less—but Tobias still hadn't awakened, and they couldn't afford to remain stationary any longer. October loomed with a significant distance left to travel before winter. At least once they reached the coast, they would not contend with snow. Or so they had been told. None of them knew for certain.

They refused to speak too much of what would happen once they reached their claim. Even if Tobias woke, his injury could leave him permanently limited in his abilities. Without his Gift, building would be more complicated and unlikely to be completed before spring.

Martha offered to drive the mules so Sarah could ride beside Tobias in the wagon bed. She slept sometimes too, her hand in his, and imagined all was well. Then she would wake, and he wouldn't and she would suffer visions of all those husbands who went before. Every glance at Tobias's pale skin wrought a fresh memory.

On the third day, when Martha brought Sarah her supper bowl, she didn't release her grip immediately. Her tone held compassion and such sympathy. "You can't stay in this wagon forever."

"I know." There was still work to be done and far fewer hands to do it. Guilt riddled that she couldn't pull herself from this spot when she knew Coraline was still grieving Oliver, and Jamison and Cade were likely as distraught over Tobias's injuries as she was. Neither of them believed Jamison's healings would have the least effect. They knew it was only a matter of time before the end and couldn't bear to be there when it happened. She couldn't bear not to be.

She met her friend's gaze. "I'm afraid if I leave, he won't be here when I return. If I only have this minute, I want to spend it by his side. It's what he would have done for me."

No, he wouldn't have, she scolded. *He would have been the leader he always was. He would have known there was a world outside this wagon.* But even her logical reprimands couldn't break her away from his side.

She tugged on the supper bowl, but Martha remained firm. "He was going to give up Larksong for you," she said.

If Sarah had been holding her bowl, she would have dropped it. "What do you mean?"

"When he followed after you. Most of the train didn't want him to. He was willing to lose everything else to prove your innocence."

"He told you this?"

"No. He told Jamison, but Alice Anne's nosy and eavesdropped from under the wagon. So pretty soon, we all knew. Tobias told Jamison to build the town without him. For him to be the new leader and he'd be a good one at that. We all knew he would. Jamison's always had everyone's best interests in mind."

"He would. He does."

"Tobias was going to follow you even if you did murder those men. He said he'd plead your case so at least you wouldn't hang. Such an honorable man."

"He purchased you!" Sarah blurted. She hadn't realized she was even going to tell Martha until the words tumbled out. She had figured if she survived Mr. Aspen, she would take the secret to the grave and pray the slave catchers never found them. But now that the laundry was airing...

"Tobias bought you from my father, but I had no idea until a few days ago. Marie accidentally told me and then I found the papers in a rice barrel. I thought you deserved to know." Her glance moved to the canvas top, anything to avoid her friend's derision.

However, derision was anything but the tone from Martha's lips. "I already knew," she said softly.

Sarah's gaze fell. Martha was...*smiling*?

"Marie told me before we left Independence. She believed I should understand who I had chosen to follow."

Then why when Sarah contradicted her, did Marie pretend to be mistaken? *Of course*, she thought, Marie held tight to the vows she made with Levi. She would never purposely sow seeds of adversity in another's fledgling marriage. She likely figured if Sarah didn't know, it was because Martha didn't want her to.

"Did it not upset you?" Sarah asked her. "Knowing he still owned you?"

"At first, it did, but what other choice did I have except to return to Hawthorn Ridge? After running, Mr. Walcott was sure to sell me off for good. At least here, I had you. It wasn't long though before I realized how my papers in Mr. Lark's hand truly did mean freedom. Look what all that man gave me." She swept her hand about the wagon, but Sarah knew she didn't only mean the space within. Martha offered a small smile, embarrassment easing across her features. "Besides, I always figured he did it for you."

For *her*. Even through eight weddings, even loving Linden with every piece of herself, Sarah didn't think she had ever understood the type of love a man could truly be capable of. Now it lay before her and she doubted if she would ever be deserving of it.

Although he offered no other indication of cognition, Tobias's chest still rose and fell with ease. Her fingers lifted a lock of sweat-soaked hair from his cheek and tucked it behind his ear. He had saved Martha for her. Changed his plans, offered up his dreams and perhaps his life for *her*. It was a debt she couldn't repay.

Her fist rose to stifle a sob. She couldn't have him awaken and hear the words she held like torture to her soul. Tripping down the wagon step, she stumbled across the circle, and through their family's concerned calls, the only members of Larksong left to care. So few remained, and she was responsible for the departure of so many.

Martha didn't stop her or ask her to slow. She abandoned Sarah's meal and allowed herself to be pulled along until everyone else appeared as children in the distance. Sarah fell to her knees in the brush, all her emotion spilt over in that dusty field, her mind and body wracked over all she lost and would still lose.

She wanted to mourn forever. Weep until she drowned. Her breath came in great heaves, drawing upon the weight in her middle and the ache of her heart.

"He's...done...exactly as...Li-Linden did," she sobbed. "Giving...up everything...for me. I can't let him...lose his dream...if he...if he..." She couldn't say the last word. *If he lives.* What if he didn't? "If I never married Linden..." No, she couldn't manage that thought either.

Martha sat back on her heels and held Sarah at arm's length. Her brown eyes were bright with moisture, but surer than Sarah had ever seen them. She wasn't looking at her shoes; she wasn't looking at her folded fingers. There was conviction reflected there and something more. The courage Sarah didn't have. Despite sorrow's insistent grip, that gaze stemmed her tears.

"You think Linden would've lived if you'd only refused him?" Martha asked. Sarah's resulting nod met a tongue cluck of disapproval. "Maybe so, but what does it do to wonder? You'd only die a thousand deaths with him instead of living the life right in front of you."

With both thumbs, she swiped the tears from Sarah's cheeks and stole her hands. "I've never had the kind of love you have. One day with him or a thousand years, don't you know how blessed you are?"

Blessed? Losing seven husbands had never felt like a blessing. Discovering her father-in-law murdered six of them seemed even less like one. But what would her life and her dreams be today if Linden had lived, if Mr. Aspen hadn't done what he did? It was no justification for the horrors he wrought or the lives he stole, but without him, she would not be sitting here. Martha would not be saved from a life of eternal servitude or have seen the beauty of God's country past their plantation line. Perhaps they both would have found true love and happiness in Hawthorn Ridge, but likely not. Sarah certainly wouldn't have married Jackson Whitticomb or then danced with Tobias. She wouldn't have become the wife of a man whose love now filled every inch of her soul. Because of her grief, she had finally discovered the faith such a love required. Believing through a list of unknown days.

Promise me, Sarah. Promise me you won't give up.

Linden hadn't wanted her to write poetry or drink from chipped wine glasses. She didn't need to live in a tenement or have a stray dog named Jacque to appease his ghost. All he ever asked was that she be happy with the man she loved.

A laugh bubbled from her throat. The action drew a cautious smile from her friend and she only laughed again. She pulled Martha to her feet and tugged her back toward the wagon circle.

As they neared, Jamison rushed forward, and it was then she ran. She lifted her skirts in both hands to meet him and those beautiful words he called.

"He's awake!"

She lifted her face to the sun, to the breeze, the mountains, the sky. It was beautiful. They were beautiful. God was beautiful.

She was blessed. Oh, how very blessed she was.

40

When Tobias next woke, darkness had fallen inside the wagon. Without his pocket watch—who knew where it had been placed in the commotion of prior days—it was impossible to tell the exact hour. It was late enough for movement to have ceased beyond the canvas cover and only the faintest odor of burnt embers slipping between the cracks.

With tender movements, he lifted his right fingers to touch the binding across his gunshot wound. His left arm lay immobilized behind swathes of fabric, binding it to his side lest he move and tear his delicate stitching. From the way the wound stung every time he shifted even a few inches, he reasoned that the decision, while inconvenient, was probably for the best. He had never been one to simply lie around when there was work to be done. A quick recovery was imperative.

A slight scratching brought his attention to the foot of the wagon bed and the sliver of moonlight passing across Sarah's slender figure. Her golden hair cascaded across her shoulders, the soft linen of her nightgown draping her torso while a blanket folded over her knees. Her attention was to the parchment in her lap, flattened upon a book for a makeshift writing desk. The pencil lead swirled across the page in her delicate script, one line then the next, its sound like an evening song for only Tobias's ears. Beautiful, and he couldn't believe he had almost lost it.

It was beyond reason for Jamison to have saved him. This

afternoon—he thought it was this afternoon—when he woke to first Jamison's, then Sarah's tearful relief, he had felt overwhelming exhaustion as they recounted the tale of Morris Aspen's treachery. When Sarah and Clinton had thundered back into camp with Tobias's bloody figure between them, Jamison said all rational thought had left him. He couldn't remember a scalpel from a jack-knife, binding a broken leg versus a sprained ankle. It was only with Sarah's quick wit, careful instruction, and insistent reprimands that he was eventually able to recall his many years of medical training. The result hadn't been the most delicate surgery or the prettiest sutures, but Tobias had survived.

After learning how Sarah's father-in-law killed her husbands, seemingly without remorse, Tobias thought for sure the man must possess some Gift. That he could charm everyone and shield their suspicions while he took six lives. But no, he hadn't been. Sometimes the devil was disguised as just a man.

Sarah on the other hand, wasn't Gifted. Tobias had been wrong just as he had all those other times before. Looking at her now, he knew it didn't matter one lick whether she was the most talented or the least capable woman in the world. He would pledge his heart to her again; he would sacrifice his life for her again. In an instant, without a doubt, as he should have from the beginning.

"Sarah," he whispered.

She startled, her eyes darting to his with concern, then softening to relief when she saw him still connected to the world. Her lips turned up into a smile, and he wished there was a way to capture the moment, to hold onto the joy in her eyes.

"How are you feeling?" she asked.

"My shoulder hurts."

Her chin tipped to the side. "An understatement, I assume."

He managed a smile this time and shrugged his good shoulder. "Yeah, it is, but I think I'll make it. Thanks to you."

She looked back down at the paper on her lap, absently running a line of lead down the right-hand margin. He thought he heard her sniff, but she covered it up with a cough, like she didn't want him to know she was hurting as much as he.

"I thought you didn't care for writing poetry," he said instead.

"Not poetry this time," she said softly. "Prayers of thanksgiving and for the future."

She was strong, he realized. So much stronger than he ever gave her credit for. Gone through the fire and been made new. It took courage to cry out to the Lord when one needed help, and humility to thank Him when He provided it. She told Tobias that she had desired his faith, but it was hers that now had him in awe.

"You're different than the woman I met at her wedding." He paused, unsure if he should voice his next thought, but he wanted to be honest. "I didn't know Linden, but I think he would be proud of who you've become."

"I think he would too." Her statement was so soft, only the silence of the night allowed him to hear. "We should get to sleep."

She tucked the parchment and pencil inside the book, then shifted to her knees so she could lift the door to the under compartment. Tobias stopped her before her fingers could lift the iron ring.

"Sarah, I'm sorry."

"Tobias, you're already forgiven. Rest, we don't need to rehash all of this."

"We do though. We haven't had a chance to talk about what happened. It has to be discussed. I *need* to discuss it."

She lifted the door and set the book inside, lowering the wooden panel back into place with barely a sound. She turned back for her blanket and as soon as her back was turned, she swiped a palm across both eyes, an action forceful enough to be visible even in the dim moonlight. Knowing he had brought those tears gutted him worse than the hole through his shoulder.

"I shouldn't have left you, Sarah. I shouldn't have believed the accusations or even doubted for a minute."

"It's understandable," she said, slowly, and he could tell she was swallowing more than half her emotion within the words. "There were testimonies against me and plenty of proof."

"Lies."

"You didn't know that."

"I should have. Our marriage wasn't only about you being Gifted, I need you to believe that."

"You've told me—"

"I need to say it again. That was the reason in the beginning, and I know when I let you leave, it probably seemed like it still was. Nothing is farther from the truth. The truth is—" He closed his eyes, trying to regain control of the sorrow, the guilt, the remorse scattered throughout every inch of him. He was acutely aware of the inability to move his arm and the possibility that he might not be Gifted anymore either. The fear that she wouldn't want him if he wasn't.

He felt, more than heard, her lie down beside him, her body molded against his uninjured side, her fingers lightly entwining with the hand that lay upon his chest. She rested her head against his shoulder and said nothing, allowing him space and time to say what needed to be said, giving him what he didn't deserve.

"The truth was," he began again, "I was afraid that my love for you had clouded my judgment of who you really were. Or who I really was. That outside of our Gifts, we weren't anything." Tears slid down his cheeks, and he was powerless to stop them. Both his hands were occupied and his will didn't want to fight anymore.

"What if I never heal? What if I can't take care of you? What if my Gift is gone and I'm not me anymore? If I hadn't promised to lift your curse, if I was just me without all the trappings, would you have still married me?"

She was silent for several moments. Only the occasional staccato rise of her chest revealed that she wept against his shoulder. When she finally lifted a hand to wipe her eyes, he pressed a kiss to her crown. "Sarah?"

"I...I don't know," she stumbled, her tears still clouding her words. "I would like to think I would have married you either way, but who knows what we would do in an alternate life? If you weren't Gifted, you wouldn't have even sought me out. We're here now, Tobias, and moving forward is all that matters." She shifted away, propping herself on her elbow so she could meet his gaze fully. "I forgive you for everything. You came after me in the end. You were willing to sacrifice your dreams and almost your life for me. When you had the opportunity to shoot Mr. Aspen, you set down your weapon down, which was something I couldn't when given the same choice. It was only Mr. Reed's actions that saved me from being what they accused me of—a murderess. I don't want to live in the past anymore. I've already spent too many years there. I finally feel like I can have peace from Linden's memory, and I want us to find it too."

She shifted, pressing her lips to his, their touch salty from her tears, and his. He didn't know how he was worthy to have found such a woman for his wife. Only God could bring together a union so unexpectedly perfect.

"As for being Gifted," she said when she finally drew away, "you always wanted a wife like you. Well, maybe instead, I received a husband like me. I will love him the same either way."

She smiled, pressing another kiss to his lips, before her body settled in beside him again. "Sleep, my love," she whispered. "We're almost home."

41

October 1852
Washington Territory

October dawned as they navigated the dangerous climb over the Blue Mountains, along the winding Columbia River to the Dalles, before finally crossing northward into Washington Territory. Due to Tobias's injuries, they no longer made twenty miles every day. Some days they were lucky if they accomplished ten, but at least they were together, headed in the same direction with the same goal. A family grown from strangers.

In the end, so few remained from their original forty-five wagons. Tobias had suspected many would leave once they learned he abandoned them for a suspected murderess, but he had also hoped they would stay for the sake of the promises they made to the town. After one too many emotional blows, he could only hope they survived the final leg of their journey wherever that might take them. That was the beauty of being free. You had the choice.

He was simply thankful to have those he did. More thankful still to be alive.

Even a month later, he still carried his left arm in a sling and could barely raise it higher than a few inches. When he was wagon-bound, Cade brought him some small twigs, encouraging him to work his strength back slowly. Every night he tried to weave them together with his uninjured hand. For weeks, he struggled to perform what should have come easily—and quickly—before his injury. Now, even mediocre tasks agonized him, the wood resisting all pliability beneath his touch. Eventually, he tossed the sticks to the side of the trail and decided to focus on what he could do, rather than what he couldn't.

Hopefully, his Gift would return as he healed, but he had a feeling the Live Oak was the last extraordinary creation he would ever build. He was sure he could still construct houses and fix broken wagon wheels, but at the rate normal men were forced to take. It pained him to think he had lost his Gift forever. He never liked his father's legacy, but he had always believed he could do better with it.

The pioneers continued northward until they arrived at the promised claim, the azure ocean at their faces and evergreen forests at their backs. Breathtaking. There would be much to accomplish in order to make the space habitable, trees to fell and buildings to raise before it could be considered a town. Still, what a vision to surround them while they built their dreams.

With his uninjured arm, he pointed inland. "Can you picture it?" he asked the group. "That way will be Reed's cattle ranch, and beyond, crop fields and an orchard. Then over there, chicken coops, and I imagine Alice Ann will even manage to capture us some fish and oysters by the shore." Alice Ann giggled at his assessment, already moving down shore to slip her toes into the surf.

He turned again, gesturing to the space where he could picture a whitewashed sign welcoming all types of folks to Larksong. His right hand grasped Sarah's and squeezed. "Right there, in the middle of it all will be Main Street with clapboard buildings and dusty boardwalks. A schoolhouse painted red and beside it, a white church with a white steeple. Someday others will join us. We'll all work together exactly as we planned."

"It will be perfect," Sarah smiled. "Even when it isn't."

She had been dealt a raw hand, but life's trials had transformed her with every mile along this winding dusty trail. In turn, it had transformed him, too. She wasn't simply the woman he selected for her Gift or to add additional acreage to their town. She was also the beautiful caring woman he wanted to spend his life with—and would sacrifice it for—Gifted or not.

In her free hand, she carried ten crosses, fitted together with sticks and twine, fashioned this time by her own hands. They weren't as gracefully wrought as the lark Tobias had made her. Their edges were hardly flawless, yet beautiful in their simplicity. Seven made for every husband who brought her to this place. Another for Oliver Shay and one for little Ephram lost beneath the wagon wheels. The last for Morris Aspen, the father-in-law whom she loved even when he did not return a father's affection.

As one, they raised a prayer and lowered the crosses to float upon the sea.

This was what he wanted his legacy to be. A mix of his father's legacy and the one he and his brothers built. He wanted to be the type of man his father could have been if he had used his Gift for others, rather than for himself.

Even though Sarah proved not to be Gifted, he wouldn't lose faith that there could be others. He and his brothers had spent their lives feeling alone. He didn't want anyone else to feel that way any longer than they had to. Someday he would scour this country for his Gifted brethren, once they established Larksong and Garrett returned. First, they needed to begin this new life without old secrets hanging over them. Their Gifts shouldn't be hidden. Not here. Not anymore.

Tomorrow, he thought. Today, they would embrace the stillness. Tomorrow would be a new beginning.

"My friends," he said. "My family. Welcome to Larksong."

42

After everyone else departed to the wagons, Coraline remained near the water's edge. Foam lapped inches from her toes while deep breaths of briny air filled her chest. How she had missed being near the ocean.

The shore here wasn't at all like that in Charleston. All manner of the city—homes and businesses and smoke and noise—was now behind her. Here the rocky beach rose through the waving grasses, meeting evergreens upon the ridge. Beyond that, silver mountain peaks framed the distant eastern horizon. A cool mist drove upon her face, spattering her glasses, reminiscent of the endless condensation of Carolina's humid summers. Farther down the shore, Alice Ann swung around, kicking up sand, she and Cade splashing in the water like a couple of tikes. It wasn't long before the Harper children caught the sound of their enjoyment and scrambled away from their mother again, practically rolling down the subtle incline to splash in the surf.

Coraline smiled with a swell of homesickness, all while knowing she could grow used to this place as well. It was such a shame she would never—

Approaching footsteps halted her thoughts before they fell into despair. She didn't want to think about the trials that lay ahead. They had already endured so much to get here.

Jamison stopped beside her, sights set on the horizon. The sun sparkled off the waves and a gull flew low, skimming its wings upon the surface. "We made it," he said.

"We did."

They fell back into silence, although every half minute, his glance shifted in her direction then darted away again. When he finally spoke again, it was with words nearly lost in gruff emotion. "Oliver would have wanted to be here." A pause. A breath. "He would have enjoyed sharing this moment with you."

"With us," she clarified. "God said it's not good for man to be alone, right?"

"Nor woman."

She looked up at him and his tender gaze met hers. "Do you really believe this will be a new beginning?" she asked. "I fear that—"

He silenced her words with his own. "We all have fears, Coraline. What's important is that we face them together." He opened his arms to her and without considering the consequences, she stepped into his warm embrace.

Her fears could wait until tomorrow.

Larksong Legacy continues with Coraline and Jamison's story in *Dusk Shall Weep*.

AUTHOR'S NOTE

Like the characters in *For a Noble Purpose*, grief, anxiety, depression, and domestic abuse affect millions of people worldwide every day. If you, or someone you know, live with these conditions, you are not alone. Hope is only a call or click away.

Focus on the Family Christian Counselor Assistance
1-855-771-HELP (4357)
https://www.focusonthefamily.com/get-help/

Substance Abuse and Mental Health Services Administration
1-800-662-HELP (4357)
https://samhsa.gov/find-help/national-helpline

National Suicide Prevention Lifeline
1-800-273-8255 or Text "TALK" to 741741
https://suicidepreventionlifeline.org/

National Domestic Violence Hotline
1-800-799-7233
https://thehotline.org

There are many additional resources available in addition to those listed. While the organizations listed above are United States based, similar organizations are available in other countries.

Have faith. Have hope. You have a beautiful purpose.

HISTORICAL NOTES

Behind the Story:

For a Noble Purpose is loosely inspired by the Biblical story of Sarah and Tobiah in The Book of Tobit. In the story, Sarah has been widowed seven times, always on her wedding night, with each husband being murdered by the demon, Asmodeus. When Tobiah learns Sarah is of his own family's lineage, his "heart became set on her" and he agrees to marry her, although understandably with some trepidation. The archangel Raphael appears in disguise with advice for how to drive Asmodeus away: place a fish liver and heart on embers for incense, then pray for mercy. Tobiah and Sarah do as told and indeed, Tobiah's life is spared and Raphael captures the demon.

In my version, I wanted to keep the essence of the story, including a taste of its supernatural elements without diving too far into the paranormal or fantasy genres. Therefore I exchanged Raphael for the concept of the Gifted and the demon, Asmodeus became the human, Morris Aspen. As Tobias says, "Sometimes the devil was disguised as just a man," which I believe is true in our world today.

In addition, most of Jamison's prayer at Tobias and Sarah's wedding is taken from Tobit 8:5-7 and is one I hold close as my husband and I used it at our wedding.

The Gifted:

Since this novel is not fantasy, but more speculative historical fiction, I wanted all of my characters' Gifts to be founded in scientific fact. Through hours of reading about real-life superpowers, one question led my research: What can we achieve by strengthening our natural God-given abilities? Therefore, while the Gifts may seem a little outside this world, they remain rooted in what's possible.

Tobias, Garrett, and Jamison's Gifts are all based on a mix between Sudden Savant Syndrome and Congenital Savant Syndrome. Like the Larks, Congenital Savants acquire their talents in childhood, which often involve mechanical or navigation skills. Many of these children also exhibit autistic traits. Sudden Savant Syndrome appears without any known cause or autistic ties. Like the Larks, these savants suddenly acquire detailed knowledge without having learned it. Both types of Savant Syndrome are more often found in men than women, but women are also able to exhibit these abilities.

Tobias's Gift is also inspired by the Loretto Chapel Staircase in Santa Fe, New Mexico. In 1878, the Sisters of Loretto had nearly completed construction of their chapel when the original architect died, leaving them without a staircase to the choir loft. They prayed a nine-day novena to Saint Joseph, the patron saint of carpenters, and on the final day, a carpenter appeared. He constructed a 33-step spiral staircase using only basic tools and wooden pegs, no nails or a central support, and with wood not native to the Southwest. He also requested to work in private, refused to give his name, and disappeared after the work was completed. Due to the staircase's miraculous nature, many believed that the man was St. Joseph himself. While it has since been proven that the staircase could be constructed within the laws of physics, the fact remains that it would have been a difficult feat, especially in that time period and without the convenience of modern power tools. I visited the chapel on a family vacation, and if you're ever in Santa Fe, I recommend a visit.

Cade's Gift is based on a concept called Barometric Pressure Sickness which occurs when a weather front is moving through, causing a significant change in barometric pressure. This shift can cause mild to severe headaches, sometimes accompanied by nausea, vomiting, vertigo, or other physical ailments. Like Cade, I experience some of these symptoms when a storm is coming, but not in the same intensity he does.

And finally, Alonzo Lark's Gift is probably the one most likely to be seen in everyday life. History is full of people who persuade others to do often unspeakable things for popularity, wealth, and/or power.

While Alonzo possesses a charisma far above those real historical figures, he is no different in his intentions.

When it comes to Geraldine Lark's suicide and the subsequent rejection of a Christian burial, it should also be noted that the Catholic Church no longer endorses the belief that victims of suicide are automatically condemned to hell. Although the Church still holds to the gravity of the suicidal act, in modern times these deaths are granted the same respect as any other and can receive a Christian burial. According to the Catechism of the Catholic Church Paragraph 2283, "We should not despair of the eternal salvation of persons who have taken their own lives. By ways known to Him alone, God can provide the opportunity for salutary repentance. The Church prays for persons who have taken their own lives."

Right Versus Legal:

For a Noble Purpose deals with several sensitive topics including race relations and slavery. I think it's important to not avoid these topics, but to be respectful while remaining true to history. For this reason, I chose to keep some historically used terms like "colored" and "Indians" while avoiding other more negative ones. I felt it was also important to show the differences between the northern and southern slave states as well as emphasize those slave owners who wanted to do right for the slaves, but felt their hands were tied due to the law.

In many states, it was illegal to free your slaves, even if you wanted to. If you helped them escape to the north, the Fugitive Slave Act stated that if captured, they could be returned to enslavement. The law also forbade masters from teaching their slaves to read or write, although some, like Sarah's parents, did so anyway. The Larks chose to settle in Washington because that territory allowed Black residents while Oregon did not.

While many slave owners did treat their servants with cruelty, there are also countless stories of those who fought for their servants' betterment. The Lark brothers' treatment of their slaves versus that of their father is an example of this conflict, which when mixed with other economic difficulties, led to the American Civil War.

The story of Oliver Shay's father keeping on the runaway slave as a paid servant was based on a true story. A Missouri slave owner was going to sell a woman and her children; however, her husband lived on a different farm. While she had earned enough money to purchase her freedom, Missouri law didn't allow it, leaving her at the mercy of her owner. Another farmer, hearing of the situation, agreed to purchase her, but allow her and her family to live on his property as freemen. She continued to earn a wage and kept her family intact.

Martha's story of the St. Louis Fifth and Myrtle Market is also based on true events. This slave market was known for purchasing children ages five to sixteen and holding them in a pen with little food and no beds, until finally auctioning them off. Sales of children were in high demand as they had many years of work potential and it was believed that their loyalties were more easily swayed toward their masters.

As a border state, Missouri played an important role in the distribution of slave and free states. While technically considered a "slave state," her people's loyalties were divided. During the American Civil War, Missouri sent troops to assist both the Union and the Confederacy and even maintained two separate rival governments.

Traveling the Trail:

Hawthorn Ridge, Missouri is not a real city but would be located in Little Dixie, an area known for its hemp and tobacco plantations which encompassed several counties across Mid-Missouri. Unfortunately, the word "Dixie" has since assumed racist connotations, and it didn't seem ideal to begin the series with that picture in readers' minds. Hawthorn comes from Missouri's state flower, the White Hawthorn Blossom.

Now known as Fulton State Hospital, Asylum No. 1 was the first public mental health institution west of the Mississippi River. Opened in December 1851, it accepted 67 patients—"lunatics" as they were then labeled—with various states of mental duress, from epilepsy and tuberculosis to the more unusual "disappointed love" and "intense study." The hospital was close to self-sufficient, raising their own food while providing the patients with jobs such as sewing and soapmaking. Today, the hospital treats patients requiring heightened security, those with developmental disabilities, and sexual offender rehabilitation.

Charleston, South Carolina is a real city, full of amazing history dating back to the American Revolution. It was known for its rice and cotton plantations, complete with Spanish-moss-draped live oaks lining the drives, and it boasts a harbor with townhouses like the one the Larks would have owned.

Finally, I could write an entire historical note on the Oregon Trail alone (but I won't). 1852 saw one of the busiest summers for the trail with 70,000 people traveling, sometimes 12 wagons across. It was a grueling journey that led to an often more challenging life in the west. The key sites described in *For a Noble Purpose* would have been seen by these travelers including Independence, Fort Kearney, Fort Laramie, Independence Rock, and Fort Hall. Diseases and injuries abounded along the way and it was not unusual for children to fall beneath the wagons. But there were happy moments as well: weddings, births, dances, sing-a-longs, and church services, to name a few.

To view an interactive map of Oregon Trail sites, visit: https://www.nps.gov/oreg/planyourvisit/places-to-go.htm

Acknowledgments

As always, a most massive thank you to all my readers, especially my amazing family. God has blessed me seven-fold!

To my husband, Scott, and our children. Thank you for watching lots of superhero movies with me and helping me figure out the finer details of the Gifted. I love you! You are my best blessings!

To my parents, Ken and Ruth, for your support with this book and every day. Your love means everything.

To my fellow historical fiction author friends: *Jennifer Q. Hunt*, whose Sorrow and Song series inspired me to take the leap of faith into Christian Fiction. Thank you for your Southern knowledge, heartfelt advice, and always pushing me to dig a little deeper. *Susan Laspe* for twenty years of friendship and tea-filled writing sessions (on occasion we actually write!). Thank you for putting up with my constant questions and ideas. *Tanya E. Williams* for advice on my *many* outline and cover design changes and for convincing me that the 1850s were in fact the right era for this story. Thanks for challenging me to step outside my comfort zone!

To all my beta readers: Ann, Jennifer, Ken, Mary, Mindy, Ruth, Sharon, Storm, Susan, and Tanya. For your many comments, suggestions, edits, and hours of discussion and debate. Thank you!

To my advance reader team, the Christian Mommy Writers group, and the wonderful bookstagram community. Thank you for your advice, reviews, posts, interviews, and well wishes!

To all the incredible authors whose own fiction I read for 1800's inspiration including Lori Benton, Lisa T. Bergren, Amy Harmon, Jennifer L. Holm, Julie Lessman, Susie Murphy, Roseanna M. White, and Karen Witemeyer.

To the many organizations who helped make my historical information accurate and believable, especially the Missouri Historical Society, St. Charles and St. Louis County Libraries, Oregon National Historic Trail (U.S. National Park Service), Oregon Encyclopedia, Wonders of Wildlife Museum in Springfield, The Metropolitan Museum of Art, The National Gallery of Art, and all those real-life pioneers whose journals were left behind. I hope you found the dreams you were searching for.

Most importantly, to my Lord and creator, Jesus Christ. Every good and perfect gift is from above. Without You, none of this could be.

ABOUT THE AUTHOR

Kelsey Gietl is the author of the early 1910s Over the Atlantic duology, the WWI War Across Waters duology, and the 1850s Larksong Legacy series. Combining faith, family, and lessons from our past, her books provide inspirational stories with a dose of romance and a dash of intrigue.

She holds a Bachelor of Fine Arts in Theatre Design and Graphic Design and has made a career in fields from event planning and proposal writing to product management and communications.

She lives in Missouri with her husband, two children, and their black beagledor.

You can connect with her online at:
kelseygietl.com

www.ingramcontent.com/pod-product-compliance
Lightning Source LLC
Chambersburg PA
CBHW022025240626
47154CB00007B/2269